THE PENALTY KILLING

Also by Michael McKinley

NON-FICTION
Legends of Hockey
Etched in Ice
Putting a Roof on Winter
The Magnificent One: The Story of Mario Lemieux
Hockey: A People's History

FOR CHILDREN
Ice Time

Michael McKinley

THE PENALTY KILLING

A Martin Carter Mystery

McCLELLAND & STEWART

Library and Archives Canada Cataloguing in Publication

McKinley, Michael (Michael B.)
The penalty killing / Michael McKinley.

(A Martin Carter mystery)
ISBN 978-0-7710-5582-9

I. Title. II. Series.

PS8625.K55P45 2010   C813'.6   C2009-905148-6

We acknowledge the financial support of the Government of Canada through
the Book Publishing Industry Development Program and that of the Government
of Ontario through the Ontario Media Development Corporation's Ontario Book
Initiative. We further acknowledge the support of the Canada Council for the Arts
and the Ontario Arts Council for our publishing program.

Typeset in Garamond by M&S, Toronto
Printed and bound in the United States of America

ANCIENT FOREST
FRIENDLY

This book is printed on acid-free paper that is 100% recycled,
ancient-forest friendly (100% post-consumer waste).

This is a work of fiction. Names, characters, places, and events are either the
product of the author's imagination or are used fictitiously.

McClelland & Stewart Ltd.
75 Sherbourne Street
Toronto, Ontario
M5A 2P9
www.mcclelland.com

1 2 3 4 5   14 13 12 11 10

For my wife, Nancy, muse of the grand adventure

Hockey is murder on ice.
— Jim Murray, sportswriter

THE PENALTY KILLING

PART ONE

1

A bell rang, and it began.

"Hello?" Martin Carter said into his office phone late in the afternoon of St. Patrick's Day. On the other end was Douglas Bleecker IV, his voice rising at the end of the sentence with a question mark, like a teenager's at the mall. "Just the man I need – Come to my office? I need you to do an intervention?"

"Doug, can't we do this over the –"

Bleecker had hung up. It sounded as if he'd asked a question, but it was a command.

Doug Bleecker ranked higher on the corporate food chain, so Carter stood up from his computer and headed for the door, dodging boxes of books and files that should have been on shelves. The office was barely big enough for Carter and a desk, and a coat of paint. On the way out he caught a glimpse of himself in the mirror next to the clock, both serving as his mortality meter. He hadn't changed. His nose sported a hat trick of breaks that hooked it to starboard, his lips were thick and full, and his head a riot of black curls. He dressed it all up as best he could in a black suit over a crisp white shirt, the tie gold with a touch of green, the team colours.

Bleecker was waiting for him outside his much bigger office – with a view of the Hudson River – and when he saw Carter round the corner, he tilted his head up like a dog sniffing the wind. "Be a pal," Bleecker said, his smoker's rasp hushed and important, "and look after this woman with a camera. Cartch?"

Carter winced. Once it had seemed as if the world had known him as Cartch, the best thing to happen to the New York St. Patricks since they had first and last won the Cup back in 1969. But now, from the lips of guys like Bleecker, it was just a reminder of all that had been lost.

Bleecker stared at him without blinking. His strangely thin head on his plump, pear-shaped body made him a walking contradiction, which Carter thought perfectly suited the media director who had come to the St. Pats as an undistinguished business reporter from the *Financial News* and who could say one thing and very much mean another.

"Love to help," Carter lied, "but I'm jammed up, selling playoff tickets." The St. Pats were a long shot to make the playoffs, and their fans, the Patsies, were not known to be optimists.

"C'mon, Cartch, she's one of yours – doing something for Canadian TV."

"And you're the media boss. If she wants to host a pancake breakfast for orphans – or buy playoff tickets – I'm your man."

Bleecker stepped closer, a quick look over his shoulder toward his office, conveying conspiracy. "Look, here's the thing. Freddie wants me to look after some VIP tonight, and I need to prep, so you'd be doing me a favour."

Freddie Hutt was the team's new boss, a money guy who had been collateral damage in Wall Street's latest failed greed grab and had brought Bleecker in with him. He had "vipps," as Bleecker called them, crawling all over Emerald Gardens, people Carter had seen on TV: actors, a couple of musicians, some models, and, he was told, a porn star or two. It was all part of Hutt's plan "to brand the St. Patricks as a team of the future." Yeah, well, good luck to him, Carter had thought when he first heard of this stroke of genius. The Pats had been the team of the future for the past four decades.

"What's in it for me?" Carter asked, plumbing his leverage.

Bleecker gave him a puckered smile, a bad poker player holding cards he thinks are worth more than they are. "Well, let's just say she's your type of woman."

His type of woman? Ever since his accident, that pretty much meant any woman between the ages of twenty and forty-five. But he'd been as chaste as a Belfast nun for more than a year now, and he didn't like Bleecker playing pimp. So Carter flashed him the killer smile he used to use on Continental Hockey League goalies as he sped in on a breakaway. Bleecker stepped back and his eyes said, Martin Carter is a head case.

Then the woman from Canada came out of Bleecker's office.

"Martin Carter. This is Hayley Rawls. From Canada."

Carter offered his hand. "A pleasure."

On the surface, it was a pleasure. Chocolate eyes, auburn curls, porcelain skin, bone structure as fine as roses, and a smile full of promise.

She cocked her head to one side. "The pleasure is mine," she said, taking Carter's hand with a firm grip. "I'm such a fan of yours."

She held on to him for a moment longer than needed. Her skin was soft and warm, her perfume lilac. She was a contradiction worth parsing, thought Carter. Her leather blazer, black and expensive, framed a string of pearls that glinted on her tanned cleavage. Under the jacket, she was wearing a baby blue scooped-neck T-shirt with the slogan "I Play," the current motto of the Continental Hockey League.

"The pleasure is mutual," he said, and just like that he was ushering her down the corridor past the Old Testament eye of Brenda, the well-fed, short-sighted receptionist who hated him. Carter gave her a friendly wave and steered Hayley on to the elevator.

"What did you do to ruin her day?" Hayley asked when the doors shut.

So she was sharp too, Carter thought. "I just said no at the Christmas party," he said, and Hayley grinned. She got the joke. Carter's favourite kind of female combo – brains, beauty, sense of humour, and, in the end, probably trouble. His.

"What brings you to this old barn?" he asked as they walked down the aisle toward the ice. He meant the seventy-five-year-old rink and not himself, though he guessed that at thirty-eight he had maybe five or six years on her.

"I'm doing a doc on Link Andrachuk," she said with a hint of a wince.

"Doc as in documentary?"

"Yup. It's for a new website on him."

Carter nodded. Further proof of a godless universe. Link Andrachuk, the power forward for the St. Pats, could shift from genius goal scorer to world-class goon in the misfiring of a neuron. He was constantly consumed with rage at everything from being called offside at the blue line to not getting passed the puck when he slapped his stick on the ice and yelled, "Hey, fuckwit!" at a teammate. When he really short-circuited, he would mete out a cross-check to the head, a hit from behind into the boards, a sucker punch to the jaw. He was the kind of player who had ended Carter's career.

"Good timing," Carter told Hayley. "This is his first game back from a five-game suspension for that, uh" – he paused to find the right words – "cheap-shit scumbag hit that nearly killed that Czech kid in L.A."

"He also nearly killed the whole damn project," she said coolly, watching a couple of maintenance guys doing a patch-up job on the ice through the LCD screen of her camera. "I guess we both got lucky."

Carter stared at her profile as she concentrated. The aquiline nose dividing high cheekbones, the delicate jaw giving way to a firm, long neck that he imagined kissing – on the way up to her full, lightly glossed lips, and then south to her tanned breasts, and then, if things went well . . .

He stopped the thought there. "Life Tourette's" is what his ex, Flavia, had called it, affectionately at first, but then at the end, she just meant that he was a head case, and what to do next was a toss-up between euthanasia and just ending their affair.

"How does a nice Canadian girl wind up with a gig on the Missing Link?" Carter asked.

Hayley Rawls touched his arm. "The producer is based in Vancouver, like me, and he's tied into the CHL, who want to showcase Andrachuk, and they hired me to help them do it."

"What are you, a sorceress?"

She laughed. "Just a lady who needs to pay the rent. And I'm not so nice."

She said it, though, in a very nice way – and it tempted him to take a step back onto the eternally thin ice of the romance game.

So he said, "I think I can help you out."

She wanted some shots of the Missing Link playing hard and fierce as his team fought for a playoff spot on Manhattan ice, and since she was shooting on DVD, she didn't have a lot of gear to park in the sightlines of the famously tolerant St. Pats fans.

Carter took her around the rink to a sweet spot, just a little to the left of what would be the opponents' goal for two of the three periods in tonight's game.

The team the St. Pats would be facing, the Sea Lions, were also from Vancouver. They had spent most of the season

dozing in the Pacific sunlight and had just awakened to find
themselves fighting for the last playoff spot in the Western
Division of the CHL. The St. Pats had the same problem in a
different time zone. If Link Andrachuk decided to play
winning hockey tonight, the boys in the green and gold
would celebrate St. Patrick's Day by clinching the last playoff
spot in the East. They were running out of time to do that,
with only six games left in the season and Toronto three
points back and surging. It had the makings of an expensive
night for someone at Emerald Gardens.

Carter told Hayley that from where they were standing she
would have the perfect view of the Missing Link doing what
got him a four-year, $24.2 million contract from the St. Pats –
cutting in from the left, from his opposite wing, muscling the
d-man with one hand and cradling the puck in his stick with
the other, then making the little red goal light shine.

"Perfect," she said, checking the angle through her
viewfinder. "If –"

"He shows up."

She smiled. "You're a mind reader."

"Nah, I've just had to watch him play for the last three
years."

She nodded sympathetically, then frowned a little. "So what
is it that you do, exactly?" she asked. "You're not a coach?"

"I'm director of community relations," he said.

"Oh? And what communities do you have relations with?"

He took a deep breath. "I get to attend fundraisers for
everyone from graffiti removers to Wall Street titans to glad-
hand parents at ice rinks from Chelsea Piers to Corona Park
on behalf of the St. Pats in the hope they'll buy corporate
suites or season tickets, or just come to a game sometime and
buy a hot dog. And I try not to squeeze too hard when I meet

those hockey dads – all of them older than me – who all loved to watch me play for the Patsies when they were kids."

She took a step back at the vehemence of his speech. Then she smiled.

"Too bad it's my last day of shooting," she said. And started the clock on Carter's future.

He took a desperation shot. "The team's having a St. Patrick's Day party tonight, after the game. Would you like to come as my guest?"

She tilted her head again, as if assessing the cost of crossing the line he was inviting her over. "I have to be up at four-thirty for my flight home tomorrow."

As it wasn't a no, he pressed on. "These parties go all night. Or until the cops come." This was a head-case thing to say, but it was true.

"Tell you what," she said with professional cool. "If Mr. Link Andrachuk gives me what I want, then I'll definitely be in the mood for a party."

2

The game that night was a slumber party – during the REM part. Both teams skated out for this "must win or else" match as if they were afraid to lose. Skate the puck to centre ice and dump it. Chase it. Gain it. Lose it. Retreat. Repeat as needed for forty minutes. God forbid anyone should actually score.

Even Hayley Rawls was bored, and she, like Carter, like the players, was being paid to be there. When Carter looked down from the team's corporate box to the spot he'd reserved for her, she was sipping a cup of coffee, her camera slung over her shoulder. He hoped, for her sake and for his, that Link Andrachuk woke up.

He looked over at Doug Bleecker sitting with the VIP whose appearance had resulted in Carter tending to Hayley Rawls. Carter didn't recognize the guy, who was clearly trying to be memorable in a black three-piece suit and matching eyepatch, his receding, grey blond hair hanging to his shoulders like a Norse hero hitting middle age. Or maybe Russian.

Carter felt his forehead go cold, fast – his involuntary response to the world's perils. He knew that there were Russians all over the league these days – players and agents and, so he had heard, gangsters. If he had to place a bet on this guy, he'd wager he was mobbed up somehow, or wanted to be.

Right now the VIP and his minder were riveted by Bleecker's BlackBerry, not by the action, such as it was, on the ice. It figured. That was the current culture of the place.

Carter looked down to the ice, where the Missing Link seemed more interested in jawing at Sasha Oblomov, the Vancouver Sea Lions' own mystery man, than he did in playing. The Russian was ignoring him. Or maybe he didn't understand the Missing Link's idiomatic English, spoken through a missing bridge, half in taunts.

Carter glanced at Link on the video monitor to see if he could make out the trash talk. He couldn't, but he did notice that Link was sporting a fat lip and a black eye. Maybe he'd been worked over by a jealous husband because Carter couldn't remember him being injured in the last game. When the siren signalled the end of the second period, the Patsies cheered in relief – those who were still in their seats and not in the beer lineup. Carter made his way to the St. Pats' entertainment suite, a glorified frat house cafeteria, where beer and chips and salsa were served in crystal glasses and pewter bowls.

"Hey, Cartch, buy you a shot and a pint of Harp if you can explain this pig fuck?"

Madz Weinfeld, colour commentator for SportsWorld TV's telecasts of St. Pats games, materialized at Carter's elbow at the bar.

"I'm a dry county at the moment," he said, pouring himself a club soda.

"Well, at least I have my post-game wrap: 'The New York St. Pats' in-fucking-difference to their playoff fate finally shocked their former great white hope, Martin Carter, to drink water without whiskey in it."

"Say that on TV, Ms. Weinfeld, and I'll sue you for slander. You know I never put water in my whiskey."

She cackled, then dangled her tie in his face, the St. Pats being the last CHL team left to insist that the media wear jackets and ties to games. Madz, who would have made a very handsome man, was a six-foot-tall suicide blonde and the only woman in the New York sports media to call them on the tie rule.

"The Pats keep this shit up and I'll finally have a use for this thing," she said, pulling the tie up over her head like a noose, her eyeballs bulging.

Carter took a closer look at the tie. It was black, splashed with flame-haired female leprechauns wearing nothing but green top hats and doing the lesbian Kama O'Sutra.

"Haven't the Irish suffered enough?"

"Hey, another gift from your tribe," she grinned. "Irish birth control. Too bad you can't try it. And speaking of tongues, who was that babe hanging out during pre-game?"

"Hayley Rawls," Carter said. "She's doing a documentary on Link Andrachuk. And she's not your type."

"Oh, so you slept with her already?"

"You romantics."

She twisted the cap off a Brooklyn Lager. "Babes with cameras . . ." She shook her head, took a swig. "Watch out, Cartch, or next thing you know your pecker'll be up on YouTube."

He laughed. "You gotta learn to tame your fantasies, Madz."

She smiled and raised the bottle in a toast. "Hey, I cover the Pats. Who can tell what's fantasy anymore?"

Carter knew that problem all too well. He smiled back. "It's not in the telling, Madz, it's in the how it all ends."

3

By the midpoint of the third period, the Vancouver Sea Lions were riding a 3–0 lead – from a three-goal orgy in two minutes and twenty-seven seconds, all thanks to Link Andrachuk. The big right winger, a true power forward at six-foot-four and two hundred and fifty pounds, had finally decided after two periods of kissing-your-sister hockey that he really was a hero. And Carter knew the type: the hero who played on a team all by himself.

Taking the puck behind his own goal net, Andrachuk skated out in front of his goalie, swung to the right, then opened the throttle at the blue line to steam across centre ice. He ignored the clear passing lanes to his linemates and continued at full tilt toward the Sea Lions' goal. The problem was that the one-on-five kamikaze routine always gives the guys on the other team a distinct advantage. In this case, the other guy. The Sea Lions' Russian sniper, Sasha Oblomov, who had ignored Andrachuk's taunts all night, was finally roused from his own torpor by the Missing Link's play.

As Andrachuk cut hard to the left to bypass the two-man wall waiting for him at the Vancouver blue line, Oblomov, shadowing him from behind, lifted Andrachuk's stick, stole the puck, and whirled back toward the New York goal. With his blond dreadlocks streaming, Oblomov swept in on the St. Pats' goalie on his forehand. Then, with the swiftness of a magician, he shifted to his backhand, and the goalie went with him. Oblomov tucked the puck between his own legs and back onto his forehand. The St. Pats goalie was still travelling west, Oblomov moved east, and the puck slid into the empty net.

Carter silently and disloyally cheered. Even on the slow-motion replay on the Emerald Gardens' aging Jumbotron, the move was almost too fast to deconstruct. It was pure genius.

Carter looked up at the broadcast gondola, where Madz Weinfeld was doing her colour commentary, and she looked down at him, smiled, and put a hand to her head like a gun. He threw her a *morituri* salute, glancing over to see if Doug Bleecker and his piratical companion had noticed the gesture, but they were still in BlackBerry land, oblivious to the din that had erupted around them. The ancient rafters of Emerald Gardens were shaking with the Patsies' surprise at this turn of events.

The mercurial Oblomov had been nicknamed the Iron Curtain by a nostalgic Russian beat guy on the *Times*, partly because of Oblomov's grey eyes, but mainly because he was, like the once-veiled country, a riddle wrapped in a mystery inside an enigma. Some nights he was an alchemist, turning seemingly leaden opportunities into golden goals; some nights he played like a coma patient who'd wandered into the game.

Link Andrachuk took another run at the wall on his next shift by trying the same solo adventure, and more or less the same thing happened: 2–0 to Sasha Oblomov and the Vancouver Sea Lions.

Then, while taking a choppy, angry skate to the Patsies' bench after being shown up again by Oblomov, Andrachuk delivered language so superior to the abuse the officials usually hear that they rewarded him with two minutes in the penalty box.

The roar of the Patsies rocked Emerald Gardens again. "You're a fuck! And-ra-chuk!" they chanted as they littered the ice with popcorn and beer. With less than five minutes left in the game, they should have been streaming up the aisles, but they wanted to give a special Patsie thank you to the Missing Link.

Carter was cursing him too, for the night he now wasn't going to have, thanks to Andrachuk's virtuoso solo on the self-destruct button. He looked down from the St. Pats' corporate box for Hayley Rawls, who would probably be sitting with her head in her hands, rocking back and forth and weeping. But he didn't see her at all. She was gone.

As Carter stood for a better look, Andrachuk skated past the Sea Lions' bench and said something to Oblomov as he went. This time, Oblomov heard him. He vaulted the boards, gloves dropped, charging at Andrachuk, who had not dropped his own gloves but held his stick out like a lance, taunting Oblomov to get past him. The Russian grabbed Link's stick and yanked him nose first into an angry fist. Link stumbled backward, and Oblomov stepped in for the knockout punch. Then another St. Pat blindsided Oblomov with an elbow to the head, and the donnybrook was on. The crowd rose to its feet in one cathartic howl. The gloveless Sea Lions were doing their best to send the St. Pats to the next world, and vice versa. Carter hadn't seen anything like it since his last game in the league.

There were players paired off in the hockey waltz, one hand clutching the other guy's jersey, the other a fist punching. There were pile-ons, with half-a-dozen players writhing and flailing and face washing at either end of the rink. The goalies and their backups were grappling, their oversized equipment making them look like sumo wrestlers. Even the St. Pats' coach, Phil Winslow, and his Vancouver counterpart, Etienne "Bunny" Blackburn, were trying to scale the Plexiglas that separated the emptied team benches to make good on their screaming threats.

The fans loved the math of it all: forty-two players fighting, four officials trying to stop them, and Emerald Gardens no longer a hockey rink but a bear pit. They pounded the glass that kept them from the battle on the ice, and then they started pounding each other – the fight in the seats a duet with the fight on the ice.

Suddenly, Oblomov came tumbling out of a scrum right by the Sea Lions' goal. He crumpled, blood spurting from his mouth. It was too much blood, coming too fast, and it stopped the brawlers two by two. The Vancouver trainer skidded out onto the ice, knelt down by Oblomov, then looked up, his face white, the ice getting redder. The Patsies, who moments earlier had been baying for blood, applauded Oblomov for having the good manners to spill some. But the applause was tepid. They didn't want him to die. At least, not in front of them. A couple of Sea Lions hoisted the bloodied player to his feet and dragged him off the ice, with the trainer holding a towel to Oblomov's mouth.

Carter checked the Jumbotron to see if it was replaying whatever the hell had just happened, but it was showing only the St. Patrick's green-and-gold shamrock logo.

The players watched Oblomov bleed his way off the ice, standing there stunned and confused, all fuelled up with nowhere to go. Everyone, that is, but Link Andrachuk. When Carter tried to find the man who had started the carnage, all he could see was the back of his jersey retreating under the awning leading to the dressing room, an awning designed to protect players from the Patsies' gifts of spit and beer. Now, to Carter, the awning seemed to protect Link Andrachuk's escape from the scene of a crime – one that Link had committed in front of nineteen thousand people. And Carter hadn't seen it.

What had the Missing Link said to Oblomov that made the Russian so angry? And what had he done to him in that scrum? Carter had a feeling that whatever it was, it was going to land badly on his immediate future. If he could find her in this mess.

4

Carter hoped to find Hayley at the post-mortem, which, from the look of Sasha Oblomov, for once might not be a euphemism.

By the time he'd made it down to the media room, a troop of reporters was crowded around Bleecker. He was lit up by the camera lights, looking even more as if his body was going to swallow his head as he blinked at their elementary questions. What? How? Now what?

"Coach Winslow will be here shortly," he drawled, question mark intact. "I'd prefer to leave the answers to him?"

The reporters seemed to buy this and shushed. Bleecker's question-mark intonation made sense to Carter now. It invited the recipient to answer the question before asking another, and in that pause, the voice of reason intruded.

Carter squeezed past Madz Weinfeld, who arched an eyebrow at him since he didn't normally come to these things, and moved toward the front of the room, looking for Hayley. It was useless. He couldn't see past the cameramen shouldering their Betacams and jostling one another to get the best shot of New York's coach, Phil Winslow, who had just stepped onto the podium.

In his late fifties, still fit but with the face of a basset hound, Winslow looked as if this were the saddest day of his life. Then he smiled and said, "Ladies and gentlemen, I won't be taking questions."

That unleashed another salvo of them, the most obnoxious coming from the portly, florid Darwin Gissing, an institution at the *Mail* who had been writing on hockey when Carter was playing junior and still considered himself the smartest guy in any room he happened to be standing in, despite the couple of successful lawsuits against him for letting gossip masquerade as fact.

"So, coach," Gissing said with a smirk, "what are you going to do without Link in the playoffs? Find time to polish up your resumé?"

Winslow's hound face lit with a smirk of his own as he held up both hands, the fingers bearing four Cup rings that glinted in the camera lights.

"As I said, I won't be taking questions. I will be making a statement." He paused and swung his eyes around the room. "The St. Pats have to play better than we did tonight if we hope to have a long run in the playoffs. And that means playing as a team. On the ice and off the ice. Thank you."

Winslow followed that cliché by hustling off the podium, chased by more unanswered questions. As the cameras shifted to follow the coach offstage, Carter thought he saw a flash of a soft black leather blazer. Then the wall closed up again when the cameras angled back on Bleecker, who had resumed centre stage.

"I might also add," Bleecker shrugged, as if the coming information was superfluous, "that our customary St. Patrick's Day party, given recent events, will not be taking place tonight."

The media booed, and Carter winced. Andrachuk had spoiled any chance he had of continuing his conversation with Hayley Rawls. If she hadn't already disappeared into the Manhattan night.

"How hurt is Oblomov?" someone yelled.

"He apparently has an upper-body injury," Bleecker said, and the reporters laughed at the catch-all term for everything from stomach flu to decapitation.

Tonight, thought Carter, anyone who had seen the blood on the ice knew that Oblomov's upper-body injury was bad.

Bleecker blinked at the laughter, then glanced offstage. "I now give you the Vancouver Sea Lions' coach, Etienne Blackburn," he said and quickly stepped down.

Nicknamed "Bunny" when he played, as a joke on the animal kingdom, Blackburn was a five-foot-six ball of pure menace with no hair and no neck and hot black eyes that bulged as if under the pressure of his rage.

"That was the worse fucken crime I see since I play, and I never even see it then!" Blackburn shouted at the media in Franglish. "Fucken scumbag Link Andrachuk, I fucken kill him dead for starter!" The reporters' jaws slackened at both the vitriol and the prospect of the editing job, all beeps and asterisks.

"He fucken slice my guy up like the Easter ham! We have like a huge less playoff chance now, for fuck sake!" He paused, breathing hard through his mashed nose. "I'll sue the fucken bastard into a million pieces, so the only good fucken thing about this fucken thing is that this happen in fucken New York! God bless America!"

And off he stomped. The room was silent, reeling from this assault on the senses. Then a voice from right behind Carter tickled his ear.

"I think I need a fucken drink."

He turned and there was Hayley, smiling as if her plans had changed. To his advantage.

"I know a place," he said, hoping his surprise and pleasure wasn't too obvious.

"I thought you might."

"I even know a shortcut."

She grinned. "That's my favourite route."

So he led her through the basement of Emerald Gardens and into the broad tunnel that connected to the exit by the loading docks.

"Ooh, down a dark tunnel with a strange man," she said.

Management had probably killed some of the lights to save money, he thought, but he said, "My life is pretty much a dark tunnel these days. Don't worry, I know the way."

As soon as he'd said it, he knew it was a crazy thing to say. He might as well have plastered a "Detour: I'm a loser" sign on his forehead. But she took his arm and said, "Well then, I'm with the right guy," and through the tunnel they went, up the ramp onto 11th Avenue and into the future that, from the squeeze of her hand on his arm, now seemed like a very good place to go.

5

"So this is New York City on St. Patrick's Day."

Hayley Rawls took a sip of her organic California Chardonnay and looked around the Black Irish, Carter's favourite bar, and not just because it was around the corner from Emerald Gardens.

It had just gone midnight, and the usual suspects were celebrating the saint's defeat of the snake with their second day of drunkenness, helped out by a few visitors toasting the St. Pats' bloody loss to the Sea Lions.

The Gobshites, a quartet from the Bronx who played Celtic music with screaming verve, were pounding back Guinness and chain-smoking in the doorway, in training for their last set. Carter knew the clock was ticking on his future with Hayley Rawls, for once the Gobshites returned, conversation would be out of the question.

"St. Paddy's Day indeed," he said, taking a sip of Harp. "Too bad you missed the parade."

"Yeah, but I did see the circus."

He raised his glass to her. "So what did you see? Anything good?"

Wary amusement lit up her brown eyes now, as if he'd asked her something too intimate, too fast. "I got what I needed," she said and took another sip, then looked around the room. Again. Twice within a minute.

"How's life in Vancouver?"

"All work and no play these days. Ever been there?"

"Long time ago."

She must be a pretty recent fan of his, thought Carter, if she didn't know that Vancouver had nearly killed him. He kept the thought to himself and was raising the Harp to his lips when some drunkard yelled, "Dere de famous Cartch!" in a bad imitation of Bunny Blackburn's Franglish.

He spun around to spot the joker and spilled beer down his shirt.

"Here," said Hayley, reaching across the table with a napkin. It was too late to sop up the beer, but her hand lingered on his chest, and Carter's eyes shifted from her hand to her eyes, staring into his. He quickly looked away, like a kid who remembers he's making out in public.

That's when he noticed two men in jackets and ties sitting at the bar and clocking Hayley Rawls. The younger one, a black guy with the broken nose of a boxer, moved his gaze from her to Carter and raised his eyebrows.

Carter gave him his killer stare, and the crazed francophone voice boomed again: "De famous Cartch, *tabarnac*, I wet my pant!" It was Madz, swaggering over to their booth as if they'd been waiting for her and the party could now start. She slid in next to him.

"You clearly need a drink," said Carter.

Madz didn't even look at him. "Tell me something, famous Cartch," she said, her hazel eyes fixed appraisingly on Hayley. "How come hockey can't get a proper TV deal in the US of A? I mean, all those strapping white men, shedding their blood at the drop of a hockey glove. It's far more entertaining than the nightly highlight reel of our gift of democracy to Jihadville, ya know?"

Hayley laughed, and Carter sighed. Madz wasn't going to make it easy for him. "Hayley Rawls, Madz Weinfeld. Does the St. Pats colour commentary for SportsWorld when she's not doing a sit-down routine in the Black Irish."

"Thank you, I'll be here all week, please try the veal, and" – she offered Hayley her hand – "remember to fuck your waitress."

"That would be a change," said the waitress, who was also the landlady. Wanda Collins deposited a shot of Jameson and a pint of Harp in front of Madz. A slender, pretty black woman, Wanda had grown up in Hell's Kitchen surrounded by Irish ruffians.

"Here's to Saint Paddy's, Wanda," Madz said, raising her glass, "the one day of the year when blacks and Jews can join the only ethnic group on the planet that combines the worst aspects of their own."

Madz tilted her glass now to Carter, who aimed the insult back at her with his, then tilted her chin toward the ceiling and shot the whiskey down her throat.

"I'd love to stay and celebrate with you," Wanda said, "but the worst of humanity here is paying for my trip to Bermuda."

She hurried back to the bar, where her right-hand man, Russell the Muscle, all rippling pecs and abs, was trying to keep up with all the drink orders.

Carter noticed Hayley noticing Russell and was on the verge of intervening – by venturing how culturally rich it was to see a gay black weightlifter working in an Irish bar – when Hayley suddenly turned to Madz. "So," she said, her Chardonnay poised before her lips, "did you see what happened to the Russian?"

"Afraid not," Madz replied. "The replays were crap too. Eight cameras in that barn and none of them could see through the love fest. All we saw was Oblomov flying out of the scrum onto the ice, apparently bleeding to death from an upper-body injury. Beyond that, it's a mystery. But then, isn't life?" She smiled and followed the Jameson with a long draught of beer.

"Hard to believe all those cameras – not to mention all the cellphone cameras – and no one saw anything." Carter was sounding like a prosecutor. Not good. "I mean, I noticed you'd moved to a new spot? No luck there, huh?'

Hayley frowned at him. "I don't think Oblomov would call it luck."

Madz smacked her lips. "He will if it gets the Linkster suspended from the playoffs. The league sees a video of whatever Andrachuk did to the Russian and I'm betting he's gone for the rest of the season, and playoffs, and maybe next year. It will cost the Pats a fortune. It'll be a nice payday for some kid with a camera phone." She took another long draught of beer and then, catching Wanda's eye, waved her finger in a tight circle for another round.

"A fortune? How?" asked Hayley, looking with interest at the naked lesbian leprechauns on Madz's tie. Carter was losing the game and he hadn't even taken a good shot yet.

"Because the playoffs are the time of year when CHL teams print money," he said. "Players don't get paid for the playoffs. Their contracts end when the regular season ends. If a team gets in the playoffs, then all that money from tickets and hot dogs and beer and parking and TV is gravy for the club. And the deeper they go into the playoffs, the more they make. So losing their best player, and that's best with quotation marks —"

"Could cost them a fortune," said Hayley in a low voice, her eyes now stuck on Carter. It was like foreplay.

The Gobshites, sufficiently revived, kicked into their final set of the evening with the old Irish weepie "Molly Malone." Their Guinness-fuelled energy managed to rouse the other drunks, and soon a few couples had lurched out onto the dance floor, flailing away as the Gobshites rollicked.

The black man at the bar drifted to the side of Carter's booth and asked Hayley Rawls if she'd like to dance.

"We're in the middle of a conversation," Carter said, smelling Jameson on the man, who eased back his sports jacket at the waist so that Carter could see the NYPD badge hooked on his belt.

"Sorry," Carter corrected himself, "we're in the middle of a conversation, *officer.*"

The cop stared hard at Carter. "Aren't you the guy . . ." he said, letting the question hang. Carter waited for the part about being a great star once for the St. Pats. But instead, the cop continued, " . . . the guy who was just leaving?"

Carter knew that getting into a fight over a woman he barely knew in an Irish bar on St. Patrick's Day with a cop was a very low percentage play. But Hayley came to the rescue. "Actually, we were just leaving," she said. Then she drained her Chardonnay and stood, taking Carter's arm.

It was hard to say who was more surprised, Carter or Madz or the cop. Carter recovered enough to toss a twenty on the table. "Here's for our drinks, Madz. And feel free to buy this gentleman a round."

Weinfeld scooped up the note while the cop shifted his stare from Hayley to Carter, smiling at him with real loathing. "The next round's on me," he said. "That's a promise."

6

It was "Molly Malone" that followed them out on to 11th Avenue and not, as Carter feared, a drunken cop with an afterthought and a gun.

"So cops drink on duty here," Hayley said. "How civilized." She gave him a half-smile as he flagged a cab, which cut across two lanes and skidded to a stop in front of them. Carter knew the gesture wasn't for him. He opened the door for Hayley and followed her in to the back seat. "Would you like a night-cap?" he asked. "Maybe back at your hotel?"

"No," she said emphatically. "I thought I made it quite clear that we were going to your place."

Then she smiled at Carter and put her hand on his thigh, and Carter said, "Weehawken, my good man," to the driver, hoping Hayley wouldn't move her hand any higher. Not yet, anyway. He could already feel the heat rising in his crotch.

The driver, catching the spirit of the moment, with Carter on the verge of losing his one-year virginity, said, "Wee what?"

"Weehawken. New Jersey. You know, the state across the river."

Hayley pouted a little at the words *New Jersey*, but on what the St. Pats paid Carter, the only place he could afford in Manhattan wouldn't be big enough to hold a double bed.

Carter let New Jersey speak for itself as they swung out of the Lincoln Tunnel onto JFK Boulevard East, known in his neighbourhood as the MDV – Million-Dollar View. The secret about Weehawken that he had found out when he moved there ten years earlier was that its perch on the pal-isades of the Hudson River gave it the kind of vista of Manhattan that makes lovers swoon.

"Wow," said Hayley in genuine awe at the illuminated might of Manhattan across the river. "It looks so much bigger at night."

She let her hand ride higher on his thigh, closing in on home.

The cab pulled up in front of his apartment building on Potter Place, a five-storey pre–Second World War folly boast-ing minarets, like a grand mosque overlooking the Hudson, an architectural statement from a more innocent age.

"I hope," Hayley said, transfixed by glittering Manhattan, "that you have a room with a view."

"Yeah," said Carter, trying to tame the tent pole rising in his pants. "I have a view. You'll like it."

"I already do," she said, her hand on his crotch. "I already do . . ."

7

By the time the tiny elevator had reached the top floor, Hayley had Carter's pants down. He had her coat and T-shirt in one hand and his keys in the other and was fumbling with the lock on his door as if he'd never been there before.

Carter had envisioned this night for months, partly as a therapeutic counterpoint to the heavy, sad melody of the end of his affair with Flavia. He'd thought that one day he would want a woman again, not from lust, but as a vote for the future, the attendant risks to self that went with it factored in and accepted. He would be over Flavia. He would be his own man, with nothing to prove, and open to whoever came his way. There would be the kind of wooing that only Manhattan can provide: Saturday afternoon at the Met, followed by a cocktail on the terrace of the rooftop bar; Broadway at night; Sunday brunch in SoHo with the weekend edition of the *Times* and nowhere else to be. There would be a meeting of minds and a consummation fuelled by the eroticism of the ritual preceding it. There would be no violent hockey game, or an assault to the senses in an Irish bar with a lesbian and a drunk cop, and then animal foreplay in an elevator, all within the space of a few hours. And the perfume of Flavia still lingering in his heart.

But Carter wasn't thinking with his heart or his head when he and Hayley finally stumbled into his apartment, the moonlight soft through the curtainless windows.

"Now that's a view," said Hayley, taking a deep breath at the sight of Midtown Manhattan sparkling on the other side of the Hudson River. Then she turned to Carter with a smile and slid his boxer shorts down.

"And so is that, Mr. Love Rocket."

Mr. Love Rocket would not be Carter's term for his cock if he was given to cute new names for bits of himself, but he was in no mind to argue. "It just looks so much bigger at night," he said.

Hayley laughed, then grabbed Mr. Love Rocket and unrolled a condom that appeared from nowhere onto him, hanging on while Carter waltzed them in a stagger toward his bedroom.

They collapsed on his bed, deep in a French kiss as Hayley helped him into her, and the newly unchaste Martin Carter gave her his example of faster than a New York minute.

"Mmm," she said afterwards, stretched out naked on her stomach. "Miss Kitty liked that . . ."

Mr. Love Rocket and Miss Kitty. Carter was beginning to get the feeling, now that his brain was working again, that maybe Hayley Rawls wasn't as grown up as she seemed.

"Would you like a drink?" he asked.

She rolled over on to her back, her small pink nipples still erect, and gave him a weary look. "Men. All you want to do is talk and cuddle." Then she chuckled. "Kidding. Got any whiskey?"

Carter went into his kitchen and hauled out his duty-free twelve-year-old Jameson, pouring them both fat shots.

"Are you sure you're not gay?" she said, surprising him from behind.

"Yeah, but thanks for asking," he said, handing her a glass. "I guess I'm just a little out of practice."

She stuck a long unpainted fingernail into her whiskey and flicked some at him. "No, I mean your apartment is so neat and clean and decorated like . . . you know. It's unusual."

He looked around. Yes, it was neat and clean, with books, photos, and furniture. Understated and uncluttered. "No cat, though. Except for Miss Kitty."

She laughed and clinked his glass, then wandered out of the kitchen and into Carter's living room. He followed, her tight, swaying buttocks his very own light of the moon.

"Actually, it's a bump on the head is what it is," he said. "I used to make cavemen look gay until my, uh, accident." It had been no accident.

She gave him a searching look, but he didn't want to talk about it, didn't want to remember it. Couldn't remember it.

She seemed to understand and strolled over to look at the photos on the wall above the lawyer's bookcases, photos from the Kingdom of Before. Perhaps she thought they would tell her what he couldn't: the smiling kid with his mother on the outdoor rink on Bathurst Street in Toronto; the serious Catholic high schooler playing for the St. Mike's Buzzers; the Ivy League scholarship hotshot Princeton Tiger; then the pinnacle, or so he thought, the New York St. Pats rookie, spraying ice toward the camera in his one-day-to-be-priceless hockey-card photo.

But the photo that had Hayley leaning closer, her golden breasts brushing the three-volume set of *Remembrance of Things Past* (a gift from Flavia, trying to impress), was of Carter on the cover of *Sporting Times*. It was taken in his sophomore year as a pro, his last year in the CHL. He was wearing his green-and-gold St. Pats home uniform in the club dressing room and reading a book: *The Sonnets of William Shakespeare.* The photo had been set up by the photographer, and Carter had been too college arrogant to see it as anything other than him, the scholar athlete, telling the world that he was not to be taken for just another toothless, puck-chasing grunt. He had book learning. He was different.

And that turned out to be true, though not quite how he'd planned it.

"It's a great photo of you," she said.

"It was the kiss of death."

"Oh yeah? You seemed pretty alive a few minutes ago."

He grinned. "There's a tradition that says if they put you on the cover of *Sporting Times* before you've won the Cup," he explained, "you'll never win it."

"So why'd you let them?"

"Because I was too busy reading fucking Shakespeare."

She nuzzled him. "Or fucking, Shakespeare . . ."

She started to refuel Mr. Love Rocket with her hand, and before he could do too much about it, she'd guided Carter to his leather couch and straddled it, facing away from him, toward the mighty city. And then she said, "Just to the right of the maple leaf."

"What?"

She pointed to her tanned left buttock, to the tattoo of the red maple leaf thoughtfully planted there to guide the exiled patriot.

"Hey," he said. "Condom . . ."

"But it's our second date," she said, turning back to the city lights across the river, not once looking back as she rode Mr. Love Rocket on a longer trip this time. And when she touched down, she gave a short, sharp yip at the moon.

She rolled away, and they lay there in sweaty silence for a few minutes. Then she propped herself up on an elbow and looked him in the eye.

"I think," she said with a pause, "I can answer your question now."

His look said, What question? so she got up and walked over to her camera bag, taking from it her DVD camera and holding it up like a trophy.

"No thanks," he said, remembering Madz's warning. "There's already enough of me on the Internet."

She sat down in front of the bulky old monitor on his desk, the Twin Towers still standing on his screensaver. Another Kingdom of Before photo.

"What are you doing?" he asked. Taking sexual advantage of a vulnerable guy with a head injury was one thing, Carter thought, but taking advantage of his computer was a whole new level of intimacy.

She just winked at him and plugged a USB cable from her camera into the computer tower.

"Don't worry," she said, as the World Trade Center gave way to the icon of his media player. "I have a condom on this thing. Your computer won't get any diseases."

"That's not what I —"

His protest was interrupted by the appearance of Link Andrachuk's enraged face seen through the glass of Emerald Gardens by Hayley Rawls's camera. He was repeatedly smashing the butt end of his hockey stick into Sasha Oblomov's chin. The Russian's grey eyes showed that he would be screaming but for the geyser of blood spewing from his mouth. He had clearly bitten through his own tongue on the force of one of Andrachuk's blows.

"Oh my God."

She hit pause and froze the geyser in mid-gush. She looked at Carter, smiling as if she'd won the state lottery. Then she hit play and let the explosion of Oblomov's blood shower the Plexiglas. "That's what I'm thinking too."

She walked over to the couch, grabbing her whiskey as she went, and sank back into its soft leather, propping her feet on the coffee table. She patted the seat next to her, but Carter stayed by his computer, staring at Oblomov's bloody face, trying to digest what he had just seen.

"Lucky I didn't just stay parked where you put me, huh? Otherwise, we'd have missed out on an opportunity."

"Opportunity?" His throat was tight.

"Or you could call it fate."

He took his whiskey and sat in the armchair facing the window, so she would look at his face, moonlit, and not out the window toward the city of Mammon. "And what does that mean exactly?"

"Well," she said, resting her glass on her flat stomach. "I was thinking about what you said about how much it would cost New York if Link were suspended."

"Yes," he said tightly, taking a sip of whiskey.

"So, I wouldn't want to hurt Link's career, but on the other hand, if I'm the only one who has evidence, it must be worth something."

He sat unblinking, letting the heat of the whiskey warm his throat, so the right words could come out.

But Hayley wasn't finished. She fingered a strand of hair into a tight curl, like a schoolgirl negotiating a treat. "Who do you think would pay me more for it? The Sea Lions or the St. Pats?"

Carter's forehead tingled with cold. The doctors said the sensation was a legacy of the hit that ended his career, but Carter had come to see it not as a legacy, but as a portent. Of trouble.

Before he became a head case, he saw only what he needed to see, but that handy little censor had been flattened by his headfirst collision with a goalpost. Now there was just Carter, defenceless and exposed to things he didn't want to see. Because then he had to do something about them.

He should have realized that Hayley's sudden enthusiasm for a trip to New Jersey to get to know Martin Carter better was based on his use to her as a broker. He downed the rest of his Jameson.

"Maybe some kid with a cellphone camera is already out there flogging it," Carter said, his head cold, his throat hot.

She grinned and shook her head. "Nope. The scrum was blocking everything but my camera and Link and Oblomov. It was our own perfect threesome."

"Selling this footage will kill your documentary deal," he said, trying to slice into her certainty with doubt.

"Not if I sell it to New York," she said, walking over to his chair, then straddling him, her face right in his. "They'd bury it. And I'm thinking, with your help, they'd be very happy to get it. I'll cut you in for a percentage of whatever you can get."

She smiled and shifted backward, glancing down at the rising Mr. Love Rocket, which, despite himself, Carter couldn't stop from responding to her heat. "Of course," she said, taking him in hand and guiding him into her again, "the bigger, the better."

8

It had happened nearly fifteen years ago and it was still beautiful. Nothing but open ice between Martin Carter and the Vancouver goalie, the puck like a yo-yo on his stick as he pushed it ahead, then caught up with it, closing in on that perfect moment when, with a snap of his wrists, he'd fire the little black disc into the net.

But it was much more than a goal. It was the Cup-winning goal for the New York St. Pats, the goal he had already scored in his head thousands of times, ever since he had understood as a little kid what it would mean.

But then, and no matter how hard he tried to dream the outcome differently, Andy Jack's lunging stick always nicked his right skate, launching him in a twisting arc toward the net. And Martin Carter was the puck now. But he wasn't going to bulge the twine and win the Cup and be the hero — he was going to ram headfirst into the goalpost. And in those days goalposts didn't forgivingly pop off their pegs but fought back with cold, hard steel.

Then darkness fell, followed by more darkness when the lights came back on. It was his Before, and his After. It was Game Over.

Carter had this nightmare with such infrequency it made it noticeable. It wasn't the effect of too much whiskey, or jalapenos on a midnight pizza, but a subconscious barometer of doom. He had it when his father died. He had it when Flavia chose her career as a lawyer over him. And now he had it after his night with Hayley Rawls. In the Kingdom of After, it was a forecast of bad weather ahead.

There was no "Just Kidding" note from Hayley scrawled in scarlet lipstick on his bathroom mirror. There was just Martin Carter looking at himself, and judging. Guilty of being a head case.

He wandered into his living room to survey the scene of his latest brain-damaged adventure in the cold March sunlight. Hard to believe that only a few hours ago he had been

rolling around there naked with Hayley and actually imag-
ining a future with her, one that didn't involve extortion.

Her business card was on his desk, sitting where she had
left it when he sent her off in a cab in the middle of the night,
her cellphone number circled as a reminder of what to do once
he had slept on her proposition and his good self-interested
sense had prevailed.

Carter tried to do his morning ritual of fifty pushups, but,
exhausted, distracted, couldn't get past thirty, then showered
and dressed. The sports reports were mystified about what
had levelled Sasha Oblomov and certain that the Sea Lions'
playoff hopes had just taken a huge hit.

On his way out, Carter grabbed his copies of the *Times* and
the *Mail* from the lobby and was pushing the door open when
he spotted Carlito, the building's superintendent.

"Hola, boss," Carlito said, looking up with a grin from his
one-kneed perch in the front garden. "Nam nam pichon." He
pumped a cupped hand up and down, and the sack of dog
shit he was holding jiggled like Hayley's buttocks had done
not so long ago.

Carlito was an illegal from somewhere in Central America,
and his English was peppered with Spanish phrases that
Carter could only guess at from his body language. His fist
pumping gave Carter a pretty good idea that he meant Hayley
Rawls. But Carter didn't recall seeing Carlito when they
entered the building night before.

"No comprende, Carlito."

"TV!"

He dropped the plastic bag and grabbed Carter by the arm,
hustling them into his little office next to the elevator, and
proudly flicked on a new TV, attached to a VCR. On TV,
Carter was staring at himself and Carlito, staring at the

monitor, then the screen shifted views to the lobby and then the elevator.

"New security! With replay." Carlito punched a code into the remote controller, and now Carter was looking at himself and Hayley Rawls making out in the elevator the night before. The image was embarrassingly clear, showing Mr. Love Rocket ready for takeoff.

Carlito's smile invited Carter to tell him more than the picture did, but instead he slipped the super a twenty and said, "Nuke it."

"What?"

Carter pointed at himself and Hayley frozen in foreplay on the TV screen, then waved goodbye at it. "Hasta la vista. Por favor."

Carlito nodded, looking a little sad, and Carter watched while he erased the tape.

"No mas, amigo," he said.

No more, indeed, thought Carter. The security camera would send them all back into the Dark Ages – hiding from its indiscriminate eye. But he also knew, deep in his cold head, that he couldn't hide from Hayley Rawls. And he couldn't erase what her camera had seen.

Carter tried to read the papers on the bus ride through the Lincoln Tunnel, but it only brought on nausea. And none of the sports reports could tell him anything he didn't already know about Link Andrachuk's assault on Oblomov. Because they didn't know.

So that made Carter the member of an exclusive club: himself, Hayley, Oblomov, and Andrachuk. And, thought Carter, from the look of his sliced-up tongue on the video,

Oblomov would be testifying with a paper and a pen. If, of course, he remembered anything.

That was the other thing about Before. Carter didn't remember the hit that had ended his career. He just remembered what he had seen of it on TV sports highlights, one of those infernal reels that he believed were the reason why the golden age of sports began with television. You don't have to see the game, just the great replay of the great play, and you have instant and permanent nostalgia.

Watching the replay of himself flying headfirst into the Vancouver goalpost was like watching someone else get injured, and he winced in sympathy every time he saw the poor bastard's helmet split in two and – slow motion was best for this – his body go rigid and pause, cartoonlike, in mid-air, before it, before Carter, crumpled to the ice with a fractured skull and a grade-three concussion.

Carter had Nurse Nature to thank for erasing that bit of footage from his brain, just as Carlito had erased him and Hayley Rawls from the security tape. Perhaps Oblomov's memory of Andrachuk's savage attack had been erased too.

But Carter hoped not, because then Oblomov could be the messenger, and not him.

9

The thing with being a head case, Carter had discovered, was that while he couldn't always remember everything, the stuff that he could remember often careered through his mind like a movie directed by a meth head. While Carter couldn't remember the hit that sent him into Afterland, he remembered exactly what Link Andrachuk had done to Sasha

Oblomov. He knew he owed it to the Cardinal to tell him.

In fact, Carter owed pretty much everything to John J. O'Connor, the Cardinal. O'Connor's father had built Emerald Gardens a long time ago, just before the Great Depression, on a chunk of land that may as well have been in New Jersey, way out on 23rd Street and 11th Avenue.

The St. Pats had been the city's immigrants' team, which tugged its forelocks before its gilded better, the New York Aristocrats, who played out of the old Madison Square Garden. But the Aristos had folded during the Second World War, and Manhattan had muscled its way westward. Now Emerald Gardens' location looked like a work of visionary genius, as the city was making noise about needing a new stadium complex on the west side, and the arena was already there, ripe for renewal.

Or demolition. To Carter, Emerald Gardens was a museum encompassing both decades and the huddled masses, an Ellis Island of hockey. But right now, with the green-and-gold dome atop a working-class brick rectangle looming into view as he walked down from the Port Authority, it seemed less a bold vision than a relic. The filigreed iron marquee that presided over the plaza in front, even with its shiny new coat of black paint, was more suited to the era when hockey players held down jobs on beer trucks in the off-season, and knew what the fans thought of them because they worked with them, than to the new world of multimillionaire players like Link Andrachuk, who couldn't hear anything but the roar of their own egos.

The mood around the Gardens that morning was like a St. Patrick's Day hangover without the booze the night before, a grim silence that hit Carter as soon as he walked through the glass doors to the executive offices.

"Tell me you know, Cartch," pleaded Bleecker, who suddenly appeared outside Carter's office. It was a real question this time, and Carter's forehead throbbed coldly. Know what? That Link nearly killed a man? And what does Bleecker know?

"It was a bad night," Carter said evenly.

"You don't know where Link is?" Bleecker continued, his tone suggesting that Link and Carter were inseparable. But that was because he was genuinely worried; no jaded ex-business reporter now but a man in fear.

"I don't. Why?"

"Well, because we can't find him. He was supposed to be here for the media conference, damage control and all that, but he's *nowhere*."

"I'm sure he'll turn up. He'll want his last cheque of the season."

Bleecker moved in close to Carter, whispering now, "He has issues."

"Don't we all?"

"No, I mean" – he looked over his shoulder – "he's got personal problems."

Carter wasn't surprised to hear that. And he could see where Bleecker was going. "That accounts for his black eye and fat lip, huh?"

Bleecker held his finger up to his lips, as if Carter had spoken the unspeakable.

"Well then," Carter said, "call the cops."

Bleecker put his hand to his heart. "We might as well call the media conference at the same time at Link's place. No, this is an internal matter."

"Okay, but how can I help?"

Bleecker sighed. "You were with the woman doing the documentary on him, so maybe you can call her? Like, now?"

So he didn't know. But Carter didn't want another dose of Hayley Rawls quite yet. And there was something wrong with the picture.

"Why don't you call her, Doug? You're the media guy."

"Yes," he agreed, "but she didn't go home with me."

Carter's forehead tingled again. How did Bleecker know that Hayley had made a midnight trip to New Jersey? Before he could form a response, Brenda, the Cardinal's receptionist, hissed, "Mr. O'Connor is here!" from down the hall and gestured toward the boardroom. If the Cardinal had come in this early to hold an audience with the staff, it wouldn't be because the Missing Link was missing. It would be worse than that.

The Cardinal, in his customary black suit, white shirt, and green tie, gaunt and grey-faced and seeming about a half-century older than his eighty-one years, rolled in to the boardroom in his wheelchair – pushed along by the St. Pats' president, Freddie Hutt. It was the only time the Cardinal ever got pushed around, and the contrast between the two men was startling. The Cardinal was elegant and dignified, even if he looked as if he'd invented time itself, and Hutt looked like he was trying to deny its existence.

On the north side of fifty, Hutt had left the pinstriped suits of Wall Street behind him and now dressed as if every day were the rich man's casual Friday, sporting five-hundred-dollar jeans and a gold Duckie Brown blazer with a Rolex to match. With his shaved head, boxy horn-rims, and the black turtleneck riding high on not much neck to speak of, the chubby Freddie Hutt looked like he was being squeezed out of his own body.

He rolled the Cardinal to the heavy wooden table, where most of the front office staff had already gathered, parked him at its head, and then pulled up a chair next to him. The

Cardinal slowly angled his head and gave Hutt a glance of such dismissive eloquence that the president shuffled his chair a couple of feet back without a word.

The Cardinal shifted his eyes to the rest of the table, eyes that matched his tie, sharp and green. Still the Boss.

"Good morning, and thank you for coming," he said, and he meant it, for like the authentically powerful everywhere, he counted on nothing. "I won't keep you long."

He took a sip of water and glanced at the portrait of his father on the panelled wall, Patrick J. O'Connor, who had started the team just before the Cardinal was born. The old man smiled at the portrait of his old man, then turned back to the assembled. "I'm selling the St. Pats," he said.

The question of what would happen next had been swirling through the Gardens ever since the Cardinal's prostate cancer had spread to his bones last year. As he had no heirs that anyone knew of, the family business was about to run out of family. Even so, the Cardinal's words sucked the air out of the room.

"I know," he said, seeing the shock, "my timing could have been better, but given my current situation, time is not my friend. If it ever was."

He smiled at Carter, who smiled back. They both knew about that bastard time, the hard way. The Cardinal took another sip of water, then, having done the hard part, nodded to Freddie Hutt, who explained the rest. Starting with Link Andrachuk.

"We dodged a bullet last night, kids," he said. "The league is gonna fine us ten thousand dollars for 'disgracin' the game of hockey,' but that's it."

Hutt had a high, flinty voice and an accent more suited to coon hunting in the Virginia hills than the dangerous reefs of New York. He carefully cultivated it to keep the Manhattan sharks off guard.

"There's gonna be no suspension for Link because" – Hutt smiled broadly at the Cardinal – "we had the luck of the Irish on our side. Not one of our friends in the media managed to capture on tape – or otherwise – just what happened between Link and Oblomov."

Now he smiled at everyone, going face by face around the table. "And we live in that magical age where if the camera didn't see it, well, then it didn't happen, now did it?" He paused to let their appreciation of his insight ripple through the room.

Carter said, "You mean no kid with a cellphone camera caught it?"

Freddie looked at him as if he were toilet paper stuck to his shoe. "This is New York, Cartch," he said. "Anyone who had such a thing woulda sold it already to the highest bidder, and it'd be all over the media by now. But it isn't. So as I was sayin', the luck of the Irish was with us. Of course, if anything should turn up that shows Link did something, uh, deliberate to injure Oblomov, then we could lose him for the rest of the season – and the playoffs. And I don't need to tell you that we *need* Link Andrachuk because we *need* to make the playoffs."

The St. Pats hadn't won the Cup in forty years, but that was an ongoing existential fist shake at a hostile cosmos. Their practical problem was that they had missed the playoffs for the past six seasons. This had caused their famously loyal fans to drop their season ticket subscription by 30 per cent, which cost five jobs in the front office. Carter knew that making the playoffs would mean the St. Pats were worth quite a bit more if you were looking, for instance, to sell them.

"As Mr. O'Connor has said, he'll put the for-sale sign out once the season ends, but we already have a couple of buyers interested. So if – when – the team makes the playoffs, and goes deep, goes, please the Good Lord, all the way to game seven of the Cup final, with each of the four series to get there going seven games, that would give us twelve home dates." He smiled at the thought. "Twelve home dates in the playoffs gives us a projected revenue stream of more than sixteen million dollars from ticket sales and another four million from concessions. That's twenty million dollars from bums in seats and beers in bellies, and that twenty million will bump up the value of the team." He paused, for effect. "And if the team is worth more, so are you and your jobs to the new owners, whoever they may be."

He looked right at Carter when he mentioned their jobs, for it was no secret that Hutt had wanted to replace Carter with one of his marketing guys when he took over the St. Pats, and that O'Connor wouldn't let him. The Cardinal had given Carter a front-office job when he couldn't play anymore and told him then, on a handshake, that it was a job for life. He hadn't said whose, and Carter hadn't ever asked.

Hutt's look told Carter that he would be the first to go under any new regime. Unless O'Connor had the good manners to die right now and Hutt could simply fire him.

The Cardinal had noticed Hutt's glare and said, in a surprisingly firm voice, "It will be a condition of sale that all of you remain here. Unless you choose otherwise."

"On that note, it will also be, excuse me, Mr. O'Connor," interrupted Hutt, "a condition of your employment that you keep what you heard here this morning absolutely confidential." He started passing around sheets of paper. "Anyone who leaks any information about the proposed sale will be subject to immediate dismissal with a seriously diminished severance package. As this clearly spells out."

The paper was a non-disclosure agreement, the first Carter had ever seen in his years with the St. Pats. He looked to the Cardinal for confirmation that this was some mistake, but the Cardinal was gazing at the portrait of his father.

"When my father started this club in 1926, as one of the original teams in the Continental Hockey League, he said it would be a family in the family of New York City." He took a sip of water. "And while patriarchs come and go, families continue. I do not want any dishonour brought on my family, ever, by anyone, and that's why I want to sell this team while I'm still here to make sure it goes to a good home. On my terms. It's my last season in more ways than one, and it would be nice to say farewell with a sip or two of champagne from the Cup."

He didn't have to add that he never had the chance to drink from the Cup in his long tenure as managing owner, and Carter knew that to bring up Hayley Rawls and her kind offer to part the St. Pats from their money in exchange for preserving the family honour might send the Cardinal to his reward right here.

"Any questions?" asked Hutt, his tight smile suggesting that asking any would be a bad idea. So Carter said nothing. What he had to say, he would now say to Hayley Rawls.

10

The cramped media room at Emerald Gardens was packed with sweaty print and radio reporters and half-a-dozen network cameras as Freddie Hutt offered up a tutorial in the language of sports management newspeak – a language that made it seem as if the St. Pats had no responsibility in starting the bench-clearing brawl but had been innocent bystanders.

Carter marvelled at how Hutt could keep a straight face as he told the bug-eyed reporters that the CHL would be fining both teams for last night's "unfortunate event." The St. Pats had been "hornswoggled" by good old-fashioned emotion as they made their glorious run for the playoffs, but they also made all their fans proud with their grit and determination in the face of adversity. Amen.

Hutt had asked Carter to sit up on the podium with senior management, the green-and-gold St. Pats banner draped behind them as living proof that the St. Pats looked after their own. Which meant that Carter couldn't wink at Madz when Hutt said, in response to her question about Link Andrachuk's whereabouts, "No, he's up at the Metrocorp Children's Hospital today. He does great work for kids with cancer."

It was the unblinking naming of the hospital – the detail, as with all lies – that sold it. Carter almost believed it too.

"Then will you tell us what charitable thing he said to Oblomov to start the riot?" Madz shot back.

Carter could feel Hutt's body stiffen from three seats away. "Link Andrachuk is a great asset to the New York St. Pats, but the beauty of hockey is that there's no *I* in the word *team*, and our team wins as a team."

Carter nearly laughed out loud. A press release had listed Hutt's favourite sport as NASCAR before he joined the St. Pats and hockey became his one true love. How hillbillies careering around in circles in the souped-up family sedan counted as any kind of sport eluded Carter, but it explained why Bleecker soon took over the media shop and recast Hutt.

"I have a question for Mr. Carter . . ." said a woman in her early thirties, looking at him with a friendly smile fronting the bluest eyes he had ever seen.

She wore a Burberry raincoat over a dress, though Carter

couldn't see what kind of dress, just her athletic legs beneath the coat, descending elegantly into black pumps. She wore her straight blond hair in a ponytail and accessorized those striking eyes with tortoise-shell glasses and a splash of scarlet across a mouth that was not going to wait for permission to speak to him. "Gracie Yates, *Vancouver Gazette*," she said, identifying herself in a strong alto. "How did you feel about what Link Andrachuk did to Sasha Oblomov?"

Before Bleecker could step in with a prophylactic "I think that's all for today," Carter started talking, and there was no way they could stop him, he knew, with all those pesky reporters in the room.

"Well, Ms. Yates," he said, "the first thing that comes to mind is that I hope Sasha Oblomov is okay. And the second thing is that I didn't see what, if anything, Link Andrachuk did to Oblomov. Did you?"

Hutt was looking at Carter with the smile of a hangman, but his gamble paid off. She said, "No, I didn't, but clearly, they were in the middle of that scrum, and Oblomov came out seriously injured, and Andrachuk did not."

Carter nodded. "And I would think Link Andrachuk considers himself lucky, for I understand Sasha Oblomov is no slouch when it comes to defending himself."

"Neither were you," she said quietly, "and look what happened when your back was turned."

On that, Bleecker ended the party. Carter tried to catch up with Gracie Yates as she left the room, but his way was blocked by an immoveable object known to the team's insiders as Hopalong.

"A word please, Mr. Carter."

Eamon Lynch had been the security chief for the St. Pats for nearly a decade but still had an Ulster accent as thick as his neck. Rumour had it that the Cardinal had helped him out when he was in trouble back home with the Irish Republican Army. Apparently, it had resulted from Lynch's knee-capping – his specialty, hence the nickname Hopalong – a Derry drug dealer, who happened to be the boyfriend of the cousin of the niece of an IRA brigade commander. Lynch had had to leave home in a hurry.

"Sure," Carter said to Hopalong, who gestured for Carter to precede him out of the media room.

"If this is about –" Carter began once they were in the corridor, but Hopalong held a rough finger to his lips.

"It is," he said. "But since it's such a nice day . . ."

They went outside into the March sunshine, like two gangsters evading eavesdroppers. Or, Carter corrected the thought, one gangster and one head case.

"So," Hopalong said as they strolled up 11th Avenue toward the Black Irish, "what do you know about that woman you were with?"

"Hayley Rawls?"

"Have there been other women in the past" – Hopalong glanced at his watch – "seven hours?"

The lights flickered on a screen in Carter's imagination. He saw Lynch outside his apartment smoking a cigarette, the moon beaming down on him in perfect film noir complicity. Otherwise, how did he know what time Hayley had left?

"I don't know much."

"No revealing pillow talk then?"

Carter stopped walking and just stared at him.

"Have you been following me?"

Hopalong's lips curled in a slight, tight smile. "Relax, Mr. Carter. I'm on your side."

"My side? I didn't know I had a side."

"We both work for the same man. And you were last seen in the company of a woman we don't know that much about, a woman with a camera." He flashed the cold-eyed grin of a sadist.

"She was just getting some shots of Link Andrachuk for a DVD she's making for some website about the guy."

"It should have gone through me," Hopalong said, still smiling.

"Talk to Doug Bleecker about that."

"Oh I have, Mr. Martin. He said she was your special request."

The lying shit, thought Carter. He had an impulse to let Hopalong know that Bleecker had once told him that the old knee-capper was also a British spy, and that was the real reason he had to leave home, but he figured the messenger might have to pay for that one, so Carter let the lie stand.

"It was a busy day. I was helping out."

Hopalong lit a cigarette and stared off toward the Hudson River. Carter stood there, still in the gravitational pull of the Irishman's general menace.

"In the future," Hopalong said, exhaling the word as if Carter's future was as evanescent as the plume of his cigarette smoke, "you come to me with any problem."

"She wasn't a problem."

Hopalong smiled for real at Carter, a crooked, yellow-toothed, toxic grin. Then he ground his cigarette into the pavement. "Well," he said, the smile flattening into a grim warning, "you come to me if she becomes one."

11

Hayley Rawls surprised the hell out of Carter by answering her cellphone on the second ring.

"You can't be home already?" he said, by way of hello.

"Good thing I'm not," she said, and he could hear the smile in her voice. "I knew you'd miss me."

She said she was still in town and suggested they meet for coffee in Brooklyn, where she was staying "with friends." Carter was still at work and counter-offered that they meet for lunch closer to his office. But not too close, just in case Eamon Lynch should hop by and spoil the mood.

"This is your treat?" she asked a couple of hours later, surveying the menu at Hearth, his favourite restaurant in the East Village, or in Manhattan for that matter. The small, real-brick joint on East 12th Street had just started opening for lunch, and its no-fakery food was matched by its democratic discretion – everyone, from king to cur, was a customer.

"Call this lunch an investment," he said.

"In that case," she smiled at the waiter, "I'll have a glass of champagne to start."

"Club soda for me."

Hayley shot him a look of mock disappointment, clearly revelling in her upper hand.

"But aren't we here to celebrate?" she said, leaning toward him.

"That would be up to you," he said, leaning toward her. May as well keep the blackmail civil, he thought.

"Well," she said, running her fingers along the edge of the linen tablecloth, brushing away imaginary crumbs, "make me an offer I can't refuse."

She was wearing a black dress with a string of pearls. Last night's funkster had given way to an Upper East Side duchess, her knee-high leather boots adding a touch of dominatrix. It was a remarkable transformation, as if she was not only running the show but already in the money.

"The thing is . . ." He paused as the waiter delivered their drinks. "I don't know the first thing about blackmail."

She angled her champagne flute toward Carter, not in a toast but to let the bubbles rise, then took a sip. "Hmm. Nothing like the Widow Cliquot to take the edge off. And I prefer your first term, by the way."

"What?"

"An investment," she said, running her tongue over her lips, her gaze meeting his.

"Like last night?"

She laughed. "No, last night I wanted to fuck. And if I like the terms of your investment, I'm sure I'll be in the mood again."

To anyone who didn't know her, to anyone who fancied a beautiful woman, she was the perfume of a spring afternoon in Manhattan, and she knew it. But all that Carter wanted now was to redeem his mistake the way he'd been taught – by scoring a goal.

"The thing is," he countered, "if this footage you have of Link slicing up Oblomov . . . if it's made public, and he gets suspended by the league and crucified across the land because the tape plays all the time on YouTube and on sports shows, and maybe even ends his career, how can that help your project?"

Hayley looked at Carter as if he were the stupidest child in a class of idiots. "Because, as I tried to tell you last night," she said, stretching out the syllables, "if Link Andrachuk gets suspended – and he certainly will if the league sees what you've seen – then that will cost your team a lot of money . . ." She sipped her champagne, giving him time to think about how much. "Much more than you'd have to pay me. Same thing if I sell it to the Vancouver Sea Lions and they have real legs for their fucken God bless America lawsuit. No matter how you slice it, it's a lot more than I'm making for this crappy little documentary."

Carter stared at her, so confident and patronizing and downtown, when less than twenty-four hours ago she was a wide-eyed girl from the West Coast.

"Do you know where Link is right now?" Carter countered.

"No, where?"

"I'm asking."

"Why? You think he's going to step in and buy my bargain footage?"

No, Carter did not. The famously cheap Link wouldn't even step in to buy a round of beers for his linemates. But Link's participation in the blackmail would be moot if he were dangling from a rope.

"How much do you want?" Carter whispered, the words sticking in his throat.

"Oh, let's eat first," she said, opening the menu. "How's the gnocchi?"

It was going to be a long game.

"The food is all very good," Carter played along. "Old family recipes of the chef. He's Sicilian – revenge is a dish best served cold and all that."

She didn't even glance up from the menu. "You come here a lot, then?"

"Only when I can't get into the Black Irish." Truth was, Carter came here as often as he could, but it was hard to expense it six times a week. This one, though, the Cardinal would understand.

"I think I'll have the gnocchi and the marinated sardines," she said. "That way I can keep drinking champagne."

Carter hadn't had much of an appetite when he'd arrived, and now he wasn't hungry at all. It was going to be painful to sit through lunch while she toyed with him before she named her price. And she knew it.

Hayley smiled triumphantly at him across the table, the fragrant yellow orchid in the middle of it no match for the stench of blackmail. Carter felt nauseated.

"Let me get started on it," he said. "Tell me what you want, and I'll go to the bank."

She didn't even blink. "Okay. A million. U.S. dollars, of course."

"You're" – he nearly said "joking" but that wouldn't have been smart – "pretty generous in your estimation of what this footage means to us."

She leaned on one elbow and smiled at him as if he'd been born yesterday. "Even if you only play two home playoff games – and you can't have any less than two home dates, even if you only go one round – it would mean millions to the St. Pats. I can count. No Link, no playoffs. I think it's a fair price."

She wasn't wrong about the economics, but there was no way to gauge Andrachuk's value. Sure, he could command the St. Pats' run in the playoffs, or he could take them on an egomaniac's suicide mission. It was hard to say which, and she knew it.

So Carter had to gamble, and the one sure thing here was that if he didn't do something, the footage would be lighting up the screens of Times Square by this time tomorrow.

He wished his cellphone would ring with some huge crisis that pulled him out of the restaurant and back to the office.

And it did.

It was his turn to smile as he rose from the table and slid open his phone, noticing the display said, "PRIVATE CALLER." It could be someone selling him a credit card, or Flavia begging forgiveness, but either way he was going to say, "Gotta take this outside."

It was Madz. "Hey, Cartch, you heard?"

This was getting to be an increasingly loaded question, he thought.

"Heard what, Madz? They find the guy who nearly killed Oblomov?"

She was silent.

"Madz?"

"That's the thing, Cartch. I have someone inside St. Mel's. Bad news. They've downgraded Oblomov's condition from serious to critical."

Carter could see Link's stick smashing into Oblomov's face. And Oblomov dead before he could give a statement.

"Do you think I could see him?" Carter blurted.

"Cartch, critical means they think he's going to die."

"I know what it means, Madz," he said, his voice more tenor than baritone. "But can I talk to your source? In person? Get me in there and I'll owe you one. Please."

She paused again, this time to gauge his urgency.

"Okay," she said. "Meet you there in an hour."

Carter headed back into the restaurant, his head thumping.

Hayley had ordered another glass of champagne and was tucking into some pagnotta when he sat down.

"Who died?"

Carter waved at the waiter.

"Yes, sir?"

"Bring the bill, please. I've got to go. She can stay."

The waiter looked at Hayley with sympathy. Just another jilted woman in the city with a glut of them.

"What's wrong?" she asked.

"Oblomov's dying."

She put down her wineglass, her face flushed, her brown eyes hot with indignation. "Yeah? Well, all the more reason to buy what I'm selling."

She was all heart.

"Keep the change," he replied, slapping a fifty on the table.

"You walk out on me and it's over," she said.

"Hayley," he said, trying to keep calm, "you told me your price. Now I'm going to figure out how to get it. But I have to go. I'll call you."

She shook her head. "You have until midnight," she said. "If I hear nothing, I'm going back to Vancouver. And my first call will be to the Sea Lions. They've got money too."

12

One of the many nice things about Manhattan, Carter thought, was that no one notices when you talk to yourself, and he was doing a lot of muttering as he paced in front of St. Melchior's Hospital on 7th Avenue, waiting for Madz. But talking about his problems, even to himself, wasn't helping.

The Cardinal was the only one who could sign over a million bucks for a ten-second piece of blood-soaked video, and he could not face the Cardinal with blackmail. He couldn't bring the deal to team boss Freddie Hutt either; he'd be gleefully booted into oblivion, lucky to coach doughnut-shop hockey in Foam Lake, Kentucky.

He stared up at the statue of the saint above the hospital entrance. That's what he needed, thought Carter, the intervention of a saint, or some kind of magic to save the day.

"Jesus, Cartch," said Madz, getting out of the taxi and catching his smile. "Tell me the joke."

"I was just thinking I needed a miracle," he said, "and here you are."

"You got me mixed up with that other Jewish chick. The lady in blue, with the crown and the intact hymen."

They went inside and headed for the cafeteria, where Madz's contact was going to meet them.

She was a lanky black woman in surgical scrubs, standing by the entrance, cradling a paper cup of coffee.

"Hey, Bobbi," Madz said. "I appreciate this. Dr. Bobbi Washington, Martin Carter."

Bobbi didn't shake Carter's hand and gave him a wary look.

"It's okay," said Madz. "He's from the St. Pats. And he's an honorary dyke."

Bobbi gave him a slight nod, then turned back to Madz. "What do you want to know?"

"How bad is Oblomov?"

"Well, he's got one mother of a TBI. Traumatic brain injury."

"Can he talk?"

She glanced at Carter, then turned back to Madz. "If he comes out of his coma."

"And how's that looking?" said Madz, evenly.

"We put him under. He has a grade-three concussion and a fractured skull, with serious brain swelling. He could have died from the blood loss due to his partially severed tongue, and it's going to take a lot of surgery to get his tongue back in order. That is, if he survives the next week."

"And I know you're a betting woman, Bobbi," Madz poked.

"Yeah, I am, and I'd say that the chance of Oblomov seeing Moscow again is a long shot."

Carter and Madz were silent for a moment.

"Can we see him?" Carter asked.

"Why?"

"I need to see him so I can convince the St. Pats to do the right thing. I had a grade-three concussion once too. Call it team spirit."

He could feel Madz's sidelong glance, but he just smiled sincerely at Bobbi. She thought about it, took a sip of coffee, then nodded.

"Elevator's this way," she said.

At the nursing station in Neurology, two NYPD uniforms blocked their way.

"What's up?" Bobbi asked.

"Security for Mr. Oblomov."

"They're with me," Bobbi said.

"Sorry, doctor," the younger, Latino cop said. "Only hospital tags get past this point."

Carter looked down the hall and saw another cop standing outside what he assumed was Oblomov's door.

"It would seem there's been a change of plan," Bobbi said.

"What's the security for?" Carter asked the cop.

"If I could tell you that, sir, it wouldn't be security, would it?"

Madz waited until they were outside St. Mel's and on 7th Avenue before she pounced.

"'Convince the St. Pats to do the right thing' is, I think, what you said."

Carter stopped and turned to her. "'I owe you' is what I actually said."

"How's that?"

"Tell me," he continued, "is it usual to have NYPD uniforms guarding the room of an injured hockey player?"

She touched him on the arm. "You don't know?"

"There's a lot I don't know."

"Oblomov has been on the wrong end of the Bratva for some time now."

"The Bratva?"

"The Russian Mafia. Some gambling thing. He didn't throw a game he was supposed to have thrown. So they say."

Carter's heart was pounding, and he started to sweat. "You don't think Link is in the pay of the Russian Mafia?"

"Who knows? But then, the one guy who could tell us can't talk."

Sweat was dripping into Carter eyes, the salt making them tear up. It looked like he was crying.

"Cartch? Are you okay?"

He took a deep breath. "What would you say if I told you what happened?"

She stared at him. "You mean to Oblomov?"

He nodded and wiped away a tear of sweat. "I can get you some footage of just what happened to Sasha Oblomov last night. I saw it."

She took a deep breath. "I'd say that we both need a drink."

They parked themselves in the back of a little bar on 7th Avenue, and Madz drank a shot and a beer while Martin Carter told her the story of the night before.

"Christ, Cartch," she said when he'd finished, her eyes wide. "You need more than a miracle. What the fuck are you going to do?"

"I'm going to get the footage from her."

"With what? Your pension fund?"

"No, with your money. I mean, SportsWorld's money."

Madz gave him a lunatic stare. "Let's go back to Neurology and check you in."

He explained the plan, such as it was.

"A million dollars?" she said, her face pale. "Sorry, a million *fucking* dollars?"

Carter leaned forward. "You don't need a million. Not yet. Maybe just a hundred K. I'll talk to Hayley, tell her it's a down payment, no, a rental, get the footage, and you can have a look-see. This thing will earn you guys more than your money back in rights fees once you share it with the world."

She stared at him, as if waiting for him to say he was only joking. But he just stared back, wearing his broken-nosed poker face. She was his last hope.

"Okay," she said, convinced when he didn't blink that he was serious. "What's in it for you?"

Loyalty to the Cardinal, he thought. Loyalty to himself. A desire to see the bad punished and the good prevail. The worldview of a head case.

"Actually," he said, "'what's in it for you in the short term?' is the question. The way I see it is that you're going to sit on the footage until after the St. Pats get bounced from the playoffs."

"Jesus, Cartch, I see why she slept with you. Your charm is magical." She downed her beer and waved for another round.

"Madz, you drink like you're Irish."

"No, I drink because *you're* Irish. Show me the bouncing ball here, Cartch."

"I can't. I will – but not yet. Just trust me that there's a bigger story coming once the season ends for the St. Pats, and I'll give you that one on a platter while the competition is still hitting the snooze buttons on their alarm clocks. And when you put that one together with Link Andrachuk's crime, you'll be in line for a major raise, the Pulitzer, and some sweetness from all the lesbian leprechauns you want."

She smiled and sipped her second whiskey. "But first I have to convince the management of SportsWorld – whose wallets are welded shut, by the way – to pony up a million –"

"A hundred K –"

"A lot of money for something we can't use."

"Oh, you'll be able to use it. In a couple of weeks, if everything works out. And it will be much better then – trust me."

She thought about it. "I need to see the footage."

Carter nodded. "Just get me a bank draft, no corporate names on it, made out to cash. And postdate it two days from now."

"You don't think this Hayley chick will tell you to fuck off when she sees she can't cash it right now?"

"She's pressing me hard. Now that I'm playing, she'll play too. It's the first sniff of money that she's had. Oh, and for the time being –"

"Yeah, yeah, I know." She smiled. "This is all just a big lonely tree that fell in the dark and silent Canadian woods."

13

Carter sat at his desk in his windowless office at Emerald Gardens, waiting for Madz to call him back, to tell him his plan had worked. The first instalment of a plan that had several moving parts.

Link Andrachuk had to surface, alive, and then lead the St. Pats down the playoff road to profit, if not glory. Madz could get two stories, first about Link's criminal assault on the Russian and, later, the sale of the St. Pats. The Cardinal could die happy. And Carter could keep his job.

Carter hoped that the plan's parts all worked, but he also knew that hope was not a strategy.

Google helped, and it didn't. In a tenth of a second, he got more than a hundred thousand results. From one website, Carter learned that the Bratva had metastasized after the collapse of the Soviet Union and now counted as many members as Google hits, spread over eight thousand groups. That narrowed things down. Another told him that ex-KGB officers often ran the cells, and Special Forces operatives, known for their brutality, prevented any freelancing.

On a third website, he learned that the Bratva were beige flatliners, operating their business totally below the radar. Another said they were spectacularly brazen and bloodthirsty, killing snitches and their entire families, bankers, journalists, police, and each other in their lust for money. And just because they were a sporting bunch, they hired Olympic weightlifters as muscle, and sharpshooters for hits.

But, all things considered, Carter reckoned that having a professional hockey player whack Sasha Oblomov in front of nineteen thousand people would be spectacularly stupid. And the Russian Mafia were not stupid.

So the Missing Link held the answer.

Carter walked down the corridor to Doug Bleecker's office. He was on the phone and looked at Carter as if he were the delivery boy bringing the wrong sandwich.

"Did Link's personal problems include the Russian Mafia?" Carter said.

"I'll call you back," Bleecker said quickly into his phone and hung up. "What's this?"

"Apparently Sasha Oblomov was on the wrong side of the Russian mob."

Bleecker blinked at Carter, his thin head angled as if to follow the tilt in logic. "So?"

"Well, I was thinking that Link might have been doing them a favour."

Bleecker stood up, the ripple of a smile briefly crossing his face. "Thanks, Cartch." He gestured to the door.

"Did you find Link?" Carter said, not moving.

Bleecker nodded. "As Freddie said, he was up at the Metrocorp Children's Hospital. Those kids really love him."

Carter laughed. "I don't do cripples or cancer," is what Link had said the one and only time Carter had invited him to a charity event.

Bleecker frowned. "Something funny?"

Carter nodded. "Depends on your point of view."

Bleecker sat down and picked up his phone. "If there's nothing else?"

This morning there was nothing, but Carter's forehead tingled with frost. "No, there's nothing else," he said and walked back to his office.

Google was still open on the monitor, so he typed in the thing most on his mind: "Hayley Rawls."

There were only a handful of hits, including one result for her website, www.hayleyscomet.ca, featuring her bio and resumé, which was surprisingly thin. She'd been a producer for Commonwealth Broadcasting, responsible for commissioning a long-running children's show about a talking vegetable garden – probably inspired by executive meetings, thought Carter – and leapt from that to start her own production house, Hayley's Comet, which had so far churned out one promo, on needle distribution to drug addicts in Vancouver, and a cable access documentary about a local Internet pornographer made good. Sex and drugs. The perfect training for a documentary on the Missing Link.

Not missing anymore, though. Bleecker was probably right that he had never been gone, but Link's issues hadn't gone anywhere either. He'd been in trouble for possession of cocaine, and he hadn't been able to cross the Canadian border without the rest of the team until the Cardinal pulled in some favours from the high places he had once flown. It was also rumoured that Link had narrowly dodged statutory rape charges after he was caught as a nineteen-year-old junior player having sex with not one, but two fifteen-year-olds, back in Saskatchewan.

And then Bleecker had had to call the cops on him when they were negotiating Link's contract, with Link acting as his own rep to protect the principle of miserliness. Something Freddie Hutt had said about Link's erratic play had made Link pick Hutt up by his ankles with the intention of dangling him over 23rd Street. And he would have, too, if the windows in Emerald Gardens' executive offices hadn't been sealed by four generations of paint. It all made Link seem dangerous, and dangerous sold product. Everyone, especially Link, understood that.

Carter was trying to figure out how nearly killing Sasha Oblomov would help Link's commercial profile when his phone rang, startling him.

"You like kung po shrimp?" Madz asked.

"What?"

"I figure if you're gonna get all cloak and dagger here, then I can too. Enjoy."

She hung up on him, and before he could hit redial, Brenda was buzzing him to the reception desk to pick up a delivery.

At the front desk, a Chinese delivery guy was standing with a fragrant bag of food while Brenda glowered at him like he was delivering the devil's candy. Which in a way, he was. On top of the kung po shrimp, next to the fortune cookie, was an envelope containing, as Carter discovered once he was back in his office, a bank draft for one hundred thousand dollars. For the first time all day, Martin Carter had an appetite.

He ate at his desk, and instead of writing up the playoff renewals for season ticket subscribers, he typed into his computer what he was going to say to Hayley Rawls when he saw her.

I need all copies of the footage.

You'll sign a non-disclosure document that will result in an admission of guilt and repayment of all monies should you break it because that's what you'll be signing when you sign this.

And it's over between us.

He picked up his phone to call her, but then stopped; he hadn't opened the fortune cookie. He cracked it in two and retrieved the message, one that could be taken in two ways: *Congratulations! Everything is not yet lost!* Carter took it the Irish way. Not yet, but if his gamble failed, then very soon.

14

"Well hello, Cartch," Hayley said, her voice low and loose. "How's Mr. Love Rocket?"

It was a rattling change from when Carter last saw her.

"Are you okay?" His voice was tight.

"Am I?" she replied with a theatrical absent-mindedness. "I'm hoping I will be."

"Well, I think I can help you out there."

"Mmm-hmm," she said. "Then I think you'd better deliver your help in person."

She gave him an address in Brooklyn, someplace between the gentrifying dockyards of Red Hook and the aristocratic-by-bank-balance Park Slope.

Carter hadn't been out in F-train land in a while and was surprised the neighbourhood had become an urban boxing match. In the old corner, Italian pensioners in brick-faced houses with statues of the Madonna shaded by the Stars and Stripes; in the new corner, refugees from Manhattan's hovels who could pay the multimillion-dollar mortgage on a chic brownstone and have change left over to undo the years of old-country kitsch inflicted on it. Between the corners, organic bistros and overpriced bars with names like Harvest and Wave jostled with places like Mazzola's Bakery, its lard bread filled with prosciutto and cheese, and Scotto's funeral home, which took care of Mazzola's best customers.

Hayley was staying in a brownstone with a new facade, likely owned by one of the wealthy refugees from across the East River. The assault by the city's pollution and freezing water had made the delicate brownstone crumble. The stone needed expensive replacing far too often and was another reason, Carter reminded himself, why he lived in a room with a view in Weehawken.

He rang the buzzer for suite 1A, but nothing happened. He checked the front door of the building, found it was locked, and checked the address. What he had written matched what he saw, so he tapped in Hayley's number on his cellphone. His call went straight to her voicemail. Maybe she was on the phone. Getting a better offer.

Carter figured that, by New York math, suite 1A must be a garden suite, so he went down the stairs to the basement apartment entrance and knocked loudly. The door swung open from the force of his knock.

He could have stopped right there, could have walked away and let fate have its way with both him and the St. Pats, but he could see only what was in front of him – a tastefully, expensively renovated apartment with taupe walls under halogen lights that illuminated refinished oak fixtures and Mission furniture.

He kept going, calling out, "Hayley" but getting no answer.

Her camera bag was on the granite counter in the kitchen, and Hayley was in the bedroom, naked on her stomach on the king-sized bed, flashing her maple leaf tattoo right at Carter.

"Hey, Hayley," he said, keeping his distance. There was no way he was going to seal the deal by getting screwed again.

She said nothing. So he moved closer.

"Hayley?"

Still nothing. He could see a bottle of Grey Goose vodka on the bedside table next to her, and when he swung around the bed, he could see it was empty, and that she was asleep. Which he didn't find surprising, given the empty prescription bottle of Temazepam next to her. Carter had taken that particular sleeping pill once and had been dispatched into the land of nothingness so fast and so deeply that it scared him. Mix the pills with vodka though, he thought, and you stand a good chance of permanent residence in the land of nothingness.

"Hayley," he said, touching her shoulder. It was cool. Too cool.

He watched for her back to rise and fall with breath, but it didn't. He grabbed her wrist to check her pulse but couldn't find one. She was dead.

He managed to make it to the bathroom, and after emptying his stomach of kung po shrimp, he sat for a moment in that pause between stopping and going when the whole world is the sound of you catching your breath, getting ready to go back out there on the ice for the next shift.

Hayley Rawls was dead from an overdose of booze and pills. When Carter closed his eyes to think what to do next, all he could think was to get the hell out of there.

He walked out of the bedroom toward the front door but was stopped by Hayley's camera bag, which seemed to him to be lit up with flashing red lights.

What he needed was right here for the taking.

But there was no camera inside Hayley's bag. No laptop either. There was nothing. And there was no camera or laptop anywhere else in the apartment. He'd looked in every cupboard and drawer. He closed the door gently behind him and walked the couple of blocks to the Bergen Street subway station, his forehead fizzing. None of it made sense. Hayley was going to be rich, so she celebrated by overdosing on vodka and pills? Maybe she'd just meant to get in the mood for the return visit of Mr. Love Rocket, but he didn't think so. Not with her camera and her laptop gone.

Despite the fact she had played him, he wanted to do something for her, but all he could think of was to call 911. Doing that on his cellphone would be almost as stupid as playing with Hayley in the first place. So he used the payphone in the subway station and told the people who clean up human messes just where they could find her. Then he got on the F train, thinking things couldn't get any worse.

It was a head-case thing to think.

15

"Who died?"

Bleecker blinked at Carter in such a knowing way that Carter's throat clenched as if the noose was already around his neck.

"Bad night," Carter replied.

Bleecker gave him a thin-lipped grin. "Still having fun with that woman from Canuckistan?"

"Her name was Hayley Rawls," Carter said, immediately realizing he'd used the past tense. No going back now. "And she went home to Canada, to live happily ever after."

Bleecker clucked. "I hope she's happy with what she got?" This really was a question, and he smiled quizzically at Carter.

"I guess so. Link was there the other night, so was she . . . Must be a can't-miss DVD."

He nodded. "Especially if the DVD has extra footage."

The words seared Carter's brain. How did Bleecker know? What did he know? Carter decided to play it as an advantage. He played dumb.

"Extra footage? What do you mean?"

Bleecker smiled tightly. "Page Seven of the *Mail*. They think your friend got some pics of just what happened the other night, when that Russian got hammered into oblivion by Link – allegedly."

Page Seven of the *Mail* was the worst gossip slag in the city, and everyone read it because it was usually true.

"Jeezuz, someone should put that rag out of its misery," Carter said as evenly as he could.

Bleecker reached into his pocket, pulled out the tabloid page, and unfolded it slowly. He handed it to Carter.

Page Seven featured a photo of Link Andrachuk at the St. Pats' casino-night fundraiser, dark and hulking and dressed like a mobster as he ran the roulette wheel. There was no photo of Hayley. The piece itself was three lines long: "Thanks to a Canadian babe with a probing camera, you can soon check out Link Andrachuk's technique of butchering Russian meat on YouTube." Classy, as ever.

"She didn't mention any extra footage," Carter said, hoping he sounded casual, not desperate.

"Well, maybe Ms. Rawls would, if you kept your clothes on and asked her nicely. The Cardinal would be very grateful, I'm sure."

Carter wanted to grab Bleecker and throw him into the wall, but he had few friends in the world, not many at all really, since the "accident," and right now, Bleecker was the closest thing to a friend that he had inside the St. Patricks' executive offices.

"What's Link saying about it?"

Bleecker rolled his eyes. Andrachuk was so afraid of the media, he'd called the cops a month earlier when Madz had dared to ring the intercom to his loft to ask him why he wouldn't tell his side of the story on the hit that had put the Czech kid in traction. "Even if he could, he's not saying anything. Direct orders from Mr. Hutt."

"But what about the long-suffering St. Pats fans' right to know just what that stupid fuck said to start the whole thing?"

Bleecker pursed his lips. "He works for the same guy you do. Who wants you to find the footage."

"Well, she's left the city," Carter said, which was true in a way.

"Then find her," Bleecker said.

"How much are you willing to pay?" Carter said, with such force that Bleecker held up a hand in defence.

"Pay?" he said, as if this had never occurred to him.

"She's doing a documentary on the Missing Link. Why would she just hand over footage, if she even has it, of him committing the kind of foul that could have him kicked out of the league?"

Bleecker thought about this. "Well then, maybe you'll have to convince her. Try whatever worked before. Because your job and mine depend on it."

There wasn't much Carter could say. He had to play the game of finding Hayley Rawls until the game changed to finding out who killed her.

Images of her dead body had kept him awake most of the night. He had poured himself half a tumbler of Jameson as soon as he walked in his door, hoping to mask the scent of death on his skin by dulling his senses, and he'd knocked it back like a cold beer on a hot afternoon. It had made everything brighter, but not clearer.

Why would Hayley kill herself? Worse: why would anyone kill her? Whoever leaked the news of her "extra footage" to Page Seven might have an idea why she was dead. But who knew about the footage? Hayley, and she wasn't talking. Madz, but she'd trusted Carter with a hundred K of the boss's money to get an exclusive. And himself, the last guy in the world to talk about it – even though he already had, to Madz.

So someone else out there knew about the footage too, and wanted to make trouble. And now that trouble was his. To go with all the rest.

16

"The thing is, Cartch," said a harried Madz on her cellphone, "no one knows who writes Page Seven."

Carter was silent for a moment so she could say she was kidding, but all she said was, "Cartch? You still there?"

Yes, he thought, hovering over his own disbelief. "What about Darwin Gissing, the guy who never let a fact get in his way."

She snorted. "Darwin Gissing lies. He doesn't need gossip. For all I know, it could be Link Andra-Fuck writing the goddamn thing."

"You're joking," Carter said. "You media guys know everything, even before you know it."

She laughed. "Well *that's* news. Look, I have a million things to do before I go with Missing Link and Co. to the Great White North, so gotta go."

"Link's making the road trip?"

"Hey, Cartch, he's on your team, you tell me."

"No, Madz, the one thing he's not is on my team. Look, find out what you can about Page Seven and I'll buy you a drink in Toronto."

"You're going too?" She sounded surprised, as the director of community relations usually ventured no farther than Scarsdale.

"No. I'm not," he said. "But bring me the receipt and I'll give you the cash."

She cackled. "I'd love to see you expense a dyke bar."

"I just want to make sure I buy you a drink and not half of Church Street."

"I'll do what I can," she said. "And you can buy me a drink when I see you."

Carter thought about asking Brenda at reception to reserve him a seat on the team plane to Toronto, but he could see how that would go. She'd be on the phone to Freddie Hutt before Carter had hung up.

He checked the Internet again to see whether Hayley had turned up dead in cyberspace, but there was nothing new. Carter searched the *New York Mail*'s website to see what it had to say about getting in touch with Page Seven. How, in a city constantly drunk on rumour, could the identity of Page Seven's scribe be a mystery to Madz? Maybe Hayley had called in the scurrilous gossip herself, hoping to bump up the price of her footage. Maybe Darwin Gissing was doing the hockey column and Page Seven, and put all the true stuff in the gossip section. He jotted down the news-room's phone number and called on his cellphone. He was thrown into automated phone purgatory but after repeat-edly punching zero got a hostile human voice on the line. "I'd like to speak to Page Seven, please," he said. There was a beat of silence, then voicemail. So that's how they did it, thought Carter. With charm. The voice on the other end was female, British, and anonymous: "Do tell us! We'll call you back if we believe you."

What the hell, Carter thought, and said, "Hi, this is Link Andrachuk of the New York St. Pats. I read your thing about me today and you got it wrong," then recited his cell number. If Page Seven called, he would say, "That prankster, Link! But while I have you on the line . . ."

His office phone rang, startling him. But it was just Brenda. "You have a visitor in the boardroom," she said.

When Carter opened the door to the boardroom, he saw Bleecker chatting with a man in a grey pinstriped suit.

"This is Mr. Carter?" Bleecker said in his usual upspeak, and the man took the question literally.

"Yes, it is," he said. It was the badge-flashing cop who'd tried and failed to pick up Hayley in the Black Irish. "And I'm Detective Lucius Gibson. Homicide."

Bleecker looked at Carter with a whole new level of interest. Carter tried to smile as he stuck out his hand at the cop, but Detective Lucius Gibson was handing Carter a business card. Carter's business card.

"I'm here because we found this in Hayley Rawls's wallet."

Carter resisted the impulse to sit. He'd read somewhere that guilty prisoners go to sleep as soon as they're banged up in jail, even before they've been convicted of anything. Sitting down could tell Detective Lucius Gibson that he was expecting this.

"Yes," Carter said. "I gave it to her after helping her do some filming at the game the other night. In case she needed further assistance."

Gibson glanced at Bleecker. "But you're the media guy."

Bleecker didn't miss a beat. "Mr. Carter wanted to escort Ms. Rawls," he lied, "and I was happy to let him. It was game day and I had my hands full with the New York media."

Gibson stared at Bleecker, then shifted his eyes to Carter. And asked if it was true.

"Not quite," Carter said, and Bleecker reddened. "I also found her extremely attractive, and I suspect that Mr. Bleecker here did not."

It was a head-case gamble, one that Carter hoped would convince the cop of his honesty – even though he knew that honesty was, for the most part, a matter of geography. And right now, he was deep in the land of trouble.

Gibson smiled with a touch of appreciation. "Yeah, she was," he said.

"Was?" Bleecker's eyes darted from Carter to Gibson.

"I'm sorry to report that she's dead. That's why I'm here."

"But you're a homicide cop?"

Gibson nodded. "We're still waiting on the lab reports to confirm that she was murdered. But sometimes you gotta go on instinct. Right?"

He looked at Carter, who nodded. He knew from his playing days that all the strategy in the world couldn't trump instinct. So now he sat down. Calculated instinct.

"When?" he asked.

"Sometime yesterday. And when we found your card, I thought I'd come by to ask you when you last saw her."

The last time Carter had seen her she was dead, and the time before that she was blackmailing him. So Carter rewound the story and told the cop that she'd been fine two nights earlier, when she'd left his apartment in the middle of the night, off to catch an early morning flight to Vancouver.

"Well, she never made it," Gibson said.

"That's terrible," said Bleecker. "Do you have any suspects?"

"As I said, it's not officially a homicide. We don't have any official suspects." Gibson looked at Bleecker, then back at Carter. "Anything you could tell me to help put together her last moments, anyone she said she was meeting, anything like that would be a help."

Carter hadn't yet worked out just how much trouble the truth would land him in, so he said, "No, but if I think of anything, how can I reach you?"

Gibson handed over his card. "This number. But I know

how to find you." He beamed a cold-eyed dazzler. "The Black Irish. It's my round, remember?"

17

Back in his office, Carter stared at his daily calendar onscreen, watching the movie in his head. He could see himself in a prison cell. And he could see how his short, not entirely unhappy relationship with Hayley Rawls would put him there. The way a homicide cop might see it. Especially a cop who had seen Carter leave the Black Irish with Hayley after trying and failing to pick her up himself.

Carlito had erased the video of him having urgent foreplay with Hayley in the elevator, but Carter knew they could probably bring it all back to life. But what the hell, for good measure, he'd told Gibson she left his apartment in the middle of the night. After playing a chaste game of chess for a few hours.

Unless she'd had sex with someone else in less than the past twenty-four hours, traces of his DNA were all over her dead self. They'd dispensed with the condom on round two of their trip on Mr. Love Rocket, and it hadn't even been mentioned on round three. He'd touched her dead body. Then he helpfully left more of his DNA by vomiting in the toilet bowl of her borrowed apartment. And his prints were all over her camera bag. Not to mention on all the cupboards and drawers in the apartment. But his master stroke had been to call 911. From a payphone in the Bergen Station, which likely had a surveillance camera.

He'd left a trail of evidence a toddler could follow, and then he'd called Page Seven, posing as Link Andrachuk with information about the hit, and had given the dreaded gossip sheet his cellphone number. And he worked for the New York St. Pats, the team that took pity on him when he could scarcely remember his own name. He owed them his life and livelihood. He would do anything to protect the family.

Unless the NYPD were Druids who ignored the material world around them and parsed the supernatural in their pursuit of justice, he was in life-in-prison kind of trouble.

Carter wiped his sweaty face with both hands. He was glad his father was dead. His father had been a police officer, a soldier in the most iconic cop squad in the world, the Royal Canadian Mounted Police. And he'd told Carter always to remember that because justice was blind, she sometimes had to rely on some dubious friends. He'd drummed into Carter that when things go wrong – rain on the day of the summer picnic, bailiffs at the door – what you really need is a generous bartender, a forgiving priest, and a fuck of a good lawyer. Your own holy trinity. In whatever order you can find them.

When Carter wandered into the Black Irish mid-afternoon, Wanda Collins was sitting at a booth near the rear of the bar, eating a burger and plowing through a pile of receipts.

"Hey, Wanda. How's business?"

She kept tapping numbers into a calculator. "Thanks to the unquenchable thirst of your tribe, and the tolerance of mine, it's very good." She grinned and looked up. "You having the usual?"

"Nah, just popped in with a question." Carter tried to sound casual, as if he always showed up in the middle of the afternoon to shoot the breeze. Wanda played along.

"You remember St. Patrick's Day? When I was in here with a woman?"

"Two women. Madz and the looker." She remembered.

"Yeah. Well, the looker, Hayley Rawls, is dead, and the cops think she was murdered."

Wanda raised a hand to her mouth and leaned back in her seat.

Carter sat down. "Yeah, it's terrible. I'd just met her that day, helping her out with her work, and then . . ."

Wanda nodded sympathetically. "What happened?"

"The cops aren't saying. However, in the weird coincidence that this city is always throwing at you, the cop who came to tell me was the same one who tried to pick her up the night we were here."

"Lotta cops drink here," she said. "Another reason to like your tribe."

"This one was black Irish, like you."

Wanda shifted her gaze from Carter and into the past. "Yeah, I remember him. Never seen him before, but the way that copper could knock back the Jameson's, I hope I see him again."

"Well, he's the homicide cop on her case, name of Lucius Gibson, so if you do –"

She stopped him with a look that said she knew all about messing with the police.

"Don't tell me anything that he'd need to know," she said.

"There's nothing to tell."

She smiled at him, and he smiled back. It was time to see a priest.

Years ago the Cardinal had told Carter that he could come to him in his hour of need, whenever that hour was, and while blackmail didn't quite cut it, murder certainly did.

The Cardinal lived in one of the spired and gargoyled palaces on Central Park West that moviemakers liked to use as shorthand for "this is how New Yorkers live," without revealing that you'd need about a hundred million in the bank before any of their gatekeepers would stop laughing at your application to buy.

The Cardinal's father had bought the apartment in the 1930s, and the Cardinal had grown up there. It was a type of continuity Carter admired, and he was here now because of it. He didn't want it to end too soon.

The concierge, a smiling Asian lady, was politely skeptical that Carter would be admitted to John. J. O'Connor's penthouse suite without an appointment. But when the Cardinal told her to send Carter up, she punched in the code to the penthouse elevator herself and blessed him with "Have a nice day" as the doors to the elevator closed.

The doors were golden and mirrored, and while interior designers slapped up mirrors in any small space to make it look bigger – something that increasingly ruined Carter's appetite in restaurants, as watching himself chew food was not the attraction behind dining out – here the idea was to make the passenger look mythic, all angular shadows under muted ceiling lights. But, despite the effects, Carter just looked worried.

"Cartch," rasped the Cardinal as Carter stepped into his palace. "Good to see you again so soon."

He stretched out a bony hand, and Carter took it, finding the intimation of death in its weak squeeze.

"Thanks for seeing me," Carter said, and the Cardinal waved a hand in the air as if dispersing the alternative.

"Let's go into my study."

The apartment was a testament to the power of money. It

was maybe ten times the size of Carter's place and decorated with the touch of a Victorian titan: emerald and gold the dominant colours, the antique mahogany furniture surrounded by paintings that belonged in art history books, and crystal chandeliers that would suit Versailles.

The study, however, was all about the power of power. The curtains were drawn, the light low, but even so the first thing Carter saw when he followed the Cardinal through the door was a photo of the Cardinal and John F. Kennedy. They were having drinks on some sunny seaside terrace, and J.F.K.'s eyes were glinting as he laughed at what the then strapping young man had just said. It was the kind of glint you see in the eyes of worshippers.

"Now there was a man who could hold his liquor," said the Cardinal as he reached for a bottle of Connemara. "No Churchill, mind you. A cube or neat?"

"Neat is fine. Thanks."

There were other framed photos: the Cardinal with a couple of Popes – Paul VI and John Paul II – with Prince Rainier, with the King of Spain, and even one with Carter when he won the Hermes Trophy as the CHL's rookie of the year. A long time ago.

"I'm sorry," the Cardinal said. "Place is like a mausoleum. Just pull the cord, would you." He gestured to the heavy velvet curtains, and Carter opened them, revealing Central Park, the courtyard for the towers of Midtown. The view made Carter feel as if he owned New York City. He could only imagine how it made the Cardinal feel, since he did own the city. Or had, once upon a time.

It was no secret that the Cardinal had lost much of his money and power over a love affair. And the name of his lover was the New York St. Patricks, who'd built the family's fortune but had been draining it for years, the Cardinal refusing to let go of them; for that would be as good as saying he was ready to die. Which he had said that very morning.

The Cardinal poured them both generous shots of Connemara and put the bottle on the desk.

"To your health," Carter said, raising his glass.

"Ah, let's toast to something with a future – to the play-offs." The Cardinal smiled and took a shaky sip.

Carter drank half his glass.

The whiskey gave Carter's throat a warm smoky kiss. He couldn't drink too much of the peat whiskeys without feeling like he'd smoked a pack of unfiltered cigarettes. It was the smooth sweet Irish whiskeys, the ones more in line with his budget, that he liked, perhaps too much.

"So it looks like you and J.F.K. were having a good time," Carter said, looking at the photo, still working out how he was going to say what he had come to say.

"Actually," said the Cardinal, after a second, firmer sip, "I had just told him that if he didn't stop fucking around on his wife before the election, I was going to make him the first leader of the free world who could sing 'How Are Things in Glocca Morra?' as a castrato." The Cardinal smiled. "He didn't listen, of course, and I didn't do it. A photo may be worth a thousand words, but the trick lies in discovering what those thousand words are."

He took a noisy breath, gazing at the photo with real affection. Carter wondered for whom this confirmed bachelor's heart had throbbed. J.F.K.? Jackie? The pair of them? He seemed to read Carter's mind.

"I was one of life's attendant lords, Cartch. As a literary man, you'll know what I mean, I'm sure."

"And J.F.K. was your Hamlet?"

He smiled. "You're too young to remember, but when he ran for the White House, there had never been a Catholic president." He calmed a wheeze with another sip. "The bigots said, 'Elect him and you may as well elect the Pope.' I ran the money part of his campaign, and that's how I came to be known as the Cardinal. But J.F.K. was no Pope. And no Hamlet. He did what he had to do."

Carter finished his whiskey and did what he had to do. He told the Cardinal the truth. About Hayley Rawls and the footage of Link Andrachuk savaging Oblomov. About her death – maybe a party gone wrong, maybe suicide, maybe murder.

"And you fucked her," the Cardinal said matter-of-factly.

Carter smiled. The Cardinal was no sentimentalist. "Other way around, it seems," he said. "I got fucked. My own contribution to history."

"Well, Cartch, join the club. We're all fucked." He took a breath, the rattle of it giving the sentiment a morbid punctuation. "I'm selling the St. Patricks because the well is dry. The years of huge player salaries, the decades of losing, the cost of maintaining the image of an elite team have finally tapped me out. All this" – he made a feeble sweep with his arm – "is mortgaged to the hilt. Unicorp owns this swank apartment in which we find ourselves, and the city of New York will own Emerald Gardens if I can't pay the tax bill, which I hope to do by selling the team. With enough money left over for my funeral."

Carter knew this day was coming but hadn't imagined it would arrive today. "Do you have any buyers?" His voice was soft, unable to hide his surprise and his sorrow.

"There's a few sniffing around the carcass," the Cardinal said. "But nothing serious because no one thought the team was for sale. They just knew I was shuffling off. But" – he held his hands out in a dying man's shrug to the cosmos – "it all hangs now on this damning footage of that moron Link Andrachuk."

"But," Carter said, like a child imploring a suddenly fallible father, "you're the Cardinal. There must be something you can do to."

The Cardinal slowly took the bottle and, hands shaking, topped them both up. "Well, I have friends in the NYPD."

Carter's surge of hope collided with the realization that the Cardinal was now thinking of him as some kind of liability.

"But," the Cardinal continued, reading Carter's fear, "interfering with a murder investigation – if that's what this becomes, and I'd bet that it does – is like cheating in sports. It's only worth the risk of playing outside the rules if you expect you're going to lose. And, as an athlete, you know that you never go into a game expecting to lose."

Carter nodded. It was true. Even with a minute left on the clock and down two goals, he always thought he could win. What the Cardinal was telling him was to find a way to win.

"You know I didn't kill her –" Carter began, but the Cardinal held up a trembling hand.

"As well as I know my own name," he said "All I know is that somewhere, out there, is something that we both need. And given the state of things" – he paused to take a breath – "finding it sooner is better."

18

The bartender had blessed him, the priest had got him a little drunk, and now, as he walked south through Central Park, the sunny March afternoon surrendering to the dusk creeping

in from the Atlantic, it occurred to Carter that the lawyer
would probably hang him. And enjoy it.

Flavia.

He'd met her at a cocktail party for the Special Olympics,
and before he knew it, they were having their own special
Olympics at an apartment in Midtown owned by her law firm.
She'd refused to tell him her surname, or the name of the firm.

"I'm a married woman, Carter," she had said. "And this –
fun though it is – isn't going to change that. So let's just keep
it simple because complicated means trouble."

It was fitting, Carter thought, in a head-case way, that the
first adult woman he'd ever loved would be married and have
the soul of a male philanderer.

She was a thirty-five-year-old, guilt-free, red-headed,
green-eyed Sicilian American who looked like a cross between
Madonna – the mother of Jesus – and a Rubens empress
enjoying the fall of Rome. She said she was attracted to him
because he looked like one of her avenging tribesmen – the
black hair, the full mouth, the "I kill for fun" eyes. And
because he was smart enough to know that being too smart
would be the end of them.

In the end, it wasn't his head that did him in. It was heart.
He fell in love with her. Game over.

She was smart. She was funny. She was, on the whole, kind.
And she had the devil's own imagination when it came to sin.
"If we've fallen from grace, Cartch," she said, leaning her
heavy breasts across him to top up his wineglass in their borrowed bed in the middle of a Wednesday afternoon, "we're
fools not to enjoy the view from the gutter."

He hadn't talked to her since she put him into misery nearly
two years ago, and hoped she hadn't changed her phone
number when she changed her hairstyle and changed the locks

and all those other changes you make at the end of an affair.

"Hello?" she said on the fifth ring, sounding as if she was expecting bad news.

"Hello, Flavia," Carter said. "It's me." He gave her a beat to hang up on him – the whiskey buzz was quickly giving way to the notion this was a bad idea, but she said, "Thanks for getting back to me so soon, but can I call you back on my landline?" Then she hung up. He was just starting to feel the creep of nostalgia at her expert brush-off when his cellphone rang, the caller ID blocked.

"Cartch?" One syllable, and a world.

"I'm in a bit of trouble."

"Cartch," said this time with a sigh, as if he were headed down a road that no longer existed.

"No, not heart trouble. Law trouble."

"You know I can't."

"I'm not asking that."

"What then?"

Loaded question, that one. Detonators everywhere.

"I think the cops think I killed someone."

There was a long-enough pause, and he waited for the click.

"Where are you?" Reprieve.

"I can meet you at our usual place. The café, I mean."

"In half an hour. For ten minutes. Cartch?"

"Don't worry. I won't."

She was right on time, looking younger and lighter, though still joyfully Rubenesque. A lingering winter tan made her look like she'd just come from the summer vineyards of Sicily. Flavia was of the flesh, and because she loved her own, she was easy for Carter to love. Once upon a time, he told himself. Once upon a time.

Carter stood, and she sat. No kiss hello and, thank God, he thought, no handshake.

"Thanks for coming, Flavia. Can I get you a coffee?"

Her nostrils flared slightly to take in the whiskeyed air around him.

"No thanks," she said, "though I'll take a quick shot if you have any whiskey left. Been a tough day."

He smiled. He'd soon put the gloss on what a tough day meant. "Sorry, the whiskey was a gift. We could go to a bar."

She gave him a flirty smile in reply. "Nah, then you'd try to get me drunk and take me in carnal embrace in the stalls. And as much as I'd enjoy the effort, that would be a Life Tourette's kind of play. Would it not?"

He didn't blink. "How's your husband? Still gay?"

He didn't appreciate the Life Tourette's reminder, even if he was riding a whiskey buzz and was almost an accused murderer.

"Still bisexual," she corrected. "Still rich. And still not in trouble with the law. Unlike you."

"I didn't kill anyone," Carter said.

"But the police have charged you with murder?"

Her brain was the thing he had fallen for, and she reminded him now that he had come here for it.

"No, they haven't."

She ran a hand through her red hair, which she had cut short since he last saw her. The gamine look didn't suit her, he thought. He remembered telling her when he first saw her naked that she was the kind of woman who ruled seventeenth-century art, and she shut him up with a kiss so deep it reached the back of his broken head. And then she said, "Our rule continues . . ."

She gave him that imperial look now. "Well then, Cartch?"

"I slept with a woman," he said – and she didn't blink, though he hoped she might – "who wound up dead. The police came to see me because my business card was in her wallet. And they would not be wrong to think I had a motive for wanting her to be dead. Name of Hayley Rawls."

She looked at him now with professional interest. "And what would this motive be?"

He told her about Link Andrachuk's crime on ice and what its exposure would mean to the New York St. Pats and their playoff revenues. The St. Pats, who had given him a job and sense of family when his pro hockey career had ended. Yes, he was loyal to them and they to him and it was a fatal kind of Irish thing just like – he wanted to say but didn't – how he had been loyal to her when she was cheating on her husband.

But she wasn't listening to him anymore; she was thinking, her pupils expanding to make her eyes more black than green. Carter knew, from experience, that this meant beware.

"So I should be worried?" he said, as if he weren't.

She looked at him from far away, the length of an ice rink. "I think you should help the police if they need your help," she said and stood. She was a Sicilian when it came to endings. No long goodbyes, just a bullet in the heart and a quick exit.

"And for that you get a thousand bucks an hour?" he blurted, feeling a rush of heat to his head.

"Good luck, Cartch." She rose and walked out with a quick glance backward at him, as if looking on someone for the last time.

19

It's easy to be alone in a city of twenty million people, Carter thought as he stepped out of the café into the dusk. And alone he certainly was.

Ever since the accident, he'd found solitude to be safest, and he knew now that a kind of solitude is what he had with Flavia. There was always going to be an ending. But he'd never pictured one like this.

If things had been different. If he hadn't caved his head in on a goalpost, he'd still be playing hockey and pulling down millions and maybe leading the St. Pats to the glory they'd thirsted for, for so long. But that wasn't quite true. He'd be winding up his hockey career around now, thinking about retirement, thinking about what to do with the rest of his life. Really, he was in the place he would be in even if he'd not hit his head. He smiled grimly. Except for the murder bit.

He needed to eat something or he'd soon be taking Flavia's advice and talking to the police and believing that they'd believe him. He bought a hot dog from a street vendor and was balancing the mustard on the onions when his cellphone rang. He spilled the mustard on his shirt.

"Yeah," he said with a growl. Mustard was one of those death stains, like blood.

"Is this Link?" asked a woman with a British accent and polite wariness.

Sonofabitch, thought Carter. It was the gossip sheet calling him back.

"Yes, hi," he said, realizing that for Link, the growl would be appropriate. "Who's this?"

"Page Seven. *New York Mail*. You called us?

"Yes, I did, Miss . . ."

"No names, thank you."

Carter paused. Page Seven was Flavia with a British accent.

"Okay, well, I'm not going to spill it all over the phone to a stranger. You could be anybody."

"So could you."

"Then let's meet."

There was a sigh on the other end. "Look, if you have something to tell us, you can email it in, if you prefer."

"No," said Carter. "I can talk to you. But can you tell me one thing? Who was it that tipped you off to this footage of Link Andrachuk" – Carter winced. He'd referred to himself in the third person, and only delusionally grandiose ball players juiced up on steroids did that – "this footage of me, doing this thing to the Russian?"

The voice laughed. "Right. Here's that email address." She rattled it off and hung up.

That was a bad idea, thought Carter as he stared at his phone. As if a gossip sheet would gossip to him.

His phone rang again. Another blocked ID. It was bad enough people could bother him anywhere, Carter thought. The least the caller could do was give him a fighting chance with a name.

"Yeah?"

There was a pause on the other end, then Freddie Hutt asked, "Carter? That you?"

Freddie had called him only twice in his life before: to get season tickets for a friend and to ask him why he was late for some Wall Street gladhander – he and Flavia had been particularly inspired that afternoon.

"Hi, Freddie," he said. "Yeah, it's me. Tough day."

Another pause. "Well, I take it you know then."

"Know what?"

"That TV lady. She was murdered."

Carter stopped walking. "I'm sorry to hear that," he said, the cold stabbing his forehead. "How?"

"Overdose," Freddie drawled. "But she had some help. Bruising on her mouth from bein' forced to take the booze and the pills."

"That's terrible," said Carter.

"Mmm," Freddie said. "Indeed." He paused, then said, "You know anythin' about it?"

"Excuse me?"

"Doug was sayin' that you had quite the time with the lady."

Fuck Bleecker, thought Carter. His stomach hurt, his heart hurt, and he had mustard down his shirt, but he kept his voice calm. "I helped her do some shooting, and then we went for a drink. Doug was too busy helping you, so he asked me to do it."

Another pause. "Hmm. Well, it's all a mystery, Carter," Freddie said, as if he suspected that Carter could solve it. "I look forward to seein' what you bring home from the hunt."

Home from the hunt? How did he know Carter was on the hunt? Or maybe it was just one of his Huck Finn tropes. On the other hand, home was the best idea he'd heard all day. He would take the long way home, via the ferry, to clear his head with the breeze on the Hudson River.

Fifteen minutes later, he was settling in on the upper deck of the *Maid of Hoboken*, the palisades of New Jersey in front of him, the towers of Manhattan receding behind. He'd had enough of New York City for the day, chewing him up again and again like some urban reptile. Carter wasn't interested in the view tonight. He was interested in catching sight of his immediate future, which was as misty as the air rising off the Hudson.

Hayley Rawls was now the worst kind of dead, the murdered dead. He had never known a murder victim. Even the term killed you. As if your whole life had only been about its violent end, and you went with a whimper: the victim.

Carter didn't know anything about her, except for the fact that she was beautiful and liked sex, and had the mind of a gangster, and yet now, he felt her loss with real grief. He had to do something about it. Maybe Flavia was right. He had to tell the police the truth and trust in it. But the only police officer he trusted was his father, and his father was dead.

He needed to know Hayley Rawls a lot better. In death, she was going to have to give him the answer to her life. And to his.

20

The climb up the stairs at the Port Imperial docks took almost as long as the trip across the river to New Jersey, and Carter was sweating when he reached the top, the toxins of the day soaking his shirt. He stopped to catch his breath, and looked south toward home, a couple of blocks away down Boulevard East.

He snuck up on his building, to see if anyone was waiting for him. From what he could see, there were no guys from Con Edison pretending to fix power lines, no gardeners taking advantage of the dusk, no sign of the cops anywhere. Even so, he let himself into the building stealthily, checking over his shoulders, just like he used to do when he had the puck in the corner and could sense a defenceman speeding in, hoping to staple him to the boards.

"Boss!" Carlito jumped out of his darkened office as Carter crossed the lobby, scaring the hell out of him.

"Jesus!" Carter hissed, spinning.

"Sorry, man," Carlito said in a stage whisper, pointing upward. "They looking for you."

Carter's sweat went cold. "They? Who?"

"Guy with a funny accent."

Coming from Carlito, that was pretty much everyone, Carter thought. "Russian?"

"No Russian. Lots of Russian here. I know Russian. This guy old, bad eyes."

That narrowed it down.

"Show me on the video," Carter said.

The super swept his arm in grand invitation into his tiny office. He kept the lights off as he sat down in front of the VCR and rewound the tape. He pressed play. The screen showed nothing but static. He pushed fast forward and then play. More static. He rewound farther and caught an image. He pushed play again, and now Carter was watching himself make out with Hayley Rawls in the elevator two nights ago, the footage Carlito had supposedly deleted.

"What the fuck, Carlito?"

Carlito yelled, "Cerote! Hijo de puta!" at the machine, as if that would make it work. It did not. He turned to Carter with a sad-eyed shrug. "Never buy Korean shit."

"Carlito, what did he look like?"

"He got bad teeth. Yellow. And you know, *torcido*." He gnarled his fingers, but Carter understood. Crooked yellow teeth and bad eyes.

Hopalong. The Cardinal's hatchet man.

Carter felt a freezing light beam root around behind his eyes. He'd told the Cardinal everything, and his response was to send Hopalong after him? It felt like his father had died on him twice.

"He's up there now? In my place?"

Carlito shook his head, no.

"Did you see him go?"

Carlito smiled. "Yeah, boss. Maybe ten minutes ago. I think."

"You think it was ten minutes ago or you think you saw him go?" Carter was sweating.

Carlito shrugged.

"Okay, then you're coming with me. You have a gun?"

Carlito looked at Carter as if he'd lost his mind. "A gun? I don't even have green card."

"Get the gun."

Carlito responded to the killer stare in Carter's eyes by opening the top drawer, reaching deep inside, and removing a snub-nosed revolver. He handed it to Carter.

"Hey, it's your gun," Carter said.

"But, boss, you want."

"I want you, with it, to come with me. You do know how to use it?"

Carlito looked insulted. "I was in the war!"

The war, thought Carter. What war? "Sorry, Carlito. I didn't mean to insult you. It's just . . . things are bad for me right now. The lady, the one in the elevator with me, she's dead. Murdered."

Carlito's black eyes widened with alarm, then suspicion.

"I didn't do it. But maybe the guy upstairs did."

Carlito nodded. He understood. This was not a police matter. This was about honour. "Okay, boss. Andamos."

Carter made for the elevator, but Carlito clicked his teeth and pointed to the open staircase.

"Stairs, boss. You don't know who be there when the elevator door open, you know?"

They took the stairs, with Carter leading the way, five flights up. He was breathing hard when they reached the top, but Carlito hadn't even broken a sweat.

The super put his finger to his lips and took over the lead as they crept toward Carter's apartment. In the space of five flights of stairs, he'd changed from a frightened illegal to a guerrilla in some Central American jungle fighting a no-prisoners war.

The door was ajar, and it was dark inside.

Carlito turned to Carter and ran his finger across his throat. It was a question. Should Carlito kill whoever was on the other side of the door? Should Carlito kill Hopalong? Carter froze. How could this be his life?

He answered the question by taking two powerful strides, as if on ice, and surged past Carlito through the door.

Carlito ran in after him, his gun arm extended, his finger on the trigger of the revolver now aimed right at the back of Carter's head.

"Abajo, abajo!" yelled Carlito, pushing so hard on Carter's shoulder that Carter dropped to the floor as if he'd been shot. Carlito stepped over him and, clutching the gun with both hands, swept it in an arc, left to right and right to left. He looked down at Carter, pointed at himself, then pointed forward. With a flat hand he indicated to Carter to stay down. Then he disappeared into the dark apartment.

It was silent. All Carter could hear was the drumming of his pulse in his ears. He tried to get up, to help the super, but he couldn't move. He was pounded into the floor by fear.

Then he heard footsteps coming toward him. Slow, measured, confident. Had he heard a gunshot? Surely, if he could hear footsteps, he would have heard whatever the noise is that guns make when you hear them up close. If it wasn't Carlito coming, would he hear the shot that killed him?

He pushed up on his arms as hard as he could, making it to his knees, and crawled into the entry alcove, where he inched himself upright against the wall.

The footsteps were very near now, and Carter, his mind racing, readied his counter attack.

Then the hall light flashed on, and Carter could see the shadow of a man fall on the wall opposite.

"Carlito?"

"Boss, where are you?"

Carter emerged from the alcove, his torso soaked with sweat. Carlito was smiling at him and lowering the revolver. "No one here, boss. Everything okay."

Carter felt a thousand pounds lighter. He stepped into the hallway. Everything seemed as he had left it.

"Thanks, Carlito," he said, the words sounding small and weak.

"Nice Christmas tip, huh, boss?" Carlito winked.

"I'll have the fucking holiday renamed after you." Carter took a deep breath and realized he didn't know Carlito's last name. Maybe this was their cosmic sign to bond, to find out things like surnames, names of siblings, and where Carlito had learned guerrilla warfare. "Hey, Carlito, you want a beer?"

Carlito shook his head. "No, I have to fix the video machine." Drawing the line back between master and servant.

Carter understood. "Well, I think I need —" His eye caught an image. On his computer. But he hadn't left his computer on.

The image, which filled the entire screen, was of a hockey player laid out flat on the ice, bleeding from the head and apparently dead.

Carlito saw Carter face drain. "You okay, boss?"

Carter shook his head. "That's me," he said, pointing to the screen. "Turn that damn thing off!" Then he lunged into the bathroom and stuck his head under the cold water tap to chill the message that had been delivered to him on his computer. Nearly dead once, nearly dead now.

He turned off the water and towelled his face and hair. Then he heard a faint crackling, like static, coming from his living room.

Carlito was kneeling on the ground next to Carter's computer tower, his whole body vibrating from the electrical force coursing through his right hand, seemingly welded to the power button.

"Carlito!"

Carter took a step toward him, then stopped. Why had Carlito not turned the computer off by using the mouse? There was only one answer: because he couldn't, because the computer had been deliberately frozen to make sure he'd try a hard reboot. He needed to get to the fuse box, but the one person who could remind him where he could find it was being electrocuted. He needed something wooden. He ran into his kitchen, grabbed his old wooden broom, sprinted back to the computer, then, with the full force of a slapshot, he knocked Carlito's hand off the button.

The tower fell on its side, and Carlito collapsed on the floor, his black eyes staring at Carter, smoke rising from his flesh. He was dead.

Then the computer exploded, and flames spewed from the tower, licking the leg of his oak desk, leaping across to the bookshelf and onto the curtains Carter rarely closed, and then to his overstuffed armchair by the window. In seconds, the fire was out of control.

There was only one thing to save now.

Carter ran into his bedroom and grabbed the flight bag he kept packed for an emergency trip, an old hockey player's habit, in case you got traded in the middle of some sleepy afternoon.

He took the mahogany box on his dresser, the one his father had left him, and shoved it into the flight bag. Inside the box were his passports and some traveller's cheques left over from a trip he took to England and Ireland with his father while the old man was still able to travel. Carter didn't think he'd be going to England or Ireland, but the cheques could come in handy. If he got out of here alive.

The flames were climbing the walls of his living room now, and Carlito was burning too. The speed of the fire made Carter run, and he almost stumbled as he sent something flying along the hallway. Carlito's gun. Carter picked it up. It was lighter than it looked. Just holding it sent a tremor through him. He shoved it into his flight bag and ran out the door.

"Fire!" Carter yelled, punctuating the warning with a bang on each door as he sprinted past the three suites on his floor. "Fire, goddamnit!"

He knew he shouldn't take the elevator in the case of fire because a sign next to it said so. But Carter decided that this is just what he'd do. Having someone try to kill him off the ice was not that different from on it: the faster the game got, the slower everything seemed. It was going very slowly now.

You never know who is going to be on the other side when elevator doors open. For Carter's money, it would be the person who had done this. But the stairway was worse, because he'd have to pass through the lobby to get to the stairway to the basement. And he didn't want that.

Carter kept his finger on the B button as the elevator went down, hoping this would jam it, knowing it wouldn't, but it made him feel like he had some control. He watched as each passing floor lit up, 4, 3, 2, lobby, and the elevator kept going, down, to the basement.

If someone had been waiting for him in the lobby, they'd know where he was now, so he raced past the laundry to the stairwell door that led outside. It was a double-lock door, requiring a key both to enter and to exit. Carter, breathing hard, fished it out from the jumble on his key chain and turned the lock.

Nothing happened.

He heard footsteps on the staircase. He turned the key again. The footsteps came closer, harder, more urgent. The key caught, and Carter shoved open the door, dashed through, then slammed it shut and locked it. He took the stairs up three at a time, as his pursuer wrenched the door handle behind him.

Carter sprinted down the narrow pathway that edged his building. He could hear sirens, the long slow bass-to-treble howl of the fire department, not the growl and woof of the police, so that was good. At least there was a chance the building wouldn't burn down, which would knock a life term or so off his sentence.

When he reached the end of the pathway, he stopped at the sight of the crowd gathering in front of his building. He turned left and walked up and around the block, then made for the long staircase down to Port Imperial. He turned back once and saw smoke pouring from around the window frame in his living room, the window through which Hayley had seen her vision of the future – the money and muscle of Manhattan, willing to put a price on anything. She just hadn't reckoned how high a price or who would be paying. Carlito had paid with his life, paid a price that was meant to be exacted on Carter. Sweat dripped from his cold forehead and his stomach heaved with grief and fear as he ran for the ferry now, the lights of Manhattan the beacon to his desperate mission. He had to find out who had killed Hayley and Carlito. To save his own life.

21

It was early, but there were still a few people drinking inside the red brick walls of the Black Irish when Carter peered in through the front window. He wanted no witnesses, so he walked up the block to a payphone, put in a quarter, and called Wanda's cell.

"What are you doing calling me from a payphone?" she asked.

"Meet me around back and I'll tell you," he replied.

The Black Irish was a New York rarity – it had a service alley behind it, a legacy from the days when goods were unloaded from Hudson River barges onto horse-drawn wagons and pulled into the city. And right now, as he stood waiting in the shadows, Carter was grateful that this bit of the past hadn't been obliterated by the city's rampaging growth. Wanda unlocked the heavy steel door, one better suited to a bank vault, and it slowly swung open. As soon as there was enough space for him to squeeze through, he hurried in and helped pull the door shut. Wanda took a good whiff of him.

"You been pissing on some kind of barbecue?"

He shook his head, smelling on himself the smoke of the fire and the urine that had leaked from terror. "Someone set my apartment on fire. And I wasn't trying to put it out, either."

She sucked in air between her teeth. "So you're in *real* trouble."

He smiled. "That's what I was hoping you'd say."

He changed his trousers to the pair in his flight bag while she fetched him a pint of club soda, then they sat in leather chairs in the office upstairs she rarely used, a place more like an Upper East Side studio apartment than the adjunct of a brawled-in Irish bar. There was a kitchenette and a sofa, which looked like it folded out into a bed, and a bathroom with a shower, all of it with a tasteful Urban Barn touch. He could easily live here, Carter thought, now that he had nowhere to live.

On a side table, to the right of Wanda's broad oak desk, was a video monitor, transmitting images from different angles from the bar below. It was a much better monitor than the one that was probably now ashes in Carter's building. The images were clear and crisp, like HD TV.

"Can't be too careful, Cartch," she said, watching him watch the monitor. "No honour among no one these days."

Carter had never been up here before, having always done his drinking as a customer – even a favoured one – in the bar below. But tonight was different.

"That is some kind of trouble," she said after he finished his brief account of his life and Carlito's death since she last saw him. "I'm sorry about your friend," she said.

Carter nearly said, But he wasn't my friend, and that would have been true, in a head-case way. Carlito had died trying to help him. That was more than a friend. That was a martyr. So he said, "Once someone saves your life, you owe them forever."

"Hmm," she said, calculating the debt. "Better live a good long time then, Cartch. But tell me something, what the fuck ever happened to the luck of the Irish?"

"That's the second Irish joke."

"What's the first?"

"Believing there's any luck at all."

They shared a dark laugh, then Wanda fixed him with a wary eye. "Why would the Cardinal want to kill you? He's your friend."

Carter drained his water. "All I know is that at the moment, I'm an expensive friend to have."

"So what does that make me?

"A true friend."

She smiled and shook her head. "Ah ha. The kiss before the fuck." Then she heard herself and jauntily raised her glass to him, in case he thought she was speaking wishfully. The one thing he had never done was made a move on Wanda. That would have killed a friendship and his custom in one go.

Carter raised his empty glass back at her. "The kiss before the fuck off, actually. I need your van."

She glanced at the wooden peg by the safe where she kept her keys, as if to make sure they were still there. "My van? To go where?"

"North. Way north."

She tilted back in her office chair as if to get a bit of distance on a mad idea. "You want to drive a minivan that has the Black Irish plastered all over it, all the way to Canada?"

He rubbed his hand over his forehead. It was still cold and he was still sweating. "How did you know?"

"Because you're from Canada."

"Well yeah, and extradition takes forever."

She stared hard at him. "But you didn't kill anyone."

"That's right."

"And you're making a run for it?"

He shook his head. "Not running. Looking."

"Looking for what?"

"For a way out."

Wanda glanced at the TV monitor, then back at Carter. "Look, Cartch —"

He held up a hand. "I know what you're going to say. I thought the same thing. Go to the police and tell them everything. Can't do that, though, because I was hit on the head, and it's fucked up my judgment, your Honour."

"You don't have to have been hit on the head to think that, baby," she said. "What I was gonna say was that I can give you money for a plane ticket. Help you get outta Dodge faster."

He shook his head. "Thanks, but buying a plane ticket with cash is not the kind of attention I want."

She nodded, then a slow smile opened up her broad face. "But the thing is, Cartch, you're not gonna get any attention."

"What do you mean?"

"It's going to take them a while to figure out who the body is in your apartment, isn't it?"

Carter suddenly saw the news headlines: his charred apartment would contain "the body of a male, burned beyond recognition." He and Carlito were roughly the same age, same build, and Carter knew from his own eyes that Carlito didn't have any dental records. And as far as the United States of America was concerned, the illegal alien Carlito didn't exist. The missing building super might even be a suspect in the fire that tragically claimed the life of former New York St. Patricks ace Martin Carter.

"You're a genius, Wanda," he said.

"Nah, just the luck of the Irish."

He laughed, a real laugh, born of brief relief. Then he remembered the gun.

He reached into his travel bag and delicately, by the handle, extracted Carlito's revolver.

She stood up. "What the fuck?"

"It's not mine," he said, placing in on her desk.

"Well, it sure as hell isn't mine," she said, pushing her chair back.

Judging by her reaction, Wanda wasn't a gun person. Carter had never mastered the art of telling who was armed and who wasn't, save for looking at jacket bulges or at people from Texas.

"Can you just hide it until —"

Her eyes were wide, unblinking, angry. "You come back?"

He nodded. "I know. But trust me. I will."

She shifted her gaze to the gun. Then something caught her eye on the video monitor. Her jaw went rigid.

Carter stood and saw what she was seeing on the screen: Detective Lucius Gibson walking into the bar.

Gibson stopped and looked around the room, his head slowly swivelling. He was wearing that hard homicide cop street face, and he wasn't looking for a friend. Then he walked over to the bartender and flashed his badge. Russell the Muscle pointed upstairs.

"I gotta go," Carter said.

"He won't come up here," Wanda said, putting her hand on his arm. "Russell knows that I always come down."

On cue, her phone rang. "Coming," she said, then hung up, picked up the gun by the snub of its barrel, like it was radioactive, and walked over to a wall safe. She spun the combo on the lock, put the gun inside the safe, then fished out a couple of fat stacks of twenty-dollar bills and handed them to Carter.

"Thank you, but I don't —" he said, but she put her finger to his lips.

"Then just bring it all back," she said. "In one piece." She looked like she was going to give him a kiss, so he moved first and wrapped his arms around her.

"I'll see you soon."

Her head nodded into his shoulder, then she stepped back and took a long look, as if for the last time.

"Don't call," she said.

"I promise," he said, his throat tightening.

"Stay as long as you like," she said and walked toward the door. "You know the way out." Then she left.

Carter watched Lucius Gibson, just a few feet away downstairs, lean against the bar, casually watching the door, as if he owned the place. Then Gibson turned, sensing Wanda, and there she was, looking as innocent as Carter felt.

Gibson handed her his card and shook her hand, and while she studied the card, he made his case. It was brief, and all it got out of Wanda was a shake of her head. No, she didn't know. But she gestured with a smile to the bar and asked the cop if he'd like a drink.

He nodded. He would. She went behind the bar and poured him a club soda, tossing in ice and some lime. She wouldn't take his money, but when he insisted, she relented and turned her back on Gibson to ring in the sale. She took her time, though, and before she closed the cash drawer, she flashed his business card to the video camera above the till. On the back of the card she had written: "Take van." The message meant Gibson didn't know about the fire, yet, and that Homicide would be looking for him in the usual places: bus depot, train station, airport.

So Carter grabbed the keys to Wanda's minivan and took one last look at the video monitor. Lucius Gibson was looking directly into the camera, right back at him, a small smile playing at the corners of his mouth. The kind of smile that said he was a head case too.

22

It had just gone 9 p.m. when Carter gunned the engine on Wanda's minivan and pointed it in the direction of the Lincoln Tunnel.

The van, a new Honda Odyssey, was green, of course, a shiny New World metallic green, and not the rain-soaked green of the Emerald Isle. The Black Irish logo was splashed on both doors – a golden harp and the Irish tricolour flag and, thank God, Carter thought, no leprechauns. The paint job made the van hard to miss, but then again, thought Carter, it didn't look like the kind of getaway car a smart person would use. So in its way, not too bad at all.

He reckoned the drive to Toronto would take about eight hours at this time of night, depending on the whims of Customs and Immigration, which these days, Carter knew, were low on whim and high on officially sanctioned paranoia on both sides of the border.

The traffic out of the city was light, for Carter had caught that pause between people leaving the city after work, and those leaving it after play, and he made good time through the New Jersey Turnpike. The van had a navigation system built into the console, with a microphone so you could say the destination and up would pop a route map onscreen, but Carter confounded the machine by asking, "Where am I going?" and getting the flashing red message "Unknown Destination."

No, he wasn't going there, he was going home. Or rather, to the country he was from, for home as he knew it no longer existed. So, in a way, the van's computer was right. He didn't really know where he was going, only that he was on his way. It was going to be a flat, boring, and predictable drive. Carter was glad to be hymned on his way by a CD he'd found in the van's glove box, a soaring quartet by Mozart, *Soave s'il vento*, that sounded like heaven itself was singing. So that's what Wanda liked – not the faux Celtic stuff bashed out by the Gobshites.

Heaven, thought Carter. Easy to believe in when you're alone on the road at night and serenaded by angels. He knew the piece well, for it had been one of Flavia's signature seduction tunes – "gently, if the winds permit," she'd translated, when she played it for him after the first night of their "thing," as she called it. In the end, the winds had fuck all to do with their thing, thought Carter. The winds were blameless. It always came down to us and the wake of our own choices.

Carter didn't want to think about his. Not now. He wanted to get across the border and then deal with reality. See how it looked in the northern air.

Just past midnight, he was on the outskirts of Syracuse, and when he saw the De Witt Travel Plaza on the other side of the interstate, one with a twenty-four-hour McDonald's, he decided to stop for a burger. He managed to turn around so he was heading back toward New York, then drove into the Travel Plaza lot. There were a few cars parked there, including a boxy old Cadillac Seville with a group of surly looking Latino kids, eyeballing him and the van, so he parked in a stall under a light, right next to the building. The last thing he needed was for someone to steal his ride.

When Carter emerged five minutes later, a Diet Coke in one hand and dinner in the other, the kids were gone, and the van was still there – with a blue-and-gold New York State

Police cruiser parked perpendicularly behind it, boxing it in. Inside the police car was a Stetson-hatted trooper, his face lit up by the glow of his computer screen.

Carter stopped walking and took a long hit of soda. His driving had been careful and even, so this cop checkup was probably just routine. He was going to have to make his own fear look routine too, until he was safe again, should that day ever come.

He made a point of putting his dinner in the passenger side of the van, loudly thunking the door shut, then walking around behind, clocking the trooper's vehicle number as he went – 11T13. Lucky 13. He opened the rear gate to fish a sweater out of his travel bag. He took off his blazer, put on the sweater, then closed the door and turned toward the trooper, who by now had ample time to check him out. But the trooper was still hunched over his computer screen. Carter stared at him for a beat or two, but the trooper never looked up.

Carter got in the van and started in on his Quarter Pounder with cheese, large fries, and extra ketchup. He switched the radio on to give himself some company with the news, which was the usual litany of misery and the banal. There was no news about a former hockey great dying in a house fire.

Carter nearly smacked his head on the ceiling when the trooper tapped on the driver-side window. He looked for the handle to roll down the window, then realized it was electric and pushed the obvious button. The door locked. He pushed the button next to it and the side mirror inched to the left. Third time lucky, and the window opened.

"Sorry," Carter said. "Not used to driving this thing."

The trooper stared at him. He was a white guy, probably in his late twenties, but the thirty extra pounds around the middle and the military moustache made him look about the same age as Carter. "You don't look like Wanda Collins."

"No," said Carter. "She's my boss."

The trooper didn't blink. "Uh-huh. And where are you going with her ve-hi-cle?"

Carter's forehead tingled. He was going to Toronto in her ve-hi-cle, but Toronto was in the opposite direction. He'd just been saved by fast food.

"I'm going to New York," Carter said.

The trooper looked at the Black Irish logo on the door. "New York City?" He said "city" as if it were a disease.

"Yes."

"So where you coming from?"

Carter kept the story going backwards. "Toronto."

The trooper sniffed the air – for booze, for maple syrup. "What's in Toronto?"

"Uh, my mom," Carter said, which was true, and the first thing that popped into his head. "My boss loaned me her van because" – he cleared his throat – "I don't like to fly."

The trooper thought about that, then went for the jugular. "You're Canadian?"

Oh fuck, thought Carter. There were probably megatons of contraband zooming by them on the interstate and this guy was going for the illegal alien angle.

"I was born in Canada," Carter said. "But I've lived here for a long time. Green card and all. Just popped up to see my mother for a couple of days – she's not too well."

The trooper thought about this, then glanced down again at the Black Irish logo. "You wouldn't be carrying any al-co-hol across state lines now, would you?"

"No. I have all the alcohol I need in New York."

The trooper adjusted his purple tie, as if relieving the pressure building up in his neck. "Can I see some ID?" It wasn't a question.

Carter's forehead was cold. He could see his future all too clearly if he gave the guy his ID and he entered it in the system. Just like that, Carter would be in handcuffs. Alternatively, he could start the engine, put the van in reverse, and plow the cruiser out of the way, with about fifteen bullets in him by the time he'd finished his first ram (and a TV spot on *America's Stupidest Dead Guys*). He opened his wallet and handed the trooper his driver's licence.

The trooper stared at it as if he'd never seen one before, then strolled toward his car.

Carter needed something to distract the trooper, like having the sky fall right now or the Travel Plaza explode.

That was it. Thank God for the world we live in, he thought, as he grabbed his cellphone and called 911.

"Police, fire, or ambulance?"

"Police." Carter didn't even wait to be transferred. "There's a guy with a gun robbing the McDonald's in De Witt Travel Plaza," he said with his hand over the receiver. "The De Witt Travel Plaza, on I-90 East."

"Uh-huh." He heard the slow tap-tap of data entry into the dispatch computer. He had to speed things along.

"Actually, there are two guys. They look like Arabs."

"Terrorists?"

God bless America. "Oh, wow, a cop just pulled into the parking lot, a New York State Trooper. Car number 11T13!" Carter hit end and looked in his rear-view mirror.

The trooper was just getting into his car. He sat down. He switched on the overhead light. He took off his hat. Then he looked at Carter's driver's licence.

Carter looked over at the Travel Plaza. Not a gun-toting Arab in sight. He had to do something. So he stepped out of the van.

The trooper looked up at him this time and opened his door, swinging a leg onto the pavement and his head out the door. "Sir, get back in the –" He stopped. His eyes never left Carter as he listened to the news coming over his radio. Then he grabbed the shotgun from the rack in the front passenger seat and made a belly-bouncing run for the building.

Carter walked fast to the cruiser and retrieved his driver's licence. The trooper had left his keys in the ignition, so Carter put the police car in reverse, backed it up ten feet, took the trooper's keys, and ran back to his van. And then he was back on the I-90, doing a loop to point himself west and head for the border, sweat running from his forehead and down his cheeks like tears.

Tears would be appropriate, thought Carter. He'd just used his cell to call in a fake crime. He'd stolen a state trooper's car keys. And he was making his break for freedom in an easily identifiable van that would soon have every state trooper on the road looking for it. He needed to get rid of it and find another way to escape. He was, without really trying, thinking like a low-level criminal – reacting to whatever luck, bad or stupid, had been thrown his way, rather than being the strategist he needed to be. That's when he saw the exit signs for Onandaga Lake. It was a mixture of luck and strategy. He took the exit.

Carter drove along the parkway next to the lake, just to the northwest of Syracuse, and then onto the trail, parking on a rise next to a sign warning that the lake was too polluted for swimming or fishing. That suited Carter fine, those nasty chemicals would destroy what he needed destroyed. He looked around to see if anyone was watching him, then threw the trooper's keys as far as he could. They landed with a soft splash about fifty feet out. His phone made a louder splash, one that rippled through Carter's conscience: what the fuck was he doing? The answer echoed back: he was doing only what he had to do, now that he'd done everything else.

He took his travel bag out of the van, put the van in neutral, hunched down like he was at practice and the coach had announced wind sprints, then pushed. Nothing happened. He stepped back and took a run at it, lunging into it shoulder first. It hurt, but the van started to roll, slowly, and Carter dug in and pushed harder. Gravity and momentum soon took over, and the van slid down the hill and into the lake. And sat on the surface of the water.

Carter stood there, sweating and cursing. This was not how it worked in the movies, his only point of reference for disposing of troublesome vehicles. He couldn't believe that he'd managed to dump the van in the shallows. But then physics kicked in, the weight of the vehicle squeezed out the air pocket beneath it, and the Black Irish minivan bubbled down to its toxic grave at the bottom of Lake Onondaga.

Carter felt relieved – and terrible. He'd rid himself of a burden, but he'd gained a couple more – one of them, explaining to Wanda why he'd destroyed her van. Which would only be a problem if he ever saw her again.

He stood breathing hard, staring at the lights of Syracuse across the water, feeling like a better class of criminal, or at least one who had just committed a crime only because he hadn't committed a crime earlier. He stared at the few faint stars. Maybe there was a god after all, organizing the chaos.

All he had to do now was steal a car and continue on to the border, but he'd filled his quota of stupid things to do for the day. No, he needed someone else to do the driving. And by the time he'd walked three miles back into the city and found the bus station, Carter was beginning to feel lucky. The bus to Toronto left in fifteen minutes and would have him in his hometown in time for breakfast.

Carter gave the Trailways guy fifty-two dollars for a one-way ticket, then found a window seat at the back of the bus. He gazed out the window as they drove north, exhausted but not daring to sleep until he had truly escaped, if only into a future that seemed as dark as the night around him.

PART TWO

23

At the crossing between Buffalo and Fort Erie, Ontario, a Canada Border Services agent worked his way down the bus, checking passports. Carter had two in his travel bag, and which one he pulled out depended on how many points of no return he was going to have to cross. He could use his Canadian passport or the Irish European Union one, which was another legacy of his father. Right now, his intuition told him that it was the one to use.

He handed it to the agent, a Chinese guy, maybe forty, and looked out the window. They were sitting at the entrance to the Peace Bridge, with Lake Erie on one side and up river a few miles, Niagara Falls.

He had crossed the bridge many times as a kid, with his parents. "This thing will be around for your children," said his father, but young Carter couldn't imagine that far into the future.

And now the future that he once couldn't imagine was part of a past he couldn't always remember. The Kingdoms of Before and After were separated by a high and spiky wall.

"What's the purpose of your visit?" asked the agent in the flat tone they must be taught at border agent school, running Carter's passport through his portable computer.

"Visiting friends in Toronto."

"Coming from?"

A kind of hell, partly of my own making, Carter thought, but that wouldn't help speed his crossing, so he said, "Syracuse."

The agent didn't nod, didn't blink, just stared at him. "How long will you be in Canada?"

Well, that would depend on the NYPD and on how soon he'd have dug his own grave. How deep did a grave have to be?

"A few days."

"What work do you do?"

Carter smiled. They were in the "too many questions" part of this encounter. "I'm in charity work." Which was true enough, considering the kind of begging he did on behalf of the St. Patricks.

The agent stared at Carter, expressionless. "You do know, Mr. Carter, that it's an offence to make a false statement to a Canada Border Services Agency officer."

Carter felt his recent past collide with his immediate future. "No. I mean, I do, and I'm not," he said, his gut clenching.

The agent stared at him, then gave him the grin of a kid — open and deathless. "You sure you're not the greatest hockey player ever to come out of Toronto, Mr. Carter?"

Carter's mouth went dry. He'd been ID'd by a customs guy, who, unless he contracted amnesia in the next twenty-four hours, would put the brakes on any stories of Martin Carter dying in an apartment fire. Carter smiled. "Nah, I'm not that Carter, not the hockey player. I used to get mistaken for him all the time, but I can't even skate." Which was sort of true. Carter hadn't been on skates since his accident. "You must be quite the hockey fan to remember him."

The agent frowned but handed back his passport. "I am. And he was something to remember."

Yeah, he was, thought Carter, if only he could, as the bus rolled along the Queen Elizabeth Way with the early morning rush and then, once inside the city boundary, on the Gardiner

Expressway, so thick with traffic it was a parking lot. The driver eventually cut off onto Lakeshore Boulevard, running along the edge of Lake Ontario.

Carter stared at the lake, as big as an ocean, stretching out of sight in the morning haze. And now, on both sides of it, nothing but trouble. Had the agent believed him or had he immediately got on the phone to the New York State Police or Homeland Security, or both of them, alerting them to Carter's presence on the other side of the fence? He took a deep breath. They could arrest him – it would be easy to figure out where he was going – but how long would it take to send him back? All he really knew was that he had to keep moving.

Carter looked out the window at the new Golden Maple Arena tucked between the expressway and the railway tracks, an arena christened after an organic pancake syrup company, where that night the Pats would be playing against the Toronto Titans. Now the bus was passing by the dowager Royal York, the great old railway hotel on Front Street where the St. Pats always stayed, where Carter had once impressed his parents by showing them his lakeview suite, the kind no one else in his family could afford to stay in, and then hung a left up Bay Street, the mighty glass towers lining it home to the financial machine that ran the country.

They pulled into the grimy Greyhound Station farther up Bay, and Carter grabbed his bag to join the march of commuters. The sun was burning through the morning haze, and a cold wind whipped off Lake Ontario, snapping the flags to attention. He found the taxi rank and climbed into the first cab.

The red brick Victorian house on Trinity Street where he'd grown up was in need of a new coat of paint on the window frames and a weekend's worth of garden rehab. It looked

especially sore now that it was surrounded by renovated
houses, on a street that not so long ago had been best avoided.
Everyone had called his parents crazy when they bought their
old house here thirty years ago, and it had seemed that way
to Carter too when he had to dodge winos and junkies to
catch the King streetcar to get to school. But those days were
gone. The down and out had shuffled west and north, and in
their wake came people who wanted to live downtown, near
the lake. The house that Carter's parents had bought for
fifteen thousand dollars, with a foresight forced by poverty,
was now worth forty times that.

"Oh, you're back!" his mother said when she opened the
door, beaming as if he had been away to the wars for three years,
and not the three months since he was last home for Christmas.

"Hi, Ma," he said, giving her a kiss on the cheek. Her olive
skin was as unblemished as her black eyes were cloudy with
whatever they were doping her up with. Her snow white hair
was frizzed out in all directions, the Spanish princess hit by
lightning, and her pink fleecy was stained with what Carter
hoped was ketchup and not blood.

"Who is it?" his brother called out from his lair in the
basement.

"It's that nice man who comes round," Carter's mother
replied and stood there smiling at him. She'd put on some
lipstick today, in a little pink Hitler moustache where her
hand had slipped and she hadn't noticed. Carter wanted to
smack his brother for letting her answer the door at all, never
mind like this.

"Oh, it's you," Carter's brother said, huffing up the stairs
and into sight, his face puffy and haggard like he'd just come
off a month-long bender. At thirty-five, he was three years
younger than Carter, though he looked two decades older.

"Hi, Dennis," Carter said, offering his hand, but his brother's hand sailed purposefully past his to close the door. Carter caught a whiff of him. Dennis hadn't washed in days.

"Mom looks well."

Dennis glowered. "What are you doing here?"

Carter had expected a hostile welcome from his brother, who resented the fact that Carter could swan in whenever he felt like it from New York and that he had to shoulder the burden of their mother, but the truth was that Dennis was unemployed and living off the money he'd finagled when he remortgaged the mortgage-free house. Even so, Carter came in peace and had rehearsed his answer in the cab over, honing it down to a neutral "doing some league business."

"Really?" Dennis said, his eyes narrowing. "League business just before the Cup playoffs?" He was in his tenth year of who-knew-what studies at the University of Toronto and had become a professional student, skeptical of everything.

"Yeah," Carter said, "on short notice. Since all the hotels are full, I'm hoping I can stay here for a couple of days."

Dennis folded his arms. "I have power of attorney, you know. You're not getting a cent." He looked proud that he'd made a stand against whatever plot Carter was about to bring across the threshold.

"As far as I can see, Dennis, Mom's still here," Carter said evenly. "And the mortgage money seems to be allowing you both to live in style. Now, if you don't mind, I'm going to get some sleep. Early flights are murder."

Carter gave his mother another kiss and she gave him a startled smile, as if he were a bold stranger, and then he headed up the stairs to his old room.

His mother had kept it as a shrine to Carter and to hockey. There were photos of him playing hockey as a toddler, lurching along with a stick in his hand, the toddler terror on ice. There were photos of him playing under the moonlight at the Bathurst Street outdoor rink and in his freshman year at St. Mike's, flanked by his impossibly young and glamorous mother, the kind of woman who now caught his eye. And there, too, was his professionally suspicious father, who knew in his Irish way that the large St. Mike's M on Carter's jersey – the one announcing that the Carters had arrived in the world of big-time hockey, with a shot at scholarships to college and glory in the pros – was, in the end, just providing the gods with a bigger target. He'd been right.

Carter lay back on his old bed, looking at his past. Everyone in it was gone now, himself included. He was home, but it wasn't home. He had no home left.

The thought sank into his fatigue. He was as tired as if he had been double-shifted through triple overtime and then had lost the game. Fatigue and despair, that potent cocktail of bedtime misery. All he could hope for now was to dream, to find, deep in his damaged subconscious, a way out. His bitter smile turned into a yawn. That thought was a dream in itself.

24

No matter how hard they tried, Hayley Rawls and Carlito couldn't make Martin Carter stand up. They kept drop-ping him, his head whacking the white ice with a cold and bloody thunk.

"One more hit on the head and you'll be dead," the doctor was saying over the PA system. It's what the medics had been saying to Carter from the time he was able to understand what they were saying after his head caved in. His concussion was so bad, had scrambled so many delicate life networks, that they didn't think he could risk another concussion without doing fatal damage.

"One more hit on the head and you'll be dead."

And if his head kept hitting the ice like this, he'd be more than dead. He'd be destroyed.

He'd had enough. But he couldn't make them stop because when he tried to speak, his head smashed into the ice, and the pale, ghoulish faces of Hayley and Carlito would look at him in puzzlement, expecting him to rise up.

"Time to go, Mr. Love Rocket," Hayley said.

"Time to go, boss," Carlito said.

"But where?" the Cardinal's voice replied from behind them, from somewhere in the dark of the stands. "There's nowhere."

Carter could see stars when he woke up, not because he was floating through a heaven he no longer believed in but, he realized after a moment of panic, because he was again lying on his childhood bed, and his curtains were open on the evening sky.

He swung his legs over the edge of the bed and wobbled when he stood. He looked at his watch. It was a bit before 6:30 p.m., so he'd been asleep for nearly eleven hours.

And he was hungry. He hadn't eaten anything since his too-fast-food dinner at the Travel Plaza outside Syracuse.

He walked stiffly down the stairs to the kitchen, happy to discover that his mother's famous Drawer of Not Cooking Tonight was still functioning. There were takeout out menus so old they should have been in takeout museums, but Carter found one for the Wokker that had been printed this century.

"I had a wonderful breakfast!" Carter's mother shouted at him when she wandered in. "I'm not hungry!"

"You gotta eat, Mom, if you want to keep going."

"But I don't," she said, and Carter didn't pursue whether she meant eating or going.

He checked the fridge on the off chance elves had stocked it with beer, but no, there were just rows of Coke cans, so he walked the few blocks to the local liquor store to grab some cold takeout Sleeman's ale and arrived home in time to pay the Wokker delivery guy.

"Oh, you're back!" Carter's mother beamed again, and he went through the whole *Groundhog Day* ritual that is Alzheimer's and then sat them both down with a Szechuan feast and himself with enough beer to get through the St. Pats game on TV.

"You couldn't get into the game, Mr. New York Executive?" his brother said; and his mother answered, "I wish Carter were here too"; and Carter wished he had bought some whiskey, but then he got a break from the unlikeliest of sources: Link Andrachuk.

The Missing Link, in his first outing since his bloodying of Oblomov and his brief disappearance, was in the kind of form that had made him a first-round draft choice a few years ago. He made Carter forget, for the moment, the way good games do, all of his problems and dulled the roar of the Szechuan-fuelled chorus of the demented and the depressed sitting next to him. Link made him forget by playing hockey like he was inventing the game, skating around and through the Toronto Titans as if they were a Saturday-night beer league teleported onto the ice of the sold-out Golden Maple Arena. Where they ran smack into Link Andrachuk's sudden marriage between his talent and his desire to play, only in this honeymoon, it was the Titans who were getting fucked.

By the end of the first period the St. Pats were up 3–0 on

three unassisted goals by Andrachuk. Each goal was a variation on a theme, with the Missing Link illustrating that while there may be no "I" in "team," there was certainly an "I" in "ego." He took the puck behind his own net, surveyed the two hundred feet of ice before him as if it were his and everyone wearing the blue and red of Toronto was trespassing. He'd take a half-dozen choppy strides, like a sprinter off a starting block, and then he was at full speed, deking, dodging, streamrolling, scoring.

He played as both hero and happy ending, freed from the snarling reality that had pursued him all season, with its snaggletooth monsters trying to hamstring him. He was a different man from the player Carter had watched embarrass himself three nights earlier, and it made him wonder if Link knew that Hayley Rawls was dead, and that this was his expression of grief.

"This one's over," Carter's brother said, reaching for the remote control as the second period ended with New York up 5–0 now and Andrachuk notching two more assists. But he paused when the announcer said, "Tonight's *Legends of the Ice* series features Martin Carter, the St. Michael's Buzzer who buzzed his way to the meridian of Manhattan – until tragedy struck!"

Carter made a grab for the remote, but his brother yanked it away with surprising energy. While the brothers wrestled, Carter's mother yelled, "Look, there's that man on TV!" and there he was, that man on TV, thirty seconds away from his crash into the goalpost.

"*From the frozen outdoor rinks of Toronto to the august altar of St. Mike's high school hockey factory, Martin Carter proved he was destined to be a star from a young age!*" the announcer boomed, as if broadcasting the apocalypse to the deaf and blind. "*Blessed with breathtaking speed, and a knack for seeing the ice as if he had a third eye, Martin Carter broke all records except those of goaltending in the Ontario Junior League, and had his pick of full-ride hockey scholarships to any college he wanted.*

"But, defying convention, he chose the Ivy League Princeton Tigers – Ivy League bottom dwellers for three straight seasons – and, in his rookie year, helped lead them to an NCAA championship, the first of three in a row!"

There was Carter as a Princeton Tiger, celebrating the third of those championships, his sweat running like tears of joy as he hoisted the trophy, on his way to glory forever and ever, amen.

But he wasn't. The announcer deepened his voice to alert the audience to the coming tragedy:

"After being drafted in the first round of the amateur draft by the New York St. Patricks, Martin Carter traded the orange and black of the Tigers for the green and gold of the St. Pats and kept to his winning ways, leading the St. Pats to their first playoff berth in five seasons, and won the Hermes Trophy, as the Continental Hockey League's rookie of the year."

Carter stood to leave the room before the grand finale, but he couldn't, because even though he knew how it all ended, he was still nostalgic for that last rush up the ice. There he was, the wind chasing him, the puck on his stick, and the inevitable slow-motion replay of the Vancouver Sea Lions' lumbering defenceman Andy "Chief Hurt" Jack, the league's only Aboriginal player, getting the tip of his stick in the hollow of Carter's skate blade, and then Carter was flying into the goalpost, headfirst.

"Ooh," his mother winced. "Do you think he was injured?"

Carter was almost out of the room when he heard the studio host say, "We now join Madz Weinfeld in Toronto for some breaking news . . ."

Carter wheeled and grabbed the remote from his brother. There was Madz, looking mournful. She didn't say that Carter *was* dead, just that "the body of a man found in Martin Carter's burned-out apartment has not yet been positively identified, but New York St. Patricks president Freddie Hutt is not holding out hope."

The camera cut to Hutt, who looked like a man trying to look like a man who was sorry.

"Martin Carter was a great member of the New York St. Patricks, and we offer our prayers to his friends and family at this difficult time," he said.

Carter felt bad for Madz, but he couldn't help smiling. He was still dead.

Dennis leapt up, his face flushed and puffed. "What the fuck are you playing at?"

Carter's mother intervened. "Dennis! I won't have you talk like that to your dead brother!"

Carter walked over to his mother and put his arm around her. "Mom, I'm fine. It wasn't me."

"Martin!" she beamed. "You're looking very well! Has the mail come?"

Carter smiled back at her. Looking very well for a dead guy.

"What the fuck are you smiling at?" Dennis growled, stepping closer, looking as if he might take an ill-advised swing.

"Back off, Dennis," Carter said, holding up his hands.

"Get out. Now."

"I don't think that's a good idea."

Dennis, his eyes blazing, lunged at Carter. He was going to evict him by force, and Carter couldn't risk getting into any adolescent tussle with his brother, one that might break his glass skull forever, so he just stepped nimbly aside, and Dennis went hurtling into the wall and crumpled. He lay there on the scratched and dusty hardwood floor, eyes closed tight, breathing hard, and Carter felt sorry for him. He was only trying to protect their mother from him, but in truth, she probably needed protection from them both.

"I'd better call the police," Carter's mother said, her tone like she used to use when they were tussling little kids at the beach. "And tell them you killed him."

She reached for the phone, but Carter got there first. "It's okay, Mom," he said, taking the receiver from her. "He's not dead. I am."

25

Carter followed a wobbly Dennis down into the basement, careful on the rickety stairs, to the rough unfinished world of brick and dirt where Dennis parsed just how the cosmos was conspiring against him.

"Hey, brother," Carter said, ducking a ceiling beam. "I'm sorry."

Dennis grunted and sat down in front of what passed for his desk, where two computer monitors sat on a trestle table, surrounded by enough hardware to power a small war. Then he swung his chair around. "You've brought fucken trouble into our house. And if you don't get out of here, like now, I'm calling the cops."

Carter sighed. "I've done nothing wrong, Dennis," he said. "But someone wants me dead and I'm trying to stay alive."

"Someone wants you dead so you come here?" Dennis turned back to his computer. "I don't think so. You gotta go now."

He took a swig from a two-litre bottle of Coke that sat on his desk and stared at whatever was onscreen.

"You're right, Dennis. And I will go, first thing in the morning – but I need your help. I need to tell you my story."

Dennis swung one of the monitors toward his brother. On screen was Page Seven of the *New York Mail*. It featured a photo of Carter in black tie at a St. Pats fundraiser, looking drunk and shifty, and a headshot of Hayley Rawls, looking pure and trustworthy.

"According to this," Dennis said, "you're on the lam. A real fucken desperado."

Carter read over his shoulder.

Page Seven knew all about the NYPD's visit to him and had merrily taken the case to court. "Former New York St. Pats player and current director of community relations, Martin Carter, who is missing after a fire in his apartment yesterday, was apparently the last person to see Canadian film-maker Hayley Rawls alive. The nude body of Rawls, 32, was found in a Brooklyn townhouse, the victim of murder. The NYPD are keen to identify the body found in Carter's apartment. If it isn't him, then Carter will need to hope his famous speed and stickhandling skills are still in play, or else he could be playing on the prison team for life." Dennis stared at him as if looking down a long, dark tunnel.

"It's not what you think."

"Then what is it?"

Carter sat down and told him the whole story, and Dennis grunted and swigged Coke and just kept staring at his computer, as if a computer could solve the problem.

"Say this footage exists. How's it going to help you?"

It was a good question. What would he do, run up to Detective Lucius Gibson and say, "This is why she was killed."

If it were the motive.

"It's going to prove that she had something damaging to a lot of people, and if I turn it in, I'm not one of them. Or not the one who killed her."

Dennis chuckled. "Your faith in American justice is touching, Carter. They probably have medication to clear it up. You have health insurance?"

Dennis was deeply suspicious of every motive of the United States, which he suspected would somehow come for him, because of his relationship to Carter, when they finally jackbooted over the 49th parallel.

"Thanks, Dennis, I'll see you in the morning. I'm sorry for any trouble. Really, I am." Carter turned to leave. No use arguing with the torqued agenda of his perpetually angry brother.

But Dennis wasn't finished. "Hey, remember when we were kids how Mom warned us about being too curious?" Carter turned back. Dennis's smile was a grimace, but his tone was gentler. "'Call on God, but row away from the rocks.'"

"What the fuck does that mean, Dennis?"

"Plan B," he said, on another swig of Coke.

"Plan B?"

"Yeah. Did the lady you didn't kill do anything else on your computer?"

"Yeah, she played some Free Cell and surfed some porn. Look, I went to sleep and she left. Why?"

"She left before you fell asleep?"

"I woke up and she was gone."

Dennis grinned for real now, the smartest kid in the room. "Because, if it was so important, and could make her so much money, she'd keep a copy."

"I don't see how that's Plan B, Dennis."

He nodded. "I bet she fucken emailed it to herself."

"From my computer?"

"Why not? Or from hers. But I know where it went."

"To her email address . . ." Carter smiled now. "Which just happens to be on her business card."

Dennis narrowed his eyes, which only exaggerated the bulge. "Not a fucken chance. I'm not hacking into a server."

"Come on . . ."

"No, you can find it yourself."

"How?"

"On her server. But the easy way's on her home computer . . ."

26

Carter stood for ten minutes in the shower. He always did his best thinking cocooned within the cataract of hot water. Here, he was suspended from time and its grimy world, just himself and his thoughts to wash clean, giving him a clear shot at his future. Perhaps the footage was on Hayley's home computer in Vancouver, the city that had already nearly killed him. And "second time lucky" wasn't an expression with which he was familiar.

Page Seven had pretty much convicted him, dead or alive, of Hayley's murder, but who had convinced Page Seven? Who was Page Seven? Darwin Gissing? He worked for the rag, but surely he wouldn't be so obvious. Yet on the other hand, it was exactly the kind of thing that hack would do. But how would he know? The hot water massaged his head and Carter's more pressing troubles shifted back into focus: what to do if he managed to find Hayley's home computer? And this hypothetical email?

He was in Canada now, his old life had been demolished in the flames, and maybe he could start again. No, that wouldn't work. The Border agent hadn't shopped him yet, but the CSI guys were bound to identify the body in his apartment soon – after all, it only took an hour on TV – and then he'd look doubly guilty.

It was just a matter of time before they figured out he'd gone to Toronto, and they'd look for him at his old home. And the person or people who were trying to kill him would have an easy job to finish.

Carter turned the water off and leaned against the shower wall. He had to solve Hayley's murder in order to solve the rest of his life. And to do that, he'd have to rise from the dead.

It had just gone 5:00 a.m. when Carter, holding his shoes, crept down the stairway from his old room, keeping his feet to the edges of each step to avoid the squeaking middles. Then he slipped on his shoes, turned up his collar, and opened the door to make his escape into the chilly pre-dawn of Toronto while his mother and Dennis were still asleep. Dennis would be happy, and his mother wouldn't even remember he'd been home.

His mother was sitting on the front steps, in her winter coat, reading the *Toronto Star*. "There you are." She beamed. "The news is not good."

He helped her to her feet and steered her inside the house. He took her coat off and sat her in an armchair in the living room.

"Can I make you some tea?"

"Yes. But I don't drink tea."

Carter filled a cup with water, dropped in a tea bag, then zapped it in the microwave for a couple of minutes. He scanned the *Star* while he waited, and there he was, on page four. Dead in a fire. Maybe. Pathologists were working on identifying the remains.

The photo was a more recent one, taken from the St. Pats' media directory, and Carter realized he needed to make some changes to himself if he wanted to keep living as a dead man. Even a resurrected one.

He brought his mother her tea and a couple of Fig Newtons, then retreated, with stealth, into the bathroom. Inside the medicine chest was a little history of his mother's decline: vitamin B complex, and salmon oil, and ginkgo, then hope giving way to pharmacology and blister packs of Memantine and Aricept.

He couldn't grow a beard in the next fifteen minutes, nor could he shave his head. There was no razor; Dennis didn't shave. There was some hydrogen peroxide, but he reckoned he'd attract even more attention as a blond. The only thing of any use was a large pair of aviator sunglasses, so he put them on and checked in the mirror. Now he looked like he should be arrested on the spot. He put them back on the shelf and walked into the living room.

His mother had fallen asleep in her chair. He leaned over to kiss her goodbye, checking as he did to see if she was still breathing. The kiss woke her.

"Martin," she said, sounding more like herself than she had since he'd arrived. "You can go now. I'm fine. But be careful."

On his way out, he grabbed a Toronto Blue Jays baseball cap from a peg in the foyer. Carter believed that only baseball players should wear baseball caps, but at least this was a cap for a real team. He knew that he'd look like everybody, and nobody, if he wore it, so he put it on. And stepped out of the house and into that cold sting of the morning air in Toronto in March. The sky was a jaundiced black, night slowly ceding to the day, and both fighting the city lights.

A guy in an expensive suit was picking up after his chocolate Lab in front of the Enoch Turner Schoolhouse across the street, just down from the woman sitting in her BMW X5, its engine purring as she tweaked her makeup in the sun-visor mirror. It made Carter just a little nostalgic for the crackheads and winos of not so long ago.

He walked up to King Street, his flight bag over his shoulder, then headed west, toward the soaring towers of finance a few blocks away. He loved how one of the banks invited a zap of lightning by topping their building with a cross. Or maybe it was a church with a skyscraper for a spire. You could never tell in Toronto.

Without thinking where he was headed, he walked over to Yonge Street, which was already humming with commuters heading north, to work, and then headed down past the Hockey Hall of Fame. The floodlights at the foot of the old converted bank building led his eye up the facade, a testament to the glory of Greece and Rome as imagined, he thought, by some immigrant Glaswegian.

Once upon a time, people had said his name would be enshrined here, along with those whose talent or money placed them in hockey's pantheon. Now the only way he would get in would be if he had thirteen dollars to buy a ticket and the place were open. He didn't belong there. He didn't belong in Toronto. It wasn't his city anymore. He'd said goodbye to it a long time ago, and now he was saying goodbye again, maybe forever.

He entered Union Station as another round of commuters was pouring out of the trains and into the city. He kept his head down as he walked past them, hoping it would be disguise enough, but then realized that most of them were still sleepwalking, up at four in the morning to make it into the city by six, then heading off to do another eight hours in order to pay the bills and dream of the weekend.

The *Maple Leaf* to Vancouver left at 9:15 a.m. and arrived on the West Coast three days later. For a one-bedroom sleeper, Carter would have to fork over two thousand dollars. He had four thousand in his bag. The scenery would be great, but the price was ludicrously steep. Didn't these people know that you could fly there in five hours for a couple of hundred bucks?

He left the station and stood on the street outside, gazing across at the Royal York Hotel, debating his options. He could take a taxi out to the airport and buy a plane ticket with cash, which was risky business these days even in Canada. It got the airlines a little too interested in who you were, and the last thing he needed was people interested in him.

He could rent a car and drive to Vancouver in a week, but they'd want a credit card deposit. He could buy a car – some rusted-out Ontario jalopy – and drive to Vancouver, crossing the spring snows of the prairies and mountain passes, and if he didn't freeze to death in some whiteout, he'd be there by the time the Cup playoffs were in their final round. Or he could go back to New York and face the music.

He was just coming back to the train option when he saw across the street Link Andrachuk emerging from a Lincoln Town Car, followed by a man in an elegant black cashmere coat. It was the VIP Carter had last seen with Doug Bleecker on the night when Andrachuk changed his life.

Carter dodged a taxi and ran out onto the boulevard to get a better view. Link towered over the VIP as they lurched past the hotel's liveried doorman.

Carter knew he could turn, walk back into the train station, buy a coffee and a paper, and kill time until the train left. But he didn't. He was focused like a laser now, on the Missing Link.

27

With the brim of his Blue Jays cap riding low over his brow, Carter strode past the doorman, who tried a "bonjour" when his "good morning" got no response, and hustled up the stairs into the chandeliered lobby of the Royal York.

He knew that, after last night's game, the St. Pats wouldn't have a practice this morning, and so he was unlikely to bump into any of the other players in the lobby. Even if he did, they'd be in no shape to recognize Carter, and Link wouldn't recognize him at all, because Link refused to do cripples or cancer and had only met Carter once, and he was drunk then too, at his first and only St. Patrick's Day party a couple of years back.

Link and the cashmere-coated man, waiting for the elevator, were shouting and laughing as if they'd invented the world and were the only people in it, the way bad drunks do.

They were very drunk.

Carter could smell them from fifteen feet away. When Link turned toward him, Carter could see that the alcohol had added a ruddiness to Link's 5 a.m. stubble, to his fat lip, and to the rainbow bruise on his right eye. Then the two men stepped onto an elevator and disappeared.

Carter waited for the next car, watching the floor lights blink as Link's elevator ascended, stopping at twelve. Great, he thought as the elevator doors opened, that gave him twelve floors to think of a better plan than he had now, which was no more than the hope that Link was so drunk, he'd just spill the whole story.

The doors opened onto a sign welcoming him to the Gold Floor, the Royal York's hotel within a hotel. Across a deep-pile carpet was a check-in desk, where a winsome young Indian woman in a dark blue suit was smiling at him with professional wariness. Despite having never seen him before, she seemed to know that he wasn't a guest.

"Good morning, sir. How may I help you?"

Carter could see Link, leaning heavily now on the VIP, shuffling down the corridor, then turning the corner. The last thing he needed was a long conversation with a sharp-eyed gatekeeper.

"I need to speak to that man, Link Andrachuk."

"Are you a guest of the hotel, sir?"

Carter smiled. This was not going to be easy. He flashed his New York St. Patricks ID quickly at the young woman.

"I do media relations for the team, and uh, this is delicate, but Link, that man there, is a little drunk, and the guy with him is a journalist, and uh, Link's already in enough of a media spotlight."

She took this on board, then picked up the phone. "I'll call Mr. Bleecker for you."

Bleecker. Here? He never travelled anywhere north of Columbus Circle. What was he doing on the road with the team?

Carter knew he should run now. But he couldn't. He had committed to the play.

"No, look. I would be in trouble if you do that because I was supposed to be minding him, and uh" – he looked around conspiratorially – "I fell asleep."

She thought about this and hung up the phone. "What would you like me to do?"

"You? Nothing. I just need to have a word with him."

She picked up the phone again. "I'll call him. Your name is?"

Carter leaned in and flashed his best sheepish smile. "Look, I really appreciate this, but the world would be a much sweeter place for him, and me, if I did it in person? Please?"

She put the phone down. "You know his room number, I assume."

"12-something," Carter said.

"1213," she said quietly, as if she had her hand under the desk, on the panic button.

Carter walked down the corridor as casually as he could, but his pulse was loud in his ears and his mouth was dry. He rounded the corner and did a nimble sidestep to avoid colliding with the VIP, now doubling back.

The man was grinning to himself as he walked along, much steadier now than when Carter had seen him enter the hotel with Link. He didn't seem drunk at all, and he didn't even notice Carter as he passed.

Despite the VIP's dramatic eyepatch and black coat, he looked like a small-town guy who was pleased to have escaped the grain silos of Prairieville for the big city. He could have been a coach, or a manager, or maybe even a player agent.

Carter waited, listening for the clerk to blow his cover to the VIP, but she was talking to someone, and when he heard the ping of the elevator, he exhaled.

He moved on to room 1213 and stopped to look both ways. No one was in sight, and the door was ajar.

Carter's stomach felt hot, his forehead icy. The last time he'd gone through a door that was left open, he'd found a dead body on the bed. So he did the head-case thing and went through this door, too, hoping his luck would change.

28

Carter could hear a stream of piss splashing onto a porcelain bowl and knew from his own drunken escapades that he had maybe thirty seconds to take a look around before Link staggered out of the bathroom and collapsed onto the bed.

It was a standard hotel suite: beige loveseat and two matching chairs in the living room, a flat-screen TV, bad art, and stain-proof carpeting. Carter kept moving, spotting a wad of dead presidents on the dresser in the bedroom, maybe a thousand dollars in pocket money. And next to it was Hayley Rawls's business card.

Carter picked it up. It was the same one that she had given him – no new information. But on the other side someone had scrawled an address: 366 West Broadway. Underlined.

There was a knock on the door, and Carter's heart thudded into high gear. He'd shut it, but he hadn't locked it. Then the door opened and a man said, "Link? You all right?"

It was Eamon Lynch. Hopalong. The guy trying to kill him.

Link didn't answer.

Carter's heart was pounding as if he'd been bag skating for ten minutes. He looked quickly around for an escape route, but there was none so he dropped to the floor. There was an eighteen-inch gap between the box spring and the carpet. He shoved his flight bag in and slid in after it.

"Link? It's me, Eamon Lynch," Hopalong said, sounding as if he was now in the bedroom.

"What?" Link said, then flushed the toilet.

"It's Eamon. You with anyone in there?"

Carter could see Hopalong's feet. He was wearing running shoes, laces untied. He'd been summoned in a hurry.

"Party's over, dude," Link replied, loud and slurry. The bathroom door clicked shut.

"What party?"

The bed rocked over Carter's head as Link flopped onto it. "What time's the plane? Fuck, I need to sleep."

"Who were you with?"

"Jesus, what's the fucken problem?"

"The clerk said some media guy just came in to see you."

"He's gone, dude. Take the hint."

"Who was it?"

"What the fuck are you, my mother? I was with Erik. And no one fucking died –" He stopped and sounded like he was being strangled, but Hopalong's feet hadn't moved. Link rolled off the bed and hurried back to the bathroom. Moments later, Carter heard him vomiting the rest of his evening into the toilet.

Hopalong started to follow him into the bathroom, and Carter watched his shoes recede, waiting for his moment to get out of this alive. That's when he heard Bleecker's flat, familiar voice.

"Hello? Eamon?"

"In fucken here," Hopalong hissed.

"Jesus," said Bleecker, whose black slippers were now in sight, plump bare legs riding above them. He'd come here in a hurry too. "What happened to him?"

"Fuck," Link groaned weakly. "Can't move . . ."

"He was out on the razzle with that one-eyed fucker," Hopalong said. "Gimme a fucken hand before he chokes on his own sick."

Hopalong spoke as if he were describing unchanging weather, his Ulster inflection the only blips on the radar.

"I have a bad back."

"Well I'm fucken fifty-seven years old and I have bad every-thing including a temper, so grab his legs, would youse?"

Bleecker sighed and with heavy, staccato breathing, like he was preparing to lift for Olympic gold, helped Hopalong hoist the gasping, groaning Link from the bathroom floor onto the bed.

"Shall we get his clothes off?" Bleecker asked.

Hopalong paused, and in the pause was everything he thought about that idea.

"So," Bleecker said, trying to be cheerful under the cir-cumstances. "What was the Linkster doing?"

"Making more messes for me to clean up, Doug."

"Not again?"

"I have no fucken idea, except every time he's with that fucken cunt . . . What are you doing here?"

Bleecker cleared his throat. "I got a call from the desk saying a media guy was trying to get into Link's room."

"You're the only media guy," Hopalong said.

"That's why I'm here. You didn't see any pesky reporter on your way in, did you?"

Hopalong said nothing.

"What are you —" Bleecker began, but whatever Hopalong had gestured to shut him up like a punch to the mouth.

Carter saw Bleecker's slippers move away from the bed. Then he heard a closet door slide open, and close, and then a second one. They were making a sweep of the living room, and there weren't that many closets. They'd be looking under the bed for the bogeyman any second now. Carter was wedged in so tight beneath the bed that if he tried to move, he'd give himself away. But if he didn't, he would probably die. He pushed his arms down hard on the floor, slowly extending them as his back pressed into the mattress. He usually did fifty pushups a day, but never with a bed on his back. He pushed down on the floor as if loading the force of all fifty pushups into just this one.

And the bed began to rise.

Holding his breath, Carter pushed harder, until he was doing a full pushup now, the mattress rising, then the bed itself. And then, Link Andrachuk rolled off it and onto the floor, headfirst, on the window side. Carter grabbed his flight bag, slipped out from under the bed and hid behind the bedroom door.

Link was yelling like a guy whose parachute hadn't opened, but then he stopped, gurgled, and started to vomit again.

Bleecker and Hopalong came running. With both of them kneeling over Link on the side of the bed farthest from the bedroom door, Carter made his move. The thick carpeting muffling his steps, he headed through the door and through the living room, running down the hall, then briskly walking past the startled clerk, head down, as if in deep thought.

"Everything okay, sir?" she asked.

"Fine, fine. Couldn't be better," Carter said, following the exit sign toward the stairs. Not looking at her, not looking back. Then he ran down the stairs and out the door. A dead man on the move.

29

To Carter, Vancouver on the late afternoon of a fine spring day was that place found somewhere over the rainbow. It was a confection of a city, ringed with snow-capped mountains and a gentle green ocean, its glass towers looking as if they'd been polished by Mother Nature herself.

He'd been on the train for nearly four days, travelling through enough postcard shots to bore even his own mother: the windswept lakes and forests of Northern Ontario; the prairies, a pancake frosted with snow; the stone wall of the Rocky Mountains, so formidable it amazed him that anyone could pass through them at all; and then the winding climax through the lush Fraser River Valley and into Vancouver.

Carter hadn't spent much time appreciating the view. He'd bought himself a sleeping berth, and a thick biography of Winston Churchill, and stayed out of sight for most of the trip – living on roasted peanuts, bottled water, oranges, and, to balance his diet, a forty-ouncer of Crown Royal he'd bought in the bar car.

Running over and over in his head what he'd heard in Link's hotel room.

"What was the Linkster doing?"

"Making more messes for me to clean up, Doug."

"Not again?"

"I have no fucken idea, except every time he's with that fucken cunt . . ."

Link and the VIP made messes, and Hopalong cleaned them up. Literally. So who was Mr. Eyepatch VIP? And was Hayley a mess in need of a little wet work? Carter had stared repeatedly at her business card as if it could connect to his soul and reveal deep and eternal truths, such as what the hell lay behind the address on West Broadway on the back of the card she'd given to Link.

When he finally emerged from the train in Vancouver, blinking in the sunlight of Pacific Central Station, he was like a sailor after too long on the seas: a bit unsteady on his feet and sporting a four-day growth of beard.

He caught a taxi out front and told the blue-turbaned driver to take him across downtown to English Bay.

The city had changed dramatically in the fifteen years since Carter had last been here. As they drove along Pacific Boulevard, past the gleaming new arena where the Vancouver Sea Lions regularly played, Carter marvelled at the green-glazed towers around him, serenely presiding over those still going up. Construction cranes, slowly turning in the moist Pacific sunlight like giant metal seabirds, seemed to be on every other block, with their attendant flag crews on the ground below causing traffic chaos.

"It's like driving in a video game," Carter said to the driver, who laughed.

"It's worse, sir," he replied in a strong Punjabi accent. "At least a video game has rules."

On the sidewalks, the beautiful people sipped coffees on patios, or walked dogs, or jogged, as if the whole place was an advertisement for the good life.

Carter began to feel as if he had really escaped his problems. But then, he knew, that's what the west was all about.

A fragment of poetry filtered into his mind: "*There is a country at the end of the world/ Where no child's born but to outlive the moon.*"

"What's that, sir?" said the taxi driver.

Carter hadn't realized he had been speaking out loud. "Just something a poet said."

"Which poet, sir?"

From the Kingdom of Before. "I can't remember."

"Ah." The driver smiled at Carter in the rear-view mirror. "It's okay, I thought you were giving me directions."

"Nah, just giving them to myself . . ."

The driver nodded. "Yes, the map of life . . ." He understood, and Carter gave him a hefty tip when he dropped him at the Sylvia Hotel, the grand dame with slightly smeared lipstick perched on the shore of English Bay. Carter knew from experience that if you sat long enough with the right company in the hotel bar overlooking the ocean, you could eventually see Japan. Even now, in early spring, people were sunning themselves on the golden sand, using the logs that dotted the beach as windbreaks against the westerly breeze speeding the sailboats along out in the bay. This would be the perfect place to stay, Carter thought, if only he had that option.

The only hotel room available was on the thirteenth floor of the new wing, with a view toward the city, which glistened with the promise of prosperity.

Carter took a long, hot shower, then he ordered a steak frites from room service and a newspaper to see what had happened in the past week while he'd been rolling west along the rails.

The *Vancouver Gazette* featured the usual litany of woe in its front section, so he slathered some more hollandaise on his steak and flipped to the sports section, the front-page headline bellowing: "SEA LIONS COULD BARK THEIR LAST TONIGHT."

The team who'd lost their star player hadn't won a game since that bloody night in New York nearly two weeks ago. If they lost against Los Angeles tonight, they'd be out of the playoffs and the revenue stream that poured in with the post-season.

The team's coach, Bunny Blackburn, had calmed himself since Carter had last seen him in a whirlwind of profane outrage, threatening to sue the St. Patricks into oblivion, and was now uttering the usual bromides about working with what you've got, though in his Franglish it came out as "playing the game with the players who play."

What would the philosophers make of that? Carter thought as his eyes slid down the page to a piece on the wounded Sasha Oblomov. He was no longer in a New York hospital. He had been moved to an "undisclosed location," and neither the Sea Lions, nor the St. Pats, nor the league was saying anything about him.

The byline credited Gracie Yates, whom Carter remembered from the press conference in New York. Hard to forget her, really, asking him if he had seen what Link Andrachuk had done to Sasha Oblomov. And he had lied to her then. Now maybe it was time to tell her the truth. See what she could tell him in return.

He grinned. He was still dead, so why not go straight to a newspaper reporter and apologize for lying to her? He was sure she'd take it in the spirit it was given and keep his presence in the city hush-hush. Bad idea. No, he was here to find Hayley's computer. He'd thought about it over and over as the train wheels clacked beneath him, the percussion to a mission that he didn't see how he could escape.

It would mean breaking into the house of the dead woman, and God knows what he'd find there – if he didn't find himself in jail soon afterwards. And then, if the B&E worked out, cracking into her computer and finding the proof that would save his life. It wasn't a very attractive future, but it was the only one he really had.

He opened the phone book, but Hayley Rawls wasn't listed. He called 411, but they didn't have anything for her – the number on her business card was for a cellphone, and her address was a web address. No bricks and mortar were needed to exist in this brave new world.

He had come all the way to Vancouver to solve a mystery

and he couldn't even find out where the mystery lived. Typical head-case mess to be in.

He walked out onto the balcony and breathed the salty air. The North Shore Mountains were a deep blue in the afternoon light, crowned with a snow pack that kept the ski runs open, even now, at the beginning of April.

He decided he needed some exercise to get his plan in shape, so he wandered down Denman Street, past the lively bars and restaurants and cafés, wondering, as he went, if anyone actually held down a day job in this town, or could stay sober, given the amount of dope perfuming the air. He found a cyber café, bought himself a coffee, and plugged the computer kiosk with coins. He typed in *www.411.com* and did a search for Hayley Rawls in Vancouver. Nothing.

He did a straight Google search for her and found a tribute page of condolences in the *Gazette*. There weren't many, and most were from her old TV network colleagues, and an odd one from some guy going by "ES," who said that her death hurt him as much as it hurt her, which, under the circumstances, was something Carter would have to take on faith.

And he noticed that her memorial service was scheduled for today. In about two hours.

He took a sip of coffee and typed in his own name. Top of the list was a hit from Page Seven. The cops were being even more tight-lipped at the moment, but there were rumblings in the Manhattan rumour mill that there had been a new development in the death by fire of murder suspect Martin Carter.

Just what that new piece of information was, the tabloid coyly didn't say, but Carter knew. His time as a dead man was almost over. And he smiled. He would start his return from the dead by going to a funeral.

30

The first thing that had to go was his hair. On his way back to the hotel, Carter bought some scissors and an electric shaver at a drugstore, and once he was back in his room, he chopped his black curls down to the thickness of a Saxony carpet, then buzzed the rest of his head with the shaver. He wasn't after the chemotherapy look, he was after a just-enlisted-in-the-Marines look.

Next came the beard. He didn't like beards, not only because they itched, but because they looked like you were trying to hide something. Which he was. Himself. So he shaved off his beard, leaving behind a thick, black caterpillar moustache.

He laughed at the result: like Freddie Mercury, with better teeth. But he no longer looked like Martin Carter, especially not after he put on the horn-rimmed glasses he'd also picked up at the drugstore, the kind with clear lenses. Now he looked like an urban professional, educated and cultured, not the caricature of a suspected murderer on the lam.

With his buzz cut, and wearing new jeans and a crisp white shirt under a black blazer, he looked good, and heads of both sexes turned a little as he passed by on his way to the funeral home. That was okay. People could notice him, just not recognize him.

The funeral chapel was a little east of Gastown, where the city was in a mad frenzy of reclaiming land from the generations of lost souls who called the neighbourhood home: junkies, whores, thieves, pimps, dealers, the mad, and the broken. Or all of the above, thought Carter, crossing Main and Hastings and wondering if he'd walked onto a movie set, some horror job set in the Middle Ages, and he was in the extras holding pit. But it wasn't a movie; it was the other side of the city, the port side, the side of dank garbage and human jetsam. And the final side of the city for Hayley.

A gleaming aluminum casket sat in front of the altar in the tiny funeral chapel. Carter found a seat at the back, behind the dozen or so people scattered among the six pews in front of him. There was a quartet of men in their late forties and fifties who looked like camera guys and grips Hayley might have worked with. There was a man in his sixties in a linen suit, whose unnaturally black permed hair made him look even older, a few women in their forties and fifties, and one who was maybe two hundred years old. None of the congregation were crying, none of them were looking like Hayley, none of them were family. And all of them older than her. Either she had no friends her own age, or they hadn't heard about today's memorial.

The chapel was decorated in ecumenical neutral, with beige walls, grey carpet, and no overt signs of any world religion, save for a raised platform bearing the casket, flanked by two electric candles that flickered with programmed regularity.

Some wild-eyed minister pushing seventy, in a clerical collar and a grey three-piece suit, appeared from a hidden door beside the altar, and the canned organ music rumbling over the speakers stopped. He wore a watch fob in his vest pocket, and his grey mutton-chop whiskers bounced along with his jowls while he memorialized Hayley Rawls in a bad Cockney accent. Or rather, while he rattled off a breathless list of platitudes written by literary geniuses – "Do not send to know for whom the bell tolls" – and hacks – "If you love something, let it go" – and everyone in between, including, Carter realized with amusement, Yoda, from *Star Wars* – "Death is a natural part of life. Rejoice for those around you who transform into the Force."

Carter hoped the minister was just drunk and didn't expect anyone to connect his babble to the woman in the eight-by-ten photo propped on the altar, smiling as if life never ended. The murder victim.

After ten minutes of his greatest-hits-of-death show, which mercifully for Carter didn't include anything from gangsta rap, the minister took a breath and asked whether anyone else wanted to speak.

"When's the fucken food?" croaked a hard-looking woman a couple of rows down from Carter, whom he'd taken to be a TV network executive. When she answered her own question with a loud belch, and the minister said, "Thank you, Rae," Carter realized she was a professional mourner, probably from the neighbourhood.

"Anyone else?" asked the minister, and a voice behind Carter said, "Sorry I'm late."

The eyepatched VIP he'd last seen escorting a drunken Link Andrachuk back to his hotel suite strode to the altar, touching the coffin as he passed it. No, thought Carter, she can't be in that thing. The cops haven't even charged anyone with her murder. Or maybe they had.

"Hello, everyone, and thank you for coming on this sad, sad day," said the man, interrupting Carter's chilly thought and swivelling his gaze from one side of the room to the other so he could make full one-eyed contact. "My name is Erik Shepherd, and I worked with Hayley Rawls – was working with her at the time of her death. I can only say how sorry I am."

So that's the guy behind the website that Hayley mentioned when he first met her, Carter thought. The name Erik Shepherd certainly suited his classic style, his eyepatch accenting a black dress shirt and charcoal suit, the only splash of colour a gold-and-purple paisley tie. He had a pleasant bass voice, and he emphasized all his consonants, which gave his flat Canadian accent a slight British military flavour and made what he had to say sound true.

"She was a fucken bitch!" yelled the woman who was keen to get to the food.

"She could be difficult, we all know that," Shepherd replied with a rueful smile, "but she was also a very gifted young woman, and we cut her a lot of slack. Until someone cut her life, so full of promise, short." He paused, looking them all in the eye again, as if waiting for a confession. "But I promise you, I will find that person, and make them pay for what they have done." Then he panned the room again, in case anyone had missed the sincerity of his promise. Carter believed him, and he felt the chill on his forehead flow like a current around the back of his skull and down the nape of his neck. Erik Shepherd was now a much bigger part of his problem.

"I know, the police and the courts must do their work." Shepherd spoke firmly and clearly – the voice of reason, "but there was a saying that Hayley lived by, and I'm going to live by it too." He paused, making sure he had their attention. "Genius plays by its own rules." He paused again, then repeated it, in case anyone had missed the point. "And that, friends of Hayley Rawls, is the best way we can all honour her memory. Play by your own rules."

Carter sucked in his breath, waiting for a response from the professional mourner to this dubious wisdom, but the chapel was silent.

"And to help us along," Shepherd continued, shifting gears with the ease of a TV news anchor, "I'm also starting the Hayley Helps Fund, with 10 per cent of the royalties from the project she was working on at the time of her . . . death . . . going to help other women in media realize their visions."

There was tepid applause, and he held up a hand. "And of course, I'll be accepting donations, which you can make online at my website, maestro media productions dot com, or at my studio, just across the street from where we are now."

Erik Shepherd bowed, his performance finished, while the applause of a dozen people followed him to a seat in the front pew. Then the minister pressed a button, the floor beneath the casket dropped like a gallows, and the casket, on groaning hydraulic lifts, sank beneath the cut-pile carpet and into the basement.

That's when Carter saw her. Her sapphire eyes were aimed right at him. His head went cold. Gracie Yates, the woman he'd last seen asking him hard questions at a press conference in New York, was standing at the back of the chapel. And from the gleam in those blue eyes, she had recognized him.

He had to walk past her to the exit, and he was aware of every step now, as if he were weighed down with leg irons.

She smiled at him as he passed, just a subtle stretch of her full lips, and touched him on the arm, like one mourner to another. "Meet me after the game tonight, Mr. Carter," she whispered, scribbling an address on her business card. "And we'll toast your resurrection."

31

My resurrection, thought Carter, as he walked out of the funeral home and into the hazy afternoon light. Resurrection meant triumph over death, and right now, that victory was nowhere in sight.

He caught a glimpse of himself in the window of Maestro Media, across the street from the memorial chapel. Erik

Shepherd ran his multimedia show out of an old bank building, its Ionic stone columns, coral with black-and-gold detail
on the capital, rising above the human misery and making it
seem not only from another age but from another planet.

Carter looked at his reflection in the window. To his eye, he
did not look like himself at all. So how had Gracie Yates recognized him? But since she'd seen him, he'd have to trust
that her journalist's instinct would be to ask him at least
twenty questions before she turned him in.

He walked a couple of blocks and through the dragon gates
into Chinatown, where the chameleon city again changed its
complexion fast, shifting from drug squalor to a bustle of
Chinese industry.

Carter found himself tailing a crew of suburbanites in ball
caps and Sea Lions jerseys as he walked up Beatty Street,
toward the Brewhouse Arena, and he realized a hockey game
might be just the place to put things in perspective.

At the Brewhouse, he found out that tonight's big and
maybe last game of the season was sold out, and the scalpers
wanted to take three hundred bucks from him. Then he
remembered his St. Patricks ID. And that he didn't look like
the guy in the photo anymore – even if he could find the media
gate at which the ID would work. It was nowhere in sight.

The Brewhouse was tucked between an elevated highway
into the city centre and yet another neighbourhood of gleaming towers and a park so new he could see the cut lines in the
sod. The arena had two different street levels – one along the
highway, one below it – and after walking the perimeter,
Carter finally found the media gate on the lower level, in the
darkest corner.

Carter flashed his ID it at the teenager guarding the gate,
and by way of distracting him from the dissimilarity between

the guy holding the ID and the guy in the photo said, "The Lions gonna do it tonight?"

"Oh yeah," said the kid, glancing at the card and its shamrock logo. "They want to play you New York guys really, really badly. Enjoy the game."

"I'm counting on it," Carter replied and walked quickly into the building before the kid could think twice.

Any executive with any CHL team could get into any game on any night by flashing his magic team plastic and could sit in either the VIP box or the media box, depending on ticket sales to the public. But Carter didn't much want to sit with a bunch of reporters for three hours, and though he knew he'd enjoy being in the VIP box, as Vancouver's buffet of organic local bounties, wild salmon, and fruity wines was the envy of the league, it was too risky – these days, anyone could be a vipp, as Doug Bleecker would say. Carter pressed his way through the crowd, stopping at the concession stand.

Five minutes later, Bleecker and the St. Patricks seemed far away from where he stood, with a beer and a burger, behind a railing in the standing-room-only section, along with a dozen people who'd forked out a couple of hundred bucks to watch the Sea Lions roar or sink into the Pacific.

That was the knock on West Coast teams. They were so seduced by la dolce vita that they forgot what it was like to suffer in winter. The desire for revenge came from the misery of blizzards and ice storms and deep snow at your door. What fury fuelled these two Pacific teams? Having no snow to shovel and not having to drive to the rink through flat, ice-bound industrial wastelands?

Tonight the teams offered the kind of hockey that Carter had played on outdoor rinks on endless weekend afternoons, before he knew there were rules and strategies, when instinct and imagination united with the kind of energy that kids have, the force of creation flowing through them like light. The ice tilted up, and then it tilted down, as rush followed rush, L.A. going this way, Vancouver going that way, sound-tracked by shrieks and yowls from the capacity crowd. The two goalies seemed like the Gumby figures of Carter's youth, able to bend any which way without breaking.

At the end of regulation time, the Brewhouse was one giant pulse of luminous energy. The score was only 1–1, but both teams had reminded fans what desire truly meant. It was a shame that someone was going to have to lose.

After five minutes of sudden-death overtime, the score was still tied, so the teams went to a shootout. Each coach selected three shooters, who would take the equivalent of penalty shots on the opposing goalie. But even then, no one could score.

Now the entire arena was standing. It was one shooter at a time until someone scored.

The fans were screaming all kinds of suggestions at just whom Vancouver coach Bunny Blackburn should put on the ice, and then, while the crowd took its collective breath, some lone propagandist inserted himself in the pause and began to chant, "Oblomov!"

In an instant the chant rolled through the Brewhouse: "Ob-lo-*mov*! Ob-lo-*mov*! Ob-lo-*mov*!" Injured or not, that's who the fans wanted, even though Oblomov had not been seen since the New York game, and Bunny Blackburn urged them on, both of his scarred hands punching the air to remind them of the injustice of it all.

One of the referees skated over to him to calm things down, which only made Blackburn heat up, his arms flapping, fists clenched, as his assistant coaches held him back. But they couldn't hold back his voice, and as the referee skated away,

Blackburn said something that made the ref spin and then make the ejection sign beloved of baseball umpires – thumbs up and an arm jerk out of here. Blackburn was bounced.

And bounce he did, jumping up and down and screaming at the ref, chorused by those fans who weren't still chanting, "Oblomov." Suddenly the mood had turned from the sweetness of imminent victory to bitter outrage of unjust defeat.

Once Blackburn had been escorted away, the Sea Lions obliged the crowd by missing their first shot, and L.A. scored on theirs.

Game over.

Now the chant of "Ob-lo-*mov*!" rose up like revolution, and plastic beer cups and popcorn bags and coins rained down on the ice, forcing the players and officials to make a quick exit for the dressing rooms.

Carter took the elevator down to the main concourse, where the crowd had become a mob, their playoff hopes killed by the unpunished injury to Oblomov and, adding insult to injury, the expulsion of their coach. He could feel the foiled catharsis backing up on itself, and he knew what could happen when it all came spewing back out.

The smart play would be to stick around the Brewhouse for a while and let any riot happen without him – he didn't need to get caught up in any police action – but Carter decided to go to the bar Gracie Yates had written on her card. It was only across the street, on the other side of the mob, which was getting doused now by the kind of downpour that lasts an hour in the tropics and three days in Vancouver.

Carter needed another way out. He knew there would be a tunnel to the street – every rink had one for the player's cars and opponents' team buses to make an easy entrance and a safe escape.

An easy, safe escape. He smiled. He was due one of those.

32

Carter took the elevator to the lower concourse and headed left along the curve of the arena toward the exit ramp. He'd gone a hundred yards when he rounded a pillar and, there it was, the Sea Lions' media room in full blast. The lights from the TV cameras spilled out of the room, along with the clamour of the eulogists there to write the epitaph on the Sea Lions' season.

Carter stopped, wondering whether to go around the other way, but he was drawn by the theatre taking place inside the room. Maybe he'd learn something new, and if he stayed out of sight, the media hounds wouldn't even get a whiff of him, so keen were they on the quarry in front of them.

He staked out a position by a pillar that gave him an oblique vantage point through the doorway, hoping to hear what Blackburn had to say. But Bunny was mum. Tonight, the voice of the Sea Lions belonged to the team's president and general manager, a deep voice that pulled Carter like gravity toward the open door.

Carter had seen recent photos of Andy Jack, of course, and in one dimension, in a hockey magazine, he was harmless. But now – commanding the podium in a three-piece silk suit made doubly expensive by his six-foot-five frame, hands as big as hockey gloves bearing three Cup rings, an air of menace amplified by his broad warrior's face – Jack was the three-dimensional nightmare that had visited Carter for the past fifteen years.

Jack had the same look in his eye now as he did the night he had ended Carter's career: a cold, unblinking righteous gaze.

In Jack's calculation, what happened to Carter hadn't been worth thinking about. If Carter had scored a goal on him, he would have had his one-way ticket to the minors punched, and he would have stayed there for the rest of his career. Instead, he got to stay with the Sea Lions, a hard-rock, stay-at-home defenceman. After he retired, he coached their farm team, then came back to the big club as an assistant, then head coach, then rising to the top where he now stood, unleashing thunderbolts.

"We can't use the fact that we don't have Sasha Oblomov in the lineup as an excuse for losin' tonight," he said. "But we can use it as an excuse for why coach Blackburn got ejected from the game. He was only expressin' the frustration we all feel with a league that doesn't protect its star players. And now, our season is over."

He paused as the media digested what he had just said.

"Yes, you heard me," he continued. "The CHL, by failin' to suspend Link Andrachuk for his vicious attack on Sasha, sent a very clear message that it's open season on the skill guys, and I don't care if the league fines me ten times ten thousand dollars for saying what's true. We've already lost much more than that."

Carter was tempted to walk right into the media room and remind him that he hadn't been punished fifteen years ago when he had deliberately injured a skill guy, but Gracie Yates got there ahead of him.

"Are you saying that you saw what Link Andrachuk is alleged to have done?"

He gave her a pitying look. "We all know Sasha Oblomov didn't get a grade-three concussion and nearly lose his tongue by accident. Who was the guy closest to him?"

There was a brief silence as the other members of the media considered whether to take on Jack, and risk being black-listed, or join his chorus. Gracie chose a third option.

"I don't know," she said, "but it's rumoured there's footage of the incident. Have you seen it?"

"Lookit," he paused, the "bitch" implied, his face darkening, "I see that I lost my best player for the season and that the guy who did it got away with it." He was growling now. "And now we're outta the goddamn playoffs. What else do you need to know? You people . . ." He turned and walked away.

"How is Oblomov?" she yelled after him. "*Where* is Oblomov?" she shouted louder, but he was gone, lumbering out of the media room on bad knees propelled by fury.

The pack of reporters moved quickly out of the room, off to file their stories. Carter had no time to do anything but step back behind the pillar and let them pass.

Gracie had clocked him on her way out of the room. She rounded the pillar and took his elbow as she passed. "Come with me," she said, startling him. "But don't speak to anyone and don't look back."

The last time a woman had snuck up on Carter at a media conference, a world of woe had crashed down upon his head. And in that collision with Hayley Rawls, Carter had made some choices that left him with just two right now. So he did as she said, hoping she knew something that he didn't.

33

Gracie drove them to her Plan B bar in her turquoise 1963 Valiant Signet convertible, the kind of automotive masterpiece that survives on the temperate west coast.

"It's not my first choice," she said as she parked outside a bar named Playerz, "but I can guarantee the mob won't be here."

Carter winced at the *z*, but the bar wasn't as terrible as the name suggested. It was a sports joint, with lots of mirrors and chrome and festooned with the banners and memorabilia of great teams that didn't play in Vancouver. And it was three-quarters empty.

Gracie ordered a pinot blanc and Carter a double Jameson from the surly bartender – doing table duty and not happy about it – who told him they didn't have that brand but didn't suggest another. He was either taking the Sea Lions' loss personally or annoyed that the place was only a quarter full. So Carter ordered a double Crown Royal.

"Still a Canadian boy at heart," Gracie said, flipping open her laptop.

"I'm pretty ecumenical when it comes to whiskey," he said. "And I'm not doing any interviews."

"Me neither. I'm just capping my piece with the reax and then it's off and into the system."

She typed fast, barely glancing at her notebook, and didn't even look up when the bartender delivered their drinks.

"Cheers," Carter said, clinking his glass against hers; she flashed him a sweet smile. "Sorry, just one more wise word from the great Andy Jack and then I'm done."

"How about 'I'm a lying asshole?'"

She glanced up at him again, serious now. "True, after what he did to you, but I don't think that thought is available to him. He's deep inside the boys club now where they all play like that, and it's pretty hard to get kicked out."

"Unless you miss the playoffs."

She nodded. "Yep. That's why he came out throwing smoke bombs tonight. Blame it all on the league, and by the time it all fades away, all of the beat reporters will be at the beach."

Carter lifted his glass. The whiskey was sweet and hot. "You think those were smoke bombs? Seemed more like missiles."

"We'll see," she said as she finished typing and hit the enter key with a flourish. She raised her glass in mock triumph and sniffed the fruity wine. "Either way, the season's done. I mean, you can only blame the referees for so long, you know?"

He knew. He'd stopped blaming them long ago. "It's the problem with omniscience," he said. "We keep demanding it of the wrong people."

She looked at him with real interest now, as if she'd heard him speak for the first time. And he liked the feel of those blue eyes on him, inviting him to reveal more.

"So," she said, leaning back in her chair, her smile easy. "Tell me how you did it."

His head tingled. She made it sound like he had something to confess. "That's a big question," he said, his mouth suddenly dry.

"Resurrection always is," she replied.

He relaxed. She was talking about him, not accusing him of murder. "Well, I was sent by heaven to redeem humankind from original sin. It was part of the deal. And I wound up here in paradise."

She almost laughed. "You should check your contract. This place isn't all that it seems. But then, neither are you."

"What do I seem like?" It sounded like he was flirting with her, so he looked away, as if the question bored him. But he could feel a little heat in his stomach. He wanted to hear her answer.

"Tell me your story and I'll let you know," Gracie replied, then she added, "Please?"

"Why should I trust you?"

"Too late for that one, Martin Carter. You're already in the game."

She was right. In coming here and *here,* he was more than committed to the play. He was practically in the net, and the realization jarred him. So he told her his story.

He told her about Hayley Rawls, from beginning to end; he told her about the fire and his brave super, Carlito; he told her about escaping to Toronto and his encounter with the drunken Missing Link.

And here he was now. Raising his glass in memory of the recently dead. "To Hayley and Carlito, may they rest in peace."

Gracie hadn't touched her wine while he spoke, but now she took a thoughtful sip, her eyes down, her face golden under the overhead spotlight, like Freya, the Norse goddess who ruled the warrior Valkyries.

"Hayley had a pretty sad memorial," she said.

Carter nodded. "If she had friends, they didn't seem to be there. And that woman, the old drunk, calling her a bitch."

"Which she was, by your account."

He grinned. "Yeah, well, if that were a reason for murder, the streets would be littered with bodies."

She smiled gently. "So who would want you dead?"

It was the essential question, the one Carter had been thinking about all week. "Whoever knows what I saw."

"But if the footage has vanished, shouldn't that be enough?"

"You mean, who's going to believe me without it?"

Her cheeks coloured. "No, I meant, why do they need to kill you for something that doesn't exist?" She flicked her long, strong fingers in quotation marks to let him know that her jury was still out on the matter.

"But that's the thing," he said. "I think it does exist."

"Really?" She swallowed some wine, but her eyes never left his.

"I think it might be on Hayley's home computer. I think she might have emailed it to herself."

She didn't laugh at him. "Why?"

"My brother is something of a computer genius; he suggested she'd likely done this. Considering the value of the footage."

She thought about this and smiled amiably. "Okay. Do you know where she lives? Better still, did she give you a key?"

"No. She's not in the phone book, and no keys were exchanged."

"Just your DNA."

"Thanks, I'd forgotten about that."

Gracie glanced at his empty glass and signalled the bartender for another round. But the bartender had his back turned, juicing the volume on the TV so the patrons could hear all about the demise of their Sea Lions.

But there, on the giant flat TV screens, was Martin Carter's picture.

The photo was terrible, which was very good as he didn't look at all like the dissipated, broken-nosed ruffian onscreen.

The announcer was saying something about murder and police and Martin Carter, and then suddenly Detective Lucius Gibson appeared on the screen like judgment itself, his black eyes looking directly at Carter.

"The body found in the fire at Martin Carter's apartment was not his, and had, uh, in fact, not died as a result of the fire."

The media gaggle surrounding him shouted out their questions, but Gibson had been down this road before and held up his boxer's hand.

"We don't know who murdered who yet," he said. "All we do know is that Martin Carter was not killed in the fire."

"So he's alive?" There was Madz Weinfeld, on the edge of the camera's eye, still looking as if her best friend had died, her black roots showing.

"He was as of last week. He made a call on his cellphone from a Travel Plaza upstate."

Carter caught Gracie's questioning eye. He nodded and held up his palms by way of saying he had a good reason.

"So, he remains a person of interest in our investigation into the murder of Hayley Rawls."

"How much interest?"

Gibson was silent, as if considering whether to answer at all. Then he stared straight through the screen at Carter. "A lot," he said. "An awful lot."

The reporter threw back to the studio.

Carter turned to Gracie. She was looking at him too, her blue eyes shaded with doubt.

"Everything I told you is true," he said.

"Yeah, but did you tell me everything?"

"Look, I forgot about using my cellphone, but I didn't really have a choice. A cop was going to run my licence."

"A cop? Why did a cop stop you?" Her tone was suddenly sharp and professional, the consonants hard.

"Because there's a war on terror going on, Gracie, and you just can't be too careful."

She didn't smile.

"Because I was driving a van advertising an Irish bar, and the cop thought I might be transporting booze across state lines."

She didn't blink. "And so?"

"I called 911 and said the McDonald's at the Travel Plaza was being robbed. The cop went running in; I grabbed my licence and took off. And I dumped the van in a lake outside Syracuse."

Gracie stared at him as if her jury was now voting to convict. "You have to admit that your behaviour is pretty suspicious."

Carter leaned toward her, his face lit by the overhead spot, hiding nothing. "What would you have done? I had to get out of there, buy some time. It wasn't a plan, it was a reaction."

"Like life itself," she said and stood. "I have to go to the washroom."

He nodded. She was going to get out of sight, whip out her cellphone, and turn him in. She read the thought. But to her credit, she didn't tell him he was going to have to trust her. She didn't say anything. She just nodded and walked away.

Carter watched her disappear into the shadows at the back of the bar. She had an athlete's body, lithe and strong. Maybe she'd been a swimmer in college. Then he remembered the athletic calves he'd glimpsed in New York. Maybe a runner.

And maybe running was what he should be doing right now.

No, Carter thought, that would be a stupid play. If she turned him in, she'd lose his story. And she wouldn't let that happen because she was too good a reporter. She wouldn't tell a story whose ending she didn't know. He could trust that.

He smiled when she returned as if he hadn't expected her back so soon.

"Meet anyone I know?" he said.

She finally smiled back at him. "You frequent ladies' washrooms too?"

"That's an idea. Maybe I should disguise myself as a woman."

She laughed. "You wouldn't fool anyone. Not even in Vancouver. You're too much of a man."

It was a statement of fact, not flattery. Either way, Carter thought, it was good to hear.

"I'm a wanted man," he said, and that, too, sounded like flirting, but she was already writing the story.

"Who wants to break into the computer of a dead woman," she said. It was both a statement and a question. Carter paused, considering his reaction. He needed Gracie to help him find Hayley. He reached in his wallet and pulled out Hayley's business card.

"Here's where you come in. I found this in Link's hotel room."

She looked at it, then at him, her eyes searching for the punchline. "Your big clue is a business card?"

"It's all I've got. But you guys can find anyone, can't you?"

Gracie nodded. "Yep. We're magic." Then she noticed the address on the back of the card.

"366 West Broadway. What's this?"

"That's what I'd like to know. I'd have to get back to New York to check it out, as Mr. Google was no help. It's on my 'to do' list."

Gracie turned the card over. "I think," she said with just the touch of a smile, "you should move it up your list."

"Why?"

"I'll show you."

34

"There it is," said Gracie, pointing across Carter's chest at a four-storey building on the far side of the street, the neon lights of its shops glowing on the rain-slicked pavement beneath. "366 West Broadway. And I'm betting it's the address on the back of her business card."

Carter had forgotten that Vancouver had a Broadway too,

which stretched the breadth of the peninsula, its main midtown artery from west to east.

She stopped the car, punched *R* on the push-button transmission, and backed into a parking spot in front of a bar called Lethe.

"Good name," Carter said. "The waters of forgetfulness."

"What?"

"That's what the name of the bar means. It's one of the rivers of Hades, in Greek mythology. If you drank from it, you forgot everything."

Gracie stared at him for a moment, the engine still running, as if gauging whether to drive off after dumping him out. "You're an interesting guy, Martin Carter," she said, then turned off the ignition.

"Life Tourette's is what someone called it once."

"Life Tourette's." She grinned, trying it out. "I like it."

"Try having it."

"I just might," she said. "If I'm right about this."

They stood in front of the building under Gracie's large purple umbrella, the traffic on Broadway sloshing past them in the rain. There were shops on the ground floor, topped by three storeys of apartments.

"It has a security system," Carter said, noticing the intercom.

"A tent on a patch of toxic landfill – which, by the way, is called a starter home and will set you back half a million – will have a security system," Gracie replied. "Half the city are drug addicts, and theirs is a portable economy."

Carter smiled. He liked her dark humour. "So we buzz the caretaker and tell him we're the cops."

She shot him a worried look.

"I'm joking," he said. "You go and see if she's listed. There's probably a video camera too, and I've had enough of those."

She kept the umbrella angled forward and down as they walked toward the doorway, shielding them from the bubble camera above the building. They checked the listings on the intercom directory. And there she was: Hayley's Comet Media.

Here was the place he had crossed the continent in search of, and he had found it by accident. And with the help of a stranger. The history, he thought, of most discoveries.

"You coming in?" he asked Gracie.

She gave him another look, half-amused, half-incredulous. "Of course. How?"

"Well, the place probably has a parkade at the back, so we can wait for someone to drive in and sneak in after them."

"And Plan B?"

"Okay." Carter suddenly put his arms around her and kissed her. She was too surprised to react, pinned as she was against the door, the purple umbrella hanging over them like a chaperone.

Carter felt a rush of heat through his body from the warmth of her lips, glossed with some kind of strawberry balm that he liked the taste of very much. He could have kept going, but he just as suddenly broke off.

"I'm sorry . . ."

"I should hope –"

He pulled her toward him, away from the door, which clicked open. A middle-aged man walking a basset hound exited. "Sorry, we got a little carried away," Carter said.

"No problem," said the guy, on a wink to Carter. "Have a nice night."

Just before the door shut, Carter wedged his foot between it and the jamb, and they were inside.

Gracie didn't speak to him until they were in the elevator. "You know, after this is over, I'll get you back for that."

Carter hoped that she would. "I'm sorry," he said, the taste of her mouth still on his lips. "It was the only thing I could think of when I saw that guy coming out. It worked for James Bond."

"Yeah, well I'm not a Bond girl," she said, staring straight and looking seriously annoyed. He said nothing.

When the elevator reached the third floor, Gracie was out of it before the doors were halfway open. She was leading now. Carter took the point.

Hayley's Comet was at the bend of the L-shaped corridor. Gracie took a key out of her pocket and eyed the nearest suite. It was about fifteen feet down the hall, on the opposite side.

"Good," she said, jigging the key partially into the lock. "They won't hear us."

"What the hell!" said Carter. "You have a key?"

"Yeah," she said. "I have a key. You don't happen to have a hammer, do you?"

"Uh, no."

"Okay, well then make a fist, pretend it's a hammer, and bump the key."

"What?"

"It's called key bumping. I saw it on TV."

"Then it must work."

She sighed. "You have a better idea? No, don't answer that."

He hit the key with the side of his fist and it flew out of the lock.

"You want to vibrate the key into the lock. Not beat the door down."

After a minute of tapping, his fist getting sore, the key popped in the lock, and Gracie opened the door.

"Always spend money on a good lock," she said, offering him the chance to enter first. Truce.

The lights of the city spilled into the curtainless studio, whose huge glass windows looked north toward the downtown peninsula and beyond that to the mountains shrouded in cloud.

The studio was sparse, no more than a room with a futon bed that looked like it doubled as a sofa, a desk, a coffee table opposite a flat-screen TV, and, along one wall, a small kitchen. There was a glass door to a narrow balcony and two wooden doors across from the kitchen, one partially blocked by the bed. Carter tried them both. One led to a closet crammed with clothes, shoes, and a vacuum cleaner; the second he could open only halfway, but it was enough to see into a small bathroom. The futon faced the window, and Carter remembered Hayley's preference for a bed with a view. There were no photographs of friends or family, and the small bookshelf held a collection of DVDs.

There were several large glossy books on the coffee table, and Carter picked one up. It was an homage to the Salt Lake City Winter Olympics, and underneath it was one about the Vancouver Sea Lions titled *Stars of the Sea*.

"Interesting taste in literature," he said.

"Those would be samples of the Maestro's work," Gracie replied.

"The Maestro?"

"This guy," Gracie said, flipping the book over to the photo on the back. "Whom you know as Erik Shepherd. And whom the good people of Biggar, Saskatchewan, know as Ricky Shepherd when he's at home."

Staring back at Carter was the stylish eyepatched guy he'd last seen hosting Hayley Rawls wretched little memorial service.

"We media hacks call him the Maestro. He doesn't like that." Her tone was neutral, but her eyes were hot.

"Sounds like he's not on your A-list."

She smiled tightly, then turned to the desk where two monitors sat above a black computer tower. "I'll boot it up."

"No," he said, grabbing her arm. "We need a broom or a spoon. Something made of wood."

She took her arm away. "Why?"

"So we have a fighting chance if this thing is wired to kill."

She thought about that. "Coming right up."

Gracie rummaged in the closet while Carter got down on his knees to see if he could spot any obvious boobytrap – a wad of plastic explosives helpfully attached to a big digital clock.

"Here," she said, offering a broom. "It's plastic."

"That works," he said, rising. "You'd better keep back, just in case."

She didn't move, standing right next to him, so he gave her a "here goes us" wink, reached out with the broom handle, and pushed the power button on.

There was a click, a long silence, and then the computer whirred into life.

He switched on one of the monitors, which asked for a password.

"Fuck," said Carter. "Which I don't think is her password."

Gracie smiled at him, as if he were new to the world, and hit the return key. The computer obediently continued.

"How'd you know that?" he asked.

"Old media trick," she said. "Sloth."

Hayley Rawls's wallpaper was a photo of herself – a head shot, professionally done. Carter tried not to meet her amused gaze, the one that he last saw full of extortionate promise over lunch in Manhattan.

"Fuck," he said again. "I don't see any email icon. Don't tell me she only emailed on her BlackBerry."

Gracie leaned in to take a look, brushing against him.

"There," she said, clicking on an avian icon. "She uses Thunderbird."

Hayley's email program kicked in, a second password request came up, Gracie hit enter again, and they were in.

"You media guys all belong to the same club?" said Carter.

"In the way you hockey guys do," she replied.

He smiled. Here he was breaking into the apartment of the woman he was suspected of killing, with a woman he barely knew, and now his future was literally staring him in the face. But there was no email from Hayley to herself.

"Sonofabitch!" Carter said. "Nothing."

"Scroll down."

"There's no point," he said. "Look, she could only have sent it on these dates." He pointed at the emails at the top of her inbox. "The game was here, her offer of blackmail was here, and by here, she was dead."

"Okay, but on the same day she made the blackmail deal to you, she got an email from Freddie Hutt."

So she had. The subject heading a cryptic "Re:"

Carter moved the pointer to click on the email, but she put her hand on his.

"Don't open it."

"Why not?"

"You don't know who's watching."

"She's dead. And they're looking for me. I'll take the risk."

He opened the email.

We should talk. F

"That's an extremely encouraging email to a blackmailer," Carter said.

"Yeah, but why is she emailing Freddie Hutt if she's going through you? Why does she need him?"

Carter thought about it. "Let's see if we can find the email she sent."

They scrolled through her Sent folder, but there was nothing to Freddie Hutt.

"Must have sent it from her BlackBerry."

Gracie nodded. "Let's see what she kept in her diary then."

Carter clicked on the My Documents icon on the desktop. He found a folder called "Link Project" and opened it.

"There's a ton of files in there," Gracie said, scanning the directory.

"Yeah, but there won't be anything new, since she didn't quite make it back to her desk."

Gracie clicked over to the desktop icons. "See those green arrows linking two computer monitors? It means she had remote access. She could access her files from wherever – add, subtract, multiply. I do it too."

Carter frowned. "There are hundreds of files here." Then he took the mouse, clicked on the start button, then on shut down.

"What the hell are you doing?" Gracie said sharply.

Porky the Pig's voice responded from Hayley's computer, stuttering, "Th-th-that's all folks!" and the wallpaper faded to black.

"Stealing her hard drive. You don't have a screwdriver, do you?"

She reached in her pocket and handed him the key they'd used to bump their way in. "Best I can do. If I'd had advance notice . . ."

Carter wedged the key into a screw head and slowly, like he was disarming a bomb, loosened it enough so he could spin it off with his sweaty fingers. Then he did the same to the rest of the screws gently disconnected the hard drive, and lifted it from its shelf inside the tower. He handed it to Gracie. "Put this somewhere safe."

She slid it into her shoulder bag.

He was putting the second of the tower sides back in place when there was a hard knock on the door.

Carter looked at Gracie, putting a finger to his lips. She nodded. There was a sliding balcony door, but that left a three-storey drop to the street. Where a police car was parked, right behind Gracie's Valiant.

The knock came again. "Hello! Police! Open up!"

Gracie took a breath, then shouted, "Just a sec."

Carter's head was ice. He'd been set up, and his burning eyes told her as much. But she shook her head and gestured for him to get in the only hiding place the room offered: underneath the computer desk.

Carter's head was cold and his body was hot, the sweat running down his back. Hiding under beds, now under desks, what's next? But he had two choices, and crawling under the desk, which barely fit his frame, was the best.

Gracie calmly walked to the door and opened it.

"Hello," she said with the demeanour of a widow receiving guests at her husband's funeral.

The cops, a man and a woman, asked her what she was doing, and Gracie explained she was a friend of Hayley's, a fellow journalist looking for clues. She said it so casually, so confidently, that Carter believed it.

He couldn't see a thing, with his knees pulled up to his chin underneath the desk and his heart pounding in an angry jungle drum rhythm.

"How did you get in here?" asked the male cop.

"I have a key," Gracie said calmly, holding up her key ring. "We were close."

"Do you have some ID?" asked the female cop.

"Sure. I have my *Vancouver Gazette* media pass."

"You really shouldn't be here," the male cop said after a pause.

"Yes," Gracie said, "but then, she shouldn't really be dead, should she?"

"Why do you say that?" asked the female cop.

"All I mean is that no one deserves to be murdered, do they?"

"The caretaker saw you entering this building with a male," the female cop replied. Carter felt the freezing band tighten on his forehead.

Gracie laughed. "I wish. As you can see, I'm all alone . . . like so many women in this city."

Carter knew was she gesturing to the empty room: "Take a look, if you like."

The blood from his heart was pounding on his skull.

"That won't be necessary," the male cop said.

"You're sure?"

If she was getting back at Carter for the kiss, she'd succeeded.

"Yes, but we'll see you out," the female cop said.

When Carter heard the door shut, he counted to twenty, then crawled from beneath the table. His legs felt like they'd been bound with piano wire as he walked to the window, circulation returning in clusters of pin pricks.

He saw the police car pull away and wiped a slick of sweat from the back of his neck. His shirt was soaked, but he was safe.

Then he saw Gracie's 1963 Valiant Signet pull away too, behind the cop car. Along with Gracie, and her bag, and the hard drive.

35

Carter stood in the pounding rain in front of Hayley's build-ing, scanning the car lights on Broadway for a sign of Gracie and her unmissable car. But he knew that he had just been played. The perfect ending now would be the cops pulling up and shooting him in self-defence.

The Kingdom of Over.

He had to get out of there, fast, but he had just learned the Law of Rainy Nights in Vancouver: the harder the downpour, the fewer the taxis for hire. He might as well have been looking for UFOs.

He was standing under a streetlight, sifting through his change to see if he had enough for the bus, when a train horn sounded to his left.

He looked up and there was Gracie in her Valiant, beck-oning him.

"What the fuck?" Carter said.

"I can take that several ways," she replied calmly. "But you probably mean my Wolo Cannon Ball Express horn. Hey, if you drive in this city, you need this thing."

"I mean, what the fuck?"

"You're welcome," she said, easing them into traffic. "Not only did the cops not arrest you, the hard drive is safe in my bag."

Her purse was sitting next to him on the turquoise-and-white vinyl seat. He reached for it, but she grabbed his hand. "Not even if we were married," she said, with a smile, and took his hand off her bag. Then she opened it, one-handed, and flashed him the hard drive.

"Thanks," he said.

"You're welcome again," she replied, then drove the car

two blocks and pulled up in front of a brightly lit box store called 24-7. "I'll be right back," she said, handing him the hard drive and taking her bag.

"Where are you going?"

"Getting a friend for Hayley's hard drive. Don't go anywhere."

Five minutes later she was back and handed Carter a plastic bag. Inside it was a box labelled External Hard Drive Enclosure. "You owe me $21.99," she said, starting the car. "But I'll waive the debt if this thing finds us the Yellow Brick Road. Now, where are you staying?"

"The Sylvia."

"Good bar. Under your own name?"

"Yes."

"Time to go."

Gracie dropped him at the ivied entrance. Carter cursed under his breath when he saw that the same clerk who had checked him in was on duty, but she didn't even blink in recognition. His short hair and moustache had changed him that much. Five minutes later he was back in Gracie's car with his duffel bag.

"So, what next?"

"Plan C."

She pushed the drive button on the transmission and aimed the car toward Beach Avenue.

"Where are we going?" he asked.

"Somewhere safe."

"'I would give all my fame for a pot of ale, and safety.'"

She smiled. "Life Tourette's?"

"My favourite line in Shakespeare."

"You'll like the boat then."

The Burrard Marina, tucked under the art deco Burrard Bridge, was deserted but for the fleet of moored sailboats. Of course it would be, Carter thought. Who but a head case and his all-too-willing accomplice would go boating after midnight, in the rain?

Gracie parked the car and set off at a determined pace. Carter followed, his eyes on her purse like a dog's on a bone.

"This is us," Gracie said, reaching down to pull the tarp off a speedboat moored at the end of a metal pier. Carter grabbed the other end of the tarp and pulled it off the boat. It was wooden and it looked about as old as Gracie's car.

"What is it?" Carter asked.

"A 1962 Rebel," Gracie answered. "Goes with the car. She's a beauty, isn't she?"

She was. And so was Gracie, the rain running from her blond hair down her cheeks, her fine broad mouth set in determination as she stood in the stern, coaxing life into the spluttering outboard. The boat's name was painted in gold just below the engine: *Hamlet*.

"Why did you call it Hamlet?" he asked.

"Because it has problems starting," she said.

The engine kicked in, and Gracie gave him a thumbs-up and motioned for him to climb aboard.

He was soaked with rain and sweat, and that was the reason for the chill over his entire body, Carter thought, and not some cosmic insight into trouble lying ahead. That's why he climbed into this spluttering old boat with this strange woman who wanted to help him. For reasons he very much wanted to know.

Gracie eased back the throttle, and away they went, dead slow, as the signs on the pilings commanded, toward open water.

"Where are we going?" Carter yelled at her over the buzz saw of the outboard.

"Bowen Island," she said, pointing ahead at the dark, churning Pacific. Carter saw only the abyss. Then she reached down beneath the wheel, fished out an ancient orange life jacket, and tossed it to him. "You'll need this," she said, opening up the throttle. *Hamlet* was doing thirty knots before Carter had managed to untangle the ties on the musty life preserver. It wouldn't make much difference, thought Carter, as he struggled into it. If he were pitched into the water on a night like this, hypothermia would get him in minutes. So he sat tight, gripping the handles on *Hamlet's* gunwales, as Gracie, the Valkyrie queen, stood behind the wheel, wiping away the spray that plastered her face as they sped into the dark.

36

Carter's hands were like cold cement when he finally saw a large island looming before them in the mist. The journey couldn't have taken more than fifteen minutes, but the turbulence and the unbroken darkness had taken him out of time and into his head, so he didn't even notice how tightly he was holding on.

Gracie eased up on the throttle and swung the speedboat in a gentle arc to starboard.

Carter could make out a beach ahead and a small pier jutting into the ocean.

"Bowen Island," she shouted over the noise of the engine. "Good thing the tide is high or we'd have to swim in . . ."

They tied *Hamlet* to the pier and climbed a wooden stairway that zigzagged up the bluff ahead of them. The rain had stopped, and moonlight now lit their steep path, one flanked by the tallest trees Carter had ever seen. He was breathing hard when they reached the top.

"Welcome to the money pit," she said as they stepped onto a stone walkway. It led through a field up to an old, three-storey house, silhouetted in the moonlight.

"This is yours?" Carter said.

"Yep," she said. "All mine. No heat and limited light, so we're safe if they've got satellites looking for you."

She fished a key from her bag and gave him a sly smile. "This key fits."

She swung open the front door, and Carter stepped cautiously inside. The house was dark and cold.

"Hang on." Gracie flicked a Zippo and held it to a kerosene lamp on a table beside the door. "There. Not quite home sweet home. Yet."

Carter could just make out a curving staircase, gracefully leading upstairs, and a fir floor underfoot.

"It's a work in progress," she said. "I hoped to have it done by now, but this life thing gets in the way."

"You're doing the reno yourself?"

"Yep," she said. "I had the house barged over from the city. Well, the suburbs. Saved it from the wrecker's ball. Only way I could afford to have a house here. You're not a builder, are you?"

"I can hammer a nail straight," he said. "Which would be my most advanced skill."

She smiled. "How about building fires?"

"I'm apparently good at starting them . . ."

She took the lamp over to a grated iron fireplace with a stack of cedar wood beside it. "Here you go, then."

Carter arranged the dry wood and some old newspaper in a pile, while Gracie expertly felt her way upstairs and back down. The cedar was soon snapping and crackling, perfuming the air.

Gracie tossed him a towel, and they sat beside the modest flame, glad of its warmth, and drying themselves.

"You tired?" she asked.

He looked at his watch. It was two in the morning. "I'm fine," he said. "A little burglary and a sea voyage are better than caffeine."

Gracie grinned and took a laptop from her bag. "I'm going to fire up the generator," she said. She paused by the front door, and the thin beam of a flashlight sliced across a desk. "There's another one in the drawer here, if you need it," she said as she left.

Carter took the lamp and walked a few paces, looking for a sign of electricity and finding a thick yellow electrical cable curving along the floor. He followed its path to where it was squeezed between a heavy leaded-glass window and its splintery sill. One outlet for the entire place, he thought, enough for one power tool at a time – or a laptop. He placed the lamp down on an old oak table he'd passed and retreated to the warmth of the hearth.

Carter fed the fire a split log and looked into the popping flames. Gracie had rescued him by bringing him here. But why, and what was her price? There was bound to be one. She had already shown a nose for criminal enterprise by breaking into Hayley's apartment, calmly deflecting the police, making off with the hard drive, then ferrying them to this island that was as far off the NYPD radar as Carter could get on this continent and still order breakfast in English.

She wanted his story. That was the price. It seemed fair, but then he remembered that he'd promised it to Madz Weinfeld as well. He was going to have to find a way to make them both happy. He needed them both, no matter what they wanted from him.

"Aaagggh!" Gracie yelled, as if she'd spotted a bear or a Russian assassin, and Carter hurried outside, grabbing the second flashlight as he went. She was standing over a portable generator, holding a gas can in one hand and the generator's gas cap in the other, and wearing the look of murder on her face.

"What's wrong?" Carter asked.

"Some bastard stole my gas!"

"Any suspects?"

"Half the island, given the price of gas."

He nodded. "So we can't use your computer."

She smiled. "I've got a reserve tank hidden away. We have two hours. That means no chatlines, okay?"

Once the generator had kicked to life they went back inside, where Gracie poured them fat shots of whiskey from a crystal decanter into coffee mugs. She clinked her mug against his. "Here's to whatever's on that hard drive."

He raised his glass. "Amen."

She plugged in the computer and powered it up while Carter placed Hayley's hard drive into the external case and connected it to the laptop with its USB cable. The computer booted up with the sound bite of an organ, playing the four-chord sequence that used to play in hockey arenas.

"So you're a traditionalist," Carter said, smiling.

"Isn't every true fan?" Gracie replied.

"Not the ones who only know smoke machines and Bono."

She chuckled, and then so did he as her screen wallpaper came up: it was a doctored photo of the Sea Lions posed around the Cup they had yet to win, and wouldn't this year.

"Fan or fantasy?" Carter said, looking at the fake champions.

"Hey, a girl can dream. And that's why God invented Photoshop." She tapped the touchpad and opened Hayley's hard drive menu. "Where do you want to look first?"

He sat down next to her. Her hair was still damp from the boat ride, faintly scented with strawberries and salt spray.

"At the beginning."

He pulled a crumpled piece of paper from his pants pocket and held it to the glow of the laptop screen.

"What's that?" asked Gracie.

"Treasure map. We need to search for AVI or MPG files, so says my brother."

She nodded and typed *avi* into the search function, and a few files popped up, stuff Hayley had downloaded from other hockey sites. Then they tried *mpg*, and the computer whirred with purpose, finding more than a hundred files.

Hayley had been meticulous, labelling each one with the subject and the date. Most identified Link Andrachuk as the subject, but no date was from St. Patrick's Day.

They looked at each other, thinking the same thing.

"Either it's not here, or she lied about the dates," Carter said, his voice low and weary.

"But why would she do that?"

"Because she was a liar. Even so, we'll have to look at them all."

"Not enough power to do that tonight."

He nodded. She was pensive in the glow of the screen.

"You look worried."

She smiled. "No. Just tired."

"You should be worried. Alone on this island with a suspected murderer. Why would you want to do that?" It was a total head-case play, having just discovered footage on

Hayley's hard drive, and the woman who would help him parse it all. But he needed to know he could trust her, even if he couldn't always trust himself.

She turned, regarding him with something more than professional curiosity. "I'm a reporter, Martin. I tell stories. True ones. I want to know if yours is true."

"Why do you care about that?" he said, pressing toward disaster.

She smiled. "Because if you're telling the truth, then I'll be able to buy a whole new life."

He thought about this. "You don't like the one you have?"

Her eyes flashed with amusement, and warning. "I'll tell you this: it certainly got a lot more interesting tonight."

"Mine too." It sounded like a play for her, and he winced as the words came out of his mouth.

To her credit, she didn't affect a theatrical yawn and stretch. She just stood. "I hope you don't mind sleeping on the couch."

"Better than a jail cell. I don't mind at all. And thanks, Gracie."

She nodded. "I like you, Martin. But if this story doesn't work out, well, you won't want to know me."

She said it with a smile, but underneath it was someone who knew how to take revenge. Reminding him of his place on this island redoubt. "It will work out, Gracie. It has to, or I'm dead."

She looked him in the eye for a beat. "Maybe me too." She let the words hang in the air for a moment, then she smiled and said, "See you in the morning."

Carter smiled back. For the first time in a while, he was looking forward to daylight.

37

The sun woke Carter, a long warm kiss on his face, and when he opened his eyes he could see blue sky out the window.

He stretched under the duvet on Gracie's sofa and felt surprisingly fresh, considering the lumps he'd slept on. He scooped his watch off the floor. It was nearly noon.

He rose and wandered outside, where he sucked in the maritime air, cool and spiced with sea salt. Above him, a bald eagle did a lazy spiral upward on a thermal, and Carter watched it with awe as it so easily defied the gravity that so weighed him down. The fresh air washed over his body, which had been hot under the duvet during the night, sweating as if fevered, and dreaming: Freddie, the Maestro, Hayley, all swirling in his head. Now he wore the night sweat like a greasy film, made even more uncomfortable by the realization that if Gracie's place didn't have electricity, then it wouldn't have a shower.

"Sleep well?" said Gracie, looking up from her laptop when he walked back inside, into the sunlit yellow kitchen.

"Every time I wake up alive I consider it a good night," he said, and she arched her eyebrows on a smile.

Carter noticed that her hair was wet. "Don't tell me you went swimming."

She kept her eyebrows arched. "Are you kidding? The shower was chilly enough."

"You have a shower?"

"Hey, I'm not uncivilized. The water heater should give you enough for a good two minutes."

It seemed like only thirty seconds until the temperature of the water started to feel like a punishment, but even so, he emerged feeling better than he had the day before. Breathing in the pungent mix of island air and coffee percolating on the wood stove in the kitchen helped too. And so did being with Gracie, even if they were together out of mutual necessity.

"You want some breakfast?" she said when he returned.

He calculated he hadn't eaten since his steak frites a day ago, which explained why he was hungry. "Thanks," he said. "I do."

"I'll make you a Bowen Island Scramble."

"What's that?"

"Eggs and anything but chocolate."

He sat down at the kitchen table and she poured him a coffee. Outside the window, the generator's engine knocked as it pumped in power. "You found more gas for that thing."

"I woke up early for some reason, so I went into town and stocked us up."

"Town?" From where he sat in her sun-dappled kitchen, surrounded by Douglas firs and the perfume of the Pacific, a mule deer fawn, still and gazing at them from the clearing, and an eagle floating above, it was hard to believe that commerce had encroached anywhere near.

"There are about four thousand year-round residents here," she said, tossing some onions into the hissing skillet. "Nearly triple that in the summer. You can get pretty much anything you need just ten minutes down the road in Snug Cove. And if not, the ferry to Vancouver will have you on the other side in twenty minutes. It's the best of city life – you can see it, but you're not there."

"I'd love to see the rest of the island."

She shook her head. "Sorry, Martin Carter. You are my prisoner." She caught his look – too close to home. "I mean, my honoured guest and, now, teammate."

His words, back at him. With a smile. His teammate

hunting for the footage that could clear his name or get him killed. And her too.

"And I have a lot of time on my hands, because as of yesterday and thanks to the Vancouver Sea Lions' pitiful failure to make the playoffs, I'm an unemployed hockey beat writer for the next few months."

She didn't seem unhappy about her immediate future as she put a plate of scrambled eggs and toast in front of him. Carter felt the temperature on his forehead change – but it didn't drop fast and cold this time. Now it was as warm as the sun spilling through the window, a vision of how his life could be, here on this island with a woman who wrote about a game he used to play, in her unfinished house. It was almost perfect.

"You okay?" she said.

"Yeah," he said, thinking about what a desperation kiss in the rain can do if you're in the right, damaged frame of mind. "I actually am."

"Good," she said, sitting down opposite him. "So, do you want to hear my game plan?"

"Sure," he said, shovelling in a mouthful of the Bowen Island Scramble, fluffy and moist with onions and cheddar.

"We hang out here for a few days until we think of one."

He laughed, managing not to spray bits of scrambled egg at her. "The Bowen Island Scramble is delicious," he said. "You have a career as a chef if the hockey writing thing dries up permanently."

"Thanks, I'll keep that in my mind. My husband hated my cooking."

Carter's heart twinged. Telling him what he already knew: She was too good to be single. But she had used the past tense. "More fool him," he said.

"I thought so too. That's why we're here."

"Oh?"

"I got the boat and the empty plot on Bowen in the divorce."

"Tough luck. What did he get?"

She smiled thinly. "A younger model."

Carter stopped eating. "What, he's a pedophile?"

She laughed. "Thank you. But no, he snagged an intern. A lot like Hayley Rawls, actually. He was a TV news anchor, and I was a TV reporter before I had my come-to-Jesus moment and wound up at the *Gazette*."

"You know what they say about newspaper reporters?"

"What?" There was a cool edge to the question.

"The best come from sports."

She smiled and looked out the window, forming a question, something personal, then turned back to him, her mouth poised to ask it. But instead, she said, "So, what's your plan?"

He drank his coffee and did the head-case calculation. He could kiss her right now and blow it all to smithereens. Or he could find a way to stay on this island for as long as she'd let him. And see where things went.

"I think we need to go through everything on Hayley's hard drive. Start with her correspondence and notes, and maybe they'll give us a clue."

"About where the footage is?" She didn't sound convinced.

"About why she'd want to blackmail anyone. We need a little CSI profiling."

So away they went, plowing through news pieces about Link and his career, which Hayley had plucked off the Internet – there was no apparent method here in arrangement of subject or date – and a draft of the website text that Erik Shepherd was writing himself.

It was as close as you could get to the usual hockey hagiography for someone like Link: the farmboy from Yellow Grass, Saskatchewan, a scrawny asthmatic who laced on the skates anyway and showed the other kids he was just as good as them on the ice.

Except he wasn't. He was better than them. Much better. Rocketing up the junior hockey charts, asthma gone, summers on the farm sculpting his Ukrainian peasant's body into athletic perfection.

There was no mention of the statutory rape charges or of Link's problems with cocaine and international borders.

"Just another happy, wholesome superstar," Gracie said, scrolling down through files. Clicking on Maestro Media.

Inside was a thread of emails between Hayley and Erik Shepherd, most of them tedious technical stuff about shot lists and coverage – with her wanting more money for the job and him wanting more job for the money.

And then there was this:

> *hey hayls, look, money's tight but I'll tell you what i'll throw in a thousand shares of Maestro Media Inc. when we do the ipo in nyc on the back of the linkster. look forward to a show of the love* ☺ *happy shooting. ES*

Carter looked at Gracie. "Does ipo mean what I think it means?"

She nodded, her blue eyes sharp with surprise. "He's going to take his company public on the release of the Link Andrachuk project."

The icy band squeezed Carter's forehead. "You mean issue stock . . ."

"In New York."

"Why would Maestro Media be of any interest to Wall Street?"

She leaned her chin on the palm of her hand. "Maybe it's because he can't do it here."

"Why not?"

"A liar never wants to wind up in a room with all the people he's ever lied to."

Carter took it that Gracie had been one of them. Her eyes were a cool blue now, maybe in warning, maybe in memory.

"Do you want to tell me about it?"

She leaned back and sighed. "I ghost-wrote one of his coffee-table books before he got into the website stuff. And no, I didn't show him the love he suggested would help him to cut me a cheque faster."

"You mean sleep with him?"

She nodded. "He still owes me seventy-five hundred dollars. I'll collect via some other means."

"That would be me."

"I fight my own battles, thanks."

Carter nodded, doing the math. If the Maestro was taking his company public in New York, he had to have some high-powered help and more to offer than a DVD of Link Andrachuk.

Freddie Hutt had been a money guy before he came over to the St. Patricks. The casualty of a Wall Street meltdown. Doug Bleecker had been a business reporter, and Freddie's guy. And the Cardinal had brought them both in.

Carter took a sip of coffee to warm the chill swirling in his head. "So what does Hayley Rawls get out of this?"

"Read on, Mr. Carter."

Carter scrolled through the files, clicking on one titled Linkdeal.

It was Hayley's contract with the Maestro for the DVD. A flat fee of twenty-five K, half up front, half at the end, with no royalty on sales. Indeed, a clause spelled out that the Continental Hockey League owned the visual rights to Link Andrachuk, and as such, all monies earned past the fee would be going to them.

Carter smiled at Gracie. "She was making peanuts. And when he told her that money was tight, she saw a way to fix that."

"But he was offering her shares."

"That weren't worth anything yet." Carter closed his eyes. "I'm betting that Erik Shepherd has got the footage I need."

Gracie looked at him as if seeing him for the first time.

"My brother was thinking like the paranoid he is. Of course she'd email the thing, but not to herself – to the guy who was paying her. I mean, if she released that footage to anyone, there'd be no Link in the playoffs, and no Link DVD on the website, and certainly no Maestro Media stock to buy."

"So you're saying that he killed her?"

"That's what we're going to find out."

"Okay," she said. "But if Erik Shepherd has the footage you want . . ." The implied question hung in the air between them, a ticking clock.

"You think he'd hand it over if we just asked him? No, first we look at all the video files on her hard drive."

She opened her mouth into an O of silent delight. "You want to find something we can trade!"

He nodded. "See? All the best do come from sports."

And she smiled like she believed him.

38

Carter lost track of time. Crisp, sunny mornings in front of the computer. Afternoons on the beach, swimming, reading, sleeping. Evenings at the kitchen table, a simple meal, a glass or two of wine, and he and Gracie parsing the day like a couple with a future. Not a bad life, he thought, for a man with a past.

He felt like his old self, the man from the Kingdom of Before. Fit, sober, rested, safe. It was the kind of contentment he knew was all too brief, and as if he were in remission, each day was shadowed by the knowledge that it could all turn terminal at any moment.

Yet rather than fear, he hoped. He hoped that his life had changed, even with two death sentences hanging over it – the natural one, and the one sent his way by Hayley Rawls. He hoped that he'd found, in Gracie, a teammate who would stick until the game was over. And they could toast a victory.

She worked hard. Navigating through Hayley's hard drive with him, watching Link Andrachuk do magical things with a little black disc and navigate the world of ice on two metal blades, with people trying to knock him into oblivion as he went.

"It's an amazing game, really," Gracie said, sitting in front of her laptop with Carter, watching Link charge in on a partial breakaway, one hand on his stick, controlling a rolling puck, while the other was pushing off a defenceman intent on chopping him down.

"How did you become a hockey person?" Carter asked, taking a bite of toast and Gracie's blueberry jam.

"My dad took me to a Sea Lions game when I was four and that was that. Skating lessons came next, and then I was playing in a league when I was five. I went to UBC on a hockey scholarship, but I blew my knee and thought, well, I need a Plan B."

So those muscular legs came from hockey. Carter was delighted to hear they'd both had university hockey scholarships, that they had playing the game in common.

"I went into sports reporting," she continued. "I figured I knew something about the subject."

"Indeed," Carter replied. "But for it to be as easy as Link makes it look when he wants to can't be learned. It's —"

"Talent?"

"More than talent. It's a gift."

"You had that."

He nodded. "And then I didn't." He smiled at her. "But that's why I'm grateful for TV and video, so I can see what it was that I lost."

Her face softened, the way he'd noticed it did when she was serious. Letting reality in, rather than deflecting it with a hard, steely gaze. "You really can't remember?"

"No, I can't," he said. "But nature abhors a vacuum. Ever since I hit my head, I see things differently."

"How do you mean?"

"My head gets cold. And not because of the weather."

He could only tell her what he'd been told about his injury, because he couldn't remember. The Kingdom of After.

His was a grade-three concussion, the worst. He was unconscious for fifteen minutes, in the hospital for two weeks. The CT scan showed brain swelling, which led the medics to tell him that he was out of the game. Not just for the season. Permanently. One more knock on the head could kill him. Yes, there'd been double vision, and sleep disturbances, and bouts of nausea, but they'd all gone away.

"My head gets cold," he told her, "like a band of cold steel right here" – he ran his hand across his forehead – "whenever something seems wrong. The light changes too – it's that winter light, you know? When the sun is low in the sky?" It made him feel strange, almost a different man. An iceman.

"The Iceman," she said, trying it out. "I like that. He could be one of those cartoon superheroes."

"Well, it often seems like I'm in a cartoon."

She stared at him, her blue eyes more aquamarine now, riding a tide of emotion. "Or a bit like being God."

"No," he replied. "God doesn't seem to want to know at all."

She smiled, her lips open in rebuttal, but she just nodded and reached for her laptop. "Speaking of omniscience . . ."

"I'll top up the coffee," he said and fetched the pot from the stove as she opened up their daily dose of post-breakfast entertainment, Page Seven.

He poured a splash of coffee into her mug, and she angled the laptop in his direction, so he could read it.

The item related Link Andrachuk's night on the town with the voluptuous Alexandra Petrova – drinks at Venus, dinner at Monjay, and a bit of tongue-to-tongue action on the dance floor at Grind. All in the middle of the St. Patricks' best-of-five playoff series against Toronto, which New York was losing two games to one.

"Who is Alexandra Petrova?" Gracie asked. "And what is Link doing out on the town in a playoff series that the Pats need to win?"

It was a good question. Why this outing of the Missing Link's dalliance with a hot Russian babe when he should have been in bed by eleven, alone and sober?

Page Seven was coy about the woman – saying only that she was "a Russian lass who knows her way around a hockey stick, gold-plated at that" – so Carter googled her name and up came a Wikipedia entry on Alexei Felixsovich Petrov. Carter opened the link. Alexei was Alexandra's father and the fourth wealthiest oligarch in Russia, a humble petroleum engineer who'd made his money after the fall of the Wall by suddenly becoming director of UniGaz, which soon owned more than a quarter of Russia's oilfields and the pipelines too.

"Sonofabitch," said Carter. "Look at this."

Wikipedia had a photo of father and daughter on a red carpet at centre ice of the Khodynka Arena in Moscow, a "state-of-the-art ice palace," where the duo presented the Yeltsin Cup to the St. Petersburg Rocket as the 2007 champions of the Platinum League. Standing behind and to one side of them in the photo was none other than Freddie Hutt, president of the New York St. Patricks.

Carter leaned back, trying to relieve the ice squeezing his skull, the light shining in his eyes. "That's who's buying the St. Pats," he said.

Gracie put down her coffee mug. "You mean they're for sale?"

Carter's jaw tensed. He hadn't told anyone that the team was for sale, hadn't betrayed the Cardinal's confidence, even though it could well be the Cardinal who was trying to have him killed. But if he was going to be on her team, he had to tell her now. "They are. The Cardinal – John O'Connor – told us the morning after Link tried to take Oblomov's head off."

She wasn't blinking, just staring with that crystalline gaze. "Why didn't you tell me?"

Carter could hear the hurt in her voice. "Because I didn't need to," he replied, with head-case honesty. "And now I do."

She bit her lip, as if not trusting her rebuttal, but he was saved by the bell of her cellphone. She picked it up and looked at the caller ID.

"I need to take this," she said and walked into the living room.

Carter tested the water temperature at the sink. It was just warm enough to wash the dishes, so he squeezed some eco-friendly liquid into the basin and gazed out the kitchen window as he scrubbed. The mule deer that hung around the clearing wasn't in sight, but Carter wasn't looking for it. His thoughts were far away.

Why would Link Andrachuk be out on the town in the middle of a playoff series with a Russian billionaire's daughter unless it had been sanctioned by the Cardinal? A kind of signal to everyone that the St. Pats had friends in high places? An indication of what they were worth if you were looking to buy?

But then, why would a hockey-loving Russian billionaire care about playoff revenue if he wanted to buy the only CHL team in the capital of the world? Nothing could stop him but the U.S. government.

And what did that mean for the Maestro? If the Russians wanted to buy the team, then Hayley's footage was a road bump they'd steamroll in a hurry.

Carter shook his head and looked at the scene through the window, at the sunlight bouncing off the firs and spruces that ringed Gracie's property and beyond to where the Pacific rippled gently under a cloudless sky. He thought he would never get used to seeing the view.

He dried the dishes and turned. Gracie was in the doorway watching him.

"You're right," she said, her blue eyes darker, warmer. "You didn't need to tell me. But if we're going to be a team, no secrets. Okay?"

He nodded. "No secrets. Except for the Bowen Island Scramble."

"I'll take that to my grave," she said, smiling. "Which might be sooner than later if the Sea Lions have their way."

"Oh?"

"That was my editor on the phone. The Sea Lions are holding a press conference at noon."

"Yeah? Is Oblomov dead?"

She lowered her chin. "I hope not. But I'm going to find out."

"I'm going with you." Carter knew it was a bad idea, but he had to hear it for himself.

"That's crazy," she said.

"That's the other thing," he grinned. "I probably am."

She walked up to him, close enough to take him by the shoulders and shake him, if she wanted. But instead she said very softly, "But I'm not."

They stood there, blue eyes to brown eyes. He could feel the power in her gaze, the message she was conveying. It said she cared what happened to him. She was protecting him. And, he hoped, not just because he was a story to her. It was a new feeling or, at least, one he hadn't felt in a long time. He liked it.

"Okay," he said. "But be careful."

She smiled. "We probably have different ideas of what that means."

He laughed. "Yeah. Go with yours."

39

Carter had to admit that Link Andrachuk, when he wanted to be, was a very good hockey player. And Hayley Rawls had had a very good eye.

He was in Gracie's kitchen, working through the last of the video files of the Missing Link on Hayley's hard drive.

There was Link at practice, doing skill drills with ease.

There was Link in a game, doing his solo act with power and grace.

There was Link off the ice, relaxed and expansive, wearing a black blazer and pink button-down shirt and telling the off-camera interviewer just what made him tick: Hockey. Hard work. Honesty. Helping the less fortunate.

That was total bullshit, and Hayley Rawls must have filmed hours of him to get thirty seconds of Link Andrachuk, Human Being. It said nothing about the demon inside the man, but that was the way the league marketers liked it. A white picket fence around every player.

It also meant that Hayley Rawls must have spent a lot longer in New York City than she'd let on to Carter, with her wide-eyed Canadian girl routine. He remembered how she'd transformed from being an ingénue into an Upper East Side player less than twelve hours after meeting him, and it wasn't just from riding Mr. Love Rocket.

He clicked on the final video file. Link Andrachuk was in an apartment, and Carter recognized the sparse decor and the big window overlooking the city. It was Hayley's apartment on West Broadway. And Link Andrachuk was naked – no, he was wearing the kind of thin, skin-coloured briefs that male ballet dancers wear. Which was fitting, as Link seemed to be doing some kind of dance.

Carter watched as Link moved his limbs slowly, carving the air like a martial artist. The camera circled around him, and Carter caught a glimpse of Hayley in a mirror as she passed opposite it. Then she was gone, like a ghost. But the ghost spoke.

"That's good, Link," she said. "I'm just going to adjust the light to get more muscle definition."

He stopped and tugged at the briefs. "These things are too tight."

"Fine with me if you take them off," she replied as the light level blasted up and back down.

Link peeled off the briefs, checked out his penis, then gave it a flick, as if to wake it up. Carter had spent a lot of time in locker rooms, and Link's penis seemed to him too small for his muscular body.

"You ready?" Hayley asked.

"Yeah," he said. "Thanks."

She swung the camera back toward him, and he did the same martial arts dance again, though this time his penis woke up as he moved.

Hayley laughed. "Okay, let's take a break," she said. "It's not that kind of game!"

Link laughed. "Oh yeah?"

He disappeared from view, and she giggled like a teenaged girl, and then the screen went black.

Carter's head temperature dropped. Hayley was making sex videos of Link Andrachuk? No, that wasn't it. But he certainly wouldn't prance around naked for any league-sanctioned DVD about his life.

"It's not that kind of game," Hayley had said. What the hell did that mean?

Carter stepped outside to clear his head. Now, in the middle of the afternoon, it was warm enough to swim and sunbathe, but Gracie hadn't returned from the news conference in

Vancouver, and he didn't feel like hiking down to the water by himself.

His bladder was pinging after too many cups of coffee, so he went back inside.

The house seemed much bigger in daylight. The entrance bisected the living room, where he had spent the better part of a week on the lumpy sofa, and the dining room, with its bay windows and wainscoting, the wood stripped and ready for staining.

He climbed the spiral staircase to the bathroom, where he stared unseeing at the claw-foot tub, its enamel peeling, as he relieved himself. "It's not that kind of game."

He washed, then started toward the staircase but turned back. What the hell, he thought. Gracie was away.

Beside the bathroom was an empty room – destined to be a study, a guest room, a nursery – and opposite was Gracie's room with a queen-sized bed topped by a puffy red paisley duvet. He wanted to lie down on a comfortable bed and close his eyes, maybe dream a little.

But he couldn't do it. That was too intimate, and right now, the last thing he needed was to stoke his budding fantasy of life with Gracie by inhaling the perfume of her pillow.

So he looked at her bookshelf. She had an eclectic taste in books, running the gamut from grad studies literature to beach books to bios and one she'd written, *Hockey's Hundred*.

It was the book she'd done for Maestro Media, a collection of photo essays about the top one hundred hockey players of the CHL's past fifty years. He flipped it open to a bookmarked page, to Number 50. And was staring himself in the face: "Martin Carter, the Golden Shadow."

The term was new to Carter. He'd been called many things, but never that. The photo was a good one, of him turning in an arc, head up, eyes ablaze, seeing the ice, seeing an entire world that was his alone.

The text was good too. Gracie had avoided the usual clichés and, instead, told the story of where he'd come from, his Princeton ascendancy, and what he'd accomplished in his two seasons with the St. Patricks. Rookie of the Year and second in points, unafraid to work the corners, or his fists, until opponents learned that tangling with him wasn't a great idea. And leading goal scorer at the time of his accident.

"Even though Martin Carter's career was cut short, some players define themselves in a series of transcendent moments that, though few, are timeless. Too often we set the bar by who won the Cup, or who recalibrated the scoring charts. And while Carter knew how to put the puck in the net, he makes our list because of play so creative and graceful it didn't matter if he scored or not, it was enough to watch him in flight, golden, and like every athlete, heading for the shadows of that day when they can play no more. The day came far too early for Martin Carter, but it does not diminish the genius of what came – ever so briefly – before."

He felt like he'd just read his own obituary. He placed the book back on the shelf and sat down on Gracie's bed.

The mattress was firm, and soft, and he lay back. He hadn't slept in a real bed in nearly two weeks. His life in New York, and the troubles that went with it, seemed as far away as the blue sky through Gracie's bedroom window.

"There is a country at the end of the world / Where no child's born but to outlive the moon."

Yeats. W.B. That's who said it. And he'd remembered the lines while lying on the bed of Gracie Yates. The kingdoms connected. Sort of.

He smiled. He'd spent days viewing Hayley's footage for something to dangle in front of Erik Shepherd as bait, and all he had to show for it was a nude dance. If that was posted on YouTube, the sales of Hayley's DVD on Link would rise up much like he had.

Carter closed his eyes. He had to find a different way through. He imagined the future, with him free, and safe, and happy. Gracie was smiling at him, with something like love in her eyes. But there was Hayley Rawls, hovering like fate, her mouth open in a silent scream for justice, a hand around her throat. Link's hand. And it wouldn't let go.

40

When Carter awoke it was dark. He sat up and looked around. He was alone.

He made his way downstairs, silently cursing the squeaky tread on the staircase halfway down. In case Gracie was asleep on the sofa.

But she was sitting in the kitchen, a glass of wine in front of her, typing furiously on her computer, the generator humming outside the window.

"Gracie," he said. "I'm sorry."

She stopped typing and flashed him a smile. "Hey," she said. "Sleep well?"

"Yeah, I did. I don't know what to say. I was just —"

She held up a hand. "You must be exhausted. I wasn't thinking. I can take the couch for a while."

"It's okay. I'm fine now."

"You *are* exhausted. I have food and drink. And news."

She served him barbecued ribs and baked potatoes and poured him a generous glass of Montepulciano. He was hungry and tucked in while Gracie told him her news. The

Sea Lions were going to sue Link Andrachuk and the New York St. Patricks for the injury to Sasha Oblomov.

"Any word on how he is?"

"He's unlikely to ever play again."

Carter knew that prognosis too well. "Any word on where he is?"

"Nope. It's still a mystery."

Carter thought about calling Madz to see if her doctor friend Bobbi Washington could give them any information. But then he'd have to explain to Madz what he'd been doing since she last saw him, and that would be hard enough to do even in person. Right now, he had more pressing problems.

"How much are they suing for?"

"Fifty" – she paused to raise her wineglass – "million."

Carter nearly choked. "What? Do they think Oblomov's made of gold?"

She smiled. "Well, he's in the second year of a five-year deal that will pay him thirty-six million, and he stands to be paid in full if he has to retire because of injury. Plus, there's the lost playoff revenue from this season, and whatever Oblomov could have done for them in the next three years. So, on the whole, they're in the ballpark. Or the arena."

Carter shook his head. The pro hockey world had changed so much since he made his brief arc across it. When he'd been injured, the team insurance barely covered his hospital bills. The idea of a contract that would pay you full salary for retiring wasn't even in the fantasy file of the most deluded agent, and because Carter hadn't played four hundred games in the league, his pension was only twenty-five hundred dollars a year.

"It's crazy, isn't it?" she said.

"Yeah. It certainly is."

He washed down his rising anger with wine. "Unless they offered proof that Link did it deliberately."

She shook her head. "Nope. Not even a hint."

A huge lawsuit, and proof of nothing.

"Well," he said, "do you want to see what I found?"

She caught the look in his eye. "Not the smoking gun?"

Carter smiled. "That would depend on your choice of euphemism."

She saved her document and angled the laptop so they could both see the screen.

Carter had renamed the file "Link dancing" and he double-clicked it.

And there was Link, in his dance belt, doing his number.

"What the hell is this?" Gracie said.

"It's the last video file of him on her hard drive."

She watched as Link stripped, her glass of wine poised mid air. "Oh my God."

"It gets better."

She stared unblinking as the video came to an end, with Link tumescent and Hayley giggling behind the camera.

"What do you make of that?"

She kept her eyes on the screen. "Did she film you too?"

Her tone was professional, a journalist asking a question. But Carter could hear the squeak of personal curiosity. He blushed. "She did not. But what I'm wondering is, what the hell was she filming him like that for? What does she mean, 'It's not that kind of game'?"

Gracie nodded. "So she gets him hot by having him dance around naked, and then they have sex."

"So it would seem."

"And she left it on her computer. There's nothing else like it?"

He shook his head. "Not that I could find. Unless –" Carter felt a chill.

"She's hidden something." Gracie said

Carter nodded grimly. "What time is it?"

"Just gone ten."

Carter thumbed a number on his cellphone, then pushed the speaker phone key. After half a dozen rings, Carter's mother said, "Hello, it's me."

"Hello, Mom," Carter said, surprised to hear her voice. "It's me too, Martin."

"Martin's dead," she replied cheerfully.

Gracie gave him a sympathetic look.

"Okay," he said, "can I speak to Dennis then?"

"Fine," she replied.

"Don't put down the phone, Mom!" he yelled. "Mom!"

"Yes?"

"Just take the phone to Dennis, okay?"

"To Dennis?"

"Your son."

"Martin's dead."

"Mom, please just do what I tell you, okay?"

"Okay."

"Keep the phone to your ear and walk to the top of the stairs, then call down to Dennis. Okay?"

"Okay."

She put the phone down, and they could hear her footsteps patter away.

"Fuck!" yelled Carter. "Why does that crazy fuck let her answer the phone?"

"What the fuck do you want?"

"Dennis?"

"No, it's the FBI, who are probably listening in to this."

Carter shook his head. Dennis had been listening in the entire time. "Then we don't have long before they trace the call."

"They can trace numbers instantly. But you're on a cellphone, 778 area code, that's a British Columbia cellphone, so that takes a bit longer. They'll figure out what cell tower's relaying the call, and from there it's a matter –"

"Dennis," Carter cut in, "what is Mom doing answering the phone at one in the morning?"

"What the fuck are you doing calling here at one in the morning?"

Carter took a breath. "You sleep during the day."

Silence on the other end. Dennis wasn't disagreeing. "So I thought I'd call and ask you how to recover files hidden on a hard drive?"

Dennis burped. "You're in B.C., huh? How's the weather? How's the dope?"

Gracie's eyes widened. Carter gave her a reassuring smile.

"Weather's great, the dope I don't know about." Silence on the other end. "Dennis, please?"

"Is it a PC or a Mac?"

"PC."

"What kind of file are you looking for?"

"What kind? Well, we looked for AVI and MPG files, as per your instructions."

"But you didn't find what you were looking for."

"We found enough to think there might be more, in a secret location."

"We?"

Carter mouthed a "sorry" to Gracie. "I meant you and me. I'm counting on you to help me through this, Dennis."

More silence.

"Dennis?"

"You could never lie convincingly, Martin."

"I'm not lying. So what do I do next? Please? Mom doesn't need to spend her final years getting postcards from me in prison.

"She thinks you're dead."

Carter made a strangling motion to Gracie. She jotted something on a piece of paper and slid it toward him. "Conspiracy," it said.

"Dennis, I think I've found a conspiracy."

"Really?" He was interested now. Gracie had made a quick read. Carter was impressed.

"Really. I'll fill you in if you help me find the hidden files."

"Okay," Dennis said pleasantly. "If I were hiding an MPG or AVI file, I'd probably lose the suffix and hide it by calling it a PDF file."

"So we search all the PDF files."

"Yup, and when you find one that seems too large, that's probably an AVI or MPG. But don't try to open it as a PDF, because it won't work. Try opening it with the application that you think it is."

"You mean AVI or MPG."

"Yup. My bet is that it will be in the same format as the file you found that made you think there were others in hiding. Try using RealPlayer." He burped again. Carter could picture him working through a two-litre bottle of Coke as he sat before his deepest emotional connection to the world, his computer. "So what did you find?"

Carter looked at Gracie and she nodded. "I found footage of Link Andrachuk doing a naked dance."

Dennis laughed. "Don't fuck with me, Martin."

"I'm not. Trust me on that. Dennis?" Silence. "And thanks very much for this."

"It's the least I can do for a soon-to-be-dead man."

"What do you mean?"

"Guy was here looking for you."

"Who?"

"Didn't say."

"What did he look like?"

"Said you were in trouble, and needed to find you."

Carter felt relief flood his body. "So, he was a cop."

Dennis laughed. "Pretty funny cop. Irish guy with bad teeth."

Carter's forehead froze. Hopalong had been to his mother's house.

"What did you tell him, Dennis?" Carter's pulse was pounding in his ears.

"Same thing I told the cops." Carter felt like he was going to vomit.

"The cops?"

"Yeah, that you were probably dead. Glad you're not."

41

As the computer searched for PDF files on Hayley's hard drive, Carter's mind played over Hopalong's visit to his mother's house from every angle he could conceive. And the end result was always the same. Dennis had told Hopalong he was dead. And Hopalong, being a sentimental sort, would figure that by tapping into Carter's mother's phone line, he could find out where he was.

"He won't come looking for you here," Gracie said, reading the worry on his face.

He glanced up from the screen. She seemed confident, despite what he had told her about the St. Pats' chief of security, or chief executioner, depending on what you'd seen.

"Oh? He only tried to kill me at my apartment, and then he shows up at my mother's place, and I bet you he was listening in."

She nodded. "But if he thinks you're in Vancouver, he'll wait for you to make a move. There's no way for him to know you're lying low at Gracie's Island Hideaway. He'll be counting on you to make a mistake."

"Well, that's something I'm good at."

She put her hand on his shoulder and her touch made him flinch.

"Hey," she said softly. "I'm on your side."

"I know you are," he said with a half-smile. "Here's to my only ally." He raised his wineglass to her.

She clinked his glass. "Hard to believe, that."

"You mean my current life?"

"I mean that I'd be your friend in need."

He nodded. She was right. He'd had friends once, but they were scattered and out of touch, hockey guys for whom he would have done anything, and they for him, but who now were part of the hazy Kingdom of Before. "Aside from my brother, and you just got a taste of the state of that relationship, I don't really have friends."

"There was that woman, Flavia?"

"She wasn't a friend in the end, either. Life Tourette's, remember?"

She smiled. "Right. Let's find that footage so you can prove her wrong."

"What makes you think I want to prove anything to her?" he snapped.

"Sorry. You spoke of her like she still matters to you."

Carter blushed at the velocity of his reaction. He did want to prove something to Flavia. He wanted to prove that the loss was hers. And she did still matter to him.

"The search engine has found more than a hundred fucking PDF files," he said, glaring at the results, instantly regretting his profanity.

"Any of them called Missing Link?"

Carter laughed. He liked her wit. And it had been a long time since anyone had made him laugh in pleasure.

Carter selected the fifteen biggest PDF files, then opened them with RealPlayer. The first few were clips of Link skating around, not doing much of anything. Carter knew that if Hayley had hidden these, she'd probably have hidden much more.

There was a short take of Link being reamed out by Phil Winslow after an opposition goal – or reamed out in the St. Pats coach's lugubrious monotone, about as far as you could get from Bunny Blackburn's profane tirades but, as Carter listened, much more lethal.

"Nice giveaway, Link. Charity's good. But you want to know what's better than charity, Link?" Winslow paused and looked to his left, right into Hayley's camera filming from the first row of seats behind the bench. He flashed a slender, brief smile, then turned back to Link. "Paying for things, Link. Make the other side pay the price. Because we're certainly paying you enough. You going to let that little shit show you up like that? Make him pay the price. You know how to do that, don't you, Link? Or does he scare you? Does he? Play like a man, Link. Play like a man."

Link just stared straight ahead through the whole tirade, watching the faceoff at centre ice.

"Is that the same guy who tried to kill Oblomov?" Gracie asked, staring at the screen.

"Yeah, and that's not a clip for the kids buying the DVD." Carter realized he was feeling sorry for Link. He'd never seen a player called out like that, so intimately, by anyone.

"And 'pay the price'? What was that?"

"Well, it usually means to take punishment in front of the net while you try to score."

"I know what it means, Carter," she smiled. "But when you follow it with 'play like a man' it seems to mean something else."

"If someone said it to me, I would take it to mean they thought I was soft. My first response would be to smack them in the nose."

"But Link didn't even react."

Carter nodded. "Maybe he's heard it before. Maybe that's what he heard before he attacked Sasha Oblomov."

"Oblomov attacked him though," Gracie replied.

"Yeah, but he'd been goading Oblomov all night. If you don't want to 'pay the price,' maybe that's how you get it on, as it were."

She nodded and topped up their wineglasses. "Let's see some more."

Carter opened the next file, and the whole world changed.

Onscreen now was a naked woman, her back to the camera, bouncing up and down on a large penis belonging to a guy lying flat on his back, his face obscured by the woman. There was no sound.

"That's Hayley Rawls," Carter said, the words catching in his throat as he watched her maple leaf buttock tattoo rise and fall.

"And that's not Link," Gracie said quietly. "Not unless he's had penis enlargement since the last time we saw him."

The clip ended, and he looked at Gracie.

"You okay?" she said.

Carter's cheeks were flushed. He wasn't a porn surfer, and watching Hayley's sex tape while sitting next to Gracie made him feel dirty, ashamed.

"Yeah, I'm fine," he said. "You?"

She smiled. "Yeah – I've seen naked people having sex before. And these two were at least nice to look at. Sorry."

"It's okay. She and I weren't in love. And she is – was – nice to look at. Shall we?"

She nodded.

He opened another file. Again, Hayley was naked, and this time she was giving a blow job to someone with a paunch. The camera didn't show his face.

The next two files also showed her having sex with a man who's face couldn't be seen.

Gracie exhaled. "It looks like she had a sideline in home-made porn."

The camera was static and looked to be on automatic. But for each video, Carter noticed, the angle was different.

"It's as if she was experimenting with a hidden camera," he said.

Gracie nodded. "The blackmailer learning her art."

Carter leaned back. His memory of Hayley was colliding with the reality of her in action. She'd had sex with him because she wanted something in return. Was she having sex with these faceless guys for the same reason?

He opened another file. This time, Hayley was staring into the camera as she was getting penetrated from behind. This time, the man's face was visible. It was none other than Sasha Oblomov.

"Oh my God," Gracie said.

Carter leaned in closer. "Look," he said, "you can see some-one reflected in the mirror."

Hayley had placed the camera so it was facing the mirror, and while she and Sasha Oblomov were facing the camera, the mirror reflected another man, in shadow, watching them. Carter recognized the shape of his body.

"It's Link."

Gracie squinted for better focus. "It can't be . . ."

Carter nodded. "But it is."

The clip ended. There was one more.

"She was having sex with both Link and Oblomov," Gracie said. "Maybe the fight was some kind of lover's quarrel."

"But we haven't actually seen her having sex with Link," Carter reminded her. "You ready for the finale?"

She nodded. "Yeah. Makes you appreciate how hard it is to do good smut, though, doesn't it?"

Carter played the last file. This time, the camera angle was perfect. Onscreen, Hayley was naked, with two men in front of her, Link Andrachuk and Sasha Oblomov.

As Hayley bobbed from one man to the other, Carter's eye wandered to the two champagne bottles and four glasses on a table next to her.

Link tapped Hayley on the shoulder, and she increased the speed of her mission, then she leaned back on her heels, moving her head out of the way so the camera could catch him climax with his hand. He wasn't wearing a condom.

Oblomov wasn't quite there yet, his eyes closed tight in concentration, and he reached out for Hayley, but now she'd moved out of frame.

Then something even more extraordinary happened. Link knelt down in front of Sasha Oblomov and picked up where Hayley had left off. Oblomov's face was flushed with lust, head tilted back, pelvis thrusting out as he rode the mouth before him.

Then suddenly his head jerked forward, as if his mother had walked into the room and called his name. He looked down and recoiled as if he'd been kicked in the balls. His mouth opened in a scream, and he swung his fists like pile drivers down on a laughing Link, who jumped up and ran. In the space where they'd both been, there was a reflection in the mirror of a third man, a plump guy in the shadows, naked too, watching.

Then the screen went black.

"Oh my God," said Gracie. "Oh. My. God."

There was dead silence for a couple of minutes, neither of them looking at the laptop, or at each other. Then Carter murmured, "I think we know what Link said to Sasha that got him so angry."

"Oh. My. God." Gracie said again. "Hockey girls can be gay . . . I mean, it's almost expected –"

"But hockey boys cannot. Ever."

They lapsed into silence, and Carter could hear the waves on the beach a hundred yards away.

"Why would these guys allow Hayley to film them with her?" Gracie finally said.

"Hey," Carter replied. "You cover hockey. You know what they get up to. It was all fun and games until Link decided to play for the other team."

"But the two of them, with her . . ."

"It's the guy in the background I'm wondering about."

"What guy?"

Carter replayed the final seconds of the video. "There, that shadow in the mirror."

Gracie leaned toward the screen and squinted. "So there is . . . but who?"

"I'd say it's the fat guy she was, uh, orally servicing a couple of clips back." He right-clicked on each fake PDF file. Hayley's sex tapes were all made in the last weekend of January.

"And guess who was playing here in Vancouver that weekend?"

"The St. Patricks," she said, smiling at him with surprise and a flicker of admiration. "If this fugitive thing doesn't work out, Carter, you have a career as a detective ahead of you."

He smiled back. "It's in the blood."

"It is?"

"My father was a cop. The Royal Canadian Mounted Police"

She gave him that wide-eyed smile again, warmer this time, reaching deeper into him. "So now the question is, detective, why wasn't she using this footage as blackmail?"

"Well," Carter said, "if I was doing a DVD on Link, the last thing I'd want out there is footage of him giving a blow job to another guy. As you well know, the hockey world is more afraid of a gay player – especially a gay superstar – than they are of a player who kills women."

"You're not saying Link killed her."

"If he was aware she had this, who knows?"

"So that's why she hid it."

"Yeah, and if you know how – and she did – then it was easy to find. And used, if needs be. But then Link obliged her with a much better blackmail opportunity. Hockey may be afraid of homosexuals – scared to death, in fact – but violence, that's different."

The cold band tightened around his skull.

"Are you okay?" Gracie asked.

He nodded. "I think I am. Can this thing burn DVDs?"

"Yes. Why?"

He sat back in his chair.

"Tell me, Gracie," he said. "Do you believe in ghosts?"

"I can't say I do."

"Well, then, I'm going to introduce you to one."

42

Andy Jack's black eyes bore into Carter as if he were the ghost.

He also looked like a man who wasn't going to let either a phantom or the past ruin his future. His dark silk suit was generously cut to fit his considerable bulk and he seemed at home with his office's antique mahogany furniture around him.

His eyes never left Carter, even as he reached into the top drawer of his desk for a cigar. The desk was so large that the six-foot-five Jack could have slept on it with room to spare. Jack's beefy fingers clipped the end of the long Cuban, fired up his lighter – a miniature tomahawk – and pulled on the cigar until he had the right mixture of fire and tobacco, then he settled back in his leather chair.

"Why," he finally said, "would I do that?"

"Yeah, for fuck's sake!" barked the Sea Lions' coach, Bunny Blackburn, fidgeting in his seat next to Carter.

Jack's eyes shifted to Bunny, pinning the little cannonball to the back of his chair.

"Because," said Carter, "I've seen the footage in question, and believe me, you've got a better chance of getting" – he smiled at the number – "your fifty million if you were to have that footage."

Jack blew a ribbon of smoke between Carter and Bunny, whose head looked like it was going to launch from the nylon shoulders of his Sea Lions tracksuit. Then he looked at Gracie, sitting on Carter's right.

"This some sorta media prank?"

Gracie shook her head. She'd made the call to the Sea Lions' boss, telling him she had some information that might help them get what they needed from the St. Pats.

And when the information walked through the big mahogany double doors of the president's suite, Andy Jack looked, for a brief flicker of his black eyes, to be trapped by his past. But Carter had offered his hand, and Jack had warily taken it. Then he'd summoned Bunny Blackburn, just to make sure he had backup for whatever Carter had in mind.

"So you're telling me," he said, his eyes unblinking above a rictus smile, "that I go to Erik Shepherd and do a horse trade. I drop the lawsuit, he gives me the footage of Link smashing in Oblomov's face – which he might not have – then his company goes public and makes a nice profit, then I use the footage to nail the St. Pats?"

"You're a quick study, Andy," Carter said.

"You're crazy," he said, smiling, as if this would make the assessment more polite.

"That would be a matter of opinion, though if I am, you can thank yourself."

The smile on Jack's broad mouth disappeared. He took a deep breath and shifted his gaze to Gracie. "And what's in it for you?"

"A good story," she said.

"Fucken vultures after garbage," said Bunny.

"I thought he was a superstar worth fifty million in damages," she shot back, and the coach's mouth opened and then closed as he caught his boss's eye.

"A good story, huh?" Jack mulled, blowing smoke at them. "Your ancestors must have been the ones who told mine that exchanging half the Pacific Coast for some trinkets was a good idea."

"Look, Andy," Carter said, "you have a problem and I have a problem, so here's a chance to solve them both. And Gracie – Ms. Yates – gets to write about it. Nothing more sinister than that."

Jack frowned. "Why should I help you?"

Carter's head tingled. He'd given the guy who'd ended his career a chance to redeem himself, sort of, and Jack was too caught up in his own story to see beyond its gilded walls.

"Because," Carter said, "they're trying to pin the blame for Hayley Rawls's murder on me. Having this footage would help me show the cops that a lot of people had reason to kill her. And that I wasn't one of them."

"So you'd go against the Cardinal?"

Carter sighed. "I didn't say the Cardinal had anything to do with her murder. But when you see the footage, you'll see why others did."

Jack took a long drag on his cigar, then spun his chair to look out the window at the North Shore Mountains, still capped with the winter snows. Bunny grabbed the armrests of his chair and leaned forward, the cannonball about to smash himself into Carter's head. "This smells like horseshit inside a dead fish," he growled.

"Well then, Bunny," Carter replied calmly, "why don't you leave us and go golfing?"

Bunny took the dig about missing the playoffs more personally than Carter meant it and leapt up, bouncing beside Carter's chair on the balls of his feet. "You fucken come in here and insult me like that after your fucken guy nearly kill my Russian?" he shouted, fumbling in his tracksuit pocket for his cellphone. "I call the fucken cops right now and tell them where you are. Make a fucken citizen arrest."

"Not a bad idea, Bunny," Jack said.

Carter needed to hit the punchline before this duo decided to do what Gracie had warned him they might.

"You have a DVD player on your computer, Andy?"

"What?" It wasn't the question he'd been expecting.

"You know, the slot that plays silver disks like this." He held up a DVD in its jewel case.

"What's that?"

"I'll show you."

Jack took the DVD and slid it into his computer. Carter rose and strolled round behind his desk. Bunny rocked on his heels like a schoolboy but stayed where he was standing, not daring to go behind his boss's desk.

"This better not be some kinda virus," Jack growled, his hand poised on the computer mouse.

"It's the future," Carter replied.

Jack's media player popped up and he clicked on the play button. And up on the screen popped Hayley Rawls's sex tape. And there was their superstar, Sasha Oblomov, getting a blow job from Link Andrachuk.

"What the fuck?" Jack yelled, his face red now. Bunny scuttled behind the desk. "Holy fucken fuck!" he exclaimed, his neck straining at his tracksuit collar. "It's a fucken trick!"

In a way it was. Carter and Gracie had cut the footage so that it began just after Hayley went out of the frame and ended before Oblomov started hitting Link.

"No, Bunny," Carter said, "that is indeed your Russian wonderboy showing off his stamina with Link Andrachuk."

Andy Jack looked like he was going to punch Carter in the head, so Carter strolled back to the other side of the desk. "You can keep that. I have copies."

Jack stared at Carter, breathing hard. "So now you're goin' to blackmail me."

"No, not blackmail. Let's call it an incentive. I didn't count on you to help me because you owe me. I mean, but for a detail or two, you're my very own Link Andrachuk" – Bunny started to lunge forward, but Jack stopped him with one of his massive arms – "and so I figured I'd appeal to your clearly considerable business sense."

Jack let Bunny go and stood there, his fists clenched, his mind running.

"You mean you're going to put this on the Internet if I don't do your bidding with Erik Shepherd."

Carter smiled. "Or if your friend Mr. Blackburn here were to call the cops on me."

"You fucken faggot!" Bunny screamed, the worst insult he could think of.

"Now, now, Bunny," Carter said calmly. "That's no way to speak of your half-dead Russian superstar, whose injury is worth fifty million."

He turned to Gracie. "Well then, Ms. Yates, I think we're done here." He turned a smile on the Sea Lions duo, who were still gaping at him in disbelief, and gestured for Gracie to lead the way out. "I'll be in touch this time tomorrow. Get me what I need and this show never happened."

43

"Here's to a happy ending," Gracie said, reaching over from her Adirondack chair and clinking her wineglass against Carter's. Carter had sprung for a couple of bottles of Sandhill Syrah to go with the thick rib-eye steaks they'd picked up on

Granville Island, before they launched *Hamlet* back to the safety of Bowen Island.

"Amen," he said, though he was thinking of a different ending than she was. They'd just blackmailed the president of the Sea Lions, and there were a hundred ways it could go wrong.

"Regrets already?" Gracie asked, reading his expression.

"A little," he said, "about doctoring the footage."

"Hey," she said, touching his arm. "It was edited for, uh, length. But we didn't make up Link Andrachuk going down on Sasha Oblomov."

He was grateful she didn't add, "And the blackmail was your idea."

Gracie leaned back in her Adirondack and closed her eyes. "That steak smells wonderful."

It did smell wonderful, its aroma mingling with the dark spice of the Syrah and the cool mint of the fir trees. Carter knew that if he stayed here on this magical island, watched over by a mule deer and soaring eagles, it would not be a happy ending but a promising beginning.

But that was impossible. They had just spent the day risking his liberty, if not his life, to set up a shaky plan that would, if all went well, rip Carter from his island hideaway and send him back into the maelstrom to deal with being a suspect in two murders, his presumed death and resurrection, and one destroyed minivan from the Black Irish. If he could dodge the violent death that was chasing him.

Despite it all, Carter was feeling more than resurrected, just as he used to on the ice when he'd see the sliver of an opening and, suddenly, be back in the game. He could make a pass, take a shot, maybe even score. He had a chance. He had a future.

He'd felt like celebrating and had offered to make Gracie a feast, which he now served: steak with russets fried with onion and parmesan, spinach sautéed in lemon and olive oil, and thick slices of toasted Italian bread drizzled with garlic butter. And of course, French steak sauce, Béarnaise.

It was fat and rich, but Gracie loved it and ate seconds. And he loved the fact she had an appetite.

"Where'd you learn to cook?" Gracie asked.

"From my mother. She could just make up a recipe from whatever we had in the house, and it was brilliant. She could see how ingredients fit together, you know? Not anymore, though. Her Alzheimer's is pretty far gone."

Gracie's face softened in sympathy. "I'm sorry."

"Me too."

"It's just you're too young to have . . ." she trailed off, her eyes fixed on him as if testing where the "dead end" sign on this road might be.

"I thought so too," he replied, finishing her thought. "She got it five years ago when she was still in her sixties. My brother sort of looks after her from his hideout in the basement, and I've pretty much bailed on the notion of a happy ending, as far as family stories go." He raised his glass. "But then, I haven't heard yours."

She set down her fork. "I'm an only child, my parents are both English teachers, living in White Rock, just on the other side of Point Grey" – she pointed languidly toward the sea – "and it's both close enough and far away enough that we all get along. They came here during the Vietnam War."

"Really, draft dodgers?" He winced. "I mean, war resisters?"

She smiled. "The latter. My father did a tour, got a Purple Heart – from friendly fire – and my mother told him if he went back for a second tour, she'd come to Canada and marry a draft dodger. He took her point."

"The classic combination. Love and war."

"And love won out. For once."

Maybe it was the wine, but Carter sensed she had opened a door. So," he said, taking a delicate step through it, "anyone since your marriage ended?"

"Yeah, I threw myself into the arms of work."

"Me too." He laughed. "Though work and I have reached the point of irreconcilable differences."

She looked him dead in the eye. "You were great today. You got that bastard back a little."

He hoped his embarrassment didn't show in the dusk. "Today was easy. I let Mr. Oblomov do the talking with his stick, as they say."

She laughed, then topped up their wineglasses from a second bottle of Syrah. "It scares them to death, doesn't it, the idea that one of their almighty hockey stars could be gay?"

He nodded. "The CHL just denies they exist – no gay players, no gay fans. They seriously think that no gay man would ever give up figure skating to get repeatedly cross-checked in the ribs while standing in front of the net, or have pucks fired at his head, even for the pleasure of regular showers with the boys."

"What about when you played?"

"It was the same," he replied. That part of his life he did remember. "There was a guy who was a little out there, didn't do the groupie thing, liked to go to museums and galleries when his team was on the road, and didn't think peeler bars were the height of human accomplishment. Of course, the team tried to make him date actresses and show up at clubs on the arms of babes, just so people wouldn't think he was gay."

"What happened to him?"

He raised his glass to her. "You're looking at him."

Her blue eyes flashed with surprise and something like interest.

"They were wrong, of course, about me."

"I know that," she said.

"I'm glad."

She paused before saying, "I could tell by that kiss, even though it was only a ploy to get us into Hayley Rawls's building."

She looked away, toward the ocean, the sunlight now an orange-and-red wave washing over the sea and splashing the sky.

He leaned over and kissed her now, gently brushing her lips with his, not yet daring to explore further. Then she pulled back.

"This could be a mistake," she said, her voice low and warm.

"Yeah," he said. "But hindsight would be more of one."

She rose, then took his hand, and led him into her unfinished house, regret left at the table like an empty wine bottle.

44

When Carter awoke in the middle of the night, his bladder was throbbing and he had a purposeful erection and Gracie was naked in his arms. He smiled. If he woke her while trying not to, he at least could greet her with the offering of another course, though he was surprised he had any energy left in him after their long, luscious dessert in bed.

It had been so different than his carnal tumble with Hayley, which now seemed to him almost pornographic in its choreography.

He and Gracie were like first-timers, fumbling their way up to her bed, and then rolling around in a tangle of passion that kept them tongue to tongue and eye to eye, the climax coming with urgency, as if to emphasize the sudden change in their relationship, and then again slowly, with confidence that change was for the better.

The moon was down and it was as dark as sleep when Carter slid out of bed.

Gracie rolled on to her side, away from him. She was just a shape underneath a duvet in the pitch of her bedroom, but Carter found music in her breathing as he stood for a moment to let his eyes adjust before he crept to the bathroom.

He was about to flush when he heard something.

It was footsteps, downstairs.

He held his breath, listening. The footsteps had the syncopation of someone with a limp – heavy, light, heavy.

Maybe it was just some drunken Bowen Island teenager, stumbling around in the dark looking for more booze. Or Gracie's ex-husband, drunk and overcome with nostalgia.

Or maybe it was Hopalong who had finally found him and was clomping around in the dark to smoke him out, lure him down the stairs so he could impale him on a hockey stick.

A beam of light swept the hall ceiling from the bottom of the stairs. Carter could feel the intruder thinking about his next move. Go up the stairs and kill whatever he found. But Hopalong would be more subtle than that. This must be the Russian mafia, who didn't care what their victim heard, because they left no witnesses. The intruder was making no attempt to lighten his tread on the stairs. He wanted them to know he was coming.

Carter was stranded, naked, between the intruder and Gracie, not the worst place to be, he reckoned. He could intercept the guy, make as much noise as possible, and hope it would give Gracie time to escape.

Unless, of course, the intruder just shot him between the eyes.

The light beam levelled out now as the intruder reached the top of the stairs, and slowly limped forward, the light sweeping the floor in front of him. Carter reached behind and grabbed the plunger, aiming its suction cup toward the hallway. As soon as he saw the intruder's hand, he took two quick steps across the bathroom floor and smashed the plunger into the side of the intruder's head.

The man screamed and crumpled against the wall, his hands over his face. Carter bent down to pick up the flashlight and check if there was any gun he should now worry about.

Suddenly, the man's hands were around his neck. Carter tried to twist onto his back, so he could face his attacker. His attacker didn't seem all that strong, and Carter had swung himself halfway around, clutching at the man, when suddenly, a naked Gracie loomed behind the man and with one deft chop collapsed him in a heap on top of Carter.

Carter, breathing hard, rolled out from beneath the man. He grabbed his shoulders and rolled him over, and Gracie aimed the flashlight at the man's face. His mouth was wide open, and now Carter understood why the guy had been screaming. Blood still oozed from stitches they had put in his nearly severed tongue – what, two weeks ago?

Carter looked at Gracie, who just nodded, unable to speak. It was him all right. Sasha Oblomov, out cold on her floor.

45

"That was one hell of a chop," Carter said, surprisingly calm now, watching the shallow rise and fall of Oblomov's chest as he lay unconscious on Gracie's couch. The Russian's chin was streaked with rivulets of blood from his mouth, where he had bitten down on the sutures holding his tongue in place and reopened the wound.

"Not really," Gracie replied, staring at the bloodied, dread-locked Oblomov, still wearing his hospital ID bracelet. "It should have killed him."

Carter glanced up at her. She was serious.

"My father might have given up on war, but he taught me some things about fighting, just in case."

Carter rubbed his eyes, scarcely able to believe he was sitting by gaslight in Gracie's living room, waiting for a knocked-out hockey superstar who'd broken into her house to wake up.

"How the hell did he know where you live?"

"The whole team knows where I live – I cover the Sea Lions, remember?"

Carter thought about that. "In that case, his friends might be wondering where he is."

He dressed and went outside to look for hostiles, unsure what he'd do if he found them. And with Oblomov's flash-light in hand, he made a pretty good target.

Carter had about as much experience with survival skills as he did in finding a murderer, but he knew he needed to learn them fast in his new life as a fugitive. He reckoned that what he had to do was find tracks – then fight to the death with whoever made the tracks.

He relaxed when his flashlight tracked just a single set of footprints up the dirt path from the road. Carter swept the beam along the pavement but saw nothing, no parked car or armoured personnel carrier. So Oblomov must have walked in, hiking the mile or so up the hill from the ferry dock at Snug Cove.

Except the ferry from Vancouver stopped running at 9:30.

"That's probably why he stinks of booze," Gracie said when Carter reported the all clear. "He must have come over on the last ferry and got some courage in the pub at Snug Cove, until he figured I was asleep. Then he hiked up here."

"Interesting theory. Not very smart of him."

"Well, he's not in his right mind, is he?"

Carter thought a moment. "You didn't tell me that there's a pub at Snug Cove."

She grinned. "If I had, do you think I'd have had you all to myself last night?"

Oh yes, she would have. Carter felt himself getting aroused. This sex and violence thing was getting to him. "The night's still young," he said, nuzzling her. "And I don't think he's going anywhere soon."

She laughed and pushed him away. "You're right," she said, her eyes flickering with pleasure, "but I think I'd better get dressed for when he does."

She disappeared upstairs, and Carter took his untamed bulge for a walk to the window, puzzled. Both times he'd had sex in the past couple of weeks, Sasha Oblomov had played a role. It wasn't the kind of threesome he'd ever fantasized about, not that he was given much to doing that. He'd found it hard enough to find room for two in a bed, let alone a relationship.

"I'm hoping," Gracie said, kissing his neck after she came back down the stairs, "that we can soon pick up where we left –"

She was interrupted by a thud, and the gurgled moan of a now conscious Oblomov, who, having rolled off the couch, was crawling on the floor like a badly wounded drunk.

"We have to get him to a hospital," Gracie said.

"Sure," said Carter. "After we get to know him a bit better."

He grabbed Oblomov by his armpits and hauled him into a chair in the kitchen.

"Careful," Gracie said.

"I'm being careful," Carter replied. "Besides, you're the one who can kill him with one blow."

Oblomov moaned again, his eyes wider. They had his attention.

"Don't worry, Sasha," Gracie said. "I won't kill you for breaking into my house and scaring the . . . how do you say 'shit' in Russian?"

Oblomov gurgled some more, blood trickling from his mouth and down his chin.

"Difficult language," said Carter. "So let's make it simple. Sasha, why the fuck are you here?"

Oblomov tried to spit blood out of his mouth, but it just dangled from his chin in a strand. Carter could see that his tongue was badly swollen.

Carter raised his eyebrows to Gracie, who fetched some paper towel.

Carter opened her laptop and booted it up. "Sasha, I want you to type your answers on this," he said calmly. "It won't take long, then we'll take you to a doctor."

Oblomov tried to speak. "Fcckkkfff."

"I think he told me to fuck off," Carter said. "Maybe you should hit him on the head again."

Gracie wiped Oblomov's chin, leaning in close to him, her voice almost a whisper. "Sasha, let's try this again. You've broken into my house in the middle of the night. Now, this would be a big problem for the cops, who are just a couple of minutes down the road. But it's not a problem for me because I'm a reporter. I can write an article on it, with photos, and we all watch what happens to the Sea Lions' lawsuit and your career. Do you understand me?"

Oblomov narrowed his eyes. Then he grunted.

"Was that a yes?"

He grunted again.

"Great," said Carter, pushing the laptop in front of Oblomov and placing the Russian's limp hands on the keyboard. "Now," he said pleasantly, "why the fuck are you here?"

Oblomov sighed, blood bubbling on his lips. He wiped it off, then crumpled and dropped the paper towel on the floor.

"Thanks," Gracie said.

Oblomov typed *buny sed* like some kid texting his friends.

"What the hell does that mean?" Carter snarled.

coach Oblomov typed.

"Bunny," said Carter, rolling his eyes at Gracie. "Bunny Blackburn told him about the footage."

Oblomov nodded. Then he typed *not fag*.

Carter looked at Gracie again and she shook her head. They were thinking the same thing. Oblomov got out of his hospital bed and came here to do what? Destroy Hayley's footage?

"We know that, Sasha," Gracie said.

He blinked at her, then typed *?*.

She looked at Carter, and he nodded. "We know Hayley Rawls was there too, and she and Link tricked you. We edited her out."

Oblomov's face brightened and he blinked at Carter.

"So, you and Hayley were" – Carter searched for the right words – "lovers?"

Oblomov snorted and blood-tinged mucus now spurted from his nose. Gracie handed more paper towel to him.

Oblomov grunted again in thanks, then typed *just fuck.*

"You and Hayley just met for sex?" Carter said.

Oblomov nodded.

"What about the Maestro?" Gracie added. "Did she have sex with him?"

? Oblomov typed.

"The guy doing the DVD and website on Link."

Oblomov shrugged.

"Who was the other person there? The guy with the gut?"

?

"There was someone else there, watching. Who was it?"

link frend. link fag

"Did you and Link meet her together – I mean, before this?" Carter asked.

no her idea to bring him

"And you didn't –" Gracie caught herself. "And you thought this was okay?"

she sed 3sum how i no?

"But when you saw Link there?" Gracie pressed.

Oblomov gave her a sharp look, then typed *it her house she take me there.*

Gracie raised her eyebrows at Carter, and he shrugged. He knew well what kind of sexual antics went on between players on the road. It was not uncommon for a couple of them to pick up a keen female fan or two and share them back at the hotel. The difference here was that Link and Sasha didn't play for the same team – in more ways than one.

"So," Carter said, "had you and Link got together before to fuck Hayley Rawls?"

Gracie flinched, but Oblomov seemed keen to answer, typing fast.

no 2 bad she dead she good fuk

Oblomov was on a roll and kept typing: *you taek dvd?*

Carter and Gracie exchanged looks, and Gracie nodded. May as well tell him.

"Because," Carter said, "we wanted Andy Jack to help us, and we didn't think he would solely because of his good nature. Hayley also has footage of what Link did to you. I've seen it. And we think we know who has it now – the Maestro, the guy doing the website on Link Andrachuk."

Oblomov shook his head, as if this was all too much, and wiped his mouth. The pupils in his grey eyes were pinpricks, the effects of pain and medication and whatever he'd had to drink at the pub, not to mention the news he'd just heard.

"Do you want some water?" Gracie asked.

He shook his head.

"How about some wine?" Carter ventured, and the Russian opened his large, soft, goal-scorers' hands in a gesture that said, "Couldn't hurt."

"We drank all the wine," Gracie said. "But we do have whiskey." She poured him several fingers.

Oblomov winced as he took a sip of single malt, then washed down the pain by drinking half the mug.

tel u truth Oblomov typed.

"Go ahead, Sasha," said Gracie. "Tell us what happened with Link."

link is asshle

Gracie looked at Carter. Link's an asshole. Not news. "What did he say to you that made you so angry?" she asked

Oblomov drank more whiskey and shook his head as if to rid himself of a memory.

"Can you remember that night?" Carter asked.

Oblomov shrugged.

"What did Link say to you?" Gracie repeated, in reporter mode, on the clock.

Oblomov typed *give me fuk dvd*. Then he folded his arms on the tabletop and put his head down on them.

Gracie reached to pull him up, but Carter stopped her hand. He leaned in to Oblomov's ear.

"Just a couple more questions, Sasha," he said gently. "Then we can see about that DVD."

Oblomov raised his head halfway, blinking slowly at Carter.

"When you attacked Link, was it because of what he said about this . . . thing with Hayley?"

Oblomov laid his head back on his folded arms. Carter grabbed a handful of his blond dreads and yanked it up.

"Did Link say something about you taking money? Like, to throw a game?"

Oblomov jerked his head away from Carter's grasp and glared at him. Then he typed *give me fuk dvd.*

"Yeah, well, you need to give us something first," Carter said. "Aside from a good story for Ms. Yates here."

Oblomov sighed deeply and typed *$*.

Carter and Gracie exchanged glances.

"Who gave you money to do what?" Gracie's voice was urgent and incredulous.

Oblomov spluttered with laughter, spraying blood on Carter's shirt. Gracie handed Carter a paper towel now, but he ignored it, leaning in close to Oblomov, his hands on the Russian's collar. "Listen, you fuck," Carter said, "my life is at stake here. So tell us what you know about Link or I'm going to –"

Gracie pulled Carter off. "Sasha," she said, "what money are you talking about?"

He stared at her, as if she were an idiot: *want $ from me*

"The Russian mafia? The Bratva?"

He shook his head and winced, then drained the rest of the whiskey.

"Who, Sasha? Who wanted money from you?"

Oblomov rolled his eyes at Carter, or maybe he was just falling asleep again. Carter grabbed him again by the head, and Oblomov reached for the keyboard. *dead lady* he typed.

Then his eyes fluttered and he passed out.

Carter and Gracie looked at each other as if they'd both sniffed a strange smell and were waiting for the other to say whether it was rotten.

"Hayley Rawls was shaking him down too?" Gracie said.

Carter ran his hand through his hair. It was sweaty. "Why not? Until she lucked out with Link's attack."

"I take it you mean 'lucky' in the ironic sense."

"Yes. But why would Link want to injure Oblomov?"

"Because Oblomov had something on him."

"Yeah, he did, but it doesn't add up. Oblomov wouldn't want news of this little adventure in group bisexuality to get around."

"Maybe it was a love triangle."

Carter smiled. "I take it you mean 'love triangle' in the joking sense."

She shrugged. "The one thing we do know is that Oblomov didn't kill her. He was nearly dead himself."

They looked at Oblomov now, his breathing shallow, his chin resting on his chest.

Carter lifted Oblomov's head up and poked him in the mouth. Oblomov moaned.

"Well, he responds to pain, but he doesn't open his eyes."

"What does that mean?" Gracie said.

"It means we have to get him to a hospital now. Or we'll be burying him at sea before sunrise."

46

Carter tried to wake Sasha Oblomov as they sped across the strait from Bowen Island to the city, but all he succeeded in doing was getting wet himself as he aimed Oblomov's face into the Pacific spray. The best he could get out of him was a deep groan.

He was glad of the cover of darkness as they dragged the hockey player like a corpse from the boat to Gracie's car at the marina. Though slender and not quite six feet, Oblomov felt like he was weighed down with concrete, and Carter was sweating by the time they wedged him into the back seat of the car.

"Okay," said Carter, breathing hard. "Now we just have to get him into the hospital without being spotted."

"The things we do for a good story," Gracie replied as she started the engine.

"And some other things, I would hope," Carter said, but Gracie, her jaw tight, her lips pursed, didn't answer. She was already writing her way out of the next problem.

Once over the Burrard Bridge, Gracie turned left on Comox Street, next to the red brick pile that was St. Paul's Hospital, and pulled into a parking spot just out of sight of the Emergency entrance.

"So," Carter said, looking at Oblomov, still breathing and unconscious in the back seat. "Any idea how we make him invisible?"

"We don't," Gracie said. "At this hospital, even in his condition, he'll be one of the healthiest people in emergency."

They dragged Oblomov out of the car and sat him against the iron railing at the edge of the Emergency driveway.

"We can't just dump him in front of the door."

"We're not going to," Gracie replied. "These guys are going to take him inside."

"These guys" were a trio of street people weaving up the street toward the hospital, two men and the woman they were propping up.

"Hey," said Gracie to the older guy, bearded and ballcapped and just as strung out as the other one. "You want to make twenty bucks?"

The man narrowed his bloodshot eyes, trying to spot the trick. "What for?"

"Just take our friend inside," Gracie replied. "Drop him off at the desk, and they'll do the rest."

"What happened to him?" said the older guy.

"Too much to drink," said Carter.

"That's a problem?"

Carter smiled, but the guy gave him a hard stare, and Carter caught his meaning. "He had too much to drink when he should have been in here," Carter said, holding up Oblomov's wrist and flashing the hospital ID bracelet.

"You want us to get you off the hook for a fucken twenny?" said the younger guy.

"Okay, a hundred bucks then," Gracie replied calmly.

The two men looked at each other, and Carter looked at Gracie. Where did she learn to bargain? But it worked. The older one hauled himself to attention and stuck out his hand.

"Great," said Gracie, smiling at Carter expectantly. He

grinned tightly back as he pulled five twenties from his wallet and handed two of them to the older guy.

"You get the rest after we see you do it."

A police car suddenly swung into the driveway, making them step back. It parked by the Emergency entrance, and two cops got out and walked purposefully through the sliding doors.

"On second thought," Carter said, giving the man the rest of the money, "I trust you."

The man handed it back. "We're not going in there *now*," he said. And they hauled their friend down the block a bit and sat her against the railing.

Carter sighed. He and a trio of Vancouver drug casualties had been thwarted at the overdose hospital of choice by the same problem: the police.

"Fffk," said Oblomov, suddenly waking up and blinking hard, trying to take in where he was.

"Well, hello, Sasha," said Carter, steadying him, relieved to see him back. "You have goal scorer's timing, you know . . ."

"Fkkk," Oblomov said.

Carter bought them coffees across the street at a 7-Eleven, and they sat, all three squeezed in the back seat of Gracie's car.

"Sasha," Gracie said gently, "you said the dead lady, Hayley Rawls, was trying to get money from you? Do you remember that?"

Oblomov nodded slowly.

"Did she?" Carter said.

Oblomov shook his head.

"How many times did you and she, you know, have sex?"

Oblomov held up a hand as if to say, "Who knows?" Then he yawned. He was going to pass out again.

"Sasha, look at me." Oblomov closed his eyes. "Look at me!" Carter said, grabbing him. Oblomov opened his eyes. "What did Link say to you on the ice that night? The thing that made you attack him?"

Oblomov took a sip of coffee and scrunched his nose, as if he'd drunk better drain water. He handed the cup to Gracie and just sat there, staring into space.

"Sasha?"

He motioned to her laptop, so she booted it up. "It's running out of power," she said.

Oblomov nodded. *u give dvd*. He found and pressed each key with great effort.

"I can't do that," said Gracie, "because I can't burn a DVD on this thing. But I can do one better. I can delete it."

Carter caught her eye over the laptop, but she betrayed nothing as she opened the file and clicked play. Oblomov watched himself realize he had been fooled by Link Andrachuk that night, then shook his head vigorously and snarled.

"What's wrong, Sasha?"

He kept shaking his head. "No," he said thickly.

"That's all we've got," Gracie said.

He stopped shaking his head and fixed her with a cold eye.

"Really," she said. "That's what we showed Andy Jack."

"Is there more?" Carter asked.

Oblomov glared at Carter then smiled, his mouth a bloody grimace. *i beat sht from link* he typed.

Hayley's camera hadn't recorded the beating he'd inflicted on Link Andrachuk, though that would explain Link's shiner and bruised lip on the night of the game.

Then he tapped the delete button on the keyboard. Nothing happened.

Gracie closed the video, highlighted it, then hit delete.

The file disappeared. Gracie clicked on a Word icon on the desktop, and Oblomov's interview popped up. She handed the laptop back to him.

He sighed, as if he was about to unburden himself of a great secret, then typed *link want to beat shit from me.*

"Excuse me?" said Gracie.

Oblomov sighed again. He was struggling to stay awake. He typed *link call me fag he fag.*

Then he leaned back in his seat and closed his eyes. "No, Sasha," said Carter. "Not here. There." He pointed to the hospital. Oblomov nodded. *fag place* he typed, and leaning on Carter for leverage, he opened the car door and hauled himself out.

"Not to worry," said Gracie as they watched Oblomov shuffle toward Emergency. "I have a DVD copy. And I know how to hide files now."

"Yeah. I look forward to what he'll do when he figures that out."

"It's hard to believe that a guy could get so worked up about being called gay," Gracie said.

"But a little easier to understand if there's DVD footage of some guy sucking you off," Carter said.

"And the camera woman trying to blackmail you."

"All true, but it was the label that he was most afraid of. The caveman attitude is worst among the Russians." He thought a moment. "Hayley he could pay off, but Link Andrachuk is unpredictable."

"Then Hayley Rawls winds up dead."

"So that leaves Link."

"What do you mean?"

"I mean, we need to talk to him in person."

"And he's going to tell us?"

Carter nodded. "I think he will now that we have something to trade."

Gracie frowned. "That sounds like a dangerous plan."

"Yeah," he said. "But I don't really have a choice."

He leaned close and put her arms around his neck. She smelled like mint and coffee, and he wanted to kiss her, but she stopped him with words he had longed to hear not so long ago. "We could stay here. Hide out on Bowen."

Carter desperately wanted to say yes, but he knew that he couldn't. For her sake. "Not after tonight, we can't," he said, putting his arms around her. "It was a risk to go to Andy Jack, and he screwed me again."

"Do you think he contacted the Maestro?"

Carter shrugged. "I don't think so. I mean, Oblomov was the perfect weapon to do what needed to be done – a guy with a head injury who's been told that there's footage of him having sex with another man that's going to be all over the Internet come sunrise. But I'll find out in New York."

Gracie leaned her forehead against his. "New York?"

"I'll tell you how it ends when I come back to Bowen to cash that rain cheque," he said.

She thought about that for a second, then kissed him, soft and warm and too brief, but full of promise. "The exchange rate is good," she said. "Let's cash it in Manhattan."

47

Carter and Gracie had to laugh about the problem of actually getting to New York. He was trying to get back into the country that wanted his head, in order to save his neck. It was a Martin Carter kind of problem.

He couldn't fly, since his Canadian passport would be flagged by Homeland Security, and his Irish one needed a U.S. visa. Same with the train. Same with driving across the border, and walking across could get both of them a bullet in the head from, as Gracie put it, "some Washington State gun jockey conceived during the love scene in *Deliverance*."

So that left them where they were now, humming along in *Hamlet* on an outgoing tide, with the southern tip of Canada to port and Japan to starboard.

After dropping Oblomov back into the health care system, they'd returned to the marina and loaded on a couple of jugs of gasoline. Then, with the first lick of the sun to the east, they'd driven *Hamlet* around Point Grey, under planes from Hawaii and China swooping low over the ocean and into Vancouver International Airport, then hugged the coast along Richmond and Delta before crossing the imaginary line on the ocean that marked the U.S. border off Point Roberts.

By then the sun was up and the sky was clear. "Just another beautiful day to be making the smugglers run," Gracie shouted over the engine as she pointed *Hamlet* south, threading the narrows between Lummi Island and Bellingham Bay.

Close to the mainland, Gracie cut the engine and handed Carter a wooden paddle. "Just keep her straight," she said. "We want to land over there."

"Over there" was a lonely bay with a narrow beach bordering a steep bank studded with fir trees. Carter steered *Hamlet* to the beach, then took off his shoes and socks and rolled up his pants to help Gracie drag the boat onshore. They stood on the beach, completely alone, the sun hinting at the warmth of the day to come, the air soft and rich with birdsong. For a breath, Carter felt like the first arrivals to these shores must have felt. He also wanted to tear Gracie's clothes off and roll around with her on the beach. She read his mind.

"I think *Hamlet* will be safe here," she said. "But let's move him into the bushes until I get back."

"You'll be able to find this place?" Carter asked, urbanized long enough to find being in nature one grand mystery.

A Cessna flew over them and climbed out to sea. "Sure," she said. "We're about a ten-minute stroll from Bellingham Airport."

Eight minutes later, they stepped onto the road, within sight of the small terminal building. Leaving Carter to sip a coffee outside the arrivals gate, Gracie rented a car, then picked up Carter with a kiss, as if he were just another husband home from a business trip.

"Next stop, New York City, 2,945 miles that way," she said, pointing toward the rising sun. "Good thing we have 3,000 free miles on this thing."

They joined the I-90 East just south of Seattle and stayed on it until they reached Ohio. In between, there was road and food and sleep. Nights saw them stop in towns big enough to permit a couple of pints in a sports bar off the beaten track, where a twenty in the bartender's hand paid for one of the TVs to be switched over from basketball to the St. Patricks game.

While Carter had been on his Pacific island, the St. Patricks had been busy, and Link Andrachuk had risen to the role they always hoped that he would play – a power forward whose natural talent and muscle now combined with the desire to win the Pats their first Cup in four decades.

And win they had, knocking off Toronto in the first round of the playoffs and then taking out Philadelphia. Suddenly, the team that couldn't string together two winning periods was two games up on Birmingham, and if the St. Pats could hold on, they would be, as Freddie Hutt put it one intermission in a Madz Weinfeld feature, "ready to take on the best of the west."

Which would not include the Vancouver Sea Lions, who were well into their golf season, with the team's lawsuit against the St. Pats, right now, in the heat of the playoffs, like an ice chip in front of a puck: not about to do anything except get run over.

Gracie was just as amazed as Carter by the St. Pats' change of fortune. "What do you think happened?"

"I think," said Carter, "that something made Link Andrachuk feel awfully good. And I don't think it's Russian nookie."

"Well, nookie certainly works for Gracie," she whispered into his ear, and the warmth of her breath shot into his brain and flicked the magic switch that was seemingly on a hair trigger. They waltzed off into another night testing the mattress in an interstate motel. Most mornings, they'd awake and pick up where they'd left off the night before, with a desire that was not so much lust as a dance in the face of doom, with both of them aware that the ending might neither be planned, nor happy. It's how sex must be during war, Carter observed to Gracie during an interlude, and she'd said, "Is sex what we're doing?"

Before his damaged brain could answer that, she distracted him with a kiss, and he answered with one, and so it went as they journeyed east, toward the story he would tell her.

Along the way, there was Page Seven of the *New York Mail*, which Carter and Gracie followed daily on her laptop. The gossip column was keeping the tale of Hayley Rawls's murder alive by running a "Sudden Death" contest. Readers could guess the identity of the winning goal scorer in the next St. Pats playoff game to go to sudden death overtime, and the winner would be rewarded with the *Mail*'s implicit idea of justice for Hayley Rawls: a spa weekend at the Mohonk Mountain House ninety miles upstate. And a thousand dollars.

Freddie Hutt had pulled rank as the St. Pats' president and upped the ante, announcing a reward of a hundred thousand dollars for information leading to the arrest and conviction of Hayley's killer.

"What an asshole move," Carter said. "Usually the arrest triggers the reward, but these guys want a conviction, which could take years."

Carter felt good, even though he was heading back toward the scene of the crime. Once, he would have said it was because he was a head case, but now it was because he felt alive. Gracie made him feel clean, as if there were no Kingdoms of Before and After but just the realm of Now. The closer they got to New York City, the better he felt and not from any nostalgia for the life he had left behind, which he saw now hadn't really been a life at all. It had been a habit. Every day was new, but the prospect of getting up in the morning no longer sent him deep under the covers. Now he had no covers on him at all. He wasn't alone, he was part of a couple, and Gracie didn't have anywhere else she'd rather be. For Carter, that was the newest thing of all.

They greeted the last morning of their road trip by testing the spring action of the surprisingly comfortable bed of the Econo Lodge in Bloomsburg, Pennsylvania, about three hours outside of Manhattan.

They lay entangled afterwards in sweaty silence, the boundary of the world no farther than the edge of the bed. Gracie propped herself on his chest, her breasts warm, her blue eyes cool, and said, "We could always go back."

Carter felt the touch of ice on his forehead. Gracie read the sudden change of mood in his eyes.

"We've hit the point of no return," she said. "In the journo biz, when you hit the point of no return, to go past it means you've committed to a story so deeply that you can't stop now. Or else . . . the puppy dies, you know?"

"What are you saying, exactly?"

She ran a finger along his lips. "I'm saying, you don't have to do this."

They'd already been down that road. "I think I do. But what interests me more is why you think I don't? Now."

She lay back on the pillow. "I don't want anything bad to happen to you. I mean, the story doesn't matter nearly as much to me as . . ." she said.

He rolled onto his elbow and looked down at her. "I know, Gracie. Me too. Before, I needed to clear my name. Now, because of you, because of us, I need more than that."

She squeezed his hand. "Me too."

"And anyway, we know how it ends."

"We do?"

"Yeah, the Irish way, everybody dies."

He kissed her gently and whispered, "But not us, not yet."

"Promise?"

"Yeah, I promise. And I have a plan."

48

Part One of Carter's plan was to reach Manhattan after dark. "I used to live just up there," he said, pointing in the direction of Weehawken as they approached the city on the AirTrain from Newark Airport, where they'd dropped the rental car. No need for a car in Manhattan, they agreed, especially one with Washington State plates.

"The room with the view?" Gracie asked.

He smiled and nodded. She remembered his story better than he did.

Part Two was sanctuary with Wanda Collins at the Black Irish, until he could figure out Part Three, which was confronting the world with the truth.

There was the clunk of a lock tumbling, and the heavy metal rear door of the Black Irish opened on Wanda, looking at Carter as if she'd seen everything now.

"Hey," Carter said.

Her eyes moved to Gracie, then back to Carter, then welled up with tears. Carter put his arms around her, and she responded, hugging him as if he were her long-lost first born.

"Cartch," she said between sobs.

"Yeah," he said. "I thought it best not to call first."

She buried her head on his shoulder, then pulled her head back, took a couple of deep breaths, and let him go. She wiped a tear away and took a step back, keeping her eyes on him. She was smiling, but Carter could read something in her eyes that he hadn't seen before.

"I'm sorry about your van," he said, testing. "I'd offer to work as a bartender to pay you back, but Russell the Muscle might object."

She laughed and shook her head. "My van was stolen by thieves, so the insurance company bought me a brand-new one."

Then she held her hand out to Gracie on a smile. "Please excuse the old business. Wanda Collins."

"Gracie Yates. I've heard a lot about you."

Wanda shook her hand. "Come on in and I'll tell you how much of it is true. After, of course" – she shot a glance at Carter – "you tell me about you."

In her office, Wanda poured them each a double shot of Jameson, and with the Gobshites in the bar below them working "Brown Eyed Girl" as if on the spin cycle of an industrial washing machine, Carter told Wanda everything that had happened to him.

About breaking into Hayley's apartment.

About the Maestro taking his company public, and the stock market money riding on the success of the Missing Link project.

About finding the sex footage of Oblomov with Hayley and Link and some mystery man.

About the broken deal with the Sea Lions, and finding Oblomov himself, a speechless, drunk B&E artist.

And now, here he was back in New York, the scene of the crime.

"That's quite a tale, Cartch, but aren't you forgetting someone?" Wanda said at last, her eyes on Gracie.

Carter felt himself blushing, but Gracie calmly stepped into the question.

"I'm a sports reporter for the *Vancouver Gazette*. Carter has offered me his story in exchange for helping him prove his innocence."

"Uh-huh," Wanda said, glancing at the video monitor, which showed the action in the bar. "And how would a member of the media do that?"

Gracie kept her tone even. "Well, all thanks to meeting Martin Carter, I did a little break and entering, a little fugitive hiding, some blackmail, an assault with intent to kill on a Russian hockey star, and there was the little matter of illegal entry into the United States, but mainly I just tutor Carter in the Kama Sutra. And," she added with a nod to her appreciative pupil, "he teaches me a thing or two himself."

Wanda just stared at her, then she started to laugh. Carter laughed too, and so did Gracie, and there they were, just old friends and new having a drink upstairs in the Black Irish on a spring evening. Until Carter said, "So, Wanda, do you mind if we stay here for a couple of nights? To get things sorted?"

Wanda's face contracted. "How are you going to do that, Cartch?"

"Gracie can sleep on the couch, and I'll take the floor."

She didn't smile. Instead, she moved to top up his glass, but he held up his hand. "I'm good."

She glanced at Gracie's glass, which was still healthy, and put the bottle down.

"The thing is, Cartch, you're not. Good, that is. You're now the prime suspect in Hayley's murder, and the other guy's, the super of your building."

Carter's forehead tingled. "I thought I was a 'person of interest.' That's all that anyone has been saying."

"It's not public knowledge." Wanda's eyes flickered, then she shifted her gaze to the video monitor. It seemed to Carter like more than proprietorial vigilance. It seemed that she was expecting someone.

"Wanda, how do you know this?" Carter asked, his voice tense.

She kept her eyes on the monitor. "Don't you think the best idea might be to turn yourself in, let the police sort this out?"

Carter felt his whole face freeze. "Wanda? Are you okay?"

She turned to him with a smile, then walked over to the safe and spun the dial on the lock.

"I'll be right back," she said and made for the door to the bar below. Then she stopped and turned. "By the way, the safe is open."

Carter walked over to the video monitor to see what she was up to. And looking right back at him through the camera above the bar was Detective Lucius Gibson.

"Sonofabitch!" Carter said.

"What?" Gracie was next to him in one swift motion.

"That's Lucius Gibson, NYPD Homicide," he said, watching Gibson turn to Wanda as she came into view.

And then his entire body went cold, from his head down to the feet he should have been running on, as Gibson took Wanda in his arms and kissed her the way you kiss someone you haven't been sleeping with for long.

"He's her boyfriend?"

Carter couldn't speak. Wanda, staring directly at the camera, was sending him a message: She couldn't be his port in the storm because, now, she was part of the storm.

"Carter," Gracie said, grabbing him by the shoulders and trying to turn him to her.

"We have to go," he said, wriggling free.

"Carter?" Gracie said, confused by his change of mood.

"That guy's the cop who thinks I'm the murderer. And you can see he's running a tab here."

Gracie looked back at the video monitor. Wanda was still in Gibson's arms, laughing at something he said.

"We have to go."

He walked over to the safe and slowly swung open the door. Inside were three thick stacks of cash – twenties and fifties. And a gun. Carlito's gun. He looked at the gun, then at the money. He made his choice.

Carter left the cash and took the weapon, unzipping his duffel bag and tucking it in.

"What are you doing?" Gracie enunciated each word slowly as if dealing with a madman.

"I can't leave this thing here," he said. "She's letting me get a head start."

"A head start? To where?"

"This gun belonged to Carlito, the super of my building. I grabbed it when I ran out of my burning apartment, with Carlito lying dead on my floor. I was scared, it was instinct. Then when I made my run for Canada, I left it here. Now I have to take it because Wanda's involved with the cop, and she left the safe open to tell me that."

Gracie searched his face for the blemish of a lie. He raised his hands in surrender.

"Okay," she said, glancing at the video monitor, where Wanda was now behind the bar, tossing a lime into a glass of soda water for Gibson. "But maybe Wanda is right. Maybe you should turn yourself in."

Carter lowered his hands. This was the point of no return. "You don't have to come with me," he said.

"I know. It was a stupid idea."

Carter waited for a lethal thrust of the knife to his heart. But then she smiled and said, "I'm sorry, I should know better."

What could he say? Come with me over the edge of the abyss?

Carter took a deep breath. "I love you," he told her for the first time. Then he walked to the stairway leading to the alley. He wasn't going to look back, but then he felt Gracie's hand in his, and he turned. Her blue eyes were almost black now, her pupils were so dilated.

"Let's go," was all she said, squeezing his hand. And so they began their descent.

49

Gracie and Carter sat next to each other on the 1 train uptown, his arm draped around her like they were heading home to bed after a night on the town. They were listening to a young black guy in a hoodie and shades who got on at Columbus Circle and was playing "Somewhere Over the Rainbow" on his tenor sax with such faith that Carter gave the kid ten bucks.

They had walked a block away from the Black Irish in a silence matching the chill of the night before she asked, "Where are we going to go?"

There was only one place that Carter could think of that wasn't public, where he might just be able to bargain a welcome: Madz Weinfeld's.

"No!" Gracie said, aware of the cost.

"It was always part of my plan," he replied, buffeted by the wind whipping off the Hudson River behind him. "Just sooner than I thought."

"Well you should have told me!" she said, stopping dead. He walked back toward her. "Gracie, please," he said as calmly as he could, fully expecting Lucius Gibson to round the corner and collar him.

She didn't budge. "Why didn't you tell me?"

"I'm telling you now."

"And you think that's okay?"

The gusting wind buffered her words, but not their truth. It wasn't okay. Gracie had come a long way with him, but the prospect of sharing his story with another journalist was a step too far for her.

"Look, Gracie, I know what I need to do."

There was nothing more he could say. He turned and started walking, the wind stinging his eyes.

"Hey!" she said, grabbing his arm and spinning him with surprising force. "You can't walk away from me."

"I'm not walking away from you. I'm just going on my way. I want you to come with me, but I can't make you."

She let go of his arm and took a breath. "Then I need a guarantee."

"I just told you I love you."

"This is not a joke!" she yelled over the wind. "I'm in this up to my eyeballs, whether or not you –" She stopped.

"Whether or not I what? Whether or not I killed her?"

She moved closer to him, her face soft now. "No," she said, "whether or not you love me."

Her words ambushed his own roiling emotions. He held her shoulders and gently pulled her close. Her arms stayed loose by her side. Then he kissed her softly on her forehead, on her cheek, on her lips. She pulled away.

"I love you too," she said. "And that will have to do. For the time being."

The wind had calmed by the time they rose out of the subway at 125th and Broadway and walked west toward the Hudson River.

"So this is Harlem," said Gracie, looking around at the buildings and people as if in another country.

"Yes. Great food up here" – they were passing a Pizza Shack – "if you look for it."

"But she's not black."

"No."

"Why does she live up here?"

"Because lots of gay people bought brownstones up here at bargain prices – for this city – in the 1990s and restored them. Madz hasn't got around to the restoration part yet."

A few minutes later, they stopped in front of a house with

a cracked facade, blistered paint on its wrought-iron railings.

"What's wrong?" Gracie asked, sensing his hesitation.

"Hayley Rawls died in a house like this. In Brooklyn."

"Whose house?"

"Someone with money. It had a new facade, and those aren't cheap."

She gave him her reporter look. "You remember the address?"

He shook his head. He didn't remember it. Just everything else.

"What are you going to tell Madz about us?" Gracie said.

"I'll tell her the truth," he said. "I guarantee it." Then he walked up the stairs and rang the bell, just below the filigreed mezuzah.

After about half a minute of standing in the cold spring air, Gracie said, "Maybe she went out." She winked. "Maybe the hang-up call scared her."

Carter had called Madz from a payphone at the subway station and hung up when she answered. He rang the bell again, and seconds later the hallway light came on. Carter heard footsteps, then saw the peephole darken as someone looked through it. He heard a gasp, then the thud of a large woman falling down, then running footsteps. A woman yelled, "Baby, what happened?"

The door opened a minute later, and there was Madz, leaning on Dr. Bobbi Washington, the woman Carter had last seen at St. Mel's Hospital. They were barefoot, in bathrobes, ready for bed.

Madz's hazel eyes burned into Carter. "You bastard," she rasped. "You goddamn bastard." She was shaking, but even so, she looked like she was going to hit him.

"I know," he said. "I'm sorry."

"I thought you were dead!" Madz shouted.

"It was for your own safety," Carter said, trying not to shout himself."

"Well thanks for fucking thinking of me," she said, tears streaming down her face.

"What do you want?" Bobbi Washington wasn't the sentimental type.

"We – this is my friend Gracie Yates – would like to come in. We're on the run from the law. And some others."

Bobbi put her arm around Madz. "Come on, baby, you don't need this."

Carter put his foot in the door, in case Bobbi felt like slamming it on him. "I'm sorry, Madz, I really am. I'll explain everything." Then he took aim at her reporter's heart. "Don't you want to hear my side of the story?"

Madz shook her head, and Carter thought he'd blown it. But then came a sly smile, and she started to pull the door open. Bobbi Washington stuck a slippered foot in the way.

"Bad idea, babe."

"Yeah," said Madz, "it probably is."

Bobbi stepped between the door and Carter. "I think you should go. Now."

Madz put a hand on Bobbi's shoulder. "You moving in, sweetie?"

Bobbi turned to her. "What are you talking about?"

"Exactly. Until you do, it's my house."

Then Madz glowered at Carter, and Gracie. "This story better be good, or true," she said and, with a flourish, opened the door wide. "Even better if it's both."

50

They sat in Madz's parlour, a room that, with its copper ceiling and red walls, could have been a Harlem bordello. Madz had poured whiskey for herself, while Carter and Gracie stuck to sparkling water. Bobbi sat without a drink underneath the Tiffany floor lamp, her legs curled up beneath her and her eyes vigilant.

"So, Cartch," Madz said, "begin at the beginning and go on until the end and then we'll see if you can stop."

Gracie shot Carter a cautionary look, and he blinked back reassuringly. They were a team. He wouldn't let her down.

"When I realized that everyone thought I was dead," he said, "I used the time wisely."

"That must have been a new experience."

"There have been a few of them lately. For instance, the cops think that I killed Hayley, and the super of my building, Carlito."

"They're not alone," Bobbi said.

Carter thought his best move was to give her a role in the tale – other than as his executioner. "Why was Sasha Oblomov under police guard at your hospital?"

She stared at him and said nothing.

"The reason I ask," he continued, smiling at her now, "is that he seemed pretty free to come and go when he was in hospital in Vancouver." She rolled her eyes, but he held up a hand. "The guy was alive and kicking. Literally. He just walked out of the hospital, took a ferry to Bowen Island, and broke into Gracie's house in the middle of the night."

"Why'd he do that?" Madz asked, and Carter could see her nostrils twitch at the smell of new blood.

"My question first," Carter said.

Bobbi sighed. "Look, all I know about your mess is that there was police protection for Oblomov because the New York St. Pats asked for it."

Why would the St. Pats want to protect Oblomov? Unless putting cops outside Oblomov's door was just a smokescreen. Carter remembered the Cardinal saying that he had friends in the NYPD, and saying it in a way that sounded like he could make them do anything he wanted. Even set Carter up for a murder rap.

"What are you thinking, Cartch? That the Cardinal did it?"

Madz's tone was joking, but Carter knew she wasn't. So he laughed. "Yeah, that's it. He thought Link would show up and try to finish the job." He turned back to Bobbi. "Do you know who came to visit Oblomov while he was in your hospital?"

"I'm a doctor, not a concierge." Her tone was icy.

"Can you find out?"

Bobbi stared at him, but Madz came to his aid. "That would be good to know," she said. "Given what you just said."

"He had a grade-three concussion and his tongue was nearly severed. He had lost a lot of blood, was in an induced coma that we couldn't get him out of, and he flatlined twice. I don't think he was holding court. But then he woke up one morning, his vitals were back to normal, and aside from the post-concussive state he was in, he was fine. That's when they moved him back to Vancouver."

"Sounds like a miracle," Gracie said, and they all looked at her. "They do happen," she added.

"I'd agree with that," Madz said, topping up her glass, "as far as Cartch is concerned."

"There are some things we can't explain," Bobbi replied coolly, her eyes on Madz's half-full tumbler. "You can call them whatever you like. But I thought the whole point of this social call," she said, glaring now at Carter, "was to explain."

Carter felt the heat in his cheeks. If she wanted to drop the gloves with him, this was not the night to do it. Gracie read his face. "He's doing his best," she said, "but the story is mine."

Carter's face flushed deeper. They needed a safe place for the night, not a fight about exclusive story rights to what could still, for him, be a tale told posthumously.

"Let's see," Madz said. "My old pal Cartch here disappears from the planet, first in a fire, then on the lam, then he shows up on my doorstep with a reporter in tow, offering to tell his story, if I let him in. But I already gave him a hundred K for the story, and I still don't have it. So right now, I'd say, not only is the story mine, it's in debt."

"Oh, I think it's the other way around," Gracie said, tapping her hand high up on Carter's thigh. "And I have an advantage."

"Please, ladies," Carter said, holding up his hands. "This will all work out if we work together. I promise."

The moment simmered, with Bobbi sending eye telegraphs to Madz, and Madz smiling tightly at Gracie, and then at Carter, and Carter trying to show the beatific face of reason.

Madz broke the silence. "With platitudes like that, Cartch, you could coach the Pats."

Carter smiled in gratitude at Madz for turning the talk back to hockey. "It looks like they're doing okay without me."

"They're in the Cup final. And the only person more a-fucking-stonished than yours truly is the Patsie who wakes up from a forty-year coma five minutes before game time."

Carter laughed, and Madz turned the moment into the kind of truce she knew best. "You want another water or maybe something stronger?" she asked Gracie.

"Thank you. I'd love a beer."

"Hey, least I can do for a teammate, huh?"

It seemed the two women had agreed to keep their professional rivalry over Carter and his story on a leash. For the moment.

Bobbi Washington, though, was a problem. She was still glaring at Carter as if he were a rival for Madz's love, and in a way, he was. He was counting on her loyalty to him and the promise of his story to help him get the rest of it. He hadn't counted on Bobbi Washington being part of the mix, and now he had to find a way to keep Madz's lover from calling the NYPD and turning him in.

"When I saw Oblomov, he was like a zombie. Couldn't talk because of his tongue – he was still pretty badly concussed. But you say he was fine when he left."

"Relatively speaking." She paused, then added, "I advised against the transfer. But the St. Patricks insisted."

Carter blinked. "Wait a minute, the St. Patricks? I thought they had him under armed guard?"

"They wanted him gone as soon as he started to improve. I heard it straight from the horse's mouth."

"The Cardinal?"

"No, the southern guy, Hutt. The one who always looked at me like he's seen me somewhere before, dangling from a noose."

Carter laughed, partly in astonishment, partly in admiration for her acumen. "He looks the same way at me – but in my case he's projecting the future."

And Bobbi Washington smiled back at him. At least they agreed on something.

Madz returned with Gracie's beer. "My theory," she said, pouring the beer into Gracie's glass, "is that the St. Pats didn't want the evidence anywhere near the New York people's

court, which would be us, the media. That's why they had
the cops guarding him, just until his brain wouldn't explode
at thirty-five thousand feet when they shipped him out."

"You know, the rumour was that Oblomov had some connection to the Russian mob," Gracie said.

"Yeah, and that he was into them for quite a bit of gambling debt. Couldn't find anything on it. I think the Russkies
put that one out themselves to scare off the wrong kind
of groupies."

Gracie grinned. "Speaking of Russians, do you know anything about this Russian billionaire – Alexei Felixsovich
Petrov – whose daughter is dating the Missing Link?"

Madz snorted. "Yeah, she's dating him the way I'm dating
you. We're currently seen in each other's company."

"How do you know?" Carter asked. If the Cardinal was
selling the team to the Russian, then having his star player
squire the czar's daughter around Manhattan would be good
for the sale price.

"Because she plays for my team."

"Really?" Bobbi Washington was interested now. "How do
you know that?"

"Calm down, babe. I'm a reporter. And I go to dyke bars
when you're working." Madz winked at Gracie. "You should
try it."

"Maybe in my next life."

"When you've evolved," Bobbi said.

"Anyway," said Madz, leaning back in her chair and
twirling a strand of her suicide blond hair, "let's get back to
our favourite Russian. Remind me what Oblomov was doing
breaking into your house?"

"He wanted some footage we had," Carter said. "Of him
having sex with Hayley Rawls."

Madz let loose a low whistle. "The dead lady got around. And how, might I ask, did you come to have this footage?"

"I broke into Hayley Rawls's apartment and stole her hard drive."

"*We* broke in," Gracie corrected.

"We did," Carter said. "We were looking for the footage of what Link did to Oblomov – I thought she might have emailed it to herself."

"Yeah, that's what I would have done, Cartch. But it wasn't there, was it?"

"No, it wasn't."

"So, do you have Plan X, or Y, or fucking Z?"

"I do. It's a plan in progress."

"In other words . . ."

Carter put down his glass and leaned forward. "Hayley Rawls was working for a guy named Erik Shepherd. He has a company called Maestro Media, which he is planning to take public."

"Issue stock," Madz said knowingly to Bobbi.

"And from what we found out on Hayley's hard drive, he is going to do that here."

Madz thought about that. "Lotta media companies in Manhattan. I mean, what's so special about his that his stock would be worth killing for?"

Carter smiled at Gracie, then at Madz. "That's Plan Z. That's what we're going to ask him . . ."

51

"After we come thousands of miles you're letting her bust the Maestro? What the hell are you thinking?" Gracie stood with her back to the door in Madz's guest room, her arms folded.

"It's not what's going to happen," Carter said, regretting it the instant he spoke.

"So you're lying to her? Or to me? Or to both of us?" He opened his mouth to speak, but she was on a roll. "There's a hundred thousand dollars I didn't know about, and the promise she gets your exclusive story. Which, oddly enough, is the same promise you made to me. But hey, now that you've told her everything . . ."

"Almost everything . . ."

She opened her mouth to yell at him but stopped. There were ears on the other side of the door.

"Please, Gracie, I can explain," Carter said, realizing how lame it sounded. "We don't need to do this."

"Do what? Tell the fucking truth?"

It was the first time he'd heard her curse, and it shocked him into a sense of the future. He could lose her depending on what he said next.

"I'm trying to find the truth. I mean, I know some of it, but we're going to find the rest. And only we know the whole story."

It only made her more angry. "For all I know, Wanda's in on it too."

And that made him angry, but he turned away. Just like he used to when he got a hot, stinking glove in the face or a stinging chop in the calves from a screened goalie. But this was no game.

He sat down on the hard futon that passed for a bed in this room. "Everything I told you is true," he said softly. "When you started to help me, you wanted something. So I told you that you could have my story. Yes, I'd also told Madz the same thing, but that was before I'd met you and realized that the story had changed. A lot, thanks to your help. And now . . ."

She didn't move. Carter realized she was breathing hard and trying not to show it. He wanted to kiss her, but he didn't think she'd let him. He had dug his own grave. "Please, Gracie. Sit down, and let's talk about this."

She coughed up a short, bitter laugh. "Talk about what, Carter? You made me a promise. And right now, I'm too tired to trust myself to talk to you."

And then she was gone.

Carter slumped back on the futon and allowed himself a moment of self-pity. He had to connect the Maestro, Link, and the footage to Hayley's death, get a confession out of one of them, escape with his life, and then prove his innocence to the NYPD. And not lose Gracie in the process. Nothing to it. And now that Madz was back on the case, he needed to keep her happy too.

He walked carefully down the stairs in the dark, placing his feet at the side of the treads, just like he did at his mother's house, and checked the kitchen. Maybe Gracie was having a beer to cool down – or to stoke the flames – but no. So he moved on toward the parlour, softly calling her name. Nothing.

He stood in the front hallway, the street light spilling the red and purple and gold of the stained-glass transom on his white shirt. Blood and bruises.

Fuck, thought Carter. Surely she hasn't gone for a midnight stroll in Harlem?

He opened the door. She wasn't on the stoop. He looked up the street and down it. Nothing but parked cars and blowing garbage. The wind had picked up again. He noticed a guy sitting in a Lincoln Town Car across the street and down. A chauffeur having a snooze. Harlem had changed. Back to what it once was.

He stepped outside to let the river wind blow his hair. Clear his head, if not his head case.

He never heard the footsteps from behind.

"Well, well, fancy meeting you here," Detective Lucius Gibson said, smiling like a long-lost friend.

Carter reached for the door handle and Gibson reached for his gun. "I wouldn't do that."

Carter let go of the door.

Gibson smiled and gestured for Carter to come down the stairs. He did.

"Thank you. See, if you'd gone inside, I'd have had to come back with a warrant."

"You mean I'm not under arrest?" Carter's voice was tight and dry.

"That depends," Gibson replied, "on what happens next."

52

The only time Carter had seen the inside of an NYPD precinct house before was on TV, and this one, the 76th on Union Street in Brooklyn, looked similar, only less cluttered. It smelled of air freshener mixed with the perfume of sweat and coffee and crime.

Carter sat behind a laminated table in a tiny interview room, its only window a small rectangle in the metal door, where every twenty minutes or so for the past hour, someone would peek in.

Gibson said he'd be back soon, but that was a long time ago now. Carter avoided looking at himself in the two-way mirror on the wall to his right. He felt strangely calm, considering he might have just had his last breath of freedom. And that Gracie had vanished.

Madz wouldn't wonder where he was until he failed to appear at breakfast. She'd make some calls, and then they'd know. Unless he got a chance to call her first, but that was looking as unlikely as Detective Lucius Gibson coming back any time soon.

He was letting Carter think about things, and Carter knew that game plan all too well. Once you get inside your own head, and start second- and third-guessing, then the other team has you working for them.

A man who is unafraid of silence, Gibson had been like the other half of a bad date on the ride to Brooklyn. But then, Carter also knew the power of staying quiet. So he waited silently in the interview room, as relaxed as possible on the hard metal chair, presenting a bland expression to the mirror. And when Gibson returned fifteen minutes later, a sergeant in tow, Carter smiled at him as if he'd rather be nowhere else.

"You're still here," Gibson deadpanned as he closed the door, a manila file folder in one hand. The sergeant leaned back against the wall by the door, and Gibson crossed to the table, pulling out the only other chair with a screech.

"I am," Carter said. "If we make this quick, we can have a nightcap at the Black Irish."

Gibson didn't react. He switched on the video recorder, then sat, calm and unblinking. He must sleep well, Carter thought. Helped along by vats of Irish whiskey.

"Wanda Collins," Gibson said, "is not the reason you're here. We've been waiting for you."

Carter blushed. Gibson had read his fear that Wanda had shopped him.

"No," Carter recovered. "I was just thinking of a place I'd rather be."

Gibson nodded, then opened and closed the file.

"Hayley Rawls. Carlito Parque. Both murdered. Both connected to you."

Carter winced. That was the first time Carter had heard Carlito's surname, or even thought that he had one.

"I didn't kill them."

"Great, then we're done here." Gibson stood and walked to the door. But he didn't switch off the video recorder.

"Where are you going?" Carter didn't want to play this game, but now he had no choice.

"Home," Gibson said. "It's been a long day."

"Look, Detective Gibson, I'm sorry," Carter said and meant it. "I'm not trying to be funny. I've never been in this situation, so I need your help. Please."

Gibson came back to the table, but he didn't sit, making it clear that he wasn't going to hang around if Carter didn't co-operate.

Carter told him almost everything, from the moment he met Hayley Rawls. He thought he'd work up to the moment in which they now found themselves, leaving out a couple of things that Gibson didn't need to know yet.

He had just reached the point where Hayley had shown him the footage of Link Andrachuk's assault on Sasha Oblomov when Gibson interrupted.

"You forgot the bit about me hitting on her in the Black Irish."

Carter took this as a reminder that the cop was in on this story early.

"Right," Carter said. "I didn't want to —"

"Hurt my feelings?"

"No, hurt Wanda's."

Gibson's smile faded, but he sat back down. "Keep going."

So Carter did. He told Gibson about the damning footage of Link's assault on Oblomov, about the Cardinal's plans to sell the team, and the need to make a good run in the playoffs.

Gibson nodded. "It's been great. Andrachuk has become a new man in the playoffs."

"You follow hockey?"

"I've been a Patsie since I was a kid. Waited a long time for a Cup final."

Carter felt a flood of relief. Gibson was a genuine fan and maybe Irish himself, if he had not given up on the St. Pats during all those dry years.

"That's why I was in the Black Irish that night," Gibson continued. "I'd been to the game."

Carter's pulse picked up. "Did you by any chance see what Link did to Oblomov?"

"Gibson shook his head. "Wish I had but glad I didn't. I'd have to arrest the bast–, the man."

"You're not a fan of Link either, huh?"

Gibson stared at him for a beat, recovering command of the room. "We were talking about you."

So Carter resumed his story, telling Gibson about checking out his apartment with Carlito after the super had seen the St. Patricks' head of security there. About Carlito being killed by the computer rigged to kill Carter. And then about his escape to Canada and his partnership with Gracie Yates. He didn't tell him about what he and Gracie had found.

Gibson sat back, hands clasped behind his neck, his eyes sweeping across the ceiling as Carter spoke.

"The thing I can't quite get," he said softly, "is why you

came back. We'd never have been able to pry you out of Canada. Least not in my lifetime."

"I came back because I'm not guilty," Carter replied. "But I couldn't prove my innocence three thousand miles away."

The steel door to the interview room rattled with a perfunctory knock, and a uniformed cop stuck her head in. "Sorry to interrupt, Detective Gibson, but his attorney is here."

Gibson shot Carter a suspicious look. "How can your attorney be here?"

"You didn't call one for me?"

"What do you think this is? The Sisters of Charity?" He turned to the cop at the door. "Send him in."

"It's a she, sir."

Carter knew who would be walking though the door. Who else would it be? Gibson read his look. "You okay?"

"Don't say anything, Mr. Carter." Flavia entered the room as if it were hers.

"Counsellor?" Gibson said, offering his hand.

"Detective," Flavia replied, handing him her card and giving his hand a brief pump. She didn't look as if she'd been hauled out of bed. In her black leather blazer and jeans, she looked like this was an inconvenient pit stop between clubs. One that she was going to keep brief.

"What are the charges, detective?"

"No charges yet, counsellor. Just some questions."

"Are you planning to charge him?"

"Well, that would depend on the answers to my questions," Gibson said, looking around for a non-existent seat. "Let me get you a chair."

"Thank you, detective, but that won't be necessary. The answers are finished for tonight. Let's go, Mr. Carter."

53

"Well, Cartch, I didn't quite expect to see you back in a place like this," Flavia said with a professional smile that jarred with the use of his nickname. She was playing to a jury that only she could see.

They were standing on Union Street, the sky a jaundiced black from the city lights. Flavia had hustled him out of the police station fast "because the walls have ears."

"Where did you expect to see me?"

She fished a keyless remote out of her pocket and the doors on a black Mercedes sports car parked opposite swung up, like wings.

"Makes for an easy entry – and escape," she said. "And it's got no strings attached. It's leased."

"You didn't answer my question."

"To tell the truth, Cartch, I never expected to see you again. In person."

She smiled at him this time, and not to the jury.

He did not smile back. "So who sent you?"

"Who do you think?" She said – back in the courtroom – and walked toward her car.

"I'm not a psychic."

"No, you're not, or you wouldn't have come back here." She gestured for him to get in. "In any case, why spoil the surprise?"

He stood his ground and reached in his pockets, but his wallet was in his jacket and his jacket was in Harlem. He had no money, no phone, and a long walk north through a hostile city.

"Cartch, I just walked into a police station and got you out. I'm not going to put you in harm's way."

He got into the car.

Flavia paid no attention to the speed limit as she let the powerful Merc rip south down Hicks Street and then along the I-478. She put the top down and turned the CD player on. Freeway wind and Mozart. They made conversation impossible.

Who had sent her? he wondered. Who would know to send her? Madz and Gracie had no idea he'd been scooped up by Gibson. And Wanda had no idea he was at Madz's house, unless she was the psychic. Or Gibson had been lying.

That left Bobbi Washington. She would have met Gibson in the hospital when he'd gone to check in on Oblomov. She'd have taken his card and promised to call him if anything cropped up. But no, she wouldn't want to risk a breach with Madz, and the story Madz hoped to tell.

And Flavia had arrived just as he was telling some of that story to Detective Lucius Gibson. Just in time – for someone not in that room.

He looked over at her, staring straight ahead at the open road in front of them, her red hair a little longer now and buffeted by the eighty-mile-an-hour wind. "Flavia," Carter said, and she angled her head toward him, as if he had a confession.

"Where are we going?"

"Don't worry. We're almost there."

She turned up the volume on the Mozart aria from *Don Giovanni*. Carter remembered seeing the opera with her one Saturday afternoon: another pact with the devil. It had been their last Saturday together, though he hadn't known it at the time. Maybe it was a goodbye now too. Or maybe this, too, was a pact with the devil, should Carter be able to spot him in such a competitive crowd.

Flavia took the exit for the Brooklyn-Battery Tunnel. They were going downtown. Link Andrachuk lived downtown. Was she going to wake Link up on the eve of the St. Pats' first Cup final in forty years so he could chat with Carter? Only if Flavia had hit her head too.

They emerged from the tunnel deep in the Financial District, and five minutes later, Flavia parked the Merc in front of a greystone Neo-Gothic mansion, the kind that pops out of the shadows all over Manhattan. The Stars and Stripes hung from a flagpole above a red-carpeted entrance. "Here we are," she said.

"Where is here?"

A valet emerged from the lobby and smiled at them as if it weren't nearly 4 a.m.

"It's okay," Flavia said to him. "I'm not staying."

She flicked a toggle switch and the passenger door rose up, part science fiction, part cartoon.

"What do you mean you're not staying?" Carter said.

"I'm just the delivery girl, Cartch. And I've delivered you." She put her hand on his arm. Once, it would have meant the world. Now, it was a warning. "The rest is between you and him. He's expecting you. Just tell the concierge who you are."

Where was the woman he had loved? When had she become what he saw now: a woman in the service of no one but herself.

"Take this," she said, offering him a hundred-dollar bill, "to get wherever you're going next."

He gave her such a cold, killer smile that she pulled the money back as if shocked, then he turned and walked into the New York Club, as the discreet plaque fastened to the granite proclaimed.

He'd never heard of it, but it sounded like the kind of place where the Cardinal might be a member. Though why would the dying Cardinal be here in the middle of the night?

"He's expecting you in the Kennedy Room," the concierge

said when he introduced himself. "Take the elevator to the fourth floor and follow the sign."

Carter did so and found himself in a vaulted and chandeliered room decorated with photographs of New York's sporting history. Sitting at an antique poker table in front of a bone china tea service was Doug Bleecker.

"Hello, Cartch? Please?" Bleecker said, the question a command, gesturing for him to sit opposite in a leather wingback chair.

"Hello, Doug." If Bleecker was in business with Flavia, Carter was in more trouble than he knew. He kept his tone light.

A waiter appeared from out of nowhere.

"Drink?" Bleecker said.

"A big glass of water and a big glass of Jameson's, please," Carter said, and the waiter bowed, then disappeared.

Carter stared at Bleecker, who stared back at him, lizard-like, his head still too small for his body.

"Tell me, Doug," Carter said.

Bleecker blinked. "It's a bit unusual, I know. But I live here. Quirk of my inheritance that the family trust paid for me to live in this club."

"Tough luck, huh?"

He nodded. "It is, actually. That's all they paid for. If I don't live here, the money dries up."

"Why is that?"

"Because I'm a bastard."

Carter grinned. "What, your father, the duke, knocked up a scullery maid in 1850?"

Bleecker grimaced. "I know, but my father is very Old World."

The waiter returned with a glass of water and a whiskey for Carter.

Bleecker raised a china cup. "Here's to the New World."
Carter raised his glass but didn't drink.

"Why did Flavia bring me here?"

"I called her after the police called me."

"The cops called you?"

Bleecker nodded. "I asked Detective Gibson to reach out if you were to reappear."

"And why the fuck would you do that?"

Bleecker winced at Carter's language. "You're in trouble, Cartch. And I can help you out."

"As I recall, Doug, you were the one who got me into trouble."

"No, Cartch, that was your rather teenaged sexual appetite."

Carter wanted to punch him in the middle of his pinhead. He took a long drink of water and said, "Why am I here?"

"Well, you can help me out. Give me Ms. Rawls's footage and I can smooth things over."

Which footage did Bleecker think he had? Hayley's sex tape was his leverage, his card to play, but there was no way that Bleecker could know about that, unless he was the shadowy figure in the mirror. And he wasn't. Carter would recognize his pear-shaped body under a suit of armour, let alone naked and ready for fun. So Bleecker must be talking about the footage of Link's attack on Oblomov. Which meant that the St. Pats didn't have it. Or that they wanted all outstanding copies.

"Smooth things over how?" Carter said. "Bearing in mind they've been pretty fucking rough."

"Please, Cartch, watch your language."

Carter laughed. "Watch my language? Two people have been murdered because of this fucking footage, and I'm next on the list. Watching my back is what I'm doing, and what you'll be doing in about ten seconds if you don't tell me what's up."

"How much do you want?" Bleecker sounded cool, in control, but Carter could see that he was scared. The head case had the advantage.

"How much do I want for it? Hmm. Well, how about stop trying to kill me, for starters?"

"I had nothing to do with that," Bleecker replied.

"Who did?"

"Cartch," he sighed, "you know that Mr. O'Connor wants to sell the team. That footage, if made public, could seriously devalue the asset. Among other things."

"I haven't made it public."

"That's why we – I – think you're a reasonable man?"

Carter pondered the slip. The cops had called Bleecker and he had called Flavia. But she wasn't the team's lawyer. Then again, he'd met her at a St. Pats-sponsored function for the Special Olympics. She must have some old monied family connection to Bleecker. It couldn't be sexual, could it? But she had bailed out. She didn't want to know what was coming next. Or maybe she already knew and was just playing that lawyer's card of being above the game they were cashing in on.

"What makes you think I have this footage?" he asked

"C'mon, Cartch. Would you have come back here if you didn't?"

He might be a head case, but he wasn't suicidal. He smiled and nodded. "If I give you this footage, what guarantee do I have that I won't wind up dead?"

Bleecker's eyes flickered. "Because if we pay you a hundred thousand dollars for it, it would look awfully bad if we then killed you."

"That's reassuring. Who would pay me a hundred grand?"

"The New York St. Patricks. Who else?"

True, they were flush with playoff cash, and if they won the Cup, they'd be that much richer.

"And the Cardinal has signed off on this?"

Bleecker nodded. "And all of this goes away."

Carter drained his whiskey. "Me too."

"C'mon, Cartch . . ." Bleecker wasn't being cool. He was begging.

"Doug, I've had a long night. And as you can see, I don't have what you want in my pockets. We'll talk soon."

"But it's our first home game in the finals tomorrow night. I mean, tonight."

"Yeah," said Carter, with a tight smile. "That's what I'm thinking too. I'll know where to find you."

54

Carter made his way up Broadway, the light from the rising sun slicing across Manhattan, shifting the sky from deep purple to baby blue. Penniless, Carter had walked sixty blocks, and he still didn't have anything figured out, though he did know that, as a person of interest to the police, trying to hop a subway turnstile was not among his options.

Bleecker suddenly wanted to do a deal with him. But he didn't know what Carter knew. Or did he? Was that the reason behind this sudden "let's be reasonable" stance? Or was Bleecker just fishing to see what Carter really had, confident now that the NYPD and the courts would do the rest, making certain that no embarrassing videos were played as evidence at his trial?

Either way, he was in more danger now than he'd been

when he first set foot back in town. Bleecker and his cohort still thought Carter had what they needed. If Bleecker wasn't part of the plot to kill him, then whoever was would want to make sure Carter was dead before he could sell anything.

Carter just hoped, as he reached Central Park West and 72nd Street, that the one man who could answer a hard question wasn't dead too.

The Latino concierge on duty in the Cardinal's building looked at Carter as if he were a street person off his meds. His dress shirt was wet with sweat from his brisk, hour-long walk from Wall Street, and he hadn't shaved or slept in twenty-four hours. He'd look at himself that way too.

"Please, sir," Carter said with the sanest smile he could muster, "just call him and tell him Martin Carter is here. Martin Carter from the New York St. Patricks."

"I need some ID, sir."

Carter knew that what the guy really needed was to keep his job. Or else he'd be bounced back to his Central American hellhole and his family would go hungry.

"I have no identification on me except my face and my voice. If you just call him and tell him to turn on the security channel on his television, that will be enough. And I won't forget it."

The concierge shrugged.

"Please, sir. It's a matter of great importance."

The concierge picked up the phone.

A woman answered. Carter could hear her voice. And her reaction when she heard his name. "What the fuck's he doing here?"

It was Brenda, the St. Patricks' receptionist.

The concierge gave Carter a wary look. "She wants to know your business, sir."

Carter held out his hand for the phone. The concierge thought about it for a second, then handed it over. He knew what could befall the messenger.

"Brenda, I need to see the Cardinal."

"It's six-thirty in the morning! I'm calling the police!"

"Detective Lucius Gibson is the guy you want. And I've come here so he won't."

There was a pause, and then the Cardinal wheezed, "Cartch. Come on up."

Carter handed the phone back to the concierge, and the Cardinal repeated the invitation.

"It's the penthouse elevator, sir," the concierge said, as if Carter had suddenly become a prince visiting a king. Carter knew that he came more as a court jester. Daring to tell the truth to the mighty.

He stepped off the elevator. Brenda was waiting, the guard dog at the Cardinal's door.

"What the fuck are you doing here?" she asked again.

"Nice to see you too, Brenda," Carter replied calmly and walked past her into the apartment.

It smelled of ebbing life, musty and sour. And it was dark, the curtains closed, a sliver of light spilling into the hallway. Carter followed it into the parlour, and there sat the Cardinal in a wheelchair, the tubes from an oxygen tank running up his nose, an IV stuck in his bony arm. He was so thin and yellow that he looked like he'd been exhumed the day after burial.

"Cartch," he rasped, lifting his hand, with effort, just an inch off the wheelchair handle.

"He's trouble, sir," Brenda said, charging in behind Carter. "I'll get rid of him."

The Cardinal raised his hand again. "No, you won't," he said, and she recoiled as if he'd slapped her hard.

"Mr. O'Connor, I need to speak to you," Carter said quietly, all of his anger distilled into pity for the last of this man in front of him – even if he had tried to kill him. "I won't take long."

The Cardinal grimaced. "Take as long as you like," he wheezed. "Can't guarantee I'll be here at the end."

He beckoned Carter to sit opposite him on the antique sofa.

"Coffee," he commanded Brenda. "And the juice."

Brenda gave him a grim nod, then vanished to fill the order.

"She's my deathline," the Cardinal said. "Volunteered for the job."

Carter felt the touch of death on himself with that thought. You alone may be dying, he realized, but you can't control your audience.

"Mr. O'Connor, I was just arrested by the NYPD, then rescued by a lawyer sent by Doug Bleecker, who offered me a hundred thousand dollars for the footage of Link's attack, an offer he said you have signed off on."

The Cardinal's eyes clouded with confusion. Carter had seen morphine work on his father, and when the doctors had finally told him he had three weeks to live, his father's eyes had lit up with the clarity of fatal despair. You can't fool a man on morphine.

"You didn't know about this?" Carter said.

The Cardinal's eye shifted to Brenda, who had returned with a tray bearing two glasses, a bowl of ice, and a bottle of Connemara, – and placed it on the marble coffee table.

"You can go," the Cardinal said, and she gave him a puzzled look. "I'll call if I need you."

She opened her mouth to speak, but the look in his eye shut her up.

The Cardinal pointed to the whiskey. "Do you mind? I can't quite get there myself."

Carter rose and poured the Cardinal a double shot, then dropped in an ice cube. He handed the glass to the Cardinal.

"My oncologist says I shouldn't drink this stuff," he said, then took a slow sip, his eyes closed. "I try to limit myself to a bottle a week. Have some."

Carter laughed and poured a shot for himself, remembering the last time he had it. Here. When all this began.

"I didn't know about Bleecker's offer, Cartch," the Cardinal said, cradling the cup in his trembling hands. "And I didn't know you had the footage . . ."

"So it wasn't you who was trying to kill me?"

The Cardinal pushed a button connected to the IV drip and closed his eyes as the morphine cascaded down his vein. "Whiskey helps," he said, "but this is to die for."

Carter knew all about the magic button. In his father's last days, whenever a pain surge shocked him, he'd fumble for the button that would send him under, to sleep. If he dreamt anything, he never said.

"Do you dream with that stuff?" Carter said.

The Cardinal opened his eyes. "It's all a dream, Cartch, when you're dying." He took a breath. "And no, I didn't try to kill you. I wanted to thank you. I thought I'd never get the chance."

"Thank me? For what?"

The Cardinal took another sip of Connemara and closed his eyes again. Carter thought he'd gone to sleep, but then he said, "When they told me they were going to destroy the footage, I laughed," he said. "Don't you know matter can't be destroyed? Only rearranged."

"Destroy what footage?"

The Cardinal looked at him as if Carter was playing havoc with an old and dying man.

"You mean, they had the footage of Link's attack on Oblomov?"

The Cardinal nodded, gazing on Carter with a kind of affection. "But Freddie's a finance guy, and they think they can do anything – move money around in thin air and destroy lives as easily as they can buy a book online. Freddie said he was going to make my fortune. You could say our terms about how to do that differed."

Carter closed his eyes to block the bright cold light. Freddie Hutt was behind it all.

"And you can't go to the police and you can't fire him because he'd cost you too much?"

The Cardinal nodded again. "And I'm tired, Cartch. I want the St. Pats' winning the Cup to be the thing that kills me. Not Freddie."

"So the Russians had nothing to do with it," Carter said, working out the story.

"Oh, but they did," the Cardinal whispered. "This fellow Petrov wanted to buy the team and move it to Moscow. The league is looking to expand to Europe. But they'll have to do it without me. I have no interest in handing my father's legacy to a bunch of bandits so the league can fatten its balance sheet."

"And having the Russian's daughter dating Link was part of the business plan?"

The Cardinal gestured to Carter to top up his whiskey and took a sip. "The daughter, Alexandra, seems a nice enough girl. She's got U.S. citizenship, and so she was the front for the bid. Daddy thought that if she closed her eyes and thought of Mother Russia while Link did the business, it would help their chances of buying the St. Pats and carting the show off to Moscow. Fucking Russians."

"That must have been a surprise to Freddie," Carter said.

The Cardinal shook his head. "No, he was just driving up the bidding war. He gets a fat bonus when the team sells, you see. It's how business is done these days. You don't just get paid for doing your best at your job. You get paid for just showing up, and a bonus for not drooling on the carpet. Did I ever pay you a bonus, Cartch?"

Carter shook his head. "No. You paid me a salary. 'If you do well, it goes up, and if you don't, I'll trade you.' That's what you said when you signed me."

"Back in a world I no longer recognize." The Cardinal's voice was growing weak. Carter knew he'd be asleep soon.

"So who did you sell the team to?"

"Haven't," the Cardinal said. "There's a bid out there. Some hotshot media company."

He looked at Carter with the closest Carter had seen to a gleam in the old man's eye in a long time.

"That wouldn't be Maestro Media, would it?" His voice was so tight it sounded like he was being strangled by the thought.

The Cardinal nodded. "It came in a couple of days after you died in the fire."

Carter's head hurt. "What exactly did Freddie do on Wall Street?" he asked.

"Leveraged takeovers. Using the assets of one company to buy another."

Carter saw the plan. Freddie and the Maestro had worked it together. They were somehow going to work the Maestro's stock deal into a buyout of the team.

They weren't just taking Maestro Media public. They were

taking the St. Pats public – a company that anyone from dreamy fans to cold-eyed corporate raiders could buy shares in on the NYSE. The family business would be surrendered to the whims of the marketplace. And Doug Bleecker was the cleanup man, seeing what kind of obstacle Carter really was on the road to riches.

"Are you going to accept the offer?" Carter said, his words halting and flat.

The Cardinal managed a weak smile. "If the St. Pats win the Cup, I'll raise the price."

"But what if . . ."

"Oh, I have a will, Cartch. In fact, you're in it."

The look on Carter's face made the Cardinal laugh. "No, I haven't left you the St. Pats. If I die before I sell, then the team goes into a trust. You're one of the trustees."

Carter swallowed the sob that rose in his throat. There were tears in his eyes, but the Cardinal pretended not to notice.

"And Freddie Hutt is not one," he continued. "I have a second cousin in Philly who could well die before me, but I like his granddaughter, so she's one, and a lawyer. And you."

"I won't let you down."

The Cardinal looked at him like a dying father, proud of what they'd done all these years together and sad that they were ending so soon. "I need you to do one more thing for me before you go," he said in a voice so suddenly tender that Carter thought, for a terrifying moment, that the old man was going to ask him to hold open the morphine valve and end it all now. "No," the Cardinal said, "not that. Go into my study, you remember the way, and in the top right-hand drawer, there's an envelope, one of those padded things. Bring it to me, will you?"

Carter made his way down the hall and flicked on a light in the sepulchral study. The first thing he saw was the photo of himself and the Cardinal, when Carter had won the Hermes Trophy as Rookie of the Year. They both looked a lot younger, with the hope in their eyes that this was the beginning of a beautiful run. But no, Carter picked up the photo and looked closer. In the Cardinal's eyes, which were looking far away into the distance, the end was already in sight.

He found the small padded envelope and took it back down the hall. The Cardinal's head had fallen back against his chair, and for a moment Carter thought he was gone. He crouched down in front of him and touched him lightly on the wrist, and the old man roused himself.

"Did you find it?" he asked.

Carter handed it to him, and the Cardinal placed it in his lap.

"I'll see you at the game tonight, Cartch? In my box?"

"I don't know if that would be a good idea."

"What are you afraid of? That they'll kill you there? That would send a message."

"Yeah, well, I've been sending a lot of bad messages lately. It's not my strong suit."

The Cardinal nodded. "You know where to find me." Then he handed Carter back the padded envelope. "In case we miss each other, open this when you need to. And do the right thing."

55

Carter walked into Central Park, the padded envelope tucked inside his shirt.

The sun was warm, and people in the park had shed the calcified misery of a long winter in favour of spring's flirty eye contact. Even iPod-ed, sunglassed female joggers deep inside the autism of exercise seemed to smile at him.

The budding of flowers, the rising of dead gods, and Romeo and Juliet.

There they were, the star-crossed duo, sculpted in a perpetual embrace, outside the open-air theatre where Carter went to watch Shakespeare in the summer.

He sat down on the lovers' marble plinth, feeling as if he'd been awake for three days straight, and leaned his head on Juliet's skirt. The steel was cool on the back of his neck, and he closed his eyes, just for a second, to see if not seeing would help him put together a map of the world in which he now lived.

She awoke him with a kiss. Then put her arms around him.

"Gracie," he said, squeezing her tight, to make sure he wasn't dreaming.

"Cartch," she said, her voice soft and thick. "I thought you were . . ."

"I know," he said. "My departure was rather sudden."

He'd made one call before leaving the Cardinal's, and when Gracie answered, and heard his voice, and he heard her relief, he knew he never wanted to have another night, and make another phone call, like that.

"I knew it was you," Gracie said, sitting down beside him. "When the phone rang. I knew it was you."

He nodded. He believed her. "I would have called you from the police station, but they didn't give me that option."

"I still can't see how they found you."

"They knew I was back. They knew I had few places to go."

"Wanda?"

He shook his head. "Why would she?"

"Maybe Madz's friend called them?"

"Doesn't strike me as the type."

He read her thought on the next suspect and cut it off with a question. "What did Madz say about it?"

"She wasn't home. She left early. I don't even think she knew you were missing." She paused dramatically. "I knew because I came back to bed. Her couch was murder."

"Yeah, well there's a lot of that going around. I just saw the Cardinal. He gave me this."

He removed the padded envelope from beneath his shirt and handed it to Gracie. She held it gingerly. "It's okay," he said. "It won't explode. I already opened it."

She lifted the flap and extracted a key, a label dangling from it. "727, New York Bank of Commerce. It's a safety deposit box."

He nodded. "There's more."

She pulled out a letter, on Saint Patricks Hockey Club stationery. "Please grant the bearer of this paper access to my safety deposit box." Signed in the Cardinal's shaky writing, with its baroque *J*s and *O*s, and hard to forge.

"Why did he give you this?"

"These violent delights have violent ends."

"What do you mean?"

"Sorry, it's from *Romeo and Juliet*. I think it means our day of reckoning is here."

She looked at the sweaty and unshaven man next to her. Not in judgment but protectively. "It could be a trap for you," she said.

"Yeah, I know. That's why you're going to the bank, teammate."

They got a taxi to Columbus Circle, where Gracie bought him a Mets cap, a pair of drugstore shades, and a pay-as-you-go cellphone, then they walked the five blocks down to the bank, one of those old money New York banks that didn't have branches in every mall in the lower forty-eight. It had one, tall, slender tower, and a global reach. And, Carter hoped, more than gold in its vault.

Gracie took the key, checked her face in her purse mirror, dabbing at some minor imperfection in her lipstick, then shouldered her laptop bag. She was ready. Carter told her that if she wasn't out in twenty minutes, but was still dealing with bureaucrats, to call him. If she didn't call, then he'd call her. And if everything was fine, to call him Cartch. If not, to call him Martin.

Gracie had now been inside for ten minutes, and Carter had spent the time at a bus stop with the sports section of the *Mail*, which started on the back page. Hockey dominated the news, with a photo of Link Andrachuk scowling, looking as if he was about to go hunting for breakfast with a spear. The accompanying piece aimed its sharp end directly at Link's manhood, asking if he had the "desire" to carry the team to the next level and win the Cup. Link's spaceship had never ventured out into this rarefied part of the hockey cosmos in his career, and the writer of the piece wondered whether Link would look down, see how far up he was, and shrivel in fear. Link was quoted.

"We know what we have to do," he had said. "Work hard, keep pressure on the puck, and remember that there's sixty minutes in a game, no matter if it's the first game of the season or game seven of the Cup final." Link had mastered the cliché book. "Of course, we don't think it will go seven games. We're already up two games to nothing on those surfer dudes from L.A., and we figure we can wrap it up at home."

Carter shook his head. Link had just given the Los Angeles Pirates the one thing you never want to give an opponent: an insulting newspaper clipping to post on their locker room bulletin board. Every player on the L.A. squad would take that slur onto the ice and seek revenge.

Carter looked at the clock on his phone. Fifteen minutes and counting. He took a breath and opened the newspaper to Page Seven. Now he was staring at a photo of himself. Looking like a murderer.

"The New York St. Patricks can take a commanding lead in the quest for their first Cup in four decades by defeating the Los Angeles Pirates tonight at Emerald Gardens, but the victory champagne will be watered down considerably by the news that the NYPD are planning to charge former St. Pats star and team exec Martin Carter with double homicide. Sources say Carter, who earlier disappeared and was presumed dead, has returned to New York City. Could the lightning-quick Carter be looking to strike again and make murder a hat trick?"

Carter's whole being was ice. Either Darwin Gissing was a psychic or somebody very close to Carter was feeding Page Seven.

He replayed the sequence of the tabloid's revelations, each page flashing on a screen in his head.

Page Seven knew that Hayley had footage of Link's attack on Oblomov almost as soon as Carter knew. There was Bleecker, smiling like an executioner, showing him the page.

They knew he went missing after a fire in his apartment and suggested that the body "burned beyond recognition" that was found in the ruins might be his.

Then they suggested that the body wasn't his, although the NYPD were being tight-lipped about it all. But even so, someone had access to the NYPD's homicide guys.

And now there was this.

Madz knew part of the story, and Wanda knew part of the story, and Gracie knew more than anyone, but she hadn't been around at the beginning.

And where was she now? Carter's cellphone clock said she was a minute overdue. He was just thumbing in her number when she came out of the bank, her laptop case slung over her shoulder as casually as if she'd been to the ATM for grocery money.

He watched her glance left and right, checking out the street like a pro. She wasn't looking for cars, she was looking for tails. She wasn't rushing, wasn't jaywalking, so Carter knew that whatever she had taken out of the vault needed special treatment. And she wasn't looking at Carter. She just kept walking east on 54th. He followed her on the opposite side of the street, hanging back a half-block. If Gracie was walking away from him, it's because she wanted him to follow.

Gracie crossed over 5th Avenue and turned right. Carter crossed over too and closed the gap between them to fifty feet. The streets were not as crowded as they often were, but 5th Avenue was always a parade, and Carter didn't want to lose her among the clowns and the jugglers.

And then she went up the steps to St. Patrick's Cathedral. He broke into a jog, took the steps two at a time, and made it into the nave in time to see her.

He watched her genuflect and disappear into a pew masked by one of the cathedral's massive columns. She was of the tribe, too, it would seem. Just a good Catholic girl helping him on his messianic quest.

Carter genuflected for the sake of appearances when he reached her pew, then slid in next to her. She was kneeling, her eyes closed, in prayer. One strategy he hadn't so far tried.

Carter tried to settle on the uncomfortable wooden bench, then leaned back.

He gazed at the high altar and tried for a moment to reconcile the aggressive majesty of the cathedral with the humble message of the man who had inspired it, but it was useless. He couldn't do it at the best of times, and today was certainly not that. Gracie was still praying at his side, so he let his eyes wander to the votive candles flickering in a nearby chapel. They, and the spice of incense in the air, instantly took him back to his childhood, like the madeleine cake in *Remembrance of Things Past*, which Flavia had given him as a trophy of her taste and not as a book she expected him to read.

What was Flavia doing now? Worrying about whether he would do as he was bidden and take the money and run? And how did she connect to Freddie Hutt and his master plan with the Maestro?

Carter looked down at Gracie, and thought of the last time he had been in church. It had been for his father's funeral on a flawless April Saturday afternoon ten years earlier at St. Paul's Basilica in Toronto. He had spent the service staring up at the domed ceiling depicting heaven, avoiding the sight of the flag-draped casket depicting reality, his heart full of knowing that this was it, for his father, for him. Shortly afterwards, his mother had started to disappear, her mind crumbling on an incoming tide of despair. He'd never be with either of them again.

And now, he was back in a church because Gracie had something that couldn't be seen in public. The sanctuary of the cathedral was an inspired choice.

He realized that he had lost track of time while out of the country when he noticed that the statues around him were shrouded in purple cloth. Here he was, in a church for the first time in years, and he'd showed up on Good Friday. Led there by the woman he loved, who had now turned into a grade-school nun.

Gracie finally pushed herself off her knees and perched on the edge of the pew.

"Everything okay?" Carter whispered.

"It's in my laptop," Gracie whispered back.

Carter glanced at her laptop bag. It seemed empty.

"In front of me," she said.

For the first time, he looked down at the floor in front of them. Gracie's laptop was open and playing the video of Link's attack on Oblomov, with the Russian's blood spraying the Plexiglas wall just as it had when Carter first saw it. Here, in the cathedral, and not as a post-coital ambush, the assault seemed preordained. The Fall of Man, and now his redemption. The St. Patricks had come to St. Patrick's.

"The Cardinal had it," Carter said, his voice shaky.

"And he gave it to you."

"He gave it to us." He grinned at his teammate.

She smiled back. "Now what are we going to do?"

"It's Good Friday, Gracie. We're going to what you're supposed to do. Commemorate a crucifixion."

56

Before the blood came the ritual.

First, Carter and Gracie walked the few blocks from St. Patrick's to Brooks Brothers, where Gracie took out her credit card and bought him a grey herringbone two-button suit, a white cotton shirt, a green-and-gold silk tie, some grey socks, and a pair of slim-fitting Madras boxers.

"That should do the trick," she said with satisfaction, not even blinking at the twelve-hundred-dollar tab when it came time to pay. They walked to Grand Central Station and ate lunch in the Oyster Bar – a double order of fried Bluepoints, extra tartar sauce – and then popped into the Rite Aid to pick up shower gear. After that, they walked a couple of blocks west to the best public shower that Carter could think of: the Princeton Club.

"I'm afraid jeans are not allowed, sir," the doorman said politely, eyeing Carter's Levi's.

"It's okay," Carter replied. "I have my Princeton uniform in here."

Under the doorman's astonished gaze, Carter slipped his jeans off, took his suit pants out of the garment bag, and zipped them on fast and with a head-case grin.

"Three cheers for old Nassau," he said to the mute doorman as they walked past. The concierge found Carter's membership details in her computer and greeted him like a long-lost Princetonian sibling and not the double murderer the *Mail* suggested he was. She would do better than give him and Gracie a pass to the gym. She would give them a room.

Once he'd stepped out of the hot shower, cleansed and shaven and smelling like Sea Foam Sport Deodorant, they celebrated on the king-sized bed.

Afterwards, leaning on an elbow, her body curled into his, Gracie said, "So Doug Bleecker wants to buy the footage. But which footage does he mean?"

"He must mean the sex tape. He'd have to have known that the Cardinal had the Oblomov tape."

"Why?"

"Because the person who killed Hayley and stole her camera would have had the footage."

"But if Doug Bleecker wasn't in on that, and the Cardinal already has it, then what's he buying it for?"

"No, he's trying to buy the sex tape. He was testing me to see if I had it."

"How does he even know about it?"

Carter grinned. "I think that my old friend Andy Jack had something to do with that."

"You mean sending Oblomov after us wasn't enough?" Gracie was leaning on his chest now, looking him in the eye.

"He could have used it as another threat for his lawsuit."

"But buying it from you won't stop him from using it."

"True, but he'd have to prove it. They want to see that I have it. Or set me up again. Didn't quite work out the first time."

"What's Flavia got to do with it?"

He shook his head. "As my father always said, when you're in trouble you need a lawyer, a priest, and a bartender in whatever order you can find them."

She lay back, her arms behind her head. "That's good. Flavia's the lawyer, but who's the bartender and the priest?"

"Depends on who's in trouble. And my guess is the Maestro."

"It was Link having sex with another man, not him."

"Yeah, but Maestro Media had put in a bid on the St. Patricks."

She sat up sharply. "What?"

"Sorry," he said, feeling the jolt from her eyes. "The Cardinal told me earlier. I'm still trying to process it."

"It's pretty urgent news, Martin."

Martin. She was angry.

"I know, I know. I wasn't trying to keep it from you."

She exhaled and put her hand on his cheek. "I know. It hasn't exactly been a normal day." She paused. "Or maybe it has, for us."

He gave her a quick kiss, a promissory note on a normal life, soon. "Look, if Maestro Media has bid on the St. Patricks, they need money, or leverage."

"That would be their stock offering. If they goosed the price high enough by leaking word of the bid on the St. Patricks."

"It certainly would. And you know who used to work on Wall Street making money out of thin air?"

"Freddie Hutt."

Carter kissed her again. "He and the Maestro are going to use the Maestro Media stock offering to take over the team, and then take it public. The double whammy."

She inhaled. "Wow. As in, wow."

They sat in the silence of epiphany for a moment, then she said, "What are we going to do next?"

"You mean after a hot shower together?"

She put her hand on his thigh and squeezed. "That's exactly what I mean."

"We're going to a hockey game, Miss Yates. And we're going to win."

57

Emerald Gardens looked how ancient Rome must have before an evening of bloodlust, Carter thought, as he and Gracie approached the plaza in front of the old arena. There were maybe five thousand people milling about, waiting for the doors to open and the game to begin, some of them already drunk, some of them showing too much unsightly flesh on this warm spring evening, and some of them with the look in their eye of the true believer who sees heaven just over the next hill. They were all in the mood for a party, one that most of them had waited their whole lives to attend.

As usual in New York City, vendors galore had gathered to help them realize their dreams in that modern American way: by spending money. Some were hawking hot dogs, some overpriced green-and-gold hats and T-shirts and jerseys, and a few even offered baby gear in the team's colours, all of them bearing news of the home team's recent triumph: The St. Patricks, champions of the Northeast Division, the Eastern Conference, and, the day after tomorrow, the world.

For the crowd's entertainment, there were guitar players and accordionists and kids pounding on plastic buckets, all competing to perform the most annoying Irish song.

"What's that tune?" Gracie said, eyeing an Irish bagpipe band, complete with female step dancers in body-hugging green-and-gold catsuits, sounding like they were slaughtering all the cats in Ireland.

"That would be 'Danny Boy,'" Carter replied. "And if he heard these pipes calling him, he'd kill himself."

Carter and Gracie moved slowly through the amiable mob, past the stalls selling giant phallic plastic clappers and past the hookers who were cruising the punters in case any wanted a quickie in one of the porta-potties that lined the street, next to the semi-trailer TV trucks. A creation of radio days, Emerald Gardens could not accommodate TV technology, and broadcast games were run from remote by guys in these sweaty, cramped steel containers.

The entire carnival was perfumed by the scent of roasting pig and steer and boiling oil rising from a gleaming row of industrial barbecues, where men in aprons flipped Patsie Dogs and Shamrock Burgers that dripped grease indiscriminately on the fire, the cooks, and the customers who were lined up a dozen deep to get their quarter-pound of flesh.

Not even the presence of the NYPD's Mounted Unit, the officers hiding their thoughts behind their shades, could dent the hopes of the Patsies, gathering for the first Cup final at home in a long, long time.

On 11th Avenue, as they neared the media gate, the crowd parted to reveal Madz, fanning herself with her game notes so her TV makeup wouldn't run in the heat. "Jesus, Cartch, you clean up well," she said, giving him a slow once-over. "Thought I'd bump into you here. C'mon, let's get out of this pig fuck."

She handed him a SportsWorld media pass. "I brought this just in case the Patsies had cancelled your ticket."

"That's great," Carter replied. "I always wanted to be on TV."

"Never turn down a chance to have sex or appear on television."

"But not at the same time," he said, thinking of Hayley's tape.

Madz shrugged, then looked at Gracie, who'd slung her media ID necklace around her neck. "You want to come up to the booth too, Gracie?"

"Otherwise engaged," she replied. "I'll be busy with Doug Bleecker."

"Doug Bleecker? The media relations guy? Don't tell me he's the criminal mastermind?"

Gracie smiled. "I'll ask him."

Madz looked from Carter to Gracie and back at Carter again. "I really hope this is not what it's like to get screwed by a guy."

"No," Gracie said, a hand on Carter's back. "It isn't."

They flashed their IDs at the gate guard and walked through the lower concourse to the elevator.

Carter felt a small surge of triumph as they passed the team dressing rooms. He wasn't supposed to be here tonight. He was supposed to be behind bars on Rikers Island, trusting the promise of his publicly appointed defender from the Acme Night School of Law to get him a deal – say, double life with no parole even after he was dead.

It hadn't turned out like that, and Carter knew there were people who were angry about that. They would not be happy to see him here tonight, which was exactly what he wanted.

As the trio waited at the elevator, the St. Patricks came out of their dressing room to hit the ice for their warm-up. The elevator doors opened, and Madz stepped forward, but Carter put his hand on her arm. "Wait."

He walked toward Link Andrachuk, the last man out.

"Cartch?" Madz called after him in sharp warning, but he kept going.

Link was twenty feet away, and he caught Carter's eye. There was no sign of recognition.

"Link," Carter said.

Link kept going in the robotic gait of people who are in skates but not on ice, looking away as if Carter was some autograph seeker.

"I know who killed Hayley, Link," Carter said.

Link stopped and turned his scowl on Carter. "What?"

Carter walked closer. "I know who killed Hayley Rawls."

Confusion flickered in Link's black eyes. He shifted his hold on his hockey stick and placed it like a spear over his shoulder. One wrong word could bring the blade down on Carter's head.

Carter didn't blink. "It's okay, Link. I know it wasn't you."

Carter waited for the question, but instead, he got a sneer. "No, it was you," Link said, then walked up the stairway toward the white light of the rink. A roar erupted as he stepped onto the ice, the great hope of the Patsies, the man who would fill the L.A. net with pucks and the Cup with champagne.

Not, thought Carter, if he had anything to do with it. Then he smiled at Madz and Gracie and strolled back to the elevator. Going up.

58

The L.A. Pirates had been tense during their pre-game warm-up of give-and-go drills on their goalie. Half the shots missed the net, and the other half made the goalie look better than he was. Carter knew the Pirates were squeezing their sticks a little too hard, trying to perfect the shot that would break their scoring slump, which had them down two games to zip against the St. Patricks.

Carter couldn't believe that the St. Pats were the same team he'd watched self-destruct just a few weeks ago, a tentative, fragile crew who badly needed some kind of saviour to chase the demons out of their game. Now they were skating and passing with skill and passion. They had found their saviour in Link Andrachuk. He skated in on goal now, helmetless, and roofed the puck past his own goalie. Clearly, Carter thought, his message about Hayley hadn't rattled Link at all.

Link's confidence and ease was reflected throughout the team. They were as relaxed as Carter had ever seen them, skating with the sure moves of winners. He remembered the feeling. It was as if the puck and stick were part of your body and you could will them to do whatever you wanted.

"Too bad you never got a shot here, Cartch," Madz said, watching him watch the St. Patricks. "You of all people."

"I'm here now," he said, staring at the ice below. "Best view I've ever had."

Carter had been up in the Broadcast Blimp a few times when he was on the team, hanging sixty-five feet above the St. Pats logo at centre ice, being interviewed between periods.

The Blimp was divided into three sections: one for TV commentators, the other for radio, and the third for the tech guys who monitored the broadcasts and ran footage and replays on the rink's aging Jumbotron. As Carter and Madz entered the booth, a plump technician fiddling with the wiring was on his knees under the computer table, flashing his bum crack – a Winnipeg smile, Carter thought – and cursing the finicky machine.

"Fucken dinosaurs aren't extinct yet!" he yelled with a gnarly vowelled Queen's accent, then turned to see Madz and Carter. "Sorry," he said, sweat running down his red cheeks. "Just checking under the hood. Of a Model T."

Carter laughed. "Yeah, the boss was going to replace that thing last year," he said.

"What's a year when the thing's twelve years old? My kid's laptop could replace this thing," the tech replied. "I mean, you gotta run everything off fuck – 'scuse me, off a portable VCR/DVD player and link it up to this thing." He looked like he was going to smack the computer. "On the new switching boards, it's all touch screen. It's –"

Madz held up a hand. "Thanks, Jimmy, but we're mortals, remember? Don't explain the magic, just show us."

Jimmy grinned. "Okay, Madz. Just watch me." He smiled shyly at Carter. "Or rather, just watch him."

He popped a DVD into the portable player and hit play. Then he pointed to the Jumbotron, where a highlights video of the St. Patricks now filled the screen.

"It's the best of the Pats playoff history," he said proudly. "Did it myself."

It started in the 1920s, with murky black and white stills and dim footage as it ripped through the decades. In 1949, things got brighter – not for the St. Patricks, but for the camera, for that was the year when the concrete beneath the ice was first painted white.

Carter had to catch his breath as the faces of the great St. Patricks players of long ago faded in and out of view, all of them dead, their stiff, formal portraits serving to frame the playoff highlights to follow. It was as if the ghosts of Emerald Gardens had come back for this night. Including Martin Carter.

Jimmy the tech glanced up nervously at Carter when his face, in colour, looking not too different than it did now, rose like a spectre on the Jumbotron.

Carter knew the St. Pats wouldn't be so callous as to run playoff footage of the play that ended his career, not tonight. And he was right. The clip was from the game before the game that changed Carter's life, and as he watched himself take the puck behind his own net and look up the ice like a warrior pausing before the attack, tears welled in his eyes for all that he did not know then, for the pain that lay ahead. Carter's younger self slowly skated out of his own zone, and shifted to the left around a Vancouver Sea Lion trying to steal the puck from him. Then he made a sidestep to the right around another, his pace slow, fast, and slow again, fooling his opponent and the team.

They slowed down too. And Carter immediately turned on the speed, catching a defender flat-footed and racing past him to split the defence, streak in on goal. With a head fake to the left and a kick of his right leg, he had the goalie down and the puck over his shoulder and into the net.

"Fuck," said Madz. "They don't make 'em like that anymore."

Carter couldn't watch any longer. He squeezed his eyes shut and willed the brimming tears back to where they came from. Watching himself play like that made him feel as if the intervening fifteen years were just a moment, and the sense of what he had lost was heavy. He had been there, so close, and now he was here, high above the rink where he'd hoped to earn his name on the Cup

He looked away, toward the owner's box. The view from the tech side of the broadcast booth was perfect – directly opposite and a little lower – so Carter had a prime viewing of who came and went from the Cardinal's private domain while the remainder of the highlights montage played out and the crowd below slowly hushed in anticipation of the start of the game.

The box was almost full for this momentous night, the night where a victory would put the St. Patricks just one more win away from their first Cup triumph in forty years. The Cardinal, in his black suit and green-and-gold tie, sat in the front row, with Brenda next to him, fussing over the hose to his oxygen tank like it was her lifeline and not his. At his left sat Freddie Hutt, dapper in the way of a ringmaster, in his green silk suit and black shirt, and maybe a black tie too – Carter couldn't tell through the binoculars Madz had loaned him. Behind them, the Maestro and the Russian gas thief and his daughter were sharing a laugh while the wine stewards were hopping to keep the glasses filled.

"The Star-Spangled Banner" made the hairs on the back of Carter's neck stand up, as it always did, but tonight's singers, a mixed chorus of eighth graders from St. Patrick's Old Cathedral School, touched the crowd as if the bombs were bursting in mid-air right here and now, and the rafters shook with patriotic pride and the energy of expectation that tonight was going to be a victory, here, in the home of the brave.

Despite the roar of the crowd, the game, from the start, was the kind best seen while tipsy, Carter thought. For something so pivotal, a game that could dramatically shift the series either way if L.A. won, the two teams were playing as if they'd wandered into a chess match on ice. No one wanted to make a mistake.

And then sixteen minutes into the first period, Link Andrachuk did, nearly taking the head off of the Czech kid whom he'd nearly taken the head off of earlier in the season, and it woke everyone up, except the Czech kid, who crawled to the bench on his knees. Carter looked sympathetically at the kid, who probably no longer knew what planet he was on.

The two teams scrummed up in pursuit of blood, and the Patsies screamed to splinter the rafters. The referees conferred about giving Link "five and a game" for the clothesline hit, which would have parked him for the rest of the night, and maybe the next night too. That was not going to happen, not to that man, not in this game. The refs skated back to position, and the play resumed with no penalty call at all. The L.A. Pirates howled at the injustice, but the linesman dropped the puck and the game resumed. No longer a chess match but a blood feud.

Carter looked over to see how Freddie Hutt liked this turn of events, but he wasn't watching the game, he was watching Erik Shepherd. Carter followed his line of sight down to where the Maestro was setting up his camera in the sweet spot where Carter had first placed Hayley Rawls for the perfect view she needed. He glanced now at the media box, and there was Gracie, sitting next to Bleecker, scribbling something in her notepad as he stared straight ahead.

Despite the game's change in mood – with the two teams in torrid opposition and Emerald Gardens now humid and ornery, waiting for a thunderstorm to break – the first period ended tied at 0, and Carter walked the rickety catwalk from the Blimp to meet Gracie in the media room.

"He's a slippery one," she said, uncapping a Brooklyn Lager and inclining her head toward Bleecker's back.

"What did he tell you?"

"The official version. They're trying to settle this lawsuit with the Sea Lions and want to do the right thing. Etcetera."

"In other words . . ."

"Yeah, he's lying. But I did find out that he used to write about high-risk stocks for the *Green Sheets*. It's a website for stock manip– promoters."

He nodded. "I'll watch your back if you watch mine."

She kissed him gently on the mouth to seal the deal.

59

The St. Patricks came out flying in the second period, beating the Pirates to every opportunity at the puck and hitting them every chance they got. When Link Andrachuk laid a body-check on a Pirates defenceman in the corner, the Patsies roared and the Blimp rattled.

"It's okay," Jimmy the tech said. "I've felt worse. Maybe."

When Link picked the pocket of the Czech kid, still woozy from the blow, and powered in on a solo dash, finishing it with the flick of his wrists and the puck in the net, Carter thought he felt the Blimp swaying.

"Don't worry, it's supposed to move," Jimmy said, but now he looked worried too.

The goal provoked the Pirates, who started to hit anything that moved and to shoot on goal from every angle except upside down. But they couldn't score.

Carter looked over at the Cardinal. He was talking to Freddie, who was nodding and who glanced up at Carter. They'd spotted him in the Blimp.

Gracie was looking up at him too, alone now. Bleecker had vanished, and she gave Carter a thumbs-up. Happy ending.

When the siren sounded to end the second period, the Patsies cheered their heroes off the ice, their Irish fatalism banished now by the fact that all their boys had to do was get through one more period, and then one more game. Then forty years of failure would be forgiven.

No, thought Carter. Not tonight, it won't be.

The third period began with the Pats skating hard, pushing for the second goal that would put the game away. Carter could hear Madz in the adjacent section of the booth through his earphones, talking about how the St. Patricks, leading 1–0 after two periods, needed an insurance goal to put the Pirate pretenders from Los Angeles on the end of the gangplank.

Link Andrachuk was now willing himself upon the game, living up to his promise as he had mostly done ever since Hayley died. He was rushing the puck up the ice, feinting side to side and faking out the Pirates d-men with moves that a player might try on pond hockey, with no one watching, but never here. A through-their-legs pass to himself had the crowd on its feet in a roar.

Link's rushes were pretty, but the Pirate goalie repelled each one of them, and when Link took a penalty for goaltender interference after one of his solo dashes sent the L.A. net-minder flying – and the referees could hardly overlook that, no matter how much of a cut Freddie had promised them – the Pirates scored a quick power-play goal and were back in the game.

Link tried single-handedly to win back the margin, with Coach Phil Winslow double-shifting him, urged on by the Patsies, nearly twenty thousand of them vibrating the rafters and the Blimp with their fervour. They were trying to remind Link that this was a team sport, chanting, "Pass the puck! Andrachuk!" And when he didn't, they were quick to return to their old form, screaming, "You're a fuck! And-ra-chuk!"

They were still a sentimental lot, thought Carter, and while he wanted a Cup for them and for the Cardinal, he didn't want one for Link Andrachuk. Watching Link's assault on Oblomov again – in a church, no less – had opened all of Carter's wounds. He wanted to hurt Link too, and if the DVD of Link's orgy with Hayley and Oblomov didn't do it, then the other surely would.

When the Los Angeles Pirates finally caught a break, so did Carter. And it was all thanks to Andrachuk. The St. Patricks' one-man onslaught finally succumbed to the law of averages, and the Pirates got an odd-man rush, led by the Czech kid who had found his game again. Maybe he wasn't concussed, or maybe he was just crazy, but to Carter, he looked like he was on a mission too. The kid hit the blue line, and passed the puck to his wing man, who looked to Carter to be half a step offside, but there was no whistle.

The Patsies, who knew their hockey, saw it too and started to howl. The play kept on, the L.A. wingman dropped the puck back to his centreman, trailing. He faked a slap shot, then slid the puck to the side of the net where the Czech kid had magically appeared. With a flick of his stick, he tipped the puck into the goal, and the Pirates were winning.

The booing tumbled like an avalanche from the roof of the Gardens and down to the ice, along with a shower of plastic clappers and beer cups. The players scattered to their respective benches, and the refs signalled a time out and summoned the clean-up crew to sweep up the mess.

That only jacked up the booing, as if this time out were an admission of guilt by the refs. The Blimp swayed. Carter looked at Jimmy, and he flashed a brave face, but he was sweating. "OK, this might be the worst," he said.

But the worst was to come. Those Patsies who had thrown their cups and clappers now were throwing their programs and, viciously, pennies. A player could break his neck by stepping on a penny with a skate blade.

"Don't think we'll replay that," Jimmy said to the guys in the truck and then nodded at whatever they said back. "Time to sell some soap while this chills," he said to Carter and popped in a commercial for St. Pats season tickets, featuring a hockey-playing leprechaun and a pot of silver, which, of course, was the Cup.

The Patsies' assault on the refs turned into baying derision at this enticement to bring them back for next season when the St. Pats were just starting to burst the dream that was this season.

Jimmy gave Carter a seen-it-all-before shrug. "This'll take a while," he said. "Best to go dark till the natives realize management will turn off the beer sales. That will get them to shut the fuck up. I'm gonna have a smoke," he said. "Don't touch anything."

As soon as he was gone, Carter walked over to the

Jumbotron console. It was all too easy. Just pop the DVD into the console and push play.

So he did.

Suddenly, the Jumbotron screen, all four sides of it, filled with Link Andrachuk's sustained attack on Sasha Oblomov.

The Patsies didn't get it at first, but then people started pointing at the Jumbotron and the rink grew quiet.

In the owner's box, Freddie and Brenda were gaping at the images of carnage on the big screens while the Cardinal stared at the broadcast booth, meeting Carter's eye, the slightest of smiles cracking at the edges of his lips.

The footage stopped, and Carter looked down to the Maestro, who'd turned his camera on Carter and was adjusting the focus. The red light glowed on the camera as the Maestro filmed Carter for about ten seconds, and Carter, figuring he was in close-up, smiled and winked. Posterity would understand.

Now the Patsies were screaming and throwing whatever they hadn't already thrown on the ice at the Jumbotron. Many of the players had come back to see what all the fuss was about. Carter pushed play again, so they could see what they had missed.

In Carter's headphones, Madz was delivering a play-by-play, blow-by-blow account of what everyone was watching on the Jumbotron. Carter searched among the players for Link. He was watching himself brutally butt-end Oblomov, and from the little smile creasing his five-o'clock shadow, it looked like he was enjoying it.

The other St. Patricks stared as if in shock, seeing Link use his hockey stick like a piston on Oblomov's chin, Link's eyes hot with bloodlust. And it was blood that he struck. Once more it started to spurt from the Russian's mouth, then sprayed on the screens high above the ice at Emerald Gardens.

Phil Winslow – the fans' debris raining down around him, and probably sensing that Link might be attacked by his own team – barked a command, and the St. Pats shuffled down the corridor toward their dressing room. The St. Patricks were forfeiting the game, and the Patsies, seeing their dream of the Cup depart with the retreating team, started to riot, pushing down the Plexiglas separating them from the ice and then scuttling across it. Some went for the refs, who skated to safety, and some went for the L.A. Pirates, who beat a retreat to their dressing room, leaving a couple of their tough guys to fend off the rabid Patsies with their hockey sticks.

The rink announcer was imploring the Patsies to stop, please, with as much effect as asking the wind to calm down when it whipped up East River in winter. It only got worse the more you begged it to get better.

Carter looked for the Maestro in this maelstrom, but he had disappeared, as had Bleecker. And so had Gracie.

He popped the DVD out of the console and put it in his pocket. He nearly collided with Jimmy rushing in the door of the booth, but Carter gave the guy his killer stare until the tech held up his hands: he wasn't paid enough to risk his life for whatever craziness Martin Carter was up to.

Carter could hear Madz yelling into her mike, describing the riot below, and he made his way quickly along the shaking catwalk, just in case the rage of the betrayed Patsies should cause Emerald Gardens to disintegrate. He hoped it didn't tumble before he reached the plaza, where Gracie had promised to meet him, come hell or high water, simultaneous possibilities in this city. But to Carter's eye, it looked worse than that. It looked like the end of everything for the St. Patricks.

60

The plaza in front of Emerald Gardens had changed from a circus to a zoo in the space of twenty minutes. Enraged Patsies were smashing glass bottles and windows and the barbecue stands and one another, and the NYPD horsemen were beating back the hordes with the threat of raised batons. The rest of the crowd, trying to escape, was now becoming a panicked rabble with nowhere to go.

Carter watched the multitude surge back toward the doors of Emerald Gardens, which the ushers were trying to bolt before the mob crashed through. There was no way he was going outside into that, and he hoped beyond anything that Gracie hadn't either.

He couldn't call her – the Cardinal had installed jammers throughout the place to stop people from doing a play-by-play on their cellphones for people who hadn't bought tickets to the show. Carter figured she would have gone to Plan B by now. They'd meet by the tunnel next to the media room in the bowels of the Gardens. And they'd figure it out from there.

Power had been cut to the elevators to prevent the mob from reaching the corporate offices, so Carter took an access stairway down to the lower concourse of the ice palace. He opened the door on the lower level and was met by the sight of massed riot police, who had probably been on standby somewhere close in case the Patsies won. Wearing menacing black bomber jackets, their helmet shields up, rings of nylon handcuffs on their belts dangling beside an arsenal of crowd control gear, including tear gas grenades, they were checking their gas masks and didn't even notice Carter as he raced past them. He knew that the trouble above was going to meet the trouble about to come from below, and he didn't want to be anywhere close by when that happened.

The media room was empty. Any journalist who was still breathing was upstairs covering the mayhem, and both teams' dressing room doors were shut, guarded by the NYPD. And now the riot cops started beating their shields with their batons in a slow march tempo as they moved off along the tunnel toward the battle above.

Carter started running, flying past the blue and white NYPD buses that had delivered the cops to this underworld, and kept going along the lighted driveway to the tunnel exit onto 11th Avenue, next to Chelsea Waterside Park, which he realized now would be the perfect staging area for the attack force.

The tunnel rose up into a warehouse building with a delivery ramp for trucks and a door leading to the street. Carter reached the door, gasping and sweating. It hadn't been locked behind the police buses. Just as he was about to open it, he heard Gracie's voice. "Martin?" she called, sounding small and scared. She was sitting in the back of a Lincoln Town Car, tinted windows all around, but the rear window was down so he could see her face and the stark fear upon it.

"Martin!" she yelled, and a hand emerged from the dark to clamp her mouth shut. Carter stopped, parsing the danger ahead, and in the pause felt the cold steel of a gun pressed to the back of his head.

"I know you're thinking that I won't kill you here," Hopalong said, the beat of the riot police growing loud and near. "But if you don't get in that car, then those fine officers that you've unleashed will find your brains splattered all over that door and this gun in your hand."

Carter's head was colder than the steel. He was dead, if not now, then soon, but if he played the future card, he and Gracie at least had a chance. He raised his hands. "I'm going, don't shoot," he said.

And he walked toward the Town Car, the thudding batons of the NYPD a grim knell in his ears.

61

The Lincoln drove out of the Gardens and headed on to the Henry Hudson Parkway, with Hopalong hunched behind the wheel and Bleecker sitting next to Gracie and Carter in the back, staring at them through his bug lenses as if looking at two corpses.

"What are you doing here, Doug?" Carter said, his voice deep and dry.

Bleecker didn't say anything, but he widened his eyes a bit, as if Carter was even stupider than he'd imagined.

"I guess you're just following orders?" Carter could almost see Freddie Hutt's fingerprints on Bleecker's shaved head, pushing the buttons that had put them all here.

Bleecker blinked. "No, you followed your dick. And we're all grateful for that."

Hopalong laughed, the thick wet cackle of a heavy smoker.

They did a loop around Ground Zero and headed east through the Brooklyn-Battery Tunnel.

"You know where we're going?" Gracie whispered.

"Oh, I think he does," Hopalong answered, catching Carter's eye in the rear-view mirror. "Don't you?"

Carter's head grew even colder as Hopalong swung the car up Clinton Street. Yes, he knew where they were going. They were going to the house where he had last seen Hayley Rawls.

A few minutes later, Hopalong stopped the Lincoln, and Carter saw that he was right. And then, with Hopalong's gun to the back of Carter's head, they were marched into the ground-floor suite where Carter had found Hayley naked and dead. Moments later they were sitting around the dining-room table like old friends having a chat over a bottle of port: Gracie next to Carter, opposite Hopalong and Bleecker, with the Maestro himself at the head of the table, a one-eyed magician enjoying himself as he filled in the blanks.

"Yeah," he said, "it's a nice place, isn't it? But then you've been here before. When you killed Hayley."

"When *you* killed Hayley," Carter replied, his heart thudding.

The Maestro held up his hands in mock horror. "Not me! I wasn't even in town. Nowhere near this nice Brooklyn brownstone, which, if you didn't know, is owned by the New York St. Patricks."

Carter's mind was in overdrive. He had no idea the house belonged to the St. Pats. "Staying with friends" is what Hayley had told him, but she'd been lodged there because of the Maestro's project on Link. If word got out about the house's owner, it would look like Carter had access to the place as a valued team employee. It was the perfect set-up.

"Yeah." The Maestro grinned, putting his hands behind his long greying locks, enjoying himself. "You get the picture, don't you?"

"What do you want?" Carter meant it to sound tough, but his dry mouth made him sound scared. He was.

"Well, I wanted the NYPD to lock you up, is what I wanted, but they didn't co-operate. And after your stunt tonight, well." He lifted his eyepatch so he could mock Carter with both of his perfectly good grey eyes, "I think you're just so consumed by the damage that you've done, you have to make an exit. So tragic."

They were going to kill them both. Gracie felt for his hand and squeezed it.

"You think that tonight was the end of it?" Carter's voice was as strong as he could make it. This was his last gamble.

The Maestro laughed – three staccato coughs. "I do."

"You haven't seen the other DVD then."

The Maestro's eyes flicked, and Carter knew the answer. He hadn't seen it. "Trust me," he continued, bolder now, "it's one that you'll want to see."

"He's full of shit," Bleecker said. "I already tried that one, and nothing."

"Fuck you, Doug," Carter said, and Hopalong punched him in the gut with a roundhouse so fast and hard he thought he was going to vomit.

"What's on this DVD?" said the Maestro, holding up a censoring hand to Hopalong.

"It's of Link," Carter gasped.

"I have a lot of Link on DVD."

"Not like this."

The Maestro laughed. "Really?"

Carter nodded. "Maybe you were the guy behind the camera. When Link was giving Oblomov a blow job."

The Maestro's eyes flickered again, then he gave Carter a smile that he must have practised at sociopath school: mouth open, teeth bared, and his eyes plugged into a socket of rage. "And assuming this exists, you think what, you'll trade it?"

He didn't have to say for what. Carter nodded. "Yeah. Madz Weinfeld has a copy of the thing. So, if anything happens to us, then it's going to be all over SportsWorld. And while Link nearly killing Oblomov is one thing, this DVD will sure explain the motive. I'd say your plan to take over the St. Patricks would be worse than dead."

Carter could taste blood in his mouth, and his heart was beating too fast. The Maestro flashed Hopalong a look. It said, "You fucked up." But what he said out loud was, "Where is this DVD?"

"It's in Harlem."

The Maestro's eyes blinked out the algebra of this evening. He smiled now at Gracie. "When did you last fuck your friend here? This afternoon, wasn't it? That's good. If you're fucking with me."

Gracie just stared at the Maestro, her eyes wide as she strained to encompass just how mad he was. Carter could see where this was going. They'd kill them both and make it look like a murder-suicide with Carter's DNA deep inside Gracie. Just like it had been in Hayley.

"If you want that DVD, then we should go now," Carter said, trying his best to sound in command. "Madz was supposed to meet me after the game, and if I don't show . . ."

"You started a fucking riot!" Bleecker said. "Do you think she's keeping appointments?"

"Yeah, I do," Carter replied. "Who do you think helped me broadcast Link's show?"

The Maestro glared at Hopalong. "Take him to get it. Both of you. Be quick."

Bleecker rolled his eyes. "C'mon, Erik, do you really think this changes anything?"

The Maestro answered with a stare that scared Bleecker into answering his own question. "Okay, Okay, I see that Link's story can be saved here, the riot is a minor detail, compared to . . . Assuming this piece of shit isn't lying?"

The Maestro smiled at Carter. "You'd better kiss her goodbye. Just in case."

62

"Cartch? What the fuck happened to you tonight?" Madz squinted at him through her half-opened front door. "I was looking –"

Hopalong shut her up by kicking the door open. "Hello, how are you?" he said, sticking his gun in her face and pushing her against the wall.

Carter tried to calm the fear in her eyes with a smile. "I need to get something upstairs," he said, and she nodded, taking in Hopalong and his gun and Bleecker and his bug-eyed malice as if this were the most normal situation in the world.

"You're coming too, sweetness," Hopalong said, and Carter knew now just how deeply he'd drafted Madz onto the sudden death squad.

Carter led the way upstairs into the guest room. "It's in my duffel bag," Carter said, pointing to the black bag parked next to the futon.

"Then what the fuck are you waiting for?" Hopalong said, motioning him forward with the gun.

Carter, his hands trembling, slowly unzipped the duffel bag. Hayley Rawls's hard drive, which he hoped to trade for three lives, was at the bottom of the bag. Next to Carlito's gun.

"What's this about?" Madz said.

"Your friend Cartch has gone and got you all killed," Hopalong said with a snaggletoothed grin.

"I need to know something," Carter said to Hopalong, closing his hand around the gun. "Why are you doing this? I thought you were on the Cardinal's side?"

Hopalong snorted. "The Cardinal's side? The fucker was going to sell the team and leave me with nothing. And me being blood."

"What?"

"Brenda's his cousin, and I'm her cousin. Blood. Now hurry the fuck up or yours will be all over this nice floor."

Carter knew that wasn't true. They needed him back at the house in Brooklyn to make the theatre of their crime work. For now, he had the upper hand. So, with his body concealing the bag, and his right hand clutching the buried gun, he grabbed the hard drive with this left hand and turned, offering it to Hopalong. "Here it is."

Hopalong lowered his gun and held out his hand. Carter spun and aimed Carlito's gun at his forehead.

"Change of plan," Carter said, his voice tight.

Bleecker flinched, but Hopalong grimaced in disdain. "Give it to me, Cartch. This is over."

"Yes," said Carter. "It is." He squeezed the trigger, and the click of the gun sounded like a trapdoor snapping shut on him.

Hopalong laughed. "It's not even loaded, you stupid fucker."

He lunged at Carter, and Carter squeezed the trigger again. The gun fired this time, and a puff of red mist burst from the back of Hopalong's head onto Bleecker, who shrieked. Hopalong dropped to his knees and tumbled sideways, his eyes open and a bullet through his forehead.

Carter turned the gun on Bleecker. "Now," he said, "you call Erik Shepherd and you tell him we have it."

"Cartch . . . ?" Bleecker said, stepping forward, and Carter squeezed the trigger again. The bullet tore a hole in the wall.

Bleecker fumbled with his cellphone, and Carter stood opposite, the gun levelled at him. He didn't know whether there was another bullet inside the chamber, but he was prepared to find out if Bleecker tried anything funny. "Put it on speakerphone."

Bleecker nodded and thumbed in the number. It rang once.

"You have it?" It was the Maestro.

"Yes," Bleecker said, staring at the gun.

"It's the real deal?"

"Uh-huh."

There was a pause. "Let me speak to Eamon."

Bleecker's eyes narrowed to panicked slits.

Carter held out his left hand. He wanted the phone.

"Yeah?" he said, in a wet growl.

"Eamon?"

"Yeah."

"Is everything okay?"

"Fuck no," said Carter, keeping his voice low and his vowels large. "Fucken Link."

The Maestro paused. "Get back here soon."

"Yeah." Carter ended the call and pocketed Bleecker's phone.

"Oh my God." Bobbi Washington was standing in the doorway, bathrobed, fresh from the shower, her eyes moving from the dead guy on the floor, to Carter with the gun, and back again.

"Carter needs our help, babe," Madz said, her voice as soft as Carter had ever heard it.

"It's okay," Carter said, his voice calm now, as if he shot people all the time. He saw the future. He knew what he had to do. "It's okay. But Gracie's not. I have to go."

Bobbi spluttered. "You've gotta go? And leave a dead man on our floor?"

"On my floor," Madz replied. "I'm coming with you, Cartch."

"Oh no you're not," Bobbi said.

"You can come too," Carter said. "We just might need a doctor."

63

"You drive," Carter said to Bleecker as he marched him out of Madz's brownstone.

"I can't," he said.

"Then why the fuck are we taking you?" Carter replied, jabbing the gun into Bleecker's plump ribs. He was so jolted with adrenalin that he felt he could do anything. But he only had to do one thing, get to Gracie fast.

"I'll drive," Bobbi said, looking sleek in the silver tracksuit she'd hurriedly thrown back on.

"You sit in the back," Madz said to Bleecker, pointing a DVD camera at him. "You, I want to talk to."

Bobbi drove the Lincoln down the Hudson Parkway as if she were cutting into the brain of her own child. "Can we go a little faster?" Carter said. "It's a matter of life and death."

Bobbi sped up a bit, her eye on Carter in the rear-view mirror "If we get pulled over, you kidnapped me."

Carter nodded. If they got pulled over, kidnapping was the least of his problems. Especially with a recently fired pistol in his hand.

Yet despite the mortal urgency, everything had slowed down for him, the way it used to when he had the puck and was looking to make a play with opponents hurtling toward him to separate him from the puck, and maybe even his head. But now that head was working for him, the frozen band around it not so much a vise as a caress, calming him down, letting him see the ice before him in a way no one else could.

It was the only thing he could trust right now.

And right now, Carter thought, this was taking a long time. Too long. The Maestro thought so too because he called Hopalong's phone, which Carter had taken from his body. He knew he couldn't fool a fraud twice, so he turned the phone off, hoping, at best, that the Maestro would think they'd gone into the tunnel, and then he did the same with Bleecker's phone in his other pocket.

As the city flashed passed him like one long commercial for American genius, and as Madz filmed her interrogation of Bleecker about just what he had done to bring them both to the edge of doom, Carter thought about his own gift for self-destruction.

Here he was, on the wrong side of thirty-five, with a life that had only become good because it had gone so awfully bad. And now he had killed a man. He was as culpable as his enemies. Gracie was his only hope and dream, and he had gambled on that future by leaving her with the Maestro. Even if she were still alive, still okay, would she ever forgive him?

When Bobbi finally parked them around the corner from the St. Patricks' brownstone, nearly ninety minutes had elapsed since he'd left as Hopalong's prisoner.

"Fucking television," Carter muttered as Bobbi turned off the engine.

"What's that?" Madz said.

"If the camera doesn't see it," Carter replied, "it never happened."

"You got it, Cartch," she said, climbing out of the car.

"No!" he said, swinging around, gun in hand, making Bleecker duck. "It's just me and him. That's how we finish this."

"But –"

"If I'm not out in five minutes, call the police. Then turn your camera on whoever does come out."

Madz shot him a look but did as he said. Bobbi shook her head. "Call the police now. This is crazy."

"No," Carter said, "this is a head case saving his own life. There's a difference. You should know."

He walked behind Bleecker toward the door, Carlito's gun aimed at his back. "No head shot for you, Doug," he said. "If I have to shoot, I want you to feel it." Bleecker shuffled on miserably, his Wall Street swagger long gone.

Carter could feel his skull pulse, the beat of a plan being hammered out. He'd walk into the house behind Bleecker, put the gun to the head of the Maestro, free Gracie, call the cops, and take his chances. If the Maestro had a gun too, well, then he'd have to start shooting.

The front door was open. Just an inch, light from the foyer spilling out. This was a trap. The Maestro had seen Carter coming. He was going to ambush him. If he walked through the door he was dead. If he didn't, Gracie was.

With Carlito's gun cocked in his hand, he pushed Bleecker through the door, then followed him inside fast, sweeping the gun left to right and behind, like he'd seen so many times on TV, ready to shoot the first thing that moved.

But nothing moved. There was no sign that anyone had been here at all. Except for the trail of blood spots on the floor. A trail from the front door leading to the bedroom.

Carter's head felt like it was going to burst. "Walk," he said to Bleecker and pushed him forward, following the splatters, thicker and larger as they got closer to the bedroom door. Maybe Gracie had escaped, bleeding. Then Carter saw her laptop bag, leaning against the bedroom door.

Carter kicked the bag aside and pushed Bleecker through the door. Gracie was face down on the bed, an empty bottle of vodka and a vial of pills on the nightstand beside her, and a dark red stain on the crown of her golden head.

Carter froze, the weight of his failure pressing down. And Bleecker seemed to pick up on Carter's anguished pause. He slowly turned. "I'm sorry, Cartch," he said, his hands up, "it wasn't supposed to –" Carter smashed him in the mouth with the handle of the gun, and Bleecker crumpled on the floor beside the bed.

Carter kneeled on his chest, aiming the gun at his head, and looking to Gracie for forgiveness at what he was going to do next.

Then he saw Gracie's back rise.

He jumped up and reached for Gracie, turning her over and lowering his face to hers till he could feel the wisp of her breath on his lips.

64

Carter was back inside the 76th precinct house on Union Street, wearing a paper bunny suit that Detective Lucius Gibson had given him when he sent Carter's clothes to be tested for gunshot residue. His stomach hurt from the adrenalin pooling and fermenting and burning slow holes of worry.

Gracie had looked as good as dead when he last saw her being rushed out of the house of death on a gurney, Bobbi running beside her, and Madz speaking to a uniform. Carter had sat handcuffed in the back seat of a squad car, trying to avoid eye contact with curious neighbours, woken by the sirens, who were now on the street in their robes or hastily snatched coats, watching the New York action.

Carter felt his eyes fill with tears. He had seen too much, been on the run too long, and now he'd killed a man and Gracie was probably dying. He felt guilty about a lot of things, but most of all, he felt guilty about her, about leading her to death's door on a mad quest to prove something that now seemed unproveable.

"I underestimated you," Detective Lucius Gibson said as he re-entered the room and shut the door.

"How is Gracie?" Carter asked.

Gibson sat down. "She was in critical condition last I heard."

"When was that?"

"About an hour ago."

An hour. Fortunes could be made and lost in an hour. Games. Lives. "Can you check again? Please?"

"You can check yourself," he said. "Your lawyer is here."

"What?" Carter said. The cop read his stare and held up his hands in truce.

"I called her."

"She's not my lawyer."

"She seems to think she is."

"What's going on?" Carter said.

"I've just been talking with the prosecutor. No charges. Not today anyway."

"But Hopalong, I mean, Eamon Lynch?"

"Looks like self-defence so far." Gibson leaned forward, looking weary. "We've been watching them watch you all day." He paused, letting the words sink in. "Now go finish it," he said.

"You've been following them? And me?"

Gibson nodded. "Sorry about the paper suit, but your lawyer looks flush enough to get you some clothes."

Carter shook his head, then closed his eyes hard, as if when he opened them again all this would be gone. But of course, the lights were only brighter.

"I've just been through sudden death," Carter whispered.

"I know. But the game's not over. I'll see you at the Irish Bar when it is. It's still my round."

65

"We've got to get you out of those clothes," Flavia said with a smile that Carter would have thought flirty if he hadn't just started a riot, nearly got killed, nearly got Gracie killed, and killed a man himself.

"Just take me to the hospital," he said, once he was in the passenger seat of her Merc.

"Hospital?"

"Gracie's in St. Mel's."

Carter didn't look back, but he knew that the cops were out there, following. Gibson himself, probably.

"How are you?" she said in a conciliatory tone. She'd left the top up. There'd be no yelling tonight.

"What are you doing?" he replied. "What's your game?"

"No games, remember? I came to get you because the cops wanted you fetched. You're off the hook."

"They told you that?"

"They did. But don't trust the police, Carter, despite the fact you're the son of one."

So she remembered what his father had done for a living, but her memory usually was called on only to make a point in her favour.

"Who do you think I should trust?"

"Me." She smiled.

He was too tired to fight her. He'd remembered that when captured, the guilty sleep and the innocent pace, but to hell with that theory. He just wanted to sleep for a while, until they got to the hospital. But he wasn't going to sleep with Flavia next to him ever again. Not even in a moving car with her at the wheel.

He looked out the window, Manhattan muscling in on them at speed. Then they dipped into the tunnel below the East River.

Flavia navigated the labyrinthine exit with ease, and now they were heading north on Park Avenue, with Grand Central in front of them and history on the other side.

Carter had made this drive before, in taxis, with Flavia in out-of-work mode and in the mood for love, a hand riding his thigh, a hot whisper in his ear. She was taking him to the Midtown apartment where they had ridden passion and promise, as it turned out, in opposite directions.

"No!" Carter yelled.

"Trust me," she said, pulling into the underground garage. "I have what you need."

"No, Flavia, you don't."

"Relax," she said. "I'm not trying to seduce you. That takes a willing accomplice, Carter, and you" – she looked at him with soft eyes, as close as she came to regret – "you have found a woman you deserve. I'm happy for you."

He stared at her. Only Flavia could be happy for him under

the circumstances. "Then what are we doing here? I want to see Gracie. The game is over."

She put her hand on his thigh, touching his skin where the paper suit had disintegrated in his sweat. "Almost Carter. Almost."

She swiped the card to the parking elevator and tapped in the floor code that would take them to their destination. No concierge to pass, no troublesome witnesses.

"It's changed," Carter said, once they were in the apartment. The paint, once amber, was now beige, edged with white. The burgundy sofa and chairs smelled of new leather.

"I live here now," she said casually, "with my husband."

And around the corner from the bedroom, like a punchline, came Freddie Hutt.

"That would be me, Cartch," he drawled, still wearing the green silk suit from the night before, his cheeks flushed, his drawl lazier and sibilant, as if he'd been nursing a bottle of Jack for the past few hours.

Surprise pushed Carter backward, into a leather armchair.

"Please," said Freddie, gesturing with drunk speed to where Carter was already sitting. Then he sat too.

"I know you're exhausted," Flavia said and catching the flash of Carter's eye added quickly, "and need something to eat. Can I offer you some fruit? Some coffee?"

Carter was at a loss for words. He was in Flavia's apartment, with his boss, who was her husband, and she was acting like he was her only client on a private jet.

"Water. Please," he said eventually.

She nodded and went behind a vast marble island, keeping an eye on him as she fetched a bottle of San Pellegrino from a silver fridge half the size of his burned-out kitchen.

"Ice?"

He shook his head and took the glass, cradling it as a kind of defence against these two.

"Why am I here?"

Flavia glanced at Freddie, and he took the cue, clearing his throat. "There's no delicate way to put this, Cartch, but I'm grateful for your discretion."

Carter kept his sorority-killer face fixed as his mind flipped through images of what he'd been discreet about. And he came up blank.

Freddie read his silence and hard stare as a bargaining tactic, and did what he had been trained to do.

"Name your price."

"How do you know I have a price?"

Freddie hunched forward, but Flavia stepped in. "How much do you want for the DVD? Of the" – the words caught in her throat – "the sex party?"

There was an unfamiliar tone in her voice, which it took Carter a moment to understand. Then he had it. She was begging.

The man in the shadows of Hayley's video. The fourth champagne glass in the frame. Now he saw it clearly. Freddie Hutt must have been the fourth man at the party. And both Freddie and Flavia thought Carter had seen him there. That's what Doug Bleecker and Flavia had been trying to buy.

Carter realized that he suddenly had something he hadn't had for a long time. Real power. And while he knew that the true might of power was how you used it against the defenceless, Freddie Hutt wasn't defenceless. Carter could see behind his bloodshot eyes a bloodstained knowledge.

"You knew who killed Hayley, and why, didn't you?" Carter said evenly to Freddie.

Freddie nodded. "I did," he drawled. "But that's not what concerns me."

Anger washed over Carter. Link had nearly killed Oblomov because of Freddie's sex party, and Hayley and Carlito had both been killed because of it. He had killed a man and had nearly died himself because of Freddie's fear, and Gracie was in the hospital in a coma because of it, and the Cardinal would never drink from the chalice now because of it, but Freddie didn't care. He only cared about himself.

"Besides," Freddie added, mistaking Carter's silence for more bargaining, "you took care of Link. And now I'm just trying to take care of the team. Preserve the Cardinal's legacy."

"Is he dead?"

Freddie shrugged. Carter stood up and punched him in the jaw.

"For Christ's sakes, Carter –" Flavia yelled, but Freddie held up a hand. "I had that coming." He said it as if he'd insulted Carter's honour over juleps and had not been the greedy accomplice to murder.

"You do have the footage, Cartch, don't you?" Flavia asked.

"You mean of the sex party?"

A solitary blink was her answer.

But Carter had a head-case question. For himself. He didn't know where the DVD was. He'd had the hard drive with him in the Maestro's brownstone, but if the police had taken it, Gibson would have mentioned it. Or maybe he didn't know what he had.

Carter took another sip of water to smooth his gamble. "Tell me something, Freddie," he said. "Just why were you having a sex party" – he was now enjoying the term – "with Hayley Rawls and the boys?"

"You should know," Freddie responded, the boss again, for a moment. "She's a very . . ." He stopped and cleared his throat. "She was a very compelling woman. When she wanted something, well . . ."

Carter looked at Flavia as Freddie spoke, but she didn't react. He could imagine what she was thinking. How could any woman be more compelling than she was? And that, he realized, was the real embarrassment here. Freddie had been caught with his pants down by a woman with a camera. His cheating, bisexual self she could take, but committing it to film smacked of middle-class ambition.

"Who else has seen it?" Flavia said.

"Just me and Gracie." He left out Madz.

"And Andy Jack," Flavia added.

Carter nodded. Jack had only seen an edited version, but it had been enough. Betrayed again. Though this time, the betrayal might just save him.

"Do you want to sell it or not?" she asked

Carter remembered how Flavia could turn the advantage in a conversation as easily as she might ask the time or comment on the weather. She was part of some kind of conspiracy Carter was just beginning to fathom, and now she was talking as if he were some shameless blackmailer.

He turned to Freddie. "What I want, for a start, is to know why."

"Look, Carter," he said, exasperation creeping into this drawl, "I've been seeing Link, uh, socially for a while. There was a party at Hayley's place, with Hayley and Oblomov and Link and a couple of hookers, we all got pretty loaded, and one thing led to another . . ." He half-smiled, as if Carter knew how it was when friends got together. "Name your price and we can make this go away."

"I don't think he has it," Flavia said, gambling a bit too far.

Carter stood. "Then I won't keep you any longer. Say," he said brightly, "can you loan me fifty bucks for the cab ride to Harlem, where I keep Hayley's hard drive?"

Freddie stood, taking over from his wife before they were both ruined. "How about half a million dollars for the hard drive?" he said. "You could buy a New York City cab licence."

He chuckled, trying to lighten the mood. Carter decided to stay silent.

"And of course," Flavia added, "you'd sign a non-disclosure agreement, and if any copies ever surfaced, then I don't think there'd be a place safe enough –"

Freddie interrupted. "Cartch," he said. "I trust you. I trust your loyalty, not to me, but to what Mr. O'Connor has built. What will it take to preserve your integrity?"

Carter was going to take the half million until Freddie tried to make it seem as if he, Freddie Hutt, was rescuing Carter's honour. So he said, "I want a million dollars."

Flavia opened her mouth, but Carter kept going, fuelled now by their own greed. "In ten separate bank drafts of a hundred thousand dollars each. No cheques that can bounce, no electronic transfers that magically disappear once you've got the hard drive. A million dollars."

He could almost hear the air pressure drop in the room. "Done," Freddie said.

"No, not done," Carter replied. "There's still the why."

"No," Flavia said, but Freddie just sighed. "Hayley Rawls was makin' noises to Erik about that footage of the, uh, party. We thought we had an understandin' with her, but when she caught Link's hit on the Russian, she got bold. And – I didn't know this, mind – but they thought you'd be the perfect guy to kill two birds with one stone."

"Who's they?"

Freddie looked small and weak.

"The Maestro was the theory, and Hopalong was the practice. He killed Hayley and the janitor fella."

Carter nodded. Suddenly, he felt much better about having split Hopalong's evil brain with a bullet. Now he wanted to hurt Freddie too. "You have until five today to get me the money."

"Today's Saturday."

"Right," Carter said. "The banks close early. Make it three."

Flavia just stared at him, then gave him the hint of a smile. It seemed that they'd made a deal.

66

The ER waiting area at St. Mel's was practically empty early on the Saturday morning of the long Easter weekend, just a Latino couple with a toddler coughing like a three-pack-a-day man, a woman cradling a bandaged hand, Carter, and Madz, who'd brought him his clothes and wallet.

They didn't have to wait long. Bobbi Washington swept into the room as if she had a few things to say to Carter and they'd been fuelling her momentum all night long.

But all she said was "Come" and beckoned a long gloved finger at him like fate.

They followed her silently into a restricted zone, down a green corridor, to a set of grey windowless doors with a sign above: Intensive Care Unit.

Bobbi swiped her card, and the doors swung open. She led them to a sink, flanked by surgical glove and mask dispensers.

"Wash your hands and put on gloves and a mask." Her tone was professional, but her body language seethed with anger.

They did as she asked, and then she scrubbed and masked herself and led them to a darkened room just past the nursing station.

"You need to see her," Bobbi said to Carter, her eyes cold above her mask. "So take a look."

Carter entered the room and his eyes started to tear up. Gracie had an IV stuck in her arm and an oxygen mask on her face. An artificial respirator by her bed was pumping air in and out of her lungs. Her head was shaved and bandaged where they had sewn up the wound.

She looked as if her rescue had nearly killed her.

"Jesus," Madz said.

"Jesus had nothing to do with it," Bobbi said, glaring at Carter.

"I didn't —" he began but stopped himself and tried to staunch Bobbi's anger. "Thank you for saving her. Thank you."

So Bobbi turned her unblinking wrath on Madz. "No story is worth that much."

Their silence was broken only by the sighing of the respirator and the dirge of Gracie's pulse, beating on the heart monitor above her bed.

"Will she —" Carter's words jammed.

"We don't know," Bobbi replied. "We got the vodka and Temazepam flushed out, but she has a triple skull fracture. It was a terrible blow. But she put up a mighty fight — there was skin and blood and what looks like eyeball tissue under her fingernails. It's being analyzed."

Carter approached the bed, his initial shock already subsiding. "Gracie," he whispered, touching her hand. "It's Cartch. I'm here now."

"We'll have her out of the coma soon," Bobbi said, leaving his hand where it rested.

"Have her out the coma?" Carter said, his throat tight.

"We put her in one as soon as we got here."

"Not in the ambulance?" Madz said, still the journalist.

"No, there I was busy trying to keep her heart going," Bobbi said. "You need a team to put someone out, to stop brain swelling. You can drill a hole, too, but this was the better option."

Carter looked up at Bobbi, and she read the question in his eyes. "I don't know. I haven't had any experience like this before. And hope to never again."

"Baby, please," Madz said, reaching out for her, but Bobbi walked out of the room and held the door for them. Her eyes and tone both calmed when they were outside the room.

"Look, I'm sorry," Bobbi said to Carter. "I know this is all bad for you, but I'm usually not part of the story, you know. It's hard for me too."

He nodded. He knew. He hadn't been part of his own story for a long time, then suddenly he was trying to outskate it, and now he felt he'd run out of ice.

"I can't say what she'll be like," Bobbi continued, softly, a little sadly. "All I can say is that if we keep doing what we're doing, and she keeps fighting, then she'll live."

67

Emerald Gardens looked like the scene of an urban battle.

"Jesus," said Madz, scanning the boarded-up windows. "Think what would have happened if the St. Pats had actually won the Cup last night."

Or lost it, thought Carter. He and Madz wandered through the broken glass sparkling in the warm morning sun, the dried blood on the pavement beneath it, and the air still spiced with tear gas and burnt iron, where the flames had licked the gold paint off the colonnades holding up the portico. The neon sign above it had been broken in two and. now advertised St. Pats vs.

"That's appropriate," Madz said, following his gaze.

"What do you mean?" Carter was feeling the hangover of the past few hours – of the riot, the murder, the near-murder, and his dubious release – but the thing hitting him hardest was the shiv of guilt in his weary heart. He had only been trying to save himself but might have destroyed everything.

"I mean, the league suspended Link indefinitely, which, first of all, was unusually quick and decent of them in the face of, like, massive criminal evidence. The DA's considering whether to charge him with assault or attempted murder. Second, without Link, and given all that's happened, the St. Pats are totally, royally, utterly –"

Madz stopped, and Carter saw what she she'd spotted at the other end of the concourse: the Cardinal, in his wheelchair, his oxygen tank clamped to the side, staring at his ruined palace. Brenda at the handlebars.

Madz grabbed Carter's arm and tried to pull him out of sight, but the look in his eyes made her let go. She followed as he walked over to the broken man who had once ruled the city.

"Cartch," said the Cardinal, his face as grey as his suit. He moved to raise his hand, veined and bony, but Carter reached down and clasped it.

"I'm sorry," Carter said, his voice small. "I never meant for it to end like this."

"You should be sorry," Brenda hissed, but the Cardinal raised an admonishing finger, and she said no more.

"Has it ended?" he rasped. "There are still four games to go. Last night" – he smiled as broadly as Carter had seen in weeks – "doesn't count, apparently."

Carter realized he'd just been given absolution, in the Cardinal's cryptic way.

The Cardinal turned to Madz. "I gather you got more of a story than you anticipated last night, Ms. Weinfeld."

"Well, when it comes to the St. Patricks," she began, then caught herself. "I had hoped for better days."

"That was your mistake right there," he said. "Looks like I'll have to watch them win the Cup in goddamn Los Angeles for my sins."

Two games was the magic number for the St. Pats to win the Cup, which they all knew was as likely as Link being unsuspended.

"Do you want to come to Los Angeles with me?" the Cardinal asked.

"I'd love to, Mr. O'Connor, but I have some things to do here," Carter replied.

The Cardinal nodded. "I hear she'll be okay."

"From God's lips to your ears, sir," Carter said and then winced. Head-case thing to say to a guy who was nearly dead, but the Cardinal smiled again with real pleasure.

"When Voltaire, that great apostate who had been excommunicated and consigned to hell, was dying," he said, pausing to take a breath as deep as his ravaged lungs could manage, "his friends ringed his bed with candles. When Voltaire awoke from his death slumber and saw the candles, do you know what he said?"

Carter did not know what Voltaire had said but knew this was goodbye.

"'What? The flames already?'"

Carter couldn't tell whether the Cardinal was winking at him or blinking away a tear, but then he raised his right hand and pointed west toward the Hudson River, and Brenda wheeled him away.

68

Carter knew what effect apparitions have from the look on Wanda's face when he and Madz walked into the Black Irish.

He greeted her with an easy smile, as if he were wandering into her bar at his customary hour and not for the first time since he saw her two nights ago in the embrace of the NYPD detective, when Gracie was alive and well and he wasn't a murderer.

But she wasn't buying it. Her eyes were a kaleidoscope of shifting emotions – affection and regret and more than a little fear.

"I'll have a club soda," he said, "and my friend Ms. Weinfeld here will have the usual."

"No," Madz said, "I'll have a club soda too."

Carter and Wanda waited for the punchline, but she just shrugged. "Never date a doctor if you want to drink like a sportswriter."

"You work in TV," Wanda said.

"In my heart, I'm still in print," she replied. "Kinda like the thousand-dollar bill."

Wanda delivered the pints of soda water to their booth and sat down next to him. "Why are you back here?"

"I came to finish some business," Carter said.

"Oh?"

"Between me and recent history."

"Ah," she said. "He's asleep upstairs."

"Gibson is here?"

She grinned like a schoolgirl. "He's here a lot."

Carter nodded. "He had a late night."

"Well," she said, her eyes flicking with pleasure, "he's used to late nights."

"I'm happy for you, Wanda. I really am."

"Me too. He's a good man." She nodded slowly to emphasize the thought, not to suggest that Carter was a bad man, but that he was a good man too. "Cartch?" she began, but he held up his hand.

"No need. We're okay."

"I was gonna say, give me a shout when business has turned into pleasure and I'll buy you a drink."

"Thanks. I will. Maybe Detective Gibson can join us."

Wanda gave him a funny little smile, then walked behind the bar and started to empty the glass washer.

Madz looked at her watch. "They're late. And I want some pleasure soon."

"Don't worry," Carter said. "They'll be here. They want what I've got. Thanks to you."

"You can buy me drinks all night for that," she said. "I got the hard drive out of the house of death about ten seconds before cops showed up. Didn't want to shock those innocent boys in blue and all."

"If this works out, I can buy you more than drinks. Which your doctor girlfriend might even thank me for."

Carter put Gracie's laptop on the table and booted it up, the screen casting a blue glow over him in the dark bar. Then he hooked up the portable hard drive and opened the file with Hayley and Link and Oblomov and Freddie.

"Jesus," Madz said. "Watching this thing makes you realize that pornography really is an art form."

"Well, we don't want it for the aesthetic value," Flavia said coolly.

Carter had seen her come in the door and survey the bar as if it were the kind of place you might send someone to do community service. Making her come here now was part of her punishment.

He wanted to punish her, for the sins of her husband, the person he wanted to punish most of all, but there was no sign of Freddie. "Where's the sex-party boy?" Carter asked.

"He's indisposed. Who's this?" Flavia said, looking at Madz.

"Madz Weinfeld. She's my witness. She's also a reporter." Carter knew that Flavia had no interest in sports and wouldn't recognize Madz.

"Ah," Flavia said sliding in next to Madz. "Then she'll know all about what happens to reporters who break non-disclosure agreements."

She opened her briefcase and took out a sheet of paper with two yellow tabs stuck on the margin. "Speaking of which," she said, sliding it across the table.

"It's shorter than I thought it would be."

"Many things are," Flavia replied. Madz squawked.

"I wasn't speaking about inches," Flavia said sternly. "I was speaking of footage. Is what I just saw all you have?"

There was disdain in her voice, as if she'd wasted a lot of time and energy to get him to this place only to find a bit of harmless fun on a DVD that wouldn't convict anyone in the court of public opinion.

But Carter knew that she was bluffing. Even in the dimness of the bar, he could see the desperation in her eyes.

"Well then," he said, closing the laptop. "I guess your work on my behalf last night was all for nothing."

Flavia smiled thinly. "You'd better read the agreement," she said, "before you sign."

She slid the document in front of him, then reached back into her briefcase for an envelope. In it, he knew, were bank drafts totalling a million dollars. It was a gambit to make him lose his concentration while reading the agreement, but he could have been half-dead and still not missed the point: Flavia now owned the footage, and its copyright.

She was buying it from Carter, who had stolen it from Hayley Rawls, "now deceased." If he betrayed the deal, he would pay her two million dollars and admit legal responsibility to indemnify any media outlet for their losses from the lawsuits she would bring against them. If he tried to ruin Freddie, he would ruin himself.

He looked at her and smiled. "I see your point," he said.

"Thank you," she said. "So, no posting on YouTube or" – she glanced at Madz – "on SportsWorld, should you have made any copies."

"Don't worry, Flavia. It's not something I ever want to see again." He moved to sign the document, then paused, the pen hovering above the paper. "Tell me one thing, though."

"I didn't know he was fucking Link, no," she said, the slightest of tremors in her voice.

"No, what I want to know is, when did you know that Freddie had seen the tape of Link's attack on Oblomov? When you met me that day in our café?"

She smiled at Carter, something like affection. "No, I didn't know. But after you told me what you told me, I knew that he probably would have seen it. If it existed."

"Well it did . . ."

She shrugged and opened the envelope. "As you can see, Cartch, I don't know too much about anything. No strings attached."

She counted out the ten bank drafts. "Here you go — each worth a hundred thousand dollars, making a total of one million."

He nodded, signed the document, and Madz scrawled her witness signature as Carter unplugged the hard drive. "And here you go," he said, handing it to her.

She dropped it into her boxy briefcase as if it were trash, then slid out of the booth. Carter slid out too and faced her. He knew that only coincidence would ever put them in the same place at the same time again. She knew it too, and that a handshake was too formal, and a kiss, too false. So she just smiled at him, then walked out the door.

Carter slid back into the booth and grinned at Madz, who looked as if she was seeing him for the first time. "Jesus, Cartch, it's true what they say about the Irish."

"That we're immune from psychotherapy?"

"And all of your wars are merry and all of your songs are sad."

He laughed. "Yeah, well it's merry when you win the war."

"No kidding. You have a million dollars sitting there."

"Not quite," he replied, sliding a money order toward her.

"What's this?"

"Matter cannot be destroyed," he replied. "Your hundred grand went up in flames, and now, from the ashes . . ."

"But it wasn't my money."

"Now it is," he said and looked over to the bar to summon Wanda to bring more soda water for a toast to success.

But Detective Lucius Gibson was standing in the way, and he, too, was looking at Carter as if seeing him in a cold, hard light.

"Detective Gibson," Carter said.

"Mr. Carter. Looks like you've been busy."

Carter pocketed the money orders. "Let's call it a windfall."

Gibson nodded. "I watched the whole thing on the security monitor upstairs."

Carter's head went cold. Gibson was going to seize the money and hunt down the hard drive in Flavia's bag, and Carter would soon be on his way back to the precinct house to answer murder and conspiracy charges.

"It's too bad a spouse can't be compelled to testify except in cases of adultery," Gibson said. "Imagine that one, if Flavia Hutt named Link Andrachuk as the co-respondent."

"She won't do that," Carter replied, his head tingling with the chilly wonder of where Gibson was going with this.

"'Course she won't. That's why a million bucks in exchange for your sex tape was a very good deal."

"You saw the tape?"

"We did. Took a peek while you were busy showing the Patsies the other DVD about Link. Don't worry, we didn't make any copies."

"You broke into my house?" Madz snarled.

Gibson jerked his head back in mock surprise. "This from the woman who did a little freelance evidence removal at the scene of a crime? I'd say we're even."

Madz grinned and held up her hands. "Busted!"

Carter suddenly saw the whole picture. "So when exactly did you know that I didn't kill Hayley? Or Carlito?"

"When you came back. 'Only robbers and thieves fear to go where they've once been.'" He smiled at Madz. "Dostoyevsky. Very popular crime writer in the precincts. And you can quote me."

"You were following them?"

"Remember the night you came back and went to Ms. Weinfeld's house?"

"Call me Madz," she said. "I think this might be the beginning of a beautiful friendship."

"I remember," Carter said.

"There was a Town Car out front. Did you see it by any chance?"

"I did."

"Eamon Lynch. He was staking out Ms. . . . Madz's house. Waiting for you. We were staking out him. As soon as I saw a bad IRA dude like him spending quality time with Erik Shepherd, I knew something was up."

"The Maestro," Carter replied, the cold band around his head now dissolved in sweat. Gibson could see the world the way Carter could see the ice. He smiled. "You've got him, don't you?"

Gibson nodded. "Yeah, he scored on his own net. He staggered into the ER at Long Island College Hospital just a little while after you arrived at the house where Hayley Rawls died. His right eye looked like it had been on the wrong end of a corkscrew. Apparently your friend Ms. Yates got him pretty good, and now he can wear his fucken eyepatch for real. Should impress the other inmates on pirate night at Attica."

"You've got him," Carter said again, still amazed.

"That's right," Gibson said. "And Doug Bleecker's a very talkative bird. We have them all. The Maestro gets murder one for Hayley and attempted murder for Gracie, and the others get conspiracy charges."

"What about Link?"

"Dunno yet. Those lawyers at the league offices seem to think that sport is outside the law. And the Cardinal does have friends. But so do you – Freddie can keep his sex tape. Wouldn't want to make you unrich if I didn't have to."

Carter laughed, feeling now as if he was on the ice again, doing graceful arcs with the puck toward an open net. "Can I buy you a drink, detective?"

"No," Gibson said. "It really is my round."

69

Carter awoke to the sound of bells ringing and sunshine in his eyes. He was either dead and heaven existed and St. Peter had made a clerical error or he was hungover on a sunny Sunday morning in Harlem. That would be Easter Sunday, he remembered.

After a long hot shower that only made him aware he was even more hungover than he'd first thought, he dressed in his best clothes, a black jacket, black jeans, and an electric blue shirt, and went downstairs to the kitchen.

"Off to church?" Bobbi said, looking up from her coffee and the Sunday edition of the *Times*.

"Not exactly," Carter replied. "But I am hoping to roll away the rock from the tomb."

"Madz told me that everything turned out okay."

"Yeah, well, we know how it ends."

"We do?"

"Everyone dies. But while there's life . . ."

She smiled. "Tell me about it."

"Where's Madz?"

Bobbi put down the paper. "How much did you guys have to drink last night?"

Carter didn't want to get in the middle of a domestic temperance tussle, so he just shrugged amiably. "Not much, but it was on an empty stomach, so to speak."

Bobbi gave him her doctor's stare but then realized it wouldn't have any effect on an Irish guy. "Madz's at the airport, remember? Off to L.A.? To cover that hockey thing."

He remembered. She'd asked if he wanted to go with her to Los Angeles, and that was before he and she and Lucius Gibson had killed a bottle and a half of Jamesons between the three of them, and he'd said no. There was only one place he wanted to be.

But when he arrived in the Intensive Care Unit of St. Mel's, there was a tall guy sitting beside Gracie's bed. Carter knew the man wasn't a doctor because doctors usually don't hold the hands of patients and stroke their heads.

"Hello," Carter said, when the man didn't turn.

"Oh, hello," the guy said with an easy smile, offering his hand. "I'm Rob Richards. Gracie's husband."

Carter kept his hand by his side. "I didn't think she had a husband," he said evenly.

The man had a smooth, classically handsome face, the angles in the right places, the dimple in the chin not too deep, the eyes friendly, in a what-can-you-do-for-me? sort of way.

"We're divorced, actually, but we're still very close. And you would be?"

"Martin Carter," he replied, offering his hand, which Rob Richards grasped and squeezed hard. "I'm her friend."

"Ah," Rob Richards said, "I see."

"Hey, Gracie," Carter said, walking to the side of the bed where the respirator had been and taking her other hand. She was breathing on her own now, and her eyes were open, her gaze on her former husband.

"She's going to be fine, aren't you, babe?" Rob Richards said to her.

"I was just telling her that she's in hospital in New York," he told Carter. Then he stroked her hair. "You're going to be fine, babe. Just fine."

Gracie turned her blue eyes to Carter. "Thank you," she said, smiling at him so tenderly he thought he might weep. "Thank you, doctor."

70

Carter had just settled into his first-class compartment of the *Maple Leaf* service to Toronto out of Penn Station when there was a knock on his door. On the other side stood Lucius Gibson, and for a second Carter was sure the cops had shown up in the nick of time to tell him they'd found the evidence to charge him.

"I came to say goodbye," Gibson said. "I heard you were heading home."

"How'd you hear that?"

"I have my sources."

"Not home exactly," Carter said. "To a neutral corner for a while." With his angry brother and demented mother. He could handle that. What he couldn't handle was the loss of Gracie.

"Yeah," Gibson said. "In the end, that's all you can ask for."

He handed Carter a copy of the *Mail*. "I brought you some reading for the train. Thought you might like to read about yourself."

Carter smiled. "Page Seven strikes again?"

Gibson nodded. "That damn thing is the best detective in the city." Then he shook Carter's hand, and Carter said, "Thanks for everything. Next round's mine."

Gibson opened the door, then turned back, a hand to his head just like Columbo.

"I forgot to tell you that Eamon Lynch, who you knew as Hopalong was really murdered. And we know whodunit."

"You do?" Carter said, his throat thick. What game was Gibson playing?

The detective nodded. "The Cardinal called me from Los Angeles. Said he'd killed him and will turn himself in when he gets back. If he lives that long. Just thought you'd like to know."

Tears were dribbling down Carter's cheeks as the train pulled out. He knew altogether too much, and all he wanted now was to forget. Like Gracie had forgotten him. As the train passed through the Bronx, Carter wiped his eyes and opened the newspaper to Page Seven. There he was, gazing back at himself as a rookie, the future still before him. As he read the article, he realized he knew just who had written it. For Page Seven had him a free man, cleared of murder, and heading north to the land of the Maple Leaf on a train of the same name.

"Godspeed to you, Cartch," Madz had written. "Come home soon."

ACKNOWLEDGEMENTS

The Penalty Killing had many helpers, and while space prevents gramercies to all of them, there are some whom it would be criminal not to thank here. So, to David Bieber, Karen Bower, Kate Fillion, David Gibson, David Harrington, Karen Powell, Barbara Shearer, Don Winslow, Lori Williams and the Book Club Ladies, Charles Wilson, Stefan Winfield, David York, and my agent, Richard Pine, thank you for your generosity of time and wisdom. Special thanks to Dinah Forbes, who manages to be both editor and friend without losing sight of the plot, and who always finds a way to make it better. And of course, great thanks to my wife, Nancy, and daughter, Rose, for providing me with such excellent alibis while I was in my study, committing murder. I couldn't ask for finer accomplices, and hope the story makes for a worthy escape.